W9-BDD-107

afterlove

afterlove

ROBERT ROSENBLUM

NEW AMERICAN LIBRARY

NEW AMERICAN LIBRARY
Published by New American Library, a division of
Penguin Putnam Inc., 375 Hudson Street,
New York, New York 10014, U.S.A.
Penguin Books Ltd, 80 Strand,
London WC2R 0RL, England
Penguin Books Australia Ltd, 250 Camberwell Road,
Camberwell, Victoria 3124, Australia
Penguin Books Canada Ltd, 10 Alcorn Avenue,
Toronto, Ontario, Canada M4V 3B2
Penguin Books (N.Z.) Ltd, 182–190 Wairau Road,
Auckland 10, New Zealand

Penguin Books Ltd, Registered Offices:
Harmondsworth, Middlesex, England

First published by New American Library, a division of Penguin Putnam Inc.

Copyright © Robert Rosenblum, 2003

Ⓡ REGISTERED TRADEMARK—MARCA REGISTRADA

ISBN 0-451-20786-6

Designed by Leonard Telesca

Printed in the United States of America

For Julia—
who told me this story, I'm sure,
after she was gone.

1

An earring, that was all. But for the earring, everything would have been different. Life would have gone on as it had before—not perfect, not without problems, but a life like most people had. Normal, happy most of the time, filled with small but mainly satisfying events.

The greatest irony was that Kate's desire to wear the earrings that morning at the end of September arose out of her belief in them as a proven good luck charm. Jim had bought them for her during the trip to London three years ago, gold ovals set with cabochon amethysts— her birthstone—from Asprey's, no less, a spur-of-the-moment splurge conceived as they strolled down Bond Street the day before their return. The vacation was the first they'd been able to manage alone since the birth of the twins. Tom and Chloe had recently turned four, and with their choice in foods not quite so finicky, night fears subsiding, Kate had decided that Jim's folks were finally up to the challenge they had been begging to take on—to have the children to themselves so that Jim could take Kate away. So for those precious ten days at the end of that June, Kate had agreed to let the twins go to the elder Weylands' summer place in Maine.

Nervous as she was at the start, the getaway had been ideal. Visiting the museums, seeing *Macbeth* at the National Theater, satisfying her passion for English history with trips to Westminster Cathedral, Hampton Court, and the Tower. With nothing to do but pleasure themselves, all the weariness and tension that had built up since the twins were born fell away, passion and romance were fully reborn. After such a perfect vacation, she had tempted fate perhaps when she said as they boarded the flight home, "Whatever happens, Jimbo, we'll always have London."

Jim had smiled at the twist on Bogart's "Paris" line to Bergman in *Casablanca*, but it was a nervous smile. Basically a practical man, he nevertheless had a superstitious streak that made him anxious to counteract any negative thought. "Nothing's going to happen that'll keep us from having plenty more times like this one," he said.

But two hours into the flight they'd gone through a patch of unusually severe turbulence. The plane dropped so fast in one air pocket that a steward who wasn't buckled into his seat had been launched violently into the ceiling of the galley, his head badly cut. The bustle of other attendants aiding their injured coworker heightened the air of emergency. One stewardess did a "refresher" demonstration of the ditching procedure, and the captain came on the intercom telling passengers not to leave their seats, and advising parents to make sure children and babies were secure. That made Kate painfully aware of being parted from her own children, and her mind was suddenly filled with dire visions of Jim's folks having to tell the twins that Mommy and Daddy weren't ever coming home. . . .

"If we do have to . . . leave the kids," she burst out, "I guess it's better now than when they're older. They won't really understand it now, won't miss us so—"

"All right, that's enough!" Jim cut her off, sounding much more angry than scared. "We'll be fine. I promise you: tomorrow morning we're going to be having breakfast with the kids just like always."

He said it with such force that it was as if he actually *knew* for sure, and Kate felt instantly calmer. A minute later, she pulled the carryon out from under her seat, reached inside, and pulled out the little box from Asprey's.

He didn't look pleased when he saw her putting on the earrings. "Don't let me hear a word about how you hardly got to wear those."

"That's not it, darling. But they're so lovely, I did think if God could see how good they looked on me, it might clinch a few more nights out. . . ."

He looked at her lovingly then, and grabbed her hand in his, and they sat in silent wishful communion. Kate actually went beyond wishing to form a silent prayer, a vague deal with God that she'd try even harder to do all the right things if only the plane could land safely and she could hold the children again. Less than ten minutes later, the turbulence eased, and the captain came back on the intercom with every bit of that irritating tour-guide jollity back in his voice. "Well, folks, that sure was a nasty patch back there. But we're on the other side of it now, and the radar shows smooth sailing from here on to Logan. . . ."

They had breakfast the next morning with the kids just as he'd promised, and she wore the earrings while she made the pancakes. Maybe it was the holy deal that had brought them through, but she thought luck—and lucky tokens—played a part, too.

After that, she wore them on any important occasion, especially when there was something at stake. Like the night they'd gone to dinner with Harry Parker, who was thinking of inviting Jim to be his partner. The Parker Agency did three times as much insurance business as Jim's office, so it would be a windfall; Harry wanted no compensation, only someone who'd be a good shepherd for the business while he eased into retirement. But he'd been dangling the merger possibility for almost a year, and dinner with the wives seemed to be some sort of final test of how comfortable Harry could be leaving the business in Jim's hands. Kate had worn the earrings, of course, and the evening had been wonderful. It was that night she and Harry's wife, Meg, had struck up the friendship that had since become Kate's closest. Harry had called the next morning to say an agreement for the deal would be on Jim's desk after the weekend.

So naturally on this Wednesday morning, Kate planned to wear them for her interview. Not that she wasn't perfectly happy with her position at Fairhaven's public high school, teaching upper-grade history, along with serving as assistant principal for the past five years. But Ashedeane Preparatory was considered one of the finest private schools in all the Northeast, if not the country. She'd been thrilled when the letter came early in the summer informing her that a search committee had her name on a list of people to replace a retiring Assistant Head of the middle school, a position that would not only allow her to continue teaching, but put her in line to replace the current Head when he retired. Her salary would double; yet what she cared about most was the chance to teach in smaller classes, in a well-endowed institution free from the stifling oversight that the local public schools had been saddled with under the strict community board. Her two preliminary interviews had now led to this morning's invitation to appear before a group of Ashedeane's trustees—one of only three contenders short-listed. It was a good sign, too, that they had accommodated her when she'd asked to schedule the meeting at a time that wouldn't interfere with her current teaching duties. On Wednesdays, she had no classes until early American history at 10:25, so they had agreed to set the interview for 8:30 to make sure she was done by 10. The timing would also allow her to drive the twins to school as she always did.

The morning started on schedule. Before waking the twins, Kate showered, packed their lunches, had her own fruit and yogurt, and made Jim's coffee and toasted oat muffin. Then she went upstairs, woke the children, left them in their father's hands for breakfast, and went to get into her good clothes and brush out her hair.

Finally, she took the earrings from her jewelry drawer, leaving one atop the dresser while she fixed the other to her left ear, checking herself in the mirror. When she reached to pick up the second, her attention was still concentrated mainly on her reflected appearance, a little worried as always that perhaps she'd be judged *too* chic and good looking to be taken seriously as the best of teachers. She'd had that all her life, going back to boys who couldn't believe she didn't want to be on the cheerleading squad, and would rather turn down dates to stay home with a book. Not that she was so all-fired beautiful, she knew, but her height, the "lucky" bone structure, and the reddish-brown hair with blue eyes, made her striking.

Now, her gaze held by the mirror as her hand went for the earring, instead of her fingers landing gently on target, they collided with it, flipping the earring over onto its polished gem to send it shooting across the smooth top of the dresser and off the edge like a hockey puck on ice. A moment later, she heard the earring *clack* against a hard surface—a nearby wall, perhaps, or the sill of the bathroom door a few feet to the right of the dresser, or the leg of a night table on the far side of the door—she hadn't seen the flight of the object. Then it must have fallen to the bedroom carpet, because there was no further sound.

Dropping into a crouch, Kate swept her gaze over the surrounding area. It must have gone behind something, because she didn't spot it at once. She bent lower, peered under the dresser, behind the legs of the night table, looked through the door into the bathroom. Or had it sailed even farther away than she'd first assumed, bounced off the bed frame, wound up somehow under the bed? Soon she was lying flat, eyes at floor level, searching for a glint in the darkness beneath the bed. How could it have vanished? It had to be right under her nose!

It was that belief which kept her hunting—tossing the bedclothes, going around the bed to look by the windows, behind the curtains— when she should have just let it go. Except, these were the *lucky* earrings: losing one now seemed to guarantee that the interview wouldn't go well.

When Kate stood up finally—only to discover dark green carpet lint all over the fawn wool skirt and a run in her pantyhose—she'd given more than ten minutes to her search, and now she would need extra time to change clothes, straighten her hair again, and just simply compose herself. And Ashedeane was six miles away, on the far side of town from Windridge, their own neighborhood—

"Jim!" she shouted.

He heard the ring of emergency in her voice and bounded upstairs quickly from the kitchen to the bedroom.

"Will you drive the twins to school?" she asked when he appeared at the door.

"Oh, Katie," he groaned. "It's not so much out of your way, and I have an early appointment to discuss a fire policy with—" It suddenly registered on him that she was barely listening as she hastily removed her clothes. "Why on earth are you getting *un*dressed?"

"I got all messed up crawling around on the floor."

"Crawling—?"

"Look, I don't have time to explain." She ran into her closet to get fresh pantyhose off a shelf, calling out as she continued to dress, "The point is I've just blown fifteen minutes, and I mustn't be late for this interview." She emerged from the closet with her hands, one gripping a dark gray skirt, extended in appeal. "I know it's not convenient, but it would help so tremendously if you'll do the run to school." She jumped into the skirt, and started hitching it up.

He watched silently as she darted to the dresser to grab her hairbrush and whisk it through her chestnut hair. Her frazzled disarray was puzzling to him. She was usually so organized and punctual. He liked that about her, just as he liked contemplating her now, his wife, who probably could have had a career as a model if she wasn't so modest about her looks, and didn't have a passion for history and teaching. "Okay, babe, sure," he said, with a sigh. "I'll take the kids if it helps."

"You're an angel." Half hobbling as she slipped into her heels, she came over to give him a quick kiss before veering back to the dresser to rummage in her jewelry drawer.

"I'd just like to know what happened here. You seem really upset."

"Oh . . ." She bowed her head, her spirit sagging totally. "I wanted to wear the earrings, and I dropped one. It's around here somewhere—I went crazy looking, but I couldn't find it."

He knew, of course, which pair was "the" earrings. He moved up behind her. "Well, don't make it such a big deal. It'll turn up later. And, if you ask me, wearing those wouldn't be appropriate, not today. Even at that gilt-edged school, I don't think they want teachers who show up glittering as if they're going to the opera."

"They're just earrings!"

He was silent, and she raised her head, her eyes meeting his in the mirror.

"There's no one better, Katie," he said then, with a wink and a smile. "You'll get the job."

Her rock, her comfort, her friend, booster, partner, lover. She smiled back and looked deep into his mirrored gaze for another moment.

"I'm a very lucky man," he said, quietly, and not for the first time, but with an evident passion and pride that expressed a fresh appreciation of the simple miracle of having met and married her.

That was a mirror, too, of her own feelings of good fortune at that moment, and she turned and they kissed. Then Kate rested her head on his shoulder—a moment's calm to restore herself from the whirlwind. Until, over his shoulder, she saw the clock on the night table showing 8:10.

"Oh, hell!" she erupted, tearing loose. "I've got to get out of here." She spun back to the jewelry drawer and started raking through its contents. "And I still haven't picked out something to replace—"

"C'mon," he said, "you don't need any special charms except your own." He pulled her gently away from the dresser. "I'll find the earring later, I promise."

They went downstairs together. The twins looked at her in near disbelief as she gave each one a lightning hug and nuzzle, then dashed for the back door.

"Daddy's taking you this morning, lovebugs," she explained, then stopped to glance back at him for one more brief second. "Thanks again, lover."

"Hey," he said, "anytime. Now, go knock 'em dead."

"See you all later," she said, blowing a quick kiss.

As Kate turned for the door again, her glance caught the kitchen clock. It was 8:13, her time really growing short.

2

At the same time Kate was saying good-bye to her family, a young woman named Janet Curtis was just leaving the checkout counter of the supermarket in the Centerstop Mall. Janet rarely went grocery shopping before work, but at the local bank, where she was assistant manager, a favorite teller was leaving to move with her husband to the Sun Belt, and Janet had offered to pick up food and drinks for a farewell party after work that day. Pushing a cart loaded with four bags of sodas, pretzels, and potato chips, Janet left the supermarket and headed toward the edge of the parking lot. She always left her new Jeep Cherokee at a distance, parked on its own, a precaution against possible dings and scrapes caused by other cars.

Halfway to her car, Janet heard a voice behind her say, "Hi." She turned to see a young man trailing along.

"I thought you might need some help putting those bags in your car," he said. He smiled and moved closer.

He looked nice enough, dressed in clean jeans and a leather jacket that might be expensive, but it bothered her that he'd followed so closely without her being aware of him. It couldn't be a simple pickup attempt; she judged him to be a year or two out of high school at most. "That's very kind," she said. "But I can manage."

"It's no trouble." Before she could protest, he had moved up to the cart and started pushing it toward her Jeep. Janet hung back a second, wondering what to do, how hard to resist, or whether it was worth resisting at all.

He glanced back and saw her hesitating. "C'mon," he said. "It'll just take a second."

She decided he must hang around the mall to offer exactly this small service in exchange for tips. Janet took out her keys and joined him at the back of the wagon. She opened the hatch and turned to the cart to help with the bags.

"Don't scream," he said abruptly in a low growl. "Whatever you do, don't scream or I'll shoot."

The breath went out of her as she saw that he was holding a gun aimed at her chest. "Oh, God," she gasped.

He told her to give him the keys, then load the bags into the back of the car. For a moment, she was rigid, her eyes darting over his shoulder to see if there was anyone who might help. But they were far enough from the store that the few shoppers who came at this hour wouldn't be aware that she was in trouble. She handed him the keys, then froze again.

"Move," he snarled.

"Please don't hurt me," she said, and kept repeating it until she had loaded all the bags into the car. He slammed the tailgate shut, then told her to walk in front of him to the passenger side and open the door. He slid into the seat first, keeping the gun aimed at her as he positioned himself at the wheel and ordered her to get in.

Of all the things racing through Janet's mind, one suddenly stood out—a TV talk show on which several women told of being in situations like this, and suggestions were given on the best way to react. One key lifesaver was to avoid letting an abductor take you anywhere secluded. Empty as the parking lot was, it was still a public place; once she got in the car, Janet thought, he could take her off to a deserted spot where anything might happen.

With one hand, he slipped the keys into the ignition, while the other prodded the gun forward again. "C'mon! Get in or I'll shoot you right here."

She raised her foot to the floor of the car and turned her body as if preparing to sit. But with each fraction of a second, she was calculating when she would be in the best position to launch a run without risking a stumble or fall.

And then, without even knowing at what point the decision had been made, she was off and running across the wide-open asphalt field.

"Bitch!" she heard him scream.

Expecting a shot to follow, Janet dared not even the quickest look over her shoulder. From farther behind came the sound of the motor roaring, then the squeal of tires. He was going to run her down! She had to look now, to know which way to dodge. Grabbing a quick look backward, Janet saw the red wagon just speeding out of the parking lot, swerving right across the path of an oncoming car onto Center Road.

Officers Wayne Norstrand and Ralph Jefferson of the Fairhaven Police were having morning coffee in their car outside the Dunkin' Donuts when the dispatcher came on the radio to report a 911 call from a woman whose red Jeep Cherokee had been car-jacked at the Centerstop. The officers reported to the dispatcher that their own location was within a mile of the mall, and were told the direction in which the stolen car was last seen heading. Immediately, they tossed their cups of unfinished coffee out the window, and sped off in hot pursuit.

Freed of the task of dropping off the twins at school, Kate didn't turn onto Center Road—which went through town—but continued on Woodlands Drive. This route lengthened the drive to Ashedeane Prep by nearly two miles, but it would also allow her to go much faster, since there were no stoplights, and much less traffic.

She had gone a mile or two from the intersection when a police car went racing past in the opposite direction, its warning lights flashing. Preoccupied with rehearsing answers for her interview, she barely gave it a thought.

Jim Weyland had finally gotten the kids out the door, lunch boxes and homework remembered, scarves and hats in place against the early autumn chill. He squelched the bickering about who would get to ride with him in front very quickly: "In back, both of you—or you get no hotchafoddle for supper!"

The twins were familiar with his nonsense-word tricks, but they loved playing along. They were in back, buckled up, before Tom grumbled, "I betcha I wouldn't like hotchafoddle, anyway," and Chloe reminded him gravely, "There's no such thing, dummy!"

"Think again, Button," Jim said. "This time you're wrong."

"What's hotchafoddle?" the children demanded in chorus.

Jim paused to invent an answer as he reached the exit from the cul-de-sac and turned onto the beginning of Woodlands Drive, one block from where it met Center Road. Approaching the stop sign, he was startled by the sight of a large, bright red vehicle rocketing left to right across his vision, going so fast it was almost a blur.

"Wow!" Tom whooped from the rear seat. "Did you see that?"

"Asshole!" Jim blurted, too outraged to be mindful of his language.

"Daddy!" Chloe scolded.

"Sorry, kids. But driving like that, it's criminal!" He looked carefully up and down the crossroad now, saw that the way was clear, and began to turn left past the stop sign. Then he stomped on the brakes, suddenly aware of a car hurtling straight toward him out of the morning shadows along Woodlands. Its blue roof lights were flashing, but they had been lost until now in the dappled morning sun filtering through roadside trees. A police car, obviously, in hot pursuit of the reckless jerk who'd just passed. Now the siren began to scream—apparently to warn all traffic that the police weren't going to stop before taking the turn.

"Hey, look, cops!" Tom shouted excitedly.

Having crossed half the near-side lane before hitting the brakes, Jim debated for a second whether it was best to continue forward—or shift into reverse, and back the car behind the stop sign. Reverse, he decided, and just had time to get the car in gear before it seemed the police car was there, right there, hardly having slowed, simply expecting the path to be clear.

3

Kate was bursting with excitement. She might already be late for class, but on the drive to the high school she pulled her car to the side of the road and took out her cell phone to call Jim at the office. She let his private line ring four times, then remembered he had an appointment to pitch a fire policy and guessed he must still be there. Never mind, saving the news for tonight would be even better—feed the kids early, bring out the champagne, and tell him the news over a candlelit dinner.

Kate's elation was all the greater because during the interview she'd been so certain it was going against her. She'd done well answering the questions about curriculum and the reasons she felt the study of history was of particular importance, but once the Michelangelo thing came up, she felt her goose was cooked. She realized then that the issue hadn't been raised in previous meetings because those were with teachers and administrators, people who were already sympathetic. Her jury today was the trustees—wealthy alumni of the school—who were more concerned with avoiding controversy.

"I know it was covered in the news at the time, Mrs. Weyland, but I'd appreciate hearing from you directly about the trouble you had with the school board."

It was the trustees' chairman who'd brought it up. A man named Dudley Sherman; he was Fairhaven's richest citizen, his fortune derived from the medical products company founded by his grandfather.

"How much background do you want?" Kate began her reply.

"We're familiar with what led to the problem," he said. "We'd just like to hear how you feel in retrospect—and how your feelings might bear on the way you would instruct students at Ashedeane."

No surprise, of course, that they all knew the background. Where Fairhaven's schools were concerned, there hadn't been a bigger story. In her eleventh-grade survey course on "World History," Kate always spent a few weeks on the Italian Renaissance, during which she cited Michelangelo as the greatest creative force of the period—a master not only of sculpture and painting, but an architect to whom the Vatican had turned when building St. Peter's Basilica. In one class four years ago—just that one—she had remarked that Michelangelo's genius was such that, although he was apparently homosexual, the Church honored him with its most important commissions. Even in the halls of highest moral authority, in a much more conservative time, Kate had observed, what was deemed most important about the man was his mind, his talent, not his sexual preference. The remark had been carried home by a student—or perhaps several, she was never told—and the next day she was asked to explain to the high school's principal why she had been so foolish as to offer such superfluous information.

Superfluous? Foolish? Wasn't tolerance one of the values children ought to learn in school? she defended herself. Did it go unnoticed that many students were coping with problems of sexual identity as they went through adolescence? Was it bad for them—or those who might taunt them—to hear that, in the history of the world, people were judged only by the positive contributions they made?

She had made her case with the principal—though he advised her it wasn't prudent to crusade for these opinions. Indeed, she was soon called before the school board to explain again. The matter then escalated into a community debate on whether it was the school's place to openly "advocate" sexual freedom. If Kate had survived, it wasn't because of any reasonable defense, but because the principal had praised her before the board as a talented teacher the system couldn't afford to lose. And because there had been an outpouring of support from students she'd taught over the years at Fairhaven High—declaring in demonstrations outside the board hearings that Mrs. Weyland's classes were the most interesting they'd ever had, and that she brought history to life in ways that gave them valuable perspectives outside the classroom.

In the end, Kate had been allowed to continue even as assistant principal. It was understood, however, that she would henceforth avoid anything in the classroom that was—as Dave Kronin, the principal, put it to her—"sensitive to misinterpretation." Never mind, Kate reflected at the time, that history itself often required interpretation.

Now here she was in this interview being challenged again. Kate met Dudley Sherman's probing gaze squarely, then swept an unashamed glance over all the others in the conference room. Quietly, she said, "I can't tell you how much I've been hoping for the opportunity to teach at your school precisely because I believed that there would be less resistance here to letting your children be prepared for all the realities of the world that waits for them when they leave this safe and privileged place. Do any of you know the derivation of the word 'educate'?"

No one answered, and she continued. "It's from the Latin *educere*, which means 'to lead forth.' I don't believe we can lead our children out from behind these protective walls by being overly selective about which truths we permit them to know, and which we keep hidden. At the heart of education must be endowing students with an ability to discriminate wisely between true and false, right and wrong, what's decent and valuable . . . and what's specious and useless. Giving young people that ability, that's what I would strive to do every day for every student I educate. And I cannot believe a good beginning toward that goal would be to agree to teach only the easy truths."

There had been a long silence then, and Kate suddenly realized she'd been up on a soapbox, so wrapped up in pontificating she wasn't sure she had even replied to the question.

"Well, Mrs. Weyland," Dudley Sherman had said at last, "I think we've heard quite as much as we need." When she'd been asked to wait, Kate had assumed it was only to confirm among themselves that she could be told immediately she was no longer under consideration.

However in a highly unusual move, the board had brought her back into the room to offer her the job on the spot, and had expressed their desire for her to start, if possible, with the January term. This extra phase of the interview had lasted so long, in fact, that by the time Kate entered Fairhaven High, she could already hear the 10:25 bell announcing the start of classes. By the time she raced up to her second-floor classroom, her tenth-grade class in American history was just settling down.

"Good morning, everyone."

A ragged chorus of "good morning's" came back at her. Only as she arrived at her desk did it strike Kate that in all the rush this morning, she'd left home without her class notes, and the marked essays on the reasons for the Puritan emigration from England she had wanted to return today.

The lack of notes didn't bother her; she had no trouble speaking off the cuff on the period of early American settlement they were covering. Yet Kate found herself wordless as she looked at the rows of young students in front of her, their expressions marked by a curious sense of uneasy expectation. Perhaps because they'd noticed she wasn't going to hand back their homework.

"I'll be returning your papers on the Puritans tomorrow," she said to cover it. "They're generally very good, and they deserved a very careful reading. Now, we'd begun to discuss the settlement of—"

From the front row, Tammy Stuart piped up. "They've been looking all over school for you, Mrs Weyland."

"They? Who, Tammy?"

"Mr. Kronin . . . some of the teachers."

Of course, she hadn't mentioned the interview at Ashdeane to any of her coworkers, and ordinarily she would be at school by eight thirty, either in her homeroom or at her small office in the administrative suite.

"Did anyone mention why?" Not a routine matter, she supposed, if it wasn't the principal alone wanting to track her down.

More than a few kids said no, or shook their heads, an indication the search had been fairly extensive. Kate realized now why they were edgy with curiosity. She considered excusing herself to go and see Dave Kronin, but decided to wait until after class. If she went now, it risked being asked where she'd been the past two hours, and she'd be snared in tedious evasions, or in a conversation that would eat up all the class time. Plus, she needed to discuss leaving at Christmas.

"Well, thank you for telling me," she said. "Let's get back to the Puritans. Remember, we were talking about the period after the *Mayflower* arrived here. I wanted to go a little deeper into—"

She was interrupted by a couple of taps on the small window in the classroom door. Looking over, Kate saw Dave Kronin's narrow face behind the glass. She gave him an inquisitive glance, anticipating a sign or gesture to summon her into the hall, but the door opened, and he stepped partially inside. "Katharine," he said, "I'm sorry . . . but I need to speak to you. . . ."

His voice was tremulous and a bit husky, she noticed, the tone so obviously dejected that she could tell the need was absolutely critical. Had they been looking for her to step into his shoes because of some disaster that had befallen him?

"Of course," she said. She was about to turn to the children, and assign a section of the text to read until she returned, when Betsy Linnaker, another history teacher, came in past the principal. She walked with an odd gait, almost on tiptoe, as if she were afraid to wake someone.

"Betsy will take over your class," Kronin said, and extended his hand as if to lead Kate out of the room.

That was when she realized she wasn't being called out only for a minute. Having another teacher take over the class meant she wouldn't return to it today, hinted darkly that her absence might even last beyond. Her first thought was that Kronin must have learned she was pursuing another job without the courtesy of informing him, an action he could view as a betrayal, given the way he'd fought on her behalf in the past. In the circumstances, she wondered if she wasn't about to be summarily fired.

As soon as she was alone in the hallway with the principal, he took several paces away, plainly wanting to put some distance between them and the classroom before speaking. When he faced her again, the emanations of some unpleasant emotion consuming him were undeniable. "Katharine," he said, and coughed to clear his throat, "I hardly know how to tell you this. . . ."

"Is it about Ashedeane?" she said, to make it easier.

"Ashedeane? No." He appeared thoroughly confused. "No, I'm afraid it isn't."

"Then, what—"

A faint noise echoed along the hallway from behind Kate, and she looked around to see Judy Forrest, the school secretary, at the far end on the landing at the top of the stairs, standing and watching tensely, as though from behind an invisible barricade erected to save innocent bystanders from a bomb.

Then, all at once, for no reason Kate could ever consciously understand, the image of that police car racing past her on the road this morning loomed in her mind, filling it, the lights flashing so brightly that, seen only in memory, it seemed they made her eyes ache. At that moment—or at least she would believe later—even before she turned back to the messenger and he began to speak, she knew.

Knew some of it anyway, if not the worst.

4

A squad car was waiting outside to race her to the hospital, the police summoned even while the principal was proceeding to her classroom to break the news. An accident, he told her—Jim's car on the way to school; quite serious, apparently; and Jim and the children had all been injured and taken to the hospital. On the way there, Kate kept trying to find out more from the policemen. How had it happened? How serious were their injuries? The answers she got were only sketchy. The car had been hit during a high-speed police chase of a stolen vehicle, that was all they knew.

At the hospital, a policeman escorted her straight to an elevator. "I want to see them," she said, and he nodded and pushed a button.

Where the elevator doors opened, a sign faced her: OPERATING ROOMS A & B—over an arrow. The policeman steered her in the opposite direction. Along a hallway, Kate saw a doctor waiting by a door, the ear tubes of a stethoscope dangling from a pocket of his white coat. He was talking into a phone, but folded it up, and dropped it into a pocket as soon as she approached.

"Can I see my husband and children?" she asked at once.

"Mrs. Weyland, I'm Dr. Bittman," he answered obliquely. "Would you come in here, please?"

Kate looked through the doorway into a small waiting room. "No—I don't want to sit and wait. I need to be with them."

"Soon," he said, gentle yet firm. "I need to talk with you first."

Strong as she wanted to be, the jolt of adrenaline that had come when she heard about the accident had waned, and she let the doctor guide her into the waiting room. As she entered, a nurse in a corner looked up from a lamp table, where she'd set a small tray on which were a hypodermic, a cup of water, and some pills. At the sight, a sense of overwhelming dread came over Kate like an avalanche of cold black snow rushing down to bury her and suddenly she felt too weighted down to stand.

"Nurse," the doctor said briskly as Kate began to sway, and the nurse rushed forward to assist her to a chair.

But the very act of accepting help would somehow make her worst fears true, Kate thought. "Leave me alone," she brayed as she struggled to stay on her feet. "Just tell me!" When they hesitated, she was surprised to hear her own voice emerge in a roar: "For God's sake, *tell* me!" It drained her, so that when the doctor merely gestured to the nearby couch, she had no more will to resist and sank onto it.

Nodding toward the tray, he said, "You can have something at any time. . . ."

"No, I can't stand this anymore. I just want to know." Whatever they gave her would only dull her senses. It bound her more to her family to feel as much as she could, to suffer no less than the suffering she imagined they must be going through.

The doctor pulled a chair over in front of her. Before he could sit, the phone in his pocket chirped. "Excuse me," he said, extracting it. He said, "Yes, all right," into the phone, then dropped it back into his pocket.

Seated at last, he said solemnly, "As you already know, Mrs. Weyland, there was an accident. A very bad one, I'm afraid. I sincerely wish I didn't have to tell you this. . . ." He paused for a deep breath, and Kate felt as if her heart stopped before he went on. "Unfortunately, your husband and your little boy both expired at the scene. . . ."

In the first instant, she simply rejected it. Some mechanism of the mind raced into action, assuring her it couldn't be true, that if she merely refused to believe it, then it could be nothing more than words, meaningless words that couldn't hurt her. Then, as the doctor kept gazing at her, waiting for a reaction, the words replayed in her brain: *unfortunately, your husband and your little boy both expired at the scene. . . .* And now the fury mushroomed up within her. *Expired!* What the hell kind of word was that? Died? Was that what he meant?

Unfortunately! She glared at him, consumed by rage at the lie of language he was perpetrating on her. "What do you mean?" she demanded savagely. "Say what you *mean*!"

"Mrs. Weyland," the doctor replied evenly, "their injuries were massive. They couldn't be saved."

She began slowly scraping the nails of one hand across the palm of the other, gouging as deeply as she could into her skin. She had a reflex yearning to discover she couldn't feel it; that this was a dream, after all. And when it hurt, when she glanced down to see shreds of skin caught under her nails, the lines of blood in her palm, that too gave some sort of relief—to sacrifice the absence of physical pain. In a small way, it distracted from the agony of the spirit that was welling inside.

The doctor reached out quickly and pulled Kate's hands apart.

"Chloe . . . ?" she said in a pleading whisper and turned to the nurse. A woman—a mother herself, perhaps—must give her the answer she wanted. The nurse came and knelt beside her, taking one of her hands as the doctor released it. Kate turned back to the doctor to find his eyes were also directed to the nurse, silently asking her to perform some further benevolent service.

"Your daughter was brought to the operating room," the nurse said quietly. "The doctors were with her until just a little while ago. They did everything humanly possible, Mrs. Weyland. . . ."

And, Kate waited for her to say. *And? Andandandandandandand?* The word drummed in her brain with the quickening beat of her heart, pounding faster and faster as the silence went on, until she couldn't escape the realization there was no *and.* The nurse just gazed back silently, her own eyes filling with tears.

In the detonation of emotions that rocked Kate now, it seemed that a million memories went through her mind, each distinct, yet all packed together into an instant, so many images piled on, packed in, fused together in a mental nuclear blast. It wasn't *her* life that flashed before her eyes, but *their* lives, the life they'd had together. Blown apart and destroyed forever! Kate's head dropped back, and she stared up at the vacant white of the ceiling for a second, and a terrible primitive howl rose out of her throat. *Don't!* she meant to say. *Don't do this to me!* But she couldn't form words, could only cry out the sound, hoping, even without articulation, it would carry the plea to Jim, the children—to God, maybe—she didn't really know whom to beg for relief.

She was aware of movement around her, the sleeve of her blouse being pushed up, and she looked down to see the doctor beside her, holding the hypodermic.

"Let me give you this, Mrs. Weyland," he said. "To make it easier."

"You can't," Kate murmured, her voice dying to a whisper. "You can't. . . ."

Though she was not, the doctor understood, refusing the shot.

Whatever they gave her acted quickly. Soon, everything she perceived seemed to pass through a filter that softened the focus, muted the sound, slowed time itself. The waves of grief didn't stop coming, but she wasn't submerged in them, drowning; rather, she seemed to be floating along on their current. While she remained slumped in a chair, sobbing, the nurse put some salve and a small bandage over the wounds in her palm, then stayed to hold her hand.

She was aware of the doctor going away briefly, then returning. "Friends of yours have begun to gather downstairs," he said. "Anyone you'd like to see?"

She shook her head. "Not yet," she managed to say between sobs.

"I'm told your mother is also on her way. . . ."

She nodded dumbly, and the doctor started to turn from her, and she grabbed at his sleeve. "I'd like to see them," she said.

"I'll send them up."

"No—not friends. My—" *Family*, she was going to say. But that seemed absurd suddenly. "My husband . . . the children," she finished.

"If you'll wait a bit," the doctor said, "I'll arrange it. For your daughter. Your husband and the boy were taken . . . somewhere else." He walked out.

Those two dead at the scene, she remembered. *To the morgue*, the doctor must have stopped himself from saying. All at once, her stomach was churning, and before she could move, Kate vomited, messing her blouse and her skirt. *Damn!* she thought. She didn't want Jim to see her this way! Which then struck her as comical, and she almost laughed out loud, but stopped herself, realizing it was hysteria and she mustn't shatter now or she could never be put together again.

"The sedative can do that," the nurse said. "Sit there, dear. I'll get a cloth. . . ." She left the room and returned with a bowl of warm water and a washcloth. Kneeling in front of Kate, she swabbed the mess from her clothes. "How are you feeling, dear?" she asked after a minute.

How? What *was* the feeling? "I want to die," Kate murmured.

"Of course, you do," the nurse said, "that's understandable." She rinsed the cloth in the bowl, and dabbed some more. "It would be wrong, though."

Two wrongs don't make a right, the old saw ran through Kate's mind. But maybe in this case they did.

The doctor was back. "You can come with me now, Mrs. Weyland. If you're still sure it's what you want."

She nodded, and the nurse helped her up.

The body had been brought to a recovery room on the same floor; no chilly air, or cold marble slab. Kate asked to go in alone, but before she entered, the doctor tried to prepare her for what she'd see. His words came to her in patches as if she were hearing him through static on a radio:

. . . massive bleeding . . . insult to the brain . . . even if she'd lived . . .

In the room, the blinds were closed, but a lamp was on beside the bed where Chloe lay, her eyes closed, the blankets pulled up under her chin. Her head was in a bandage wrapped at a slight angle, almost the way Kate would jauntily set a tam when she helped dress her for cold weather. Her long blond hair trailed out from under the gauze on only one side. Kate guessed it had been cut on the other, where they had operated. She touched one cheek gingerly, afraid the lifeless coldness she anticipated could deliver a shock as lethal as high voltage. But as soon as she touched the cool skin, all she wanted to do was bring it back to warmth, the way she'd massage the kids' fingers after pulling off their mittens on a winter day. She opened her hand and rubbed it lightly over the contours of her daughter's face. Then she was overwhelmed by the need to hold the child close. Slipping her arms around the slim shoulders, Kate pulled her child up, but there was no suppleness, no "give." The small body had to be lifted almost as a piece, an object. Kate let go, fearful the memory of this last hug would adulterate a thousand others she would have to depend on remembering. She stood for a long time then, just looking at the face, appreciating how beautiful her child was.

Emerging from the dim room into the bright fluorescence of the corridor, she had the odd sensation of not remembering where she was, the kind of momentary amnesia that often occurred when she woke after a night spent away from home.

A few nurses stood talking in hushed tones, but they dispersed when they saw Kate emerge. Only the one who had been escorting her remained. "How are you, Mrs. Weyland?" she said, slipping an arm around Kate's waist.

"I don't know."

"Would you like to lie down for a while, or be taken home?"

"I don't know."

The nurse glanced at Kate. "A lie down might be good."

Kate let the nurse guide her along the hallway. The drug had taken complete hold of her mind and will. The air through which she moved seemed as thick as oil.

Suddenly, another woman was at her side, gripping her arm. "I saw her rise," she said. Kate stared at her. Another nurse, she realized—or perhaps a doctor—clothed in a blue-green smock. "I was there when she passed," the woman went on. "Your little girl. I saw her rise."

The first nurse spoke up. "Anne, please—not now."

"But I did," said the woman named Anne. Her grip on Kate tightened as her voice took on an urgent tone. "I saw her rise up. You can be at peace. She's in a far-better place." The nurse turned from Kate to her colleague. "That's all I wanted to tell her. Surely, she's glad to know."

"All right, Anne," said the first nurse firmly. "Leave her with me now."

The woman let go of Kate's arm, but remained looking at her another second, a smile of inherent sweetness on her face. Kate took in more of her aspect—small, with short brown hair, eyes behind plain spectacles with wire frames. Then the woman vanished as abruptly as she had arrived—or so it seemed to Kate, her senses muddled by drugs on top of the shock.

In a minute, she was resting on a bed in another room. The solitude, the absence of people, was a blessing. Alone, Kate felt, was the way she belonged now. Alone always, in every way.

The curtains were drawn, but through a gap she could see a slice of sky, the crisp brilliant blue of autumn. Such a lovely day, as beautiful as any could be if you went only by the weather. Was there really a heaven up in that blue?

I saw her rise.

The words echoed and reechoed in her mind. How soothing, how perfectly lovely to believe Chloe had gone there—that they were all there together.

And, oh, how nice it would be to join them, to rise up to that blue heaven. If that were only possible.

5

The agony was unbearable. Yet she had to bear it. Hour after hour, day after day. The good-byes over the bodies—Jim and Tom at the funeral home, after Chloe at the hospital. Then the church service, sitting through the long, well-meant sermon on the unfathomable nature of life's mysteries; and the graveside ceremony, watching the caskets lowered away forever into the cold ground. At home, mourners streamed through endlessly, including the delegation from the Fairhaven Police to deliver an official apology. Another visitor was the woman whose car had been stolen. For some reason, she felt a need to take Kate's hand and apologize to her, as if by any stretch of the imagination she had been responsible.

Kate could tolerate it at all only because the pain, her perception of all the events that followed unbearably one on another, was completely dulled by drugs. She drifted through a succession of days and nights, unaware of where one ended and the next began, largely unable to believe that any of what was happening was real.

Occasionally, though, the relief of the tranquilizers and sedatives and painkillers wore thin. Then her mind would teem with visions and echoes of the last time she'd been with them—the last chance, as she thought of it, to do something differently, add or subtract one minute in the schedule of fate so that they wouldn't have been at the time and the place where disaster had overtaken them. If any one person was to blame, she thought, it was she. If only she'd held them a little longer that morning, hadn't said such a hasty good-bye. *See you all later*. The parting words uttered so casually echoed a thousand times a day within Kate's mind, as maddening as a tinnitus ringing incessantly in her ears. The notion that any one of a hundred small changes in destiny's clockwork could have undone the catastrophe expanded beyond that quick good-bye to her every action. If only she'd planned the interview for another time; if only she'd driven the kids herself. Of course, there was one critical moment that she lived more than all the others: simply putting her hand out to reach for the earring. If only she hadn't been so goddamn clumsy, knocking it away . . . and then, compounding the sin, searched so long for the infernal thing—which she'd never found anyway. A minute or two less, maybe even thirty seconds, and—

If only.

There were times when she tried desperately to cling to a more objective, rational viewpoint, to tell herself that an accident was just that, an event over which no one had control. Other times, she sought relief in her knowledge of history, the lesson it taught over and over that life could be cruel, even to the best of people. Plagues, wars, "ethnic cleansings," terrorist atrocities, all down the centuries into our own newspapers here and now; she was far from alone in suffering the misery of beloved family members annihilated, saying a casual good-bye one morning to a mate or a child without realizing it was the last time you'd ever see them alive.

But in the end, to know others suffered the same misery made her feel no better. In her silent, empty home, alone in a bed too wide for one, she remained in unspeakable agony, flaying her mind and spirit with the belief that, in the final analysis, it was undoubtedly her own fault. And not just because of her actions of that one fateful morning. Deep in the night, when the leaden silence in the house and the emptiness of the bed were no less a torture than if she were being held to a flame, she decided there must be some other unforgivable wrong she'd committed sometime, somewhere. Surely such suffering as was being visited upon her would not be inflicted upon anyone except as a punishment?

But what was the unpardonable sin of which she was guilty, and for which she deserved to be plunged into such unendurable pain?

Throughout each ordeal, Kate's mother was with her. She'd been the one who brought Kate home the day of the accident. Jim's folks weren't near; they stayed at their summer house in Maine through the early autumn, so it was Sarah Ballard who had come straight from New York City, where she'd lived since the divorce from Kate's father, and moved into Kate's house. Sarah had overseen the funeral arrangements, brought in and prepared the food, opened the piles of mail to sort out condolences from bills that might need attention, and sat with Kate to read aloud the many cards of sympathy whenever Kate was up to listening.

Taking charge came naturally to Sarah. She had been at the top of her class in law school, met Kate's father there, but hadn't bothered taking the bar after marrying him. She'd done it only after the divorce; at the age of fifty-six, she'd taken refresher courses, passed the bar exam on her first try, and gotten a job doing pro bono work with Legal Aid. *Leave her to me,* Kate could imagine her mother saying in her calm, efficient way as she sent Jim's folks off after the funerals to return to Maine, and encouraged Kate's sister, Lisa, to return to Los Angeles, where her husband, a network television executive, was being pressed for decisions about the new season.

For days on end, Kate spent most of the time alone in her bedroom, crying until her lungs ached and her throat was raw. When the tranquilizers and sedatives took hold, she would lie on her bed in a haze of memories, or drift off into a half-sleep, where the awareness of her loss still lingered at the edges.

Her mother came in often to bring a light meal, or urge her to come out for a walk or join in the shopping. She offered, too, to take Kate to church. But Kate had no interest in seeing the sun or the trees, no appetite to prompt her to buy food. Nor was she able to think of church as being a refuge. While she'd had a conventional religious upbringing in her youth, enjoying occasional attendance at holiday services on Christmas and Easter, even spending a year in the children's choir, no one in her family had given much attention to churchgoing after the divorce. Faith became an abstract concept; not a crutch to cling to in times of trouble, but something you could afford to have only when things were going well. Now, if she went to church, if she even allowed herself to begin a conversation with God, Kate suspected it would only trigger an uncontrollable rage at this all-powerful deity for the cruel way her life had been destroyed.

When at last she did begin venturing out of her room, it was only to go downstairs in her robe and sit quietly with her mother in the den or the kitchen. While Kate stared into a fire, or picked desolately at some food on a tray, Sarah did a needlepoint or worked at a cross-word puzzle.

Her mother never forced her to talk, to bare what was in her mind, for which Kate was thankful. She had always been good that way, Kate remembered: never pushing in, certain that sooner or later things would emerge. She only had to keep herself available. At least, she had been good that way for Kate and her sister when they were growing up, letting them try things even when she disapproved, saying nothing until they were in over their heads and ready to seek her advice. Though Kate was equally aware that being simply patient and available hadn't worked so well with her father, who had been the one to ask for the divorce, had married again soon after it was final, and now lived in Seattle with his new family. (So committed to them, indeed, he had not come for the funerals, imagining that his obligation was ful-filled merely by sending three of the largest of the floral wreaths.)

On a Friday afternoon at the end of the third week after the acci-dent, before going downstairs to join her mother, Kate took a long shower and washed her hair, then finally dressed herself in one of the trim practical outfits she wore when teaching. As she descended the stairs, she could hear music on the radio in the kitchen, a baroque piece with a flute piping a sprightly melody.

Sarah was sitting on a bench in the kitchen nook, some papers spread in front of her. Engrossed in her work, she didn't notice Kate in the doorway, and Kate stood a minute appreciating her mother. At sixty-two, she looked damned good, still slim and well toned. She'd confessed to Kate that two years after the divorce she'd had "some tucks" done around her eyes and chin, and recently her hair had been cut in a shorter, more daring style, though she wasn't completely coloring out the swaths of silver that mingled with light brown.

Kate stepped into the kitchen and her mother looked up with a wel-coming smile. Sarah was relieved to see her daughter wearing some-thing other than rumpled nightclothes, looking at last as if ready to return to the world. She gathered up the papers from the table and stuffed them into a manila folder she set aside on the bench. "There's tea in the pot," she said, nodding at the stove. "Shall I get you a cup? Or there's some of that vegetable soup from lunch. . . ." She'd knocked on Kate's door at midday to offer the soup, but Kate had no appetite for it then.

"No thanks." Kate turned off the radio on the counter, then slid onto a corner of the bench. "I just wanted to talk."

Sarah waited. Available.

"I was thinking you ought to be going home. It's been almost a month."

"Three weeks and four days," Sarah corrected her.

"Long enough, in any case. You have a job, people depending on you."

"I'm not letting anything slide. I have people covering for me; they know this is where I need to be."

"I'll be able to manage by myself now."

Sarah gave her a probing look. "Will you, Katie?" Kate looked away, and Sarah took it for license to expand on her doubt. "What's happened, it's something so devastating that . . . well, there are no words to describe what you're going through. Of course, I loved Jim, too. . . . And losing my grandchildren is . . ." She was silent a moment. "But I know that as bad as it is for me, it has to be a thousand times worse for you. I've wondered . . ." Sarah stopped once more, a pause so long and deliberate that Kate understood she had to face her mother again to hear the rest. When she did, Sarah went on. "I've wondered if you can bear it."

Kate looked at her squarely. "I don't have a choice, do I?"

"As long as you feel you don't, I'll worry less. But I've been afraid you might decide there *is* a choice—that if I'm not here, then . . . anything could happen."

In the language of euphemism they were speaking, the translation of "anything" was obvious.

"Would you blame me?" Kate said.

"Yes, I would—for taking *my* child away from me just because yours were taken from you. I wouldn't think that's fair."

"Fair." Kate spat out the word. "That doesn't seem to have much to do with the way life works."

Sarah's tone grew firmer. "Not, perhaps, when events are out of our hands. But it has everything to do with the choices we make for ourselves and others. Fate hasn't been fair to either of us, but I want you to be fair to me, Kate—and fair to yourself. Give yourself time, and—"

"And *what*?" Kate erupted, springing off her seat to pace across the floor. "I'll get over this? In a year, two? Do you really think I can ever be whole again, Mother? And I don't see how I can go on living in

this pain. Why should I go on living? Just to have an endless proces-
sion of days in which I'll always feel like . . . like . . ." Kate clawed at
her chest as she began to weep helplessly. "Like my heart has been
torn right out of me, yet the darn thing keeps beating and it hurts,
hurts so terribly with every single beat. No, Mommy, no. That's no
way to live. My God, yes, if I wasn't so doped up on all the pills I'm
taking, I would . . . I'd . . ." A hiccup of hysterical laughter mixed with
her sobs. "I'd take even *more* pills, take every damn one!"

For a few moments, Sarah watched her daughter crisscrossing the
kitchen in a frenetic prowl for solace. "I know it's hard to imagine
now," she said finally, "but things do change. When your father left
me, I thought—"

"You're *not!*" Kate whirled on her mother furiously. "You don't
dare to compare Daddy walking out on you with—"

"No, no, of course not!" Sarah broke in. "I'm only saying that no
matter how bad things seem, they do get better."

"Do they? Or do we just get used to the pain, become hardened
and learn not to feel it as much?" Which wasn't better, Kate thought.

Sarah picked up the hint of accusation. "You think that's what happened to me?" she asked. "That I've become hard?"

Kate didn't answer. In fact, it struck her now that all the while she
had been incapacitated by her own grief, the only signs of sorrow she
had ever noticed from her mother were a few sedate sniffles during
the church service, and a trickle of tears at the cemetery, quickly dabbed
away with a handkerchief that remained neatly folded. Nor did her
mother have any trouble continuing to function: going to the supermarket to buy the food, keeping house, reading the newspaper. All
right, Kate acknowledged, it helped her; yet there was something in
her mother's stoic acceptance, her ability to go right on functioning
that she resented, too. With the magnitude of what had happened,
why didn't her mother collapse? There was nothing admirable in such
fortitude, not at a time like this. It wasn't strength, Kate felt, but a
kind of heartlessness. And it occurred to her now that, in all the traits
a child inevitably picked up from a parent, maybe this one, too, had
infected her. Was she feeling the loss of her family *enough*? Why hadn't
she actually died of grief? It seemed possible that, if she cared enough,
her own heart should break—literally.

"Well?" Sarah demanded. "Are you saying I don't feel things . . . ?"

The accusation spilled out of Kate, an indictment made harsher by fearing her mother's stoicism had molded her own emotions. "Well, I haven't seen this affect you very much. Jesus, you don't even have trouble working!" Kate waved at the file folder Sarah had laid aside on the bench. "You go right on, busying yourself with some legal file, or doing a crossword. For God's sake, Mother, how the hell can you even concentrate? Do I think you might not be feeling things as much as you should? Hell, I can *see* you aren't." Cruel to say so, Kate realized, yet it provided some vital relief to inflict pain after weeks of nothing but suffering with it.

Sarah stared back, trembling slightly as she struggled to control herself. Then her hand went to the envelope she'd laid aside on the bench. She picked it up, laid it on the table in front of her, and seemed on the verge of opening it—to expose its contents, to demonstrate what a worthy cause she'd taken on: preventing the eviction of some indigent family or saving a battered wife from her abusive husband. But then she shook her head, denying the impulse. "We all have our own way of feeling things," she said very quietly. And, averting her eyes, she broke down. Gulping air between high, keening sobs, she said, "You . . . are . . . not the . . . only one . . . who hurts."

Kate was suddenly filled with shame and regret for her callousness. She slid back onto the bench and encircled Sarah's shoulders with her arms. "Mother . . . forgive me. I'm truly sorry. But my own feelings have been so bashed around, maybe nothing that comes out of me now can be soft or kind or . . . even human." As Sarah's crying eased, Kate leaned into her, pillowing a cheek against her hair. "The way I feel . . . I've been reduced to an animal, or something even less, surviving out of nothing but reflex, without thought or will. I don't have a reason to go on living anymore, do I? It's only some primitive impulse that won't let me quit—the same mindless drive that . . . keeps tiny, one-celled organisms swimming through a drop of water." Kate leaned forward to look into her mother's face. "You want to know what this has done to me? There it is, Mom, the whole picture in microscopic detail. I'm a thing without a mind or a heart, just swimming aimlessly in a world that no longer seems any larger, or has any more to offer me than one little drop of water. I'm sorry, Mother, I truly am . . . but I can't know—can't care one tiny little bit—how anybody else feels. Even you." Kate started to pull away.

Sarah brought her arms up, and clasped to her chest one of Kate's arms before it could be withdrawn. "Now listen to how it is for me," she said. "There's a hole in my life, too. I have to do something to try and fill it . . . and the first thing I think of, the only thing that can work, comes out of *my* instinct—a mother's—to take care of you." She turned and moved her hands down to seize Kate's. "I need a promise from you, a solemn oath, or I won't be able to leave here. You have to swear to me that you will not abandon me, either . . . that you'll live with this, *try* to, instead of . . . running away."

Kate gazed into her mother's eyes and saw she meant it: without that oath, she was ready to give up her own life, and stay on and on and on, protecting Kate from herself. "I'll try," Kate said. "I will try." After a moment, she added, "I *am* trying."

They sealed their compact with a long embrace. At last, Sarah eased away. "Let's see how the weekend goes," she said. "If you're still feeling on Sunday you're ready to manage on your own . . . well, they wouldn't mind having me back in the office."

Over the next two days, Kate made an effort to demonstrate she had recovered to the point that her mother could return to the city. She dressed each morning; she accepted the invitation to go for a long walk on Saturday afternoon. And although she didn't agree to the idea of attending Sunday morning church services with Sarah, Kate rose early and made a nice breakfast, the first time in three weeks she had been the one to prepare a meal for the two of them. Kate wasn't quite certain herself if she was only "playacting" her readiness to be alone; perhaps, when her mother went, she would fall apart again. Or, perhaps, all she could ever do from now on was pretend that she would survive; as long as she kept up the pretense, she would.

Sarah stayed through Sunday afternoon. It was agreed she would catch the 5:48 to New York, and have the evening to settle in again at home. They spent the time quietly for the most part, Sarah's concerns surfacing in occasional little bursts of conversation. "Do you think you'll go back to work soon?" she asked at one point. And at another, "Have you given any thought to what you'll do with the house?" They were important questions, the kind that Kate knew had to be answered sooner or later, but answering them now seemed impossible. Though perhaps that was why Sarah had asked them, merely to test her equilibrium.

"I suppose I'll have to sell the house at some point," Kate said.

"But right now it's a way of staying near them. They're here . . . in all the corners, reminders. I'm not ready to let go of that." The tranquilizers helped her say it without breaking down.

About work, she answered honestly, "I don't know when I'll teach again. Or if I ever will."

Sarah knew her daughter was not only gifted as a teacher, but had always found immense pleasure and great rewards in her work. Yet her responsibility to the profession was such that she would need to feel she could do the job well, so Sarah didn't press her.

The taxi came twenty minutes before train time. Dusk had already settled, and the chilly air had a wetness in it foretelling rain. The gloom and the hint of a storm made Sarah anxious as she said good-bye to Kate at the door of the house and carried her valise to the taxi. After the driver took the bag from her, Sarah turned back.

Kate came down the path to meet her. "I'll be all right," she said.

"Promise me," Sarah said. "Give me your oath."

Kate understood. "I swear to try very, very hard," she said, "to go on living."

It was the best she could hope for, Sarah knew. She embraced her daughter and got into the cab.

Turning back into the house after the taxi disappeared around a corner, Kate stopped when she noticed all the dead leaves that were carpeting the lawn and piling up in drifts against the trees and the side of the house. Some well-grooved synapse in her brain sent the thought that Jim ought to rake and bag them—before she realized the leaves would continue to pile up unless she took care of them herself.

She stood in the chill evening air another minute, staring at the dead, dry remains of what had once been alive and green. Why did living things, lovely things, have to die? Why did they get reduced to insignificant dust to be swept away? *Ashes to ashes, dust to dust. Is that all that was left . . . ?*

At last, she went back into the house, took Jim's old sheepskin jacket from the coat closet, and got the rake and a couple of garbage bags from the garage. Under the light of the streetlamp and a quarter moon, Kate began to take care of her lawn.

6

Dozens of tasks kept her swimming through her drop of water driven by instinct alone. To the bank to set up an estate account; Jim's office to discuss how to keep the agency going; the lawyer's to go over the will. She'd assured her mother that Jim had left her secure, but as she dealt with these practical matters, it dawned on Kate that money was going to be a problem. For more than a year, she'd been telling Jim that the $75,000 life policy he'd taken out when he was thirty-three ought to be improved, but he'd been too busy handling everyone else's insurance to get around to it. Their savings added up to no more than $60,000 since they'd made the down payment on the new house, mainly in stocks that had declined sharply. And funeral expenses alone would take a big bite out of that—nearly fifteen thousand for the three, not counting headstones. What was left would hardly maintain her indefinitely, especially if she had trouble going back to work.

Added to those worries were the daily stresses of facing the searing reminders of her loss. People kept passing through the house—well-meaning Samaritans she couldn't rudely shut out, others with papers to sign. Chloe's ice-skating teacher came to say she was establishing a course of free lessons for a promising junior skater in Chloe's memory.

Most of the time, Kate felt as though she was a skater herself, gliding along over a cold flat surface, her momentum sustained by only an occasional small burst of effort. Then, without warning, she'd fall through a crack into a colder, darker place where she couldn't breathe. The worst plunge was at the supermarket.

Her mother had done the food shopping while she was with her, but by the end of her first week alone, Kate wanted more things she could fix without effort, throw in the microwave, and take up to bed. She drove to the mall, proud of herself to be responding normally to a private need. But then in the market, as she started to wheel a cart toward the long aisles with their vast rainbow arrays of boxes and cans and bottles, it struck her that there was no reason anymore to load up on ice cream or frozen waffles or soups with alphabet letters; she wouldn't be hauling home a dozen crammed shopping bags, but just a few paltry things, a widow's portion. In that instant, she felt the change of identity thrust upon her by events harden around her, determining the shape of her existence as immutably as if she'd been encased in cement. Here, in this place that fed her community—a crossroads where so often she met others like her—she had been wife, mother, teacher, active citizen, happy neighbor. Now she no longer belonged to any of those groups. She was nothing, every element of identity stripped away.

Glancing around—fighting for her balance on the ice—Kate caught a couple of the checkout girls giving her the same amazed examination they might give a movie star. Which brought home the realization that there was, after all, one flag of identity still flying: *there's that woman whose husband and kids—*

She raced out without buying a thing, and went to a small convenience store at the edge of town, walking past the door a couple of times until she could see from the sidewalk that no other customers were inside.

She was driving home when she happened to notice the white-brick bulk of the hospital several streets away, looming over the low roofs of the town's older buildings. As it caught her eye, that odd little scene with the nurse who'd stopped her in the hallway popped into her mind.

I saw her rise.

Abruptly, Kate swung the wheel over to the left, turning onto a street that headed in the direction of the hospital.

At the hospital, she went straight up to the central nursing station on the OR floor to inquire about the nurse whom she recalled hearing addressed as Anne. "I don't know her whole name," Kate admitted to the nurse who was alone at the station. "But she works in the operating room. . . ."

"You must mean Anne Morrissey—she's our only Anne. I haven't seen her today, though, Mrs. Weyland. Let me check the duty roster. . . ."

Another hint of her fame, Kate mused; she hadn't mentioned her own name.

The nurse finished scanning a loose-leaf binder. "Sorry. Anne's not here."

"Can you give me her phone number, or tell me where she lives?"

"I don't know offhand—but actually, Mrs. Weyland, there's a hospital policy against giving out personal information about nurses." Apparently affected by the disappointment she saw on Kate's face, she added, "But I think some nurses who usually work with Anne are on break in the cafeteria. Perhaps they can help. . . ."

In the ground-floor cafeteria, there were several groups of nurses at separate tables. But only one included a couple of women wearing the greenish-blue coveralls that Kate recognized as OR scrubs.

She didn't have to introduce herself this time, either. The five nurses at the table had been talking animatedly, but fell silent as Kate approached. "I was hoping one of you could help me get in touch with Anne Morrissey," she said.

The nurses traded glances, and one in OR garb spoke up. "I'm friendly with Anne," she said. She was about thirty, attractive, with well-cut, dark hair, and warm brown eyes. Kate also noticed a wedding band on her finger. Not the most likely friend for the spinsterish woman Kate remembered from the hallway encounter.

"I'd be very grateful," Kate said, "if you could give me her phone number?"

The friend sent one more glance at her coworkers, then picked up her coffee, and came around the table to join Kate. "Can I get you some coffee, too, Mrs. Weyland?"

She seemed to be signaling there was more to supply than just a phone number. "I'd prefer tea, thank you," Kate said.

The nurse nodded to a separate table in a corner. "Sit down. I'll join you in a minute," she said, and handed her coffee to Kate to bring over.

"I'm Sandy Pratt, by the way," she said with a smile when she came to the table. Along with the tea for Kate, she'd brought a couple of small muffins on a plate.

"Nice to meet you, Sandy."

Sandy offered the muffins, and when Kate declined, took one herself, and sipped at her coffee. "It may sound trite by now, Mrs. Weyland," she said at last, "but I'd like to say how deeply sorry I am for your loss."

"Thank you," Kate said, eager to move on.

The nurse took a bite of her muffin, and another, longer pull from her coffee. She was obviously having trouble opening a real conversation.

Kate took the initiative. "I know hospital policy frowns on giving out personal information, and I don't want to get you in trouble, Sandy, but I'm anxious to talk to your friend, and it doesn't really concern a hospital matter."

The nurse gave Kate a searching look. "Mrs. Weyland, I've heard Anne spoke to you the other day. Is that what this is about?"

"Well . . . yes. What she said was so unusual, it stayed with me, and . . . I thought I'd explore it a bit more. . . ."

Sandy gave a knowing bob of her head. "Before you do, I think you should know this isn't the first time Anne has done this kind of thing."

" 'This kind of thing,' " Kate echoed, begging a fuller description.

"What I've heard," the nurse said carefully, "is that Anne told you she'd seen your child's spirit leave her body. Is that correct?"

"Not in those words, exactly . . . but, yes."

Sandy fixed her gaze on Kate, evidently assessing what degree of candor a woman who had suffered so much might still absorb. "Anne's a very kind and sensitive person," she said, "and also deeply religious. For all the difficult things we're exposed to in the hospital, I'm sure Annie takes it hardest when . . . when it's the death of a child. She wants desperately to do something to help, and at times perhaps she wants it"—Sandy gave a little shrug—"too much."

Kate took a moment to weigh this. "Are you saying she told me what she did only to make me feel better?"

"No. I'm sure Annie believes she saw . . . something. But in the OR, with all the tension, with life and death in the air—and traces of gases that can have hallucinatory effects—some people are more susceptible. . . ." She left the suggestion hanging.

Kate sipped thoughtfully at her tea. "I'm surprised this woman is allowed to work in such an environment," she said then, "if she's unstable, prone to imagine—"

"I never said she's unstable," Sandy cut in. "Put Anne in one of the toughest work situations on earth, and she's a rock. There's no one our surgeons would rather have at their side—and no one who did more that day to—" She stopped, obviously to spare Kate from further mention of the failed attempt to save her daughter.

Kate picked up the thread. "I'm just trying to make sense of what you've told me. You insist your friend has her feet on the ground. But you started out by telling me—*warning* me, almost—that I shouldn't pursue this because it's . . . pointless."

Distress clouded Sandy's expression. "Mrs. Weyland, if you want to speak to Annie, of course I'll tell you how to reach her. I just thought it was important beforehand for you to know where she's coming from." The nurse hesitated. Then, her hands clutched around her coffee cup as if she needed to feel its warmth, she leaned forward and went on in a more tremulous voice. "I was also there . . . with your little girl. Some of them were, too." She waggled her head toward the table she'd abandoned. "We all hated losing her—hate losing anyone, of course, but children always the most. And most of us who work in the OR, who know what happens, don't think it's right for anyone in our position to do or say things that can make it even more confusing to deal with death and loss at a time when people are struggling to come to terms with it." The nurse looked searchingly at Kate.

Kate knew that what she had been told was meant to save her from that ill-timed confusion. "Thank you. I know you mean to be helpful. But all the same, I would like that phone number."

The nurse nodded, then fished a pen and a small pad from the pocket of her uniform. "That's her address, too," she said, handing over what she had written down.

Kate thanked her again, and they rose from the table together. "Sandy," Kate said, "if it's regarded as inappropriate in the hospital for Anne to say the sort of thing she did to me, why isn't she warned about it? You say it wasn't her first time."

"Oh, she has been warned," Sandy replied. "In fact, Mrs. Weyland, she's on suspension right now for doing it again—with you. And this time, unfortunately, there's some question about whether she'll be allowed to return." The nurse headed away to join the others.

Back in her car, Kate looked at the piece of paper with the phone number. It was tempting to think of hearing a beautiful fairy tale spun around her daughter, the promise of eternity spent as a little girl playing in paradise. But Kate understood, too, the reason for Sandy Pratt's concern, and the advice implicit in the information she had supplied. For some people, embracing a convenient fantasy could be the first step away from ever accepting reality.

At the moment, Kate felt she was perched precariously enough on solid ground that it could be dangerous to take that step. She folded up the piece of paper, and tossed it into the glove compartment.

She had let the answering machine take most of her calls, but at the end of the afternoon, when she heard Dave Kronin leaving a message, Kate picked up the kitchen phone.

"Your students have been asking for you," the principal said. "Have you given any thought to when you might come back to school?"

"I appreciate being wanted, David, but I'm nowhere near ready to face classes."

"I expected you'd need more time. I just wanted to assure you that whenever you are ready, we'd love to have you back."

She was touched. "Thanks. But even when I feel better, I may want to do something different."

"Ah, yes. That day—you said something about Ashedeane. Later I learned they wanted you. Hardly a surprise. You're an asset to any school, Katharine."

"David, I'm not sure about teaching *anywhere*. I don't think I'll have the concentration it requires, and I don't want to do the job if I can't do it well."

"That's why I hope you'll reconsider—because that *is* your commitment. Whether or not you come back here, you shouldn't be giving up. Our profession can't afford to lose people like you."

Giving up, she mused after the call, is that what it was? A failure to meet some essential obligation? A lack of courage?

Well, what if it was? She couldn't think of any good reason to keep going, to be brave—except the promise she'd made to her mother. Even if she could muster the will to teach, she wondered if Ashedeane still wanted her. There had been letters of condolence from people at the school, but nothing said about the position.

She went to the kitchen and took a couple of extra tranquilizers— there were bottles scattered all over the house now—then meandered aimlessly from room to room. Twilight was coming on, and in the half-light, visions of the life she'd lost clung to every corner like cobwebs. Chloe practicing her flute in the living room, Tom tracking puddles into the entrance hall after a snowball fight, Jim simply tossing a loving glance at her over some work papers he'd brought home. A lump rose in her throat, yet the worst of the sorrow was tempered by remembering that they *had* been happy here. Thank God, their time all together had been good, full, well used. There were, at least, few regrets from the past.

The familiar evening sounds of the street came wafting through the windows. A car door slammed and a man called out to his wife that he was leaving groceries at the back door while he went to collect their daughter from ballet class. A tide of bitterness rose within her, but she fought it down. She had to stop wallowing in this pool of bile, blaming people simply for still having what had been taken from her. It wasn't their fault. If it was anybody's—

The litany of *if only* she'd been through a thousand times began drumming again in her brain, all the things she might have done differently to change fate, keep them alive. Until, finally, she was fixating on the root of it all, the moment when the course of destiny had been changed by her carelessness. If only she'd been paying just a bit more attention—!

Something snapped then. She found herself charging up the stairs to the second floor. She tore into the bedroom, flipped on a light, and went to the place she'd been standing that morning when she'd knocked away the earring, then spun to look at its imagined flight. Leaping at the bed as if it were an enemy, she heaved the heavy oak piece off the floor with a burst of strength she'd never mustered before, and pushed it ahead of her until it bumped into the wall by the window. Then she fell to her knees and scoured the carpet that had been bared, a nest of dust-mice and lost coins and dry-cleaning tags that had drifted under the bed, out of reach of the vacuum.

But no earring! The murdering object—she had an insatiable need to find it now. For what? Maybe to put it under a hammer and smash it as her life had been smashed. She tore up the edge of the wall-to-wall carpet and looked there. Moved the dresser and the night tables. Went to the bathroom next. For an hour, she searched, her fury and frustration growing until she was insane with it, screaming aloud sometimes at the elusive thing. *"Let me see you! Why did you do this to me?"*

Finally, she gave up. Lying prostrate on the floor, she ached in every part of her, muscles sprained from overexertion, her mind and soul strained to breaking from having to deal with the unendurable.

Barely even aware of the transition—moving on a residue of the tranquilizers, she supposed, in a state not unlike sleepwalking—she found herself lying on Chloe's bed. Curled up, she clutched herself and surrendered fully to the grief, emitting loud banshee howls until her throat and her head ached even more than before.

God Almighty, how was she going to get through another night? Or, if she did, through the one after that?

Rolling onto her back, Kate stared up at the ceiling over her daughter's bed. Stuck to the ceiling were the "glow-in-the-dark" stars and planets Chloe had requested after a trip to the planetarium in New York. The glimmer of a do-it-yourself heaven turned Kate's thoughts to the notions of the paradise promised in one form or another by all faiths. Could there be such a thing? Was Chloe there now? Were they all surviving together in a place of eternal joy and peace?

Or was there nothing more than this fake heaven of glow-in-the dark stars shining down on her now?

I saw her rise. . . . Grappling with the question of an afterlife brought back once more that quick encounter with the nurse at the hospital. What *exactly* had she seen? The ghost of her daughter leaving her body, rising to a true heaven?

Oh, if only, if only!

Kate yearned to see that beautiful vision, too. If no other way were possible, then at least to see it through the other woman's eyes.

7

Kate stopped her car in front of 89 Lymon Street, the address provided by Sandy Pratt, and surveyed the house through the windshield. It was in an older section of town, the streets lined with narrow porch-fronted Victorians, separated by alleys, boxed-in yards beyond. In recent years, many had been bought at bargain prices by young couples, then spruced up with extensions, third floors, new outdoor lighting, and plantings. But still intermingled were several houses like this one that had remained for generations in the families of local blue-collar people. Number 89 was badly in need of repainting, and the porch eaves listed at a corner where a supporting post was cracked. Kate saw lamplight glowing in a front window behind lace curtains with gossamer backing, evidence that someone was home. At last, she pulled herself from the car and went up a path to the door. She rang the bell, a vintage mechanism that made a whirring *ching* when a knob in the door was turned.

The door was opened by the woman Kate recognized from the hospital. She was wearing a gray wool cardigan over a T-shirt bearing the faded panda logo of the World Wildlife Fund, and holding a newspaper in one hand.

"I . . . I know I should've called first," Kate stammered. "But I—"

"That's perfectly all right, Mrs. Weyland." Anne Morrissey stepped back from the door. "Come right in."

It was almost as if she'd been expecting her, Kate thought as she crossed the threshold.

"Who is it, Annie?" a woman's frail croak called from the second floor. "Who's coming at this hour?" She made it sound as if it were midnight, when it wasn't yet nine.

Anne closed the door and went to the bottom of the stairs. "Just a friend of mine, Mom," she called up.

"Don't get so wrapped up in chitchat you forget my potty."

Anne darted a sheepish glance at Kate as she called back, "I won't." She gestured to the portal that led into a parlor. "Please," she said warmly, "come and sit down."

The parlor furniture was of the same vintage as the house: lamps with china bases glazed with gaudy flower patterns, overstuffed chairs covered in dusty brown velour, frayed antimacassars draped over the arms and the back of a worn sofa. The faded decor added to the picture of Anne Morrissey's life that Kate had gathered from her first impression of the nurse, augmented by discovering she cared for a bedridden mother: a woman who had denied herself a full life of her own in favor of doing her duty. A woman, in short, who might believe in an afterlife because it was the only place where her thwarted ambitions and frustrated desires might be fulfilled.

"Can I offer you something—tea, a soda?" the nurse asked as Kate settled on one of two hard-backed chairs in the room.

"Thank you, no. I can see it's an inconvenient time—I shouldn't have barged in without letting you know."

"It's perfectly all right, Mrs. Weyland." The nurse seated herself on the sofa.

The assurance was welcome, yet now that Kate was inside, she felt a nervous impatience to leave. Perhaps it was an eagerness to escape from the vision of a life that might someday await her, too: the solitary daughter relegated to taking care of an aged, bedridden mother.

"I did try to see you at the hospital," Kate rushed on. "I learned you were in trouble for speaking to me—I mean, for telling me what you did. I realize you wanted to help, to be kind. I'm sorry if it caused a problem."

"No fault of yours. I thought you had a right to know what I'd seen."

From the upper recesses of the house came the old woman's voice. "Anne?" The single syllable was drawn out in an insistent whine.

Anne raised her eyes to the ceiling, then pursed her lips in tolerant forbearance. "Let me take care of her first," she said.

While she was alone, Kate explored the room, mining clues about the nurse. A freestanding bookshelf held a collection of ancient Book-of-the-Month club selections like *Peyton Place*. On a table in a corner was a photo album stuffed with family snapshots. Kate turned a few pages and recognized a much younger Anne in some of the candids, along with a man and woman who were obviously her parents, and another young girl and two boys who must be siblings. There was nothing in her youthful pictures to indicate she would be the one never to leave home. She had been a pretty child.

Kate heard footsteps descending the stairs, and went back to her chair. Anne came in and asked again if Kate wanted anything to drink, then took her place on the sofa when Kate declined. "Well, if you've talked to people at the hospital," she said, "then you know they regard me there as a bit . . . cracked." She let out a slight laugh, evidently to assure Kate her choice of word was meant ironically.

"I did hear," Kate admitted, "this wasn't the first time you said you'd seen . . ." What did one call it? A rising? "Had a spiritual experience," she concluded.

Anne smiled. "So perhaps they gave you the impression I see spirits fluttering through the hospital corridors night and day?"

Kate had to smile, too. Anne Morrissey's playful tone suggested a healthy sense of humor about herself. "I didn't go around the hospital talking to a lot of people," Kate said, eager to correct any impression her information came from suspicious prying. "I spoke only to a friend of yours—Sandy Pratt. All I wanted was information about how to contact you. But she understood why I was asking, and volunteered that there had been other occasions when you'd . . . had these experiences. She never said you were 'cracked,' though. She suggested they spring from your desire to make a bad time easier for people in my circumstances."

Anne fell silent, her eyes cast down, seemingly weighing her response. Finally, she looked back to Kate. "As I told you earlier, I didn't regard it as a matter of choice whether or not to let you know what happened. If we're shown certain things—if one person is able to see the light when others are in darkness—then there's a responsibility to help others to see. Wouldn't you agree, Mrs. Weyland?"

The hint of evangelical fervor underlying the words concerned Kate; yet she longed to believe that Anne Morrissey was no less purely rational than she was herself. She nodded sympathetically, and to smooth their exchange, she said, "Please call me Kate."

Reciprocating, the nurse said, "And you call me Anne."

The women smiled at each other. Kate felt that something more had happened than a simple exchange of amenities. Somehow, a bond of trust had been formed.

Anne resumed. "I don't wish to upset you, Kate, but if you'd like to hear more about what happened, then I need to speak specifically about how your daughter died. I can imagine it would be hard for you to hear, so stop me whenever you want, and forgive me if it becomes too much. . . ." The nurse paused, and Kate nodded. "Did anyone ever discuss the clinical picture with you?" Anne asked then. "Did they explain the cause of death?"

Most of it was a blur, but Kate remembered some generalities. "They said the worst injuries were to her brain."

"Yes, exactly. I was beside the neurosurgeon at the table, and I heard him discuss the prognosis. In his opinion, even if your little girl had lived, she would have had very limited faculties." The nurse checked Kate with a glance to be sure this had registered. "You need to know that to appreciate how unusual your daughter's death was. The injuries caused by trauma and intracranial bleeding had damaged a part of the brain that plays a major part in controlling speech. A point came two hours into the operation when the surgeon had to decide how much of this area he might have to cut through and possibly destroy if—" She stopped as she heard the sharp intake of breath that came involuntarily from Kate. "I'm sorry. . . ."

Kate's voice struggled up from her throat. "It's all right, go on."

"The head surgeon was discussing this decision with an assisting doctor, and as he mentioned the strong possibility of destroying whatever remained of the power of speech, a sound came from your daughter. If you asked others who were there, I expect they might say it was simply a reflex aspiration, nothing more than an escaping breath. But what I heard, Kate, was the word 'No.' I heard this child—in the depths of anaesthesia and—if you believe the doctors, with her brain already robbed of most of its ability—I clearly heard her express a wish not to . . . to be made even less human. Do you understand?" Anne aimed her gaze squarely at Kate. "I believe I heard her speak from the soul."

Were the nurse's eyes glistening with tears, or lit by religious fever? Kate wondered.

"You can suppose—I know the doctors did—that it was merely a reflex, a sound without meaning," Anne went on. "But what is a recorded fact is that half a minute later, just after the surgeons decided to risk cutting more in the interest of saving her, the little girl's heart stopped beating. All efforts to resuscitate failed."

"So are you saying," Kate asked, "that you believe Chloe *chose* to die . . . because she didn't want the kind of life she would have had otherwise?"

"Let me tell you the rest. It was during the attempt to resuscitate that I saw an aura form over the operating table. All the while, we were working to bring the heart back to life and restore blood pressure, I could see this ring of golden light around the child's body. I knew then she wouldn't come back, her decision was made. I give you my solemn oath, Kate, I never stopped doing my utmost best, but at the same time I knew. And when at last the surgeon gave up, that's when I saw her rise up."

"How?" Kate jumped in, though she knew Anne would have continued. "What did you see? Tell me exactly. Everything."

"I saw the child—her image, complete, but so . . . so luminous that I had to squint like trying to see through a mist—I saw her leave the dead shell of herself on the table, and float up, slowly. . . ." Anne's hands rose, like those of a conductor asking an orchestra for the most gradually rising crescendo, and her eyes lifted at the same pace. "Up she floated toward the glaring bright lights over the table. It hurt my eyes to look, but I did . . . and while she hovered under the lights for a moment, she smiled at me. Oh, such a glorious smile, so perfectly happy and at peace." Anne lowered her eyes again to meet Kate's. "Then she vanished into the light."

Kate was lost for a second in the image, the longing to believe. Then the doubts and questions flooded into her mind, crowding out the joyous vision.

Before she could express any, Anne said, "I know: people can say all kinds of things to explain it away. The electric charge from the heart-resuscitation attempts ionized the air and produced the aura, the lights over the table played tricks with my eyes. Or they can just say 'poor Annie's as cracked as the Liberty Bell.' " A small smile touched her lips. "But you asked me what I saw, Kate, and there it is. I have no doubt it happened. None whatsoever."

The nurse's conviction was obviously unshakable. How could it even be questioned? Yet the habits formed in the classroom impelled Kate to test the logic. "I'm grateful you've shared this with me—even though it has caused you some personal difficulty. But if it did happen, then why didn't anyone else see it? Can you explain that, Anne? Why are you the only one?"

"That's so simple, Kate: because I'm *willing* to see. I am, and the others aren't. My heart and mind are completely open. You don't see these things if you're not open to them."

Kate nodded agreeably, allowing this kind and earnest woman to think the answer was enough. She stirred in her chair. "Well, thank you again. I hope things work out at the hospital."

"I'm sure they will. But don't leave just yet, please. There's a bit more to tell. Because of the way the hospital has acted, you may have the impression it's common for me to approach people like yourself and speak of these things."

"You admitted it's happened before."

"True. But I've been a nurse at Fairhaven General for twenty-one years, Kate. In all that time I've had only two other experiences like this one."

Kate relaxed into her chair again. "Tell me about them."

Anne willingly described the two incidents with the same heartfelt conviction. The first involved a man who had suffered critical burns over most of his body after going into his blazing home to successfully rescue his wife and child. "It was my second year at the hospital," she said. "I was on the floor then, not in the OR. I was on a night shift when a light went on at the station showing me the call button in this man's room had been pressed. The signal alarmed me because I knew the man was heavily sedated—burns of that magnitude are incredibly painful—and also so heavily bandaged everywhere that it was impossible to see how he could have picked up the call button and used it. When I went to the room, the patient was still comatose, and the call button was hanging in its holder on the wall. I was standing there wondering about it when right before me a form—not as clear or luminous as your child's, more of a shadow but with more or less the shape of a man—left the body on the bed, and rose up. It hung in the air, then faded away . . . and at the same time, the heart monitor went flat, showing the patient had died."

The nurse gave a small shrug that seemed to acknowledge how insubstantial the incident could have been, the possibility that the "shadow" came from nothing more than someone in the corridor passing by the room.

"At first, I said nothing about it except to tell the man's wife that I'd been there when he died, and his death had been very peaceful. That led to the nursing supervisor inquiring how I happened to be there. I told her then about the call signal, though obviously that raised more questions. Finally, I confessed that I believed his spirit had called me to witness his passing, to be able to tell his loved ones it was peaceful. That was the first black mark against me." She fell silent, and looked down contemplatively.

"And the second time," Kate prompted.

Anne came out of her reflection. "Only last year. A young woman was brought to emergency. She was in the third trimester of pregnancy, and she'd fallen down a stairway in her home. She had to be taken in for a C-section. I was at the table. "Anne's voice trembled as she went on. "It was the baby that died, a boy child. Delivered dead, not even fully formed. But as the doctor held the infant's body, I saw . . . I swear to you, Kate, I saw this babe, as he would have been at full term, appear and hover before my eyes in a crown of light before fading away."

The use of the word "babe," and the image of the child in a crown of light conjured for Kate depictions of the Christ child she'd seen in medieval paintings, art from a time when unquestioned belief had been automatic. It seemed that the nurse's vision could have been suggested by such a painting. No doubt, Anne Morrissey believed she had seen what she described, Kate concluded, yet it could not have truly occurred. It was a picture that hung in the holy gallery of her mind, brought forth in a moment of stress, not a reality gathered from true life.

Anne continued, her voice firmer. "Again, I said nothing at first. But the mother was so depressed, she was kept in another day, and during that time I went to her. . . ." She trailed off.

Kate didn't know what to say. She was touched by the other woman's sincerity, impressed by her faith and kindness. Yet she hadn't the words or the will to endorse her idea of truth. Unable to believe now that the phenomenon of seeing Chloe's spirit rise could have been real, Kate was overtaken by sadness and the loss of hope that somewhere, in some other world, her loved ones still existed.

Anne Morrissey had no trouble reading Kate's silence. "I don't blame you, Kate—I don't blame anyone, if they can't see what I see.

But you understand, don't you, that it would be wrong for me to be ashamed of it, or hide it out of fear?"

Yes, from the nurse's perspective, believing she had a mission, it would be wrong. "I'm sorry you're being punished for it," Kate said. "I hope you don't lose your job. I'm told you're an excellent nurse."

"They'll take me back," Anne said confidently. "Though I'm sure there will be certain conditions."

"Will you agree to those conditions?" Kate asked. She realized that what they involved was that Anne Morrissey would never again tell her "tales."

"I need my job," Anne replied earnestly. "So I'm going to pray that I never have to make the decision—because I won't ever again be . . . chosen."

Emerging from the house after their good-byes, Kate reflected on the nurse's final statement. The sensible yearning she expressed to be unburdened from the obligations and trials required by her profound faith echoed words spoken throughout history by unheeded saints, martyrs. Kate wavered in the conviction she had formed earlier that Anne Morrissey was unbalanced. Suppose she *was* chosen to see what others could not? Was it her own refusal to believe in the phenomenal, Kate wondered, that kept her from seeing it, too?

Before getting into her car, Kate paused to look up at the vast, star-speckled void overhead. The concept that space went on and on without end struck her as no easier to grasp than the idea that the lives of her husband and children—the lives of all human souls through all of time—should endure through eternity. Yet by the reckoning of some brilliant scientists, space was not only infinite, but expanding. So why couldn't other inconceivable propositions be true? Where science provided no answer, the truth could reside in nothing more than what one *chose* to believe. Or, as Anne felt, in being chosen.

Kate got into her car and headed home. Perhaps it was her grounding in history, in the events and happenings of the past, that kept her from being able to accept what could not be proven. But as much as she wished she could believe in heaven, a home for the parts of her heart that had been torn away, it remained beyond her—simply too much to hope for.

8

Kate soon realized she would have to sell the house. Financial considerations aside, living here she would remain forever suspended in grief and anger, confronted by thoughts of what she had lost, all the might-have-been birthday parties and other celebrations that would never fill these rooms. She didn't list the house for sale right away, however. She needed time to get accustomed to the idea of moving on.

To test the feeling of separating from her territory, she accepted an invitation from her friend Meg Parker to spend a few days at the Parkers' vacation house on Nantucket. Since the beginning of their friendship, Meg had been inviting Kate and Jim to join her and Harry for a week during the summer, but they had never found the time when the twins wouldn't be along, and felt it wouldn't be fair to the Parkers to turn their house into a summer camp. Now, with the tourist season over, Meg warned, Nantucket could seem desolate, even somewhat forbidding, the beaches cold and lonely places. In fact, she was going to the island now specifically to close the house down until next summer. But she believed the change of scene would do Kate good, and the two women would be by themselves, since Harry would be in Miami at a convention of the Independent Insurance Agents of America— with Jim's death, he was forced to start beating the bushes for a new young associate.

Before leaving, Kate called her mother to say she would be gone for a few days.

"Getting away is a good idea," Sarah responded. "Where are you going?"

"Nantucket Island."

"But that's a summer resort, darling," Sarah observed with concern. "At this time of year, I hear it can be rather bleak and depressing."

"It'll be fine, Mother," Kate said. "I'm not looking for someplace I can get a tan and dance the limbo."

She wasn't at all put off by the picture Meg and her mother had painted of a place where there would be few people and little to do. What she needed was simply to get away from the place where everybody knew her misery and where she could have at least the comfort of anonymity.

Twelve years' Kate's senior, Meg Parker was also unlike her in temperament and every physical aspect. While Kate qualified to be called statuesque, the five-feet, three-inches that Meg had wangled onto her driver's license was stretching the truth by a good inch. She wasn't slender, either, though her avid devotion to whatever diet was currently in vogue kept her small frame from ever seeming more than reasonably well filled out. Her round face was pretty, and set off by short hair that had gone silver when she was in her thirties, contrasting with sparkling dark eyes. That she had never colored her hair was consistent, Kate thought, with a breezy candor and honesty about who Meg was, inside and out. In a way that Kate had found rare among most of her contemporaries, Meg was ready to say what she thought without sugarcoating. Married straight out of college, Meg had also had her three children early so the youngest was already finishing high school when Kate's twins were born. That had made her a good source of advice as Kate coped with the initial problems of mothering. Meg's occasional frustration with the full-time role of housewife had provided a helpful counterpoint to Kate's guilt at continuing to work through the twins' childhood.

Bubbly as Meg was by nature, she was sensitive to Kate's need for quiet and introspection, and didn't push conversation on the drive up to Hyannis to get the year-round car ferry. She listened at low volume to her CDs of Celine Dion and an audiotape mystery novel, while Kate napped or gazed vacantly at the passing view.

"I'm sorry, Meg," Kate said at one point. "I'm pretty rotten company."

"I wasn't planning a house party, hon'. I'll be around for company when you want, or leave you on your own if that's your mood. I have plenty to keep me busy."

The ferry to Nantucket took two hours, and Kate spent all of it sitting on the bow deck, her body wrapped tightly in a parka while the wind and the salt spray stung her eyes and the skin of her face. The external discomfort made a natural complement to the ache within. The November day was overcast, and the wind wove a froth of whitecaps into the gray-green of the sea. By the time they entered the harbor of Nantucket Town, the day had darkened still more, and a chill mist hung over the houses, which dated to a hundred and fifty years ago when the island had been a thriving center for the whaling industry. Conforming to a code designed to preserve the traditions of the whaling days, most of the structures were painted gray trimmed with white, which caused the town to blend into the mist. As the ferry moved toward the dock, the view became more distinct, and it seemed to Kate that the place was evolving from mirage to reality, as if emerging from the past into the present.

The Parkers' house was a drive of fifteen minutes from the main town in the small village of Siasconset—which Meg referred to in native Nantucket fashion as " 'Sconset"—a warren of narrow streets lined with small, rose-covered cottages, and driveways surfaced in crushed white oyster shell. Before being converted to vacation homes, B & Bs, and shops, Meg said, most of the houses had been fishermen's shacks. Only a hundred or so families lived in the village year-round, and as they drove through, Kate saw no more than a handful of people on the misty streets.

The Parkers' house was a classic New England saltbox, expanded with a couple of wings. It stood on a slight rise at the edge of the village, commanding a breathtaking view of the beaches and the sea beyond. With its two acres of land the value of the property was such that Meg had told Kate she and Harry could never afford it now. Meg had inherited the house from her parents, who had purchased it for a modest amount in the early fifties long before Nantucket had become a summer mecca for celebrities and the super-rich.

Meg showed Kate to one of the three guest rooms under the eaves and left her to settle in. When Kate looked out a window after unpacking, she saw her friend below in her garden already at work, wrapping and tying burlap around a number of the younger plants to protect them from the ravages of the winter. Farther away, the line of an empty white sand beach trailed away into the mist, the waves breaking over it. Even at a distance Kate could hear the sound of the surf.

Called by the sight of that lonely place, she dressed in jeans and a couple of layers of sweaters, and slipped out of the house to take a solitary walk. As she plodded along the windy beach under low gray clouds, Kate thought once more of her conversation with Anne Morrissey, as she had many times in the past week. Each time it replayed in her mind, she was freshly impressed by Anne's calm certainty. How lovely it must be to possess such rock-solid conviction about the eternal nature of the human spirit. What had she said—that she'd heard Chloe "speak from the soul"? Kate stopped walking and stared out at the vastness of the ocean. Her eyes searched the horizon that blended almost seamlessly into the louring sky, looking there for a sign of life, one boat, as if it would be proof of life surviving in any void.

"Speak to *me*, baby," the plea broke softly from her lips. "Let me hear it, too."

All that came back was the whisper of the surf. Kate walked on. But Anne Morrissey's words were still echoing in her head. What made the difference between those who could see the phenomenal and those who couldn't? The nurse had said it was nothing more than being *willing* to see. So wasn't she willing enough? Kate pleaded silently. Dear Lord, there was nothing she wanted more than to feel that those souls she had held dearest in life survived somewhere, somehow.

Or did it take more than mere willingness to receive the gift of seeing the proof? Maybe you had to be worthy of it. And maybe she wasn't.

Dusk had fallen. Kate turned and saw she had come so far along the beach that the lights of Meg's house were only pale pinpricks in the mist. She started back. As the light kept fading over the ocean, her reflective wondering went on. Every day ended with night, but the sun always rose again. So could life itself end in eternal darkness? Musing on the puzzle, Kate was suddenly reminded of something she had read years ago in the basic survey course in philosophy she had taken in college:

> "If we begin with certainties, we shall end in doubts; but if we begin with doubts, and are patient in them, we shall end in certainties."

At the time she'd come across these words—amid all the questioning that came with the fresh independence, fresh ideas, and first love affairs of college—Kate had been deeply affected by their message and copied them in a journal she was keeping. They were, she recalled, from the writings of the seventeenth-century philosopher Francis Bacon. In the age when he'd composed them, Bacon's words had probably been meant to apply more to the search for practical, scientific truths than to heavenly mysteries. But as she thought of the axiom now, Kate regarded it as a comforting reminder not to be closed to *any* possibility. After all, in Bacon's time if someone had said whole cities could be lit by millions of tiny electric globes, each of which seemed to contain a fragment of the sun, it would have been written off as far less likely than the materialization of a host of angels.

Be patient in your doubts, she instructed herself as she walked toward the steadily brightening glow of the lights in Meg's house. Perhaps a certainty would be revealed.

In the morning she slept late, took another long walk by herself, then returned to the house and sat staring into the fire that Meg had left going in the living room. She had brought some books along: a novel and a couple of the self-help manuals on grieving and loss given to her by friends. But the inability to concentrate that had afflicted her since the accident kept her from turning no more than a page before she accepted that nothing was penetrating and laid the books aside.

Meg had driven to Nantucket Town earlier to buy things needed in connection with her preparations for winter from the hardware store. In the middle of the afternoon, Kate heard noises outside and looked out a window to discover her hostess had returned without coming into the house. Meg was at a corner of her property where a small gardening hut stood, struggling to sink a fence post into a hole she had dug. Kate put on her parka and went out to help.

"I had an idea," Meg announced when she saw Kate coming, "to put up something that could be used to train some ramblers so they'd hide this shed. This old thing looks ugly sitting out here, don't you think?"

Actually, Kate thought, the weathered old shed was rather picturesque. Meg's sudden interest in building a fence for ramblers that couldn't be started until spring probably had more to do with staying busy and observing her promise not to intrude on Kate, than with hiding the old garden hut. Still, by helping, Kate could show she was ready to be more sociable. "Looks like that hole needs to be deeper," she said, taking hold of a shovel leaning against the hut.

They worked together until sundown. Kate talked in spurts about her grief, her memories, questions about her future, while Meg mainly listened, curtailing her usually active tongue. Afterward, with appetites spiked by the outdoor work, but both too lazy to cook, Kate agreed when Meg suggested having supper out.

The eating places in Siasconset were all closed for the season, so they drove to Nantucket Town. On Upper Main Street stood a number of redbrick mansions built in whaling days by the men who owned fleets of the ships that voyaged to the farthest corners of the world. The Jared Coffin House had combined a couple of these to make a sizable inn that also contained a couple of restaurants.

Meg led Kate downstairs to the more informal Tap Room. A cozy basement warmed by candlelight, with walls of wood hung with old prints and paintings of nautical subjects, it gave the illusion of sitting down to eat in a cabin of one of the old whalers. On a damp and chilly off-season night, business was scant: only two other tables across the room were occupied. To perk up the moody atmosphere, Meg was moved to vent her natural effervescence, and over pasta and salad, she delivered a stream of trivia about Nantucket to Kate. Wasn't it interesting that although Herman Melville had based *Moby Dick* and its characters on the adventures of Nantucket whalers, he'd never visited the island until after the book was published? And that the three identical redbrick mansions across the street from the Jared Coffin House had been built by a whaling merchant named Starbuck for his three sons? Yes, the source of the name for Melville's character . . . and from there into pop culture as a chain of coffee shops.

Kate tried to enjoy her friend's patter, but her mind had been on something else all day. When Meg finally wound down, Kate decided to share it. "Meg . . . have you ever been to a séance?"

Meg looked up sharply from her Caesar salad. "What?"

"You know, where people sit around in a dark room and—"

"And talk to spirits," Meg supplied. "I know what a séance is, dear. You just caught me off guard with your question."

"Well, have you?" Kate prodded.

"Are you thinking of dabbling in that stuff?"

"Answer me first," Kate insisted.

"Want me to count the times I played with a Ouija board? I had a friend in sixth grade, and I used to go over to her house, and we'd scare ourselves silly with—"

"Never mind that," Kate said, blocking any playful digression. "I'd like to know if you've ever taken part in a serious attempt to . . . make contact with the dead."

Meg shot a concerned glance at Kate before answering. "Once, come to think of it. I went with my mother to see a woman who claimed to be able to put people in touch with the dear departed—a medium, I think it's called. It was five or six months after my father died, and my mother still missed him terribly, and she got this woman's name from somewhere and took me along. . . ."

Kate knew something of Meg's background. Her father had owned a Buick dealership in Hartford, and had been a heavy smoker who died of lung cancer when Meg was in high school. Meg remained a loyal owner of Buicks, and a zealous crusader against cigarette smoking.

"Where was this?" Kate asked.

"I don't remember exactly. Somewhere in the countryside not far from where we lived."

"What was it like?"

Meg put down her fork. Her eyes roamed around the low-ceilinged room as though bits of memory were being collected from different shadowy corners. "You'd think something like that would've left an impression, even after forty years," she said, "but I don't recall very much. I do remember getting in the car with my mom, and driving awhile . . . and the woman we saw being quite ordinary. She lived in a small house by the road, and she came to the door, wearing a plain housedress. I think I was expecting to see someone with a pointy hat on, and a robe with stars and moons—you know, like Mickey Mouse in 'The Sorcerer's Apprentice.' " Kate smiled at the image, but Meg's face grew taut with concentration. "The rest is vague because I wasn't part of the whole thing. I remember now! On the way there, I asked my mother where we were going, and she told me about this woman who was going to try to help us talk with my father." She rolled her eyes at the memory. "Dad had been gone half a year by then, and I knew it had been hard on Mom, but when she said this, and started explaining spiritualism—the whole deal with spirits of the dead speaking through the living—I was sure she'd gone a little batty. I told her so, too, and we got into a tiff about it. That's why it's a blank past the point where the woman let us into her house: Mother went with her into another room—and I waited outside."

"You didn't want to talk to your father?" Kate asked.

Meg lifted her fork on which she'd already harpooned a piece of romaine. The crunching sounds as she chewed the lettuce and continued talking added to the impression of her gusto: "Katie, I was crazy about my dad. He was a prince; he doted on me, and worked his ass off to give his family a good life. To this day, forty years later, losing him is the worst thing that ever happened to me." She swallowed, and went on quietly. "But to imagine that I might be able to contact him only in a circumstance where it was impossible to really be with him again, it only seemed like asking for more sadness. Even if it could be done, that is. But—sorry, sweetie—I have to say to my mind it was a load of bananas. Even without the Mickey Mouse robe. To me, that woman had to be just a con artist out for a fast ten bucks."

"Then you think I'm a fool to be interested?"

Meg put down her fork. "Honey, you're deep in a load of pain, and you have every reason to be. Last thing I'd ever think is that it's foolish to do anything and everything that might help you dig out of it. I just hope for your sake it's something that really works . . . and doesn't only cause you more hurt."

"So it didn't work for your mother?"

"If you mean did she actually get through to my dad? I never heard her say she did. I asked her later what had happened with the spiritualist, and she said if I was going to poo-poo her beliefs, then I didn't deserve to know." Meg shrugged. "But if something amazing had happened, could she have resisted telling me? She kept mum, I think, because she was pissed at me for being right. In another way, though, the experience may have helped her. She made the effort; it might have been a disappointment, but after that, she was more able to accept things as they were."

Kate clung to that final judgment. What wouldn't she do herself if it enabled her to achieve no more than peacefully accepting things as they were?

Meg was studying her. "Have you been to one of those people, Kate?"

"No."

"But you'd like to. . . ."

"I don't know. I never would have thought I'd even consider it. I teach *history*, Meg. My whole training depends on studying the past to find the lessons I believe we can learn from it. Part of that is examining whatever is left behind by the people who make history, mostly people whose lives ended long ago. Caesar, Napoleon, Abraham Lincoln—you read their words, review their actions, but you accept that they're gone forever, and they have nothing new to tell us. With that for a background, it's hard to imagine that anyone can be summoned from some afterworld, actually contacted. No serious student of history—or teacher—should believe that a way to understand the acts or ideas of all the great figures of history could be as simple as dialing up their ghosts on some supernatural switchboard." Kate became suddenly aware of her tone, lecturing Meg too loudly—as much to convince herself, she realized. "That's the rational point of view," she went on quietly. "But something happened recently that threw me off my foundations a little. . . ."

Kate shared the story now—from Anne Morrissey's first approach at the hospital, to visiting the nurse in her home and hearing her accounts of seeing spirits separate from bodies at the moment of death. They were into their second cup of coffee by the time Kate had recounted it all.

"Since then," Kate admitted, "I can't get it out of my mind—the wish that I could have the peace of knowing my own . . . spirits are around me in some way. But I haven't done anything about it. Every time I start to think I might, I turn around and feel it's so"—she winced as she completed the thought—"so pathetic. And it is, isn't it?" She paused for her friend's answer, but Meg only gave her a sympathetic smile, and Kate answered herself. "Hell, do you know anyone who's got a more pathetic story than mine? So what if I'm pathetic? Maybe I should just go ahead, toss away my smart-ass intellectual certainties, and take a leap of faith."

Meg wanted to be encouraging. "I'll take it with you, if it helps."

"Thanks, but no." From what Meg had said already, Kate knew she'd go along just to keep her company, not because she was open to belief. Which might prevent her from being in the right frame of mind herself. As Anne had told her, without an open mind and heart, it wasn't possible to see the phenomenal. "I'll do it on my own," Kate said, "if I do it at all. But I have no idea how I'd even go about finding the kind of person who could . . . make the connection."

"You might start looking right around here." Meg glanced through a window of the dining room into the misty night. "There's a long tradition of haunted houses here on Nantucket. To hear the islanders tell it, the place is crowded with the ghosts of men who went to sea and never returned, and the women who died brokenhearted waiting for them. I've heard, too, there are people who'll come to your house— if you think you're being haunted—and talk to the ghosts and get 'em to move out. Find one of these 'ghost exterminators.' They might do the job."

Meg's description of a person dealing with ghosts as if they were little more than household pests cast the idea of consulting one into the realm of the ridiculous. Still, for Kate it seemed to offer her a chance, however small, that her pain might be lessened.

"Maybe I will try," she said. "Just for the hell of it."

9

When Kate came down the next morning, Meg was already busy with her winterizing: curtains had been taken down, sheets were thrown across furniture in several rooms. The door to the basement was open, and Kate heard the washing machine humming below. She called down: "Meg . . . need any help?"

Meg came to the base of the stairs. "No thanks, hon'. Do you mind making yourself breakfast?"

"Not at all. Coffee is all I want. If you don't mind lending me the car, I was thinking I'd drive to town, grab a cup there."

"Keys are on the kitchen counter," Meg replied.

Kate slipped into her parka, picked up the car keys, then stopped at the door to the basement again. "Is there a good library in town?" she called.

Meg reappeared by the stairs. "A great one—the Atheneum. Down on Lower India Street, near the docks—big white thing with pillars like a Greek temple."

The sun was shining today, and the wind had died to a breeze, making it warmer than usual for November. Kate drove with the windows open, the tangy smell of salt air filling the car. The road took her through long stretches of quiet shrub land dusted purple with heather, then past a large cranberry bog where a couple of men were wading up to their hips, skimming a few small blotches of ruby berries that remained from the early autumn harvest. The sight triggered an association with Thanksgiving, and sparked vivid memories of the holiday, the whole family around the table, Jim carving the turkey, the children fighting over a drumstick, Jim's mother working in the kitchen whipping up her special bourbon sweet potatoes—

Gone! Kate had to pull the car to the side of the road and sit for a few minutes before she was able to see the road again without being blinded by tears and the visions of lost laughter. Jesus, when would the day come that she could see something as simple as a cranberry without having it trigger a breakdown?

The library was indeed an imposing structure, built in the same pillared Greek Revival style that many of the wealthy shipowners had favored for their mansions. A plaque by the entrance noted that the present Atheneum had been in continuous service as a library since 1847—when a previous building had burned in the famous fire that had destroyed much of Nantucket Town—and in a hall on the second floor of this building the likes of Daniel Webster, Henry David Thoreau, and Ralph Waldo Emerson had given lectures to the people of the island. Entering the place on an off-season day when no one else was around, Kate felt especially attuned to the historical echoes. Once more she had the sense that she was stepping back into the past.

Left of the entrance, a circulation desk was being tended by a gaunt, middle-aged woman. Kate asked her where to find the section containing books on Nantucket.

"We have rather a lot," the librarian said. "General histories, guide books, related fiction like novels set on the island. If there's any particular Nantucket subject that interests you, I could be more helpful. . . ."

"Ghosts," Kate said.

"There's a lot on that, too," the librarian said evenly. "Any particular ghost?"

Standing before the librarian, Kate realized she didn't really want to spend her time reading about ghosts. She'd launched her search here simply out of academic reflex. "To tell you the truth," she said, "it's not really a book I want. I was hoping I might find someone in the area who has knowledge of how to . . . to make contact with spirits. Perhaps even . . . talks to them. Would you happen to know anyone like that?"

The librarian gazed back with a slight smile frozen on her face, the practiced look of someone whose job was to provide help to all comers. Then the smile faded; she seemed to have detected—perhaps from Kate's reddened eyes—the depth of need behind the request. Leaning over the counter, as though she didn't want to take the chance of being overheard by anyone who might pass by, the librarian said, "I think I do know of someone who might at least give you more information than I can. . . ."

Ten minutes later, Kate was on nearby Quince Street, standing at the door of a bed-and-breakfast called the Captain Markham House. Like many of the old houses on Nantucket's streets, the entrance was a double gangway, with two sets of opposing steps leading up to an entrance landing. On the evening they'd first driven through town, Meg had remarked on some of the architectural quirks of the old houses, and this one she had said was called a "welcome stairway," because it represented the fact that visitors were welcome from either direction, land or sea.

The door was answered by a very attractive young woman with green eyes and a fulsome mane of golden hair loosely gathered back by a tortoiseshell clip. She was slender, dressed in jeans and an oversize raw Shetland pullover. In one hand, she held a calibrated, wooden yardstick, and a pencil was stuck behind one ear.

"I'm looking for Edwina Thorne," Kate said.

"You've found her," the young woman said jauntily.

"Oh." Kate was unable to hide her surprise. From what the librarian had said in recommending this line of inquiry—and the old-fashioned name—Kate had pictured Edwina Thorne as an elderly, straitlaced descendant of a whaling captain.

"C'mon in," the young woman said, covering Kate's stunned silence. As soon as they were inside, she added, "I should tell you right up front if you're looking for a room, we're closed 'til spring."

"No, I don't need a place to stay. The librarian at the Atheneum sent me over. . . ." Edwina Thorne nodded and waited for an explanation. "I was asking her," Kate went on, "if there's anybody around who doesn't think it's crazy to believe in spirits." The young woman only nodded again, eliciting more. "Because I'd like to try to . . . make contact," Kate continued. "She said you might be able to help me."

The librarian had also told Kate that the B & B had once been the home of Captain Elihu Markham, captain of a whaling ship that had gone as far as the South Seas in quest of its prey. He had made numerous voyages until his ship sank in a storm. A few of the crew had survived in a lifeboat, and were later rescued, but not Markham. His wife and daughter had both lived on in the house until their deaths, and both had sworn to have seen the captain's ghost on many occasions. Subsequent owners of the house also reported sightings—including Edwina Thorne and her husband. According to island scuttlebutt reported to Kate by the librarian, the couple had been able to "deal with the ghost" in some way that put it to rest so the house was no longer haunted.

Edwina Thorne had spent a few seconds studying Kate. At last, lifting the hand that grasped the measuring stick, she said, "I was in the middle of doing some stenciling upstairs. Mind if I go on working while we talk?"

"Not at all."

"People call me Eddie, by the way," the young woman said as she turned to a staircase with beautifully polished oak banisters and started up.

Kate followed. "I'm Kate Weyland."

"What's this ghost hunting about, Kate? Do you write for a newspaper or something?"

"No. It's just . . . a personal interest."

Eddie Thorne reached the landing. "Doesn't look much like a haunted house, does it?" She glanced around pridefully. The wide hallway was bright with sunlight shining down through a leaded-glass oval skylight above the stairway. More oak, polished and oiled, gleamed everywhere in the doors, moldings, and floors partly covered by hooked area rugs with floral patterns. The walls were papered with a reproduction period pattern of trellis and vine.

"It's charming," Kate said.

"It's getting there," Eddie responded, with the keen critical reservation of one who had done the work. She continued toward the end of the hallway where a door stood open. "So . . . about our ghost," she resumed. "I'll start by telling you that when Danny—that's my husband—and I went looking for a place to buy three years ago, we heard the stories about this place, but we weren't bothered at all. We'd gotten the idea to try inn-keeping after Danny almost died from a bleeding ulcer. He was a corporate financial officer in Boston, and he just couldn't take the stress. Cooking has always been his favorite hobby, so this seemed like a good fit."

She entered a sunny room, which was empty except for a stepladder. Where the freshly plastered wall met a pale blue ceiling, some wave-pattern stenciling in dark blue had been begun, and pencil marks indicated where it should continue. Eddie Thorne positioned the stepladder, climbed up, and continued making the penciled ruling as she went on. "We'd enjoyed a few vacations on the island, so this was our first choice, but it's a prime resort and we weren't sure we could afford something here. When the broker showed us this place, he said right up front there was a ghost, and other buyers had been scared off and that's why it was a bargain."

She glanced down at Kate. "Mind you, he didn't say there were *rumors* about a ghost—he said there *was* one, just like that." She looked back to her work. "But we loved the place when we saw it, and we figured the ghost stuff had to be nonsense. Just some local folklore that got repeated out of habit more than anything else."

Kate was starting to feel a crick in her neck from looking up as she stood near the ladder She moved to perch on the windowsill while she listened.

"So last March, we bought the place," Eddie continued, "and aimed for a summer opening. To save on heat, we blocked off a couple of rooms downstairs to live in while we worked up here during the day. One night, I woke up and thought I heard footsteps overhead. I woke Danny and told him there was someone in the house. He didn't hear anything, but he went for a look around, then came back and told me everything was fine, windows and doors locked, not a sign of any intruder. He went back to sleep, and I didn't hear anything else that night. Next day, he teased me about it, said it must have been the ghost. For the next few weeks, everything was fine, but then the same thing happened again. Footsteps in the night. That time, after Danny came back from looking around, he was pretty annoyed about being woken up. So when it happened a third time a few weeks later, I let him sleep and went to look for myself."

She finished making a pencil mark above the ruler, then turned on the ladder and rested against it. "As I walked upstairs, I could see a full moon shining down through the skylight. It was so bright I didn't have to turn on any lights. We'd been working on the rooms on the second floor, so all the doors were open, and I looked in one after another as I passed by. At the end of the hallway—the end opposite this one—when I looked in the room, I saw someone sitting on the side of the bed. Enough moonlight came through the window that I could see it was a man, and he was bent over, his face in his hands like he was crying. I should've been scared but, looking at him, all I could feel was a tremendous sadness. *His* sadness, as if just looking at him put me under some kind of spell. . . ."

The sadness was even in her voice as she told it, and she paused as if needing a moment to recover. "Finally, I went to the door and said something—I think I asked him who he was. I'm not sure, I was probably in shock. But then the man sat up, and reached for something on the bed, which might've been a hat . . . though again, I couldn't be sure because as he picked it up, he disappeared." She gave Kate an embarrassed smile. "I ran down and woke Danny, and naturally he had all kinds of explanations—a trick of the moonlight, I was sleepwalking, had a nightmare. Right then, I believed his ideas more than I believed my own eyes. They were simply more logical. But later, I found out that the room where I'd seen him was originally the bedroom for Captain Markham and his wife, and in old whaling prints, you can see the ship captains wearing hats like the one I thought I'd seen."

"Of course, those prints are all over Nantucket," Kate observed. "If you'd seen one at any time, it could have planted the image."

Eddie came down the ladder to the floor. "There's more, Kate. Several times after we opened for business, guests in that room complained that in the middle of the night someone had walked in and sat right on the bed. Always women staying alone, by the way. I guess because the captain only wants to see his wife. . . ."

"Not very good for business," Kate said wryly.

"It shouldn't be, I know. Yet no one was ever terribly frightened. There was something about this . . . this ghost—if that's what he was—that always seemed sad, gentle, never the least bit threatening." Eddie gave a bemused laugh. "Some of our rooms use a bath in the hall, and most of the guests thought it was just someone who'd walked in the wrong door after using the bathroom. After a while, though, even Danny said if some weird supernatural thing was going on, we ought to do something about it. It hadn't caused us a lot of trouble, but well . . . you know, you run a business, you want to keep things as simple as possible."

"I've heard you did solve the problem," Kate said. This was what interested her most: if there was any substance to this tale, then there had been dealings with the dead.

"Yes—knock wood." Eddie rapped her knuckles four times on a door frame. "We were able to find someone who could help."

"Someone on the island . . ."

"At the time, yes, he was here. But I couldn't say if he's here right now. He comes and goes a lot. Sometimes Gabriel is away for weeks at a time. . . ."

"Gabriel," Kate echoed. "Could you give me his whole name and phone number?"

"He doesn't have a phone. But I can tell you where you might find him—if he's there."

"And his name . . . so, if he isn't, I can write to him."

A baffled expression formed on the face of Edwina Thorne. "Funny, I never realized it 'til now, but I don't think I was ever told his last name. All I know, all I ever heard was just . . . Gabriel."

10

Following Eddie Thorne's directions, Kate drove out of Nantucket Town toward the settlement of Madaket, on the western end of the island. As on the eastern end, where Meg's house was located, the landscape was basically flat yet still beautiful. Expanses of undulating moors were covered with a constantly changing texture of trees and shrubs that opened occasionally onto cranberry bog, inland pond, or views to ocean inlets. Even in November, wildflowers provided patches of color, and in empty stretches along the road marked as conservation areas, Kate saw a couple of white-tailed deer loping freely, and a family of a mother quail and four chicks marching along the shoulder in single file.

After driving seven or eight miles, she arrived at Madaket, a loose collection of houses free of any tourist attractions, its few shops intended to supply only the needs of the local residents. Roads leading to outlying areas seemed equally intended to discourage transient traffic. Many were unpaved and sparsely marked. In fact, the directions Eddie had given for finding "Gabriel" were sketchy. From Madaket, Kate was to look for a dirt road that went "off to the right, maybe half a mile, maybe a bit more," from where the main road went through the center of town. Eddie couldn't be more specific because it had been a year since she'd tracked down Gabriel herself, and her own quest had involved a certain amount of trial and error.

"When Danny and I decided to deal with our ghost problem," she told Kate, "I asked around if anyone could help, and a couple of other innkeepers told us they'd had guests who came to Nantucket to visit a man who did . . . readings, is that what they call it? Anyway, this man was supposed to be able to communicate with spirits, so we thought he could help us if anyone could."

It took some effort to find him, Eddie explained, because no one knew his exact address, only that his house was on a dead end near the ocean. Kate would know she was on the right road, Eddie said, if there were only a few houses by the turning, then a long empty stretch ending at an old shack. "Gabriel has this tiny patch of land surrounded by a nature conservancy, so he's out there all alone. Not many places like it left on the island, so you should know when you've found it."

The first road Kate tried was obviously wrong, since it led past properties that must belong to wealthy summer residents—large, architect-designed houses on spacious lots. She doubled back and tried a second turning that passed no houses before it came to a dead end at a large iron gate between stone pillars, which was certainly the entrance to a sizable estate rather than a mere shack.

The third road she tried seemed right. At the turn, there were three small houses which had the rough-and-tumble look of belonging to authentic year-round residents, then a long stretch of dirt road continuing along the edge of a bluff. But as she approached what appeared to be a dead end, Kate saw no shack, only a line separating dusty brown and green from the expanse of blue beyond a hill overlooking the sea. She was on the verge of turning around when the road swooped over a rise, and dipped down to a separate plateau not much larger than a tennis court overlooking the sea. Standing on the plateau was a wooden hut, the most rudimentary kind of dwelling, with a door flanked by two four-pane windows in the side facing the road, and a tin stovepipe zigzagging up from a roof of shingles patched in several places with tar paper. One window had a broken pane that had been replaced with a piece of blue oilskin, and while the siding was a weathered gray, the door was a faded yellow, seemingly salvaged from another house or found in a dump. Stacked against the side of the house was a pile of split logs.

Probably an authentic fisherman's shack, Kate thought, the sort of place solitary men had built for themselves long ago when there was no general appetite for living on bleak cliffs above the windy ocean. Now, seeing this hut where conservationists had made the effort to preserve a piece of unspoiled wilderness, she could only regard it as an eyesore. Which discouraged Kate from proceeding: would a man truly in tune with the spiritual world be so uncaring of the beauty spoiled by his ramshackle home?

Yet, having made the trip, her curiosity tipped the balance in favor of knocking on his door to have at least a look at the man. There was no other car outside to indicate where she should leave hers—perhaps Gabriel owned none—so she parked at the top of the rise and walked down the grassy slope to the door of the shack.

No one answered her knock. Moving to one side, Kate pressed up to a window to peer inside. The opposite wall, she saw now was largely glass, facing the sea, making it bright within. The furnishings were spare. At the center of the single room stood a table with two chairs; to one side was a bed with a large chest of drawers beside it. At the opposite end was a rudimentary kitchen with a large sink and wood-burning stove. A couple of stools, and a large wooden trunk at the end of the bed completed the modest decor, except for one more special item—a brass telescope on a tripod, positioned to look out to sea. A book was open on the table, lending the otherwise empty scene some sense of a life lived within these four walls. As a clue to the personality of the mysterious inhabitant, the book held Kate's eye—but it was too far away for her to see the title. She had an impulse to see if the door was open, but stifled it. Yet, there was enough in what she had seen that she no longer judged the man who lived here so harshly. The window onto the sea, the telescope, the book, all hinted at a man who valued solitude, but wasn't fully disengaged from the world.

Kate got back in her car and drove away, but she kept wondering what book Gabriel was reading. She had decided already she would come back.

"I'd take it with a grain of salt," Meg said. "It's good for business, after all."

It was evening and they were sitting in front of a fire in her living room, sipping dry sherry, the last third of a bottle that Meg wanted to finish off as part of her cleanup. Kate had just gotten through relating the ghost story told by Eddie Thorne.

"Good for business?" Kate countered. "You think people would rather stay in a B-and-B where a spook might wander into the room in the middle of the night?"

"You bet your bippee, sweetheart. That's one of the things that brings the tourists to Nantucket, a chance to taste the flavor of the old whaling days. So much the better if they're told they might catch a look at the ghost of an old sea captain. During the summer, there's a guy who does a huge business leading groups of tourists up and down the streets of town, pointing out all the haunted houses. And didn't you say this Thorne woman made a point of saying it was a *friendly* ghost—like a nice Disneyland type it might be fun to meet?"

Kate couldn't blame Meg for debunking the story; hearing it secondhand, she would have done the same herself. "If you'd met Eddie," she said, after a sip of sherry, "you wouldn't be so quick to assume she was just drumming up business. She struck me as genuine, not someone who'd want to scam the tourists."

"I'm not saying she's a con artist. Just that she's more inclined to keep a bit of local folklore alive than to say it's all a lot of nonsense and nip it in the bud."

"She had guests who also saw—"

"Power of suggestion," Meg cut in, and punctuated the charge by downing the rest of her glass.

"Well, Miss Doubtful," Kate asked, "if she was so happy to have a haunted B-and-B, then tell me why she hired someone to get rid of the ghost?"

Meg seemed stumped for a moment. "Any left in there?" She gestured to the bottle on a table nearer to Kate. A finger or two of the tawny liquid was visible against the background of firelight, and Kate handed over the bottle. Meg poured herself some, then emptied the last bit into Kate's glass. In the pause, she found an answer. "It still feeds the local folklore. This Gabriel character would be part of that. From what you told me about the way he works, your innkeeper is free to say her ghost has moved back in again any time she decides her business needs a boost."

True enough, Kate reflected. When she had asked what Gabriel had done to purge the unwanted spirit, Eddie replied that she had no idea: he'd simply come to the house, asked her and her husband to leave for the night while he remained there alone, and when they returned the next day, the Thornes were told the captain's ghost wouldn't bother them again. "Gabriel wouldn't explain more. All he'd say was that the job was done," Eddie reported to Kate. "And since then—no ghost."

"Sorry if I'm being a wet blanket," Meg said after Kate was silent awhile. "I understand why this stuff appeals to you right now. I'm just concerned that while you're vulnerable, you could go overboard. This man Gabriel, I assume he charged something to do this . . . ghost eviction?"

Eddie had told her that, too. "Two hundred and fifty dollars," Kate admitted.

"So if you ask him to put you in touch with . . . out there"—Meg wafted her hand through the air—"you think he won't put on a show, and hit you for a contribution to his favorite charity? Honey, you're just the kind of pigeon who gets—"

"All right!" Kate interrupted, not eager to confess yet again to her pathetic susceptibility. "I know it doesn't make sense. But I can't help it. I just want to find him and hope that somehow he can help me to—"

See them again, talk to them again, be with them again, she would have said, but her throat closed suddenly and she couldn't speak. Kate swerved her glance to the fireplace as her eyes flooded. In a gulp, she drank down the rest of the sherry in her glass, and was turning back to Meg just as her friend came out of her chair and moved across the hearth to bend down and put her arms around Kate.

"I know it's stupid," Kate whispered, accepting the embrace. "I know." The flames, blurring and refracting in the prism of her tears, made new shapes and colors that almost seemed to be figures walking toward her out of the blaze.

"Never mind, sweetie, never you mind," Meg said, crying with her now. "You just do what you have to do."

11

Light glowed through the windows of the shack, and Kate could see smoke rising from the stovepipe in curling wisps silhouetted against the three-quarter moon. A battered pickup truck stood in a small clearing to the side. She left her car at a distance from the house, and moved quietly as she came nearer. She had come this far, yet she still wasn't certain she would actually knock on his door. Some of her reluctance stemmed from the way Meg had sent her off: "What do you know about this man, Kate? These island loners can be very rough characters. Living by himself, a man can get . . . well, you know, you're a very attractive woman. Go if you must, but I'd feel better if you'd wait until morning."

Kate had laughed off the warnings. "If he's a drunken fiend who wants to ravish me, I won't be any safer 'cause the sun is shining."

Yet standing now in the dark on this isolated bluff, no other house in sight, she didn't feel nearly so brave. Still, tonight seemed her best chance to connect with this man. Meg was ready to close up her house and wanted to drive back to Fairhaven tomorrow. And wasn't night the chosen time for spirits to make their appearance?

A damp cold wind blew in off the sea, and Kate shivered as she gazed down at the shack. She felt, too, the inner chill of apprehension. Never mind whether or not this unknown man posed a physical danger; she had come to cross the frontier separating the familiar world of the living from the uncharted domain of the dead.

Or was she only poised on the brink of crossing from rationality into self-delusion?

Either way, Kate thought, she might be wise to turn around.

But her need propelled her forward.

As she walked down a grassy slope to the house, the smell of wood smoke caught at her nostrils. The smoke conjured a friendly association with the past, perhaps a summer campfire from when she was a girl, and that calmed her somehow. She stepped up to the door and knocked. The sound of footsteps crossing the wooden floor emerged from within. A strong stride, it made the whole of the small shack vibrate. The door swung open.

He took her in for a second before speaking. "Yes . . . ?"

He said the single word quietly, almost familiarly, as if she were a companion who'd merely tapped him on the shoulder. Yet Kate felt that the gaze he focused on her had a demanding intensity, as if he was immediately probing beneath the surfaces, even sensing the unseen storms deep within her. Perhaps living on the edge of an island had given him that aspect, the searching look of men who lived by the sea or on it, and were always trying to read its depths to ensure safe passage. The gray-green color of his eyes was like the ocean itself when thunderclouds hovered over it. Their almond shape, taken with high cheekbones, gave his face a suggestion of the Oriental, though his other features were hardly delicate or refined—a prominent nose that was slightly crooked, as if it had been broken sometime in the past, and a strong full mouth that complemented his square jaw. His hair, long enough to cover his ears, was mostly a silken, glossy black, but shot with a few quirky streaks of coppery red. She couldn't place his age exactly, but he could have been anywhere from five to fifteen years older than her. It was hard to tell because the lines around his eyes and the other creases in his face could derive not from age, but exposure to hard weather. His clothes were the outfit of a man who made a little go a long way: pants of soft beige leather, suede probably, that had been patched in several places with a darker, rougher hide, and a denim shirt that was faded nearly to white from years of washing. The top buttons of the shirt were unfastened so his upper chest was exposed, the skin taut, but also weathered by sun and wind. Hanging from his neck by a loop of grocery string was a pair of spectacles. Half-lenses, Kate noticed, for reading; an odd, professorial touch for such a rugged, weather-beaten specimen.

He wasn't exceptionally tall or broad, simply of medium build, well proportioned. Yet Kate's first impression was that he was a man of unusual strength. It came in part from the way he stood, an open posture that expressed not merely an absence of fear, but ignorance of it. Strength was evident, too, in the hand that came up to rest against the frame of the door as he waited for her answer—long, thick fingers, the outlines of tendon and sinew visible under the skin. As her glance grazed over that powerful hand, Kate realized that ignoring all Meg's cautions might have been unwise. She would be helpless against this man if he were to "get ideas."

At last, she found her voice. "Are you Gabriel?" He returned merely a slight nod. "I'm Katharine Weyland." She almost put her hand out, but sensed he wouldn't take it. "Mrs. Thorne at the Markham House told me what you did for her. I thought you might be able to help me, too."

"You being haunted?"

"No," she said, "there's no ghost." A gust of wind came in off the ocean, and bucked around the corner of the shack. Kate was wearing jeans under her parka, but the blast of frigid air sliced across her ankles. "Could we talk inside?"

After another moment, he stepped back from the doorway. Kate went in and he closed the door behind her. He looked at her silently, still waiting for more of an explanation.

"My problem's not the same as Mrs. Thorne's," she went on. "But I do need someone who has the ability to . . . deal with the spirit world."

"For what reason?"

"I'd like to . . . make contact with someone I lost recently." He looked at her expectantly, as if he knew there was more. "Actually," she added, "with three people."

His cool gray-green eyes narrowed and swept up and down, studying everything about her. Then he turned, ambled over to a plain straight-backed chair set near the wood-burning stove in a corner of the room, and moved it to one end of the table in the center of the shack. At the other end of the table was another chair, from which he'd evidently risen to open the door. In front of it were a plate of food and a bottle of beer. He sat down again, and picked up a fork from the plate. "I was having my dinner," he said, and resumed eating.

Placing the chair was obviously an invitation to sit down, yet unaccompanied by any suggestion to remove her coat and join him, it seemed almost a grudging gesture, the most minimal recognition of civility. He went on concentrating on his meal as if he were alone, following a few forkfuls from his plate with a long swig from the beer bottle. Kate couldn't see what was in his dish, but the shack was redolent with the robust aroma of garlic and herbs and tomato over traces of things from the sea. Though she'd eaten already with Meg, the smell still piqued Kate's appetite, which made his own oblivious enjoyment of the food seem all the ruder.

"I'm sorry if I've come at a bad time," she said, still standing. "Maybe you'd prefer it if I left."

"Who are they?" he asked, looking into his plate.

It took her a moment to reconnect to the thread she'd started to provide. "My husband and children. Several weeks ago, they were . . . they—"

It came as a sneak attack this time, the full catastrophic desolation. Her voice locked in her throat, and her eyes filled. Kate looked away sharply toward the expanse of glass that faced the ocean, and concentrated on the blackness of the sky. While she fought to regain control, it struck her it was for the best to yield no more details. After all, the spirits—if real—wouldn't need to be told what had happened.

She heard his footsteps and turned to see him carrying his plate to the kitchen. He turned on the tap in an iron sink and began rinsing his plate. "I don't think so," he said. "This isn't right for you."

She glared at his back, angered by his presumption. Then she realized his quick judgment wasn't wholly baseless. Gruff as he seemed, did he possess some insight? Was rejecting her his version of compassion? Perhaps, indeed, it wasn't right for her to look for relief in a quest like this. She had to come to grips with the reality of her loss, not retreat into believing in impossibilities.

Or did she simply need to take a leap of faith in order to find relief from her pain? "It would be right," she said, "if you could really do what you say you can."

He kept busy at the sink, his back to her, but she saw him shake his head.

She went closer. "Look, Mister . . ." She paused, realizing she had no other name than Gabriel, and she was not comfortable with that.

"It's true this isn't easy for me. But you should understand: it's not the easiest thing for anyone to believe in making contact with the dead."

He closed the tap and turned to her. "Yeah, it isn't easy. Never will be. Because there's no proof, not the kind most people want. Can't be. And I can tell right off you're the kind who needs a guarantee, who wants to be sure it's not a scam. In the end, no matter what happens, you're going to feel cheated."

The more he resisted her, the more she was intrigued. "I'll pay. Whatever happens, no complaints. Just do what you do. It's my choice, isn't it, if I'm willing to pay . . . ?"

A faint smile touched his lips. "No, Katharine," he said quietly, "it isn't that simple." Oddly shocked by hearing him use her name, Kate stood rigidly as he came over until he was right in front of her, his moody eyes fixed intently on hers. "This isn't like hiring someone to wash your windows or fix your car. It's something I . . ." He stopped, pressed his lips tightly together. It looked, Kate thought, as if he was reproving himself for nearly breaking a confidence.

"What?" she asked.

He turned away. "I'd just rather not, that's all." He got the empty beer bottle from the table and threw it with a loud clatter into an iron bucket under the sink.

"I don't understand," she persisted. "Why turn me down? It's something you do for other people. Mrs. Thorne heard about you from other innkeepers. You're known for this—there are people who visit the island just to see you. Isn't that so?"

"Not a whole lot," he said mildly. "I don't advertise."

Kate saw the hint of a smile again, faintly self-mocking. She couldn't make him out. At times, he seemed to be sincerely nervous about dealing with the cosmic mysteries, as if truly afraid of an ability he commanded without comprehension. And at other moments, he seemed to be hinting she mustn't take him seriously. Maybe it was all part of a shrewd come-on, yet it fired her interest.

She couldn't stop herself now from spilling out more, hoping it would change his mind. "It happened recently—losing them—and I still . . . I just don't know how to cope. You're right that it's hard for me to believe you—or anyone else—can put me in contact with them. But I need this so much . . . if it could only be possible . . . I might be able to come to terms, forgive myself for . . ." Her voice broke, and the abject misery swept over her once more, but this time she didn't try to hold back. She wept openly. "I miss them all so much, see? Every second of every day. There's no way to describe how much it hurts." She went nearer to him. "If I could only have some sense that . . . they were somewhere . . . together, happy. If you could give me that, I wouldn't care *how* you do it." She was as much as telling him to oblige her yearning, even if it meant his contact with spirits would be merely pretense.

And that was the way he heard it, too. "I don't put on shows for people," he declared, then turned from her and busied himself again with some task at the sink.

Kate choked down her sobs, realizing her tears might be taken by him as a device against which he had to prove himself immune. "I'm sorry," she said, brushing her face dry with her hand. "But please, I'm begging you: don't send me away. I'm afraid, you see, afraid if you do . . . I'll give up all hope in everything."

He faced her again, his head cocked as if still doubtful. "I need belief," he said. "Not accommodation."

"I'd *like* to believe."

"Sure! Wouldn't everybody. But it takes more. . . ." Abruptly, he snapped out a question. "Where do you come from?"

"Connecticut."

"Go home to Connecticut, Katharine. You don't have to come all the way out here for what you want. There are people all over who'll tell you they can do it."

Who'll tell you . . . There it was again, the insinuation of fakery. As if he was warning her not to believe in ghost stories. And again, it only raised her desire to a higher pitch. "I'm *here*," she declared. "I'm ready now. Please . . ." She held her hands together in a pose of supplication.

He regarded her coolly for several seconds. "Suppose I do," he said at last. "And suppose *they* don't tell you what you want to hear. What then . . . ?"

She stared back, her resolve suddenly shaken. His question suggested that indeed he might deliver the supernatural ability he was supposed to possess, but it carried the warning of a dark outcome she had never considered. She needed to learn they were joyfully together in heaven. She could never reconcile herself to what had happened— never forgive herself for her part in their deaths—if the message that came through was something else, a howl from beyond.

But above all else, Kate decided, she wished to know that they had not vanished into nothingness.

"Whatever happens," she said, "I want this."

He studied her another moment. Then, all at once, he was practically a blur of motion, striding around the shack, pulling curtains from one corner to the other so they blocked off the wall of glass and the view of moonlight on the ocean, and turning off one of the two lamps that had been on. The edges of the room receded into darkness.

"Sit there," he said briskly, pointing at a large wing chair covered in tattered fabric positioned along the rear wall near the telescope.

Before sitting, Kate took off her parka and muffler and laid them across the back of one of the two plain chairs by the table. Meanwhile, he had taken an earthenware jug from an open shelf above the sink and filled it with tap water. He brought the jug to the table, then picked up the other plain chair and positioned it to face Kate's, a couple of yards directly in front. He sat down. "Never done this before, right?"

"No."

"Here's how it goes. I'm going to put myself in a trance. I don't promise it'll happen. But if it does, that's when I get through. Now, there's been times when I go really deep . . . and it could happen that I faint, fall right off this chair. If I do, don't be frightened. Take that pitcher on the table and dump the water on my face. If it doesn't wake me up, get more water from the sink, and throw it right on. You clear on that?"

Kate nodded.

He sat up in his chair, put his arms straight out stiffly, with his hands on his knees. "Okay, then. Off we go."

He said it, Kate thought, as if he was simply climbing behind the wheel of his pickup to take her on a tour of the island.

For another moment, he peered at her sharply, then he gave her one more of those wry little smiles, and closed his eyes.

12

He breathed deeply in and out, in a rhythm that was slow and steady at first, then began to quicken and grow louder until it had grown nearly to a vigor and stridency suggestive of a panting horse. Kate became anxious, fearful he might hyperventilate, faint, and need reviving. But it went on long enough that she began to think he could have simply gone off into a noisy sleep. Then, suddenly, he emitted a series of low staccato grunts and his head tilted to the side, his eyes still closed, but not tightly, the lids fluttering. The grunting stopped and he gave out a soft sighing moan. His breathing eased, and other sounds began to emerge from his mouth, so quiet Kate couldn't tell if they were meaningless moans or words. She leaned closer. . . .

"Yes," he said now in a low voice. "Yes . . ." His breathing became quicker and shallower; he spoke again, short phrases in quick spurts. "I'm with you . . . no . . . no, I can't. . . . Come closer . . . I can't hear . . . you have to try . . ." Abruptly, his body pitched forward. Kate's hand twitched toward the jug on the table, but he didn't fall off the chair. Though his eyes were still closed, his attitude was the same as if he was looking straight at her. "I see them," he said. "But . . . shadows . . . hiding, maybe. They speak, but I can't hear. You're not ready, maybe. Or they're not. The children . . . one . . . two . . . I can't see in the shadows. One behind the other. One? Two? The same . . . look the same."

Kate seized on that, the first slight indication of a real vision—that he had truly seen them: she'd said nothing about them being twins.

His head went back again, listening to distant sounds that seemed to come from somewhere over his shoulder. "What? What? . . . I'm trying. . . . Can't you come closer?" The last sounded as if he was genuinely annoyed with whoever or whatever he was addressing. Again, his position changed to speak to Kate. "They won't. Or can't. Not allowed, maybe . . . not—wait!" His head tilted back quickly, and his face took on a pained expression.

"What is it?" Kate said impulsively.

"Hiding because . . . children . . . have to . . ."

"My husband," Kate pleaded, "isn't he there?"

"Trying . . . to see . . . but hard . . . so many shadows . . ." He shook his head from side to side, body swaying in a widening arc. "Too soon," he said, sounding troubled, pained. "For you . . . all . . . too soon . . ." His chair began to rock from side to side with the shift of his weight, going up on one pair of legs, then the other. "Can't . . . What? Say what . . . ? Closer!" The chair tipped higher onto two legs, and teetered as though it might topple over, but then his eyes snapped open, and he corrected his balance so the chair dropped back solidly onto the floor. He looked at Kate for several seconds with the unfocused gaze of someone coming awake from a dream.

Uncertain whether the trance had ended, still waiting to hear a message, Kate remained silent. A minute passed.

"I didn't get through, did I?" he said at last. Without waiting for an answer, he rose and went quickly to turn on the lamp again.

"You said they were in shadows . . . they were too far away to hear . . . that they had to hide. . . ." She couldn't conceal the challenge in her tone, the questioning of so many ambiguities that could have been conveniently crafted to create an impression of something glimpsed, but impossible to define.

He whisked opened the curtains across the back wall. "Sorry. I guessed it wouldn't work for you, didn't I?"

Kate stood and walked in his wake. "But you said they were the same—looked the same, the children. What did they look like, exactly, can you tell me . . . ?"

He shook his head. "Whatever I see when I'm under doesn't stay with me afterward. You should've asked when they were here."

The view of the moonlit ocean penetrating the room again, reminding Kate of the cold night through which she had come for this intense, but inconclusive happening. She found herself indeed feeling worse than she had before—cheated, sorry she hadn't gone away when he'd told her to. Yet she wasn't sure if it was because she felt victimized—by the wasted investment of hope, let alone the money— or because she felt rejected by the spirits with whom she longed to communicate, spirits who refused to impart the tiniest of signs to requite her longings.

"So that's all?" she said, hungry for something, anything, that could restore at least the stability with which she'd arrived. "You can't tell me anything else?"

"No. Sorry." He carried the jug of water to the sink and emptied it.

Kate dogged his steps across the room. "Listen, whatever you saw . . . heard . . . even a guess about what they were trying to say. Give me that, please. I can't leave without *something* more."

His hands gripped the edge of the sink as he looked down into it, the pose of a man apparently summoning patience. Finally, he turned to face her. "Look, you wouldn't take no, so I tried. But it doesn't always come out good. Leave it there. That'd be best for all concerned." He moved past Kate, and went over to the wood stove. He picked up a piece of wood from a box beside it, opened the grated door, and tossed the wood inside. It dawned on Kate suddenly that he wasn't merely cutting her off, he was trying to dismiss her.

"There's something else, isn't there?" she said. "Something you don't want to tell me." His back was still to her, but he took a breath that made his large shoulders heave conspicuously. "Whatever it is," she insisted, "if it's about them, I have a right to know."

After a moment, he faced Kate again. "It's nothing I saw. But I'm left with a feeling . . . things that may have come through." He stepped closer and his aspect changed so he seemed somehow less hard and unsympathetic. His voice softened, too. "They died sudden, in some way that hurt them very badly, isn't that right?"

She nodded, impressed by the insight.

"So they didn't want to leave, and they know how much hurt it's causing you. Maybe they're not showing themselves because they're in pain themselves, and they know letting you see that will only make it harder for you." He moved closer. "It's different when older ones cross over. They're more ready, and the message they want to give is that they're fine where they are. But that hasn't come yet to your people. They stayed back, I guess, 'cause they can't say what they know you want to hear—that it's all fine and, hallelujah, they're playing in the fields of the Lord."

Kate stared back at him, her annoyance rising again. If this stranger was only playing a role, then how cruel it was to tell her that the ones she loved weren't at peace. And what was there in anything he'd just said that couldn't have been assumed, deduced, from no more than Kate's coming with a need to communicate with her husband and children, and revealing that they'd all died together only recently?

"That's what I didn't want to tell you," he added, reading the doubts in Kate's eyes.

The anger burst from her. "Well, you *shouldn't* have! You got some damn nerve setting yourself up as the chosen pipeline to heaven. Gabriel? Is that your real name, or is it so people think you're an angel—because you know how easy it is to stir up the feelings of someone in my position, to take advantage. . . ." She stalked across the floor to grab her muffler and parka from the chair. "It's not right, not fair," she said, slipping into the coat. "I should have listened when you told me to go away. But that's why you do it—right?—to set the hook, make it all the more irresistible. . . ."

He looked back at her without expression and said nothing in his defense.

Which only infuriated her more. "I know," she snapped, imagining what he *would* say. "It's my own damn fault. I should have known better than to let myself be taken in." She started for the door. "But you can bet it won't happen again."

"Forgetting something, aren't you?"

She stopped and looked back at the chair, as if what she'd forgotten must be hat or gloves. But then she realized she'd worn none, and she understood. And that *really* lit the fire. "Oh, right!" she spat out bitterly. "You don't get conned without having to pay for it, do you? What point would there be in *that*?!"

She went back to the table, pulled her wallet from a pocket of her parka. "Two hundred and fifty dollars, wasn't it? Well, I hope you'll take a check, because—"

"Fifty," he said. "Just fifty."

She spun around. The momentum of anger began to form some biting retort about the "discount," but it vanished when she saw his face. His plain expression struck her as guileless, and in his eyes she believed she saw a hint of anguish in the wake of her abuse. "Fifty," she said, bringing her voice down. "In cash . . . ?"

"Whatever."

She fumbled in her wallet, stealing an extra moment or two to craft some words of apology. But when she held out the bills, and he stepped forward to pull them from her hand, she couldn't bring herself to say she was sorry. That would spin her right back into being a sucker. "Quite a break you're giving me," she said.

"No break at all," he said, walking away from her.

"Mrs. Thorne told me it was two hundred and fifty."

He was at the door, and yanked it open vigorously. "Gettin' rid of a ghost," he said, "that's a whole lot more work." The cold night wind blew into the shack as he stood rock still, holding the door wide, making it perfectly clear he wanted her gone.

She hesitated another second, balanced between crying out more words of damnation, or making an apology.

"And just by the way," he said gruffly, "it's real, all right. . . ."

She looked at him questioningly.

"Gabriel," he said, "Gabriel Farr."

That would have tilted her toward the apology, but she could see from the darkness of his expression it was too late for it to mean anything. Humbled, stymied, yet still angry, she said nothing before running straight out into the night. Racing ahead up the slope, she stumbled to her knees, picked herself up, and scrambled to the crest. There, at last, she turned and looked back.

The door was closed. The skein of smoke curled up languidly against the silver-white moon. And beyond, the ocean stretched out into a black nothingness. Looking into it, Kate felt, was like looking into a vision of her future.

Finally she wrenched herself around, and got into the car. Speeding away, she switched on the radio, and turned up the volume, not caring at all what music was playing, only that it was loud enough to drown out her own wretched wails.

13

Kate was still unsettled by her experience with Gabriel Farr when Meg dropped her at home the next afternoon. Feelings of regret gnawed at her, worry that she had abandoned her rationality and turned to a blatantly unreal solution for her all-too-real problems. She was embarrassed, too, at the way she'd behaved with him, so mean and spiteful; after all, she'd virtually forced him to yield to her demands. What disturbed her most, however, was the vision Farr had conjured—spirits hovering out of reach, clinging to shadows of that other world rather than showing themselves to her.

But Kate hadn't been able to confess any of this inner turmoil to Meg. When she'd returned last night and Meg inquired about her outing, Kate had dismissed it: "You were right. It's just a load of bananas. The sooner forgotten the better."

Meg didn't miss Kate's reddened eyes, but had known better than to press for details. But she didn't hide her concern after Kate kept a brooding silence on most of the trip back from the Cape. "Are you going to be all right?" she asked as they arrived in front of Kate's house. "I don't like leaving you, if you're not. . . ."

"I'll be fine. Don't worry."

"I'd hoped a little time away would be good for you, Katie."

"I liked it, Meg, thanks. Nantucket's a lovely place."

But alone at home, Kate remained troubled, her mind tossing up a strange mix of visions, some from memory, some wholly imagined. The children tussling somewhere in the house, their giggles and bickering floating down the stairs. Jim calling out to her as he went on some evening errand, that he'd be back late. Gabriel stalking around his shack after emerging from his trance. And a vision of Chloe as Anne Morrissey had described her—a diaphanous chimera rising from an operating table into . . . where?

Kate had intended to catch up with everyday matters like checking the mail undone in her absence, but this sporadic waking dream kept intruding. To escape from it, she went to her room, took a sleeping pill, even though it was barely twilight, and got into bed. It occurred to her then she ought to let her mother know she'd arrived home safely. From the bedside phone, she dialed the number, and got Sarah's answering machine. "I'm home, Mom," she said. "Talk to you tomorrow."

As the pill dragged Kate down into unconsciousness, her mind was again on the way Gabriel had spoken about spirits reluctant to show themselves to her. Hanging on the brink of sleep, she peered into the gloom of a corner by her bedroom window. Could they be here now? Always around her . . . ? The bough of a tree outside the window swayed in the evening breeze, shifting shapes projected dimly against the wall. Within the pattern, did she see a hint of figures gathered in the corner—the curve of a man's broad shoulder, an unruly thatch of hair on the head of a boy, the delicate knob of a girl's ankle down near the baseboard?

Kate might have risen for a closer look, but the chemicals in her blood were taking hold. Perhaps she wasn't awake at all, she mused as she sank down into the dark well of her mind, but already dreaming. "Don't be afraid," she whispered as she slipped down farther into the well. "Mustn't be afraid." But whether she was talking to the spirits or to herself—or if it was part of a dream—she had no idea.

The insistent ring of the phone drilled down into her drugged sleep. She groped the receiver to her ear, and mumbled a groggy hello.

"Katie? Are you all right?"

The voice brought her more fully awake. "Oh, Mom . . . fine. Took a pill, thassall."

"At this hour? That doesn't sound good."

Kate glanced at the digital clock. A few minutes after seven. "Feels good though—better'n being awake."

"Oh, Katie." Her mother sighed, then made an effort to hit a brighter note. "So didn't you like Nantucket? I've always found it the most charming place."

"Mmm-hmmm." Kate worked to clear the fog from her mind.

"I won't keep you now if you're sleepy, dear, but there are some things we should discuss, the sooner the better. Call me in the morning, all right?"

Kate detected a note of urgency. "Now's okay." She pulled herself up on her pillows and switched on a bedside lamp.

"But if you're upset—"

"Mother, upset is my natural state these days. If you're going to let that stop you, there isn't much we can talk about except the weather and the price of oranges."

"Very well. It's about next week. Your sister has invited us to come out there. We ought to get right onto making plane reservations if you'd like to go. . . ."

Next week? Why was that so important? Then it hit her. *Thanksgiving.* At the realization, Kate was cast back down into despair. She'd cried over it already within the past two days, the ruination of that marvelous time of family joy, of counting one's blessings—but that didn't prepare her to confront it again. She bit down on her lip and turned from the phone, trying to throttle down the wave of emotion.

"Katie?" Sarah coaxed her out of the silence. "What do you think . . . ?"

She envisioned it—sitting in the huge dining room of her sister's sleek Beverly Hills house, with *her* husband at the head of the table, *her* three children needing to be told to stop fighting over who got the drumsticks—

"I can't," she forced out quietly, then summoned a stronger tone. "But of course, you should go. It's been awhile since you went out—"

"No, no, dear. You mustn't be alone. I understand if you're not up to going, but then you'll be with me here. We'll be together."

"Mom, your holiday doesn't have to be spoiled because—"

"Darling, let's not argue about it. I'm not going to leave you on your own."

"Sure," Kate conceded tiredly. "What else? You said one or two 'things.' . . ."

"Never mind. I can hear you're half asleep. But maybe you can come into town and we'll talk then. In a few days, maybe, whenever you're feeling better."

Kate bridled at her mother's tone, the implication that she wasn't up to facing anything so taxing as a train ride to the city. As to waiting until she felt better, who knew if that would ever happen? "I'm not an invalid, Mother. I'll come tomorrow."

"All right. I've got to be in court in the morning. I can meet you at my place at around two."

"Fine," Kate said drowsily. The effort of fighting the sedative was becoming too much. She turned off the lamp, and slipped down again under the covers.

"You can stay over, too. There are lovely shows at the museums and—"

"We'll see," Kate said, added good night, and cradled the phone.

Two o'clock, she reminded herself. Then before yielding to sleep, she forced her eyes open and glanced once more toward the corner by the windows. Nothing there now but the soulless dark. But since she was going to be in the big city, it occurred to her she could do some more research on how to throw light into those corners.

In the morning, Kate attended to the mail and phone messages that had collected while she was away. Sorting quickly through the bills and credit card statements and the continuing trickle of condolences in the mail, she came at last to an envelope of thick vellum, engraved with the crest and return address of the Ashedeane School. Since accepting the offer to begin in the winter term, there had been nothing from the school other than expressions of sympathy from the administration and the board. But this letter, she expected, would be about the job. She eyed the envelope with trepidation. Perhaps, anticipating the psychological effects of her situation, they had decided to withdraw the offer. . . .

Suddenly, faced with the possibility of losing this passion, too, this remnant of identity, she realized how important it was to her to go on working. Fearing the worst, she shoved aside her coffee and ripped open the envelope. The letter was on the stationery of the school's Headmaster, Louis Halaby:

Dear Mrs. Weyland,

    In view of the great personal tragedy you have suffered so recently, it would be understandable if you felt a need to reappraise any plans made at an earlier time. In the event you may

*be having second thoughts about assuming a position at Ashe-
deane following the Christmas break, I trust you will let me
know soon, as only a few weeks remain for us to make alterna-
tive arrangements.*

*However, my essential purpose in writing is to assure you I re-
main hopeful, along with the rest of my faculty, that you will be
joining us. In that case, we should meet at your earliest convenience to discuss course schedule, textbook requirements, office
space, and other details. You might plan to spend part of a day so
I can introduce you properly to the staff and the campus.*

The kindness expressed in the letter boosted Kate's mood. The
doubts about returning to work that had plagued her were swept
away in a flood of hope. No denying she was in a delicate state, still
dependent on tranquilizers to function. But the end of the Christmas
break was almost seven weeks away. She ought to be steadier by then,
able to concentrate on texts, keep lessons in her head, read students'
papers, care about their problems. And total immersion in the work
she loved seemed to offer the best chance of recovering something like
a normal life.

When she called Louis Halaby to assure him she wanted to teach,
and make the arrangements, a secretary informed her that the Head
was away for a few days—it was the time of year when he visited Ivy
League colleges and talked to admissions people on behalf of appli-
cants from Ashdeane. But hearing Kate wanted an appointment to
plan for her coming term, the secretary offered her own warm comment. "It's a wonderful school, Mrs. Weyland. I know you'll be happy
here."

If she could be happy at all, Kate thought.

14

By the time she left for the city, the patchy morning sun had given way to a dreary November drizzle. The changing weather matched Kate's darkening mood as she rode the train to New York. In the past, she'd made the trip with the twins at about this time of year to see the tree at Rockefeller Center or choose toys at FAO Schwarz. The desolation that overcame her while she traveled to the city today could have been no greater if she'd been on a six-month trek alone across Arctic wastes.

Her mother had lived in the same Upper East Side building since moving to the city after the divorce, one of the newer constructions that had seemingly spent so much on marble and crystal chandeliers in the lobby that there wasn't enough left to insulate apartment walls from the sound of a neighbor's stereo.

Sarah met Kate at the door of her apartment on the ninth floor. She looked pleased as soon as she saw Kate carrying a small overnight case. "So you will stay over," she said as they exchanged a quick hug. "I'm so glad."

"Don't run and make the bed. I wanted to be prepared, but I haven't decided."

Her mother was holding a hanger by the time Kate slipped out of her wet raincoat. "I'll put that to dry in the bathroom with mine," Sarah said. She walked off, chattering as she went. "Nasty day, isn't it? Can I give you a cup of tea? I was making some—only got in myself a minute ago, and I've got the shivers." She returned to the hallway and looked expectantly at Kate.

"What I could really use," Kate said, "is a stiff whiskey." Liquor was rarely her remedy of choice, but along with feeling chilled, Kate had an onset of anxiety. She recalled Sarah mentioning something besides her sister's Thanksgiving invitation that they needed to discuss, and she had an intuition it would be no less upsetting.

Sarah cocked a critical eye, but resisted comment. "Well, if a drink is what you need, there's scotch, bourbon, and glasses on the trolley in the living room. You want ice?" She headed for the kitchen.

"Just a little water, thanks."

Kate went to the living room and scanned it quickly. Not her taste—her mother went for a more formal look: flocked upholstery, long curtains, spindly antiques—but Kate took some pleasure in seeing many of the pieces from her childhood home. At the trolley, she found a bottle of Jack Daniel's and half a dozen of different single-malt scotches, the more esoteric brands that were fashionable and expensive. She decided to try one called "Islay," described as a "lowland malt."

"Since when did you become such a connoisseur of scotch?" Kate asked when her mother returned, a mug of tea in one hand, a small pitcher of water in the other.

"Oh, Bert brings those over," Sarah said offhandedly.

Kate had heard Sarah speak of Bertram Davis, a city judge who'd taken her out for the occasional dinner or play, but nothing had been said to indicate they were seriously involved. "If this is where Bert keeps his scotch," she remarked, "he must be doing some pretty serious relaxing around here."

"We're good friends," Sarah said. "I hope you'll meet him soon."

"Who knows? He may even let himself in with his key while I'm staying over. I just hope he doesn't get into the wrong bed."

"All right, Katie," Sarah said starchily, "enough on that subject. We have other things to talk about." She sat down on the sofa. Now Kate noticed the file folder lying on the coffee table. Placed there before she'd arrived in the manner of a stage being set, it reinforced her concern. "Sit down, dear," Sarah said softly.

Kate took a chair opposite, added a little water to her glass of scotch, then tossed down a large swallow. "All right," she said crisply, "what's this about?"

Sarah hesitated, and placed a hand on the folder in front of her. Kate was suddenly reminded of her mother sitting with a manila folder in her own kitchen, nearly exposing its contents to her. *This* folder, Kate suspected now.

"I've wanted to talk about this for a while," Sarah said at last. "I never could find the right moment, but I don't think it should be put off any longer." She took a gulp of her tea, then pulled forward on the sofa. Her fingers played with the edges of the folder. "It's about the accident, Katie—"

"The accident," Kate echoed quietly. The word and its associations made her reach at once for another long swig of scotch.

"Can you manage to deal with it?"

Kate leaked a bitter smile. "Mother, in one way or another, that's all I ever deal with now." She glanced at the file. "What's in there?"

"Newspaper accounts, police reports, hospital records. Some correspondence I've had about the case. . . ."

The case. The use of the term—as it might dryly sum up a legal matter—and Sarah's reference to correspondence suddenly revealed to Kate why her mother was bringing this up, why she had even started collecting the file. "You want me to sue someone, is that it? You think someone should pay for what happened?"

Picking up on Kate's resistant tone, Sarah answered obliquely. "From what I've learned, dear, it's pretty clear that the accident didn't have to happen."

"Have to?" Kate reacted sharply. "I don't need to be told that! I don't think of my family being wiped out as written in the stars. It happened the way all accidents happen, because—" She faltered as it loomed in her memory once more: reaching out for the earring, that single instant from which the rest flowed. "Because people were careless," she concluded, sparing herself, then reached again for the scotch. Jesus, would that be the ultimate solution, to drown her sorrow and guilt in booze? She retracted her hand.

Sarah went on making her case. "There's a difference between carelessness and negligence, letting things happen that might have been easily prevented. It's clear to me that the accident *wouldn't* have happened if the police had exercised a reasonable amount of common sense in the circumstances."

Kate stared dully at her mother. She ought to be grateful to be given a scapegoat other than herself, she realized, and yet she couldn't bear to think about the accident having been preventable. Not when so much had been lost that could never be recovered. "Mother, I know you mean to help, but a lawsuit won't do any good."

"Won't it? Kate, with Jim gone your security isn't as—"

"I'll take care of myself," Kate declared stridently. "I'm not looking to find a pot of gold at the end of my . . . my river of tears."

"It's not just about money. It's about doing what's fair and right—justice, I believe it's called."

Under her mother's steady gaze, Kate felt as if she was a witness on the stand, caught in a lie and uncertain whether to defend it or recant. Could she take care of herself? Might there be some healing balm in making someone pay for her loss? Avoiding Sarah's eyes, Kate cast her own toward the file. *Newspaper accounts, police reports, hospital records.* It struck her now that she'd never read anything about the accident: all that time Sarah had been nursing her, she must have kept such things tucked out of sight. Could she bear to confront them now?

"Don't make me read it," Kate said. "Just sum it up for me."

"From my analysis of the facts," Sarah began, "I believe we'd be justified in bringing a charge of criminal negligence. Newspaper accounts and the police report of the accident give the estimated speed of the squad car at impact as seventy miles-per-hour. It's also stated their car was taking a curve at the time, so it's fair to assume the driver slowed, maybe from ninety or more on the straightaway. At that hour of the morning—on roads traveled by commuters and schoolchildren—it's fair to say that driving at that speed, even by the police, is highly irresponsible." Sarah's delivery became colored by indignation. "As bad as that is, the most inexcusable thing was that the police gave no warning they were engaged in what's called 'hot pursuit.' The officer who was driving is quoted in one report as saying he turned on his siren as soon as he saw a car—Jim's car—turning across his path. So Jim heard no siren until *after* he'd started his turn. It seems likely he had no idea they were bearing down at high speed until they were practically on top of him. . . ."

Kate listened with a certain detached admiration. Not since her mother had begun practicing law had Kate ever heard her present a legal argument. The accomplishment of resuming a career after the divorce had impressed Kate enough that anything beyond seemed irrelevant. Now she perceived Sarah must be quite capable in her work; she could imagine her being very effective in front of a jury.

"At that point," Sarah went on, "Jim made an effort to get out of the way, but obviously he froze for a second, uncertain which way to go. An examination of his car revealed that he'd thrown the gear into reverse, and tried to—"

Kate couldn't stand it anymore. "Enough!" she cried, bolting from her chair to pace the room. "My family is gone. What's the point now in estimating speeds, blaming this on men who were only doing their job?" She stopped and put a hand to her forehead to massage a throbbing pain that had begun. "The truth is," she murmured, "if anyone's to blame for what happened . . . it's me."

"You?" Sarah looked at her, wide-eyed with astonishment. "How on earth can you *possibly* blame yourself?"

Kate was silent, lost in a mental replay of her scrambling search for that cursed earring, persuading Jim to drive the children to school.

"Katie?" her mother's voice intruded. "What on earth are you talking about?"

Kate tossed up her hands, expressing the futility of any explanation. Her throat tightened, and tears began to spill from her eyes. She turned to see her mother waiting for the answer. "They wouldn't have been there—in that place, at that moment—if it wasn't for me. I was running late that morning, so I asked Jim to drive the twins to school."

"Oh, sweetheart!" Sarah said sympathetically and pulled forward on the sofa, as if to rise and embrace Kate. But at once Kate turned away and retreated across the room, unready to accept comfort or forgiveness. "You can't possibly blame yourself for that," Sarah went on. "That's like saying . . . if you'd only set the alarm ten minutes earlier, boiled the eggs a minute less . . ."

"Cereal," Kate murmured. "They had cereal."

"Listen to me," Sarah said firmly. "The one and only place to affix blame here—"

Kate only wanted to end the argument. She whirled to face her mother again. "So what do you want to do about it?" she demanded. "Sue someone for their last penny? Is treating me to your precious 'legal aid' going to do one goddamn thing to bring them back? No! So I'm sorry, Mother. You can forget about turning this into your golden opportunity to handle a big gazillion-dollar lawsuit!"

"Kate!" Sarah glared at her daughter for a second, then swept up the file folder, and stood. "You think this is for *me*? That I don't have enough to do—enough people who need my help, and *want* it? Never mind, then." Her voice became tremulous. "I'm sorry I ever thought of it. Sorry, sorry, sorry—how often will I have to say that?" She spun away to hurry from the room.

"Mother!" Kate called after her. "Mom! Wait!" Then louder, more regretful: "Please!" Sarah halted, but didn't turn around. Kate crossed the room to her. "I seem to have gotten real good at hurting your feelings. It's petty. I'm suffering, so I want everyone else to suffer, too. I know you were only thinking of me."

Slowly, Sarah turned around and they embraced.

When they separated, Kate saw that her mother's cheeks were wet. She brought her hand up, brushed one side dry with her fingers as she went on. "I suppose I've just proven why you were right to avoid bringing this up the first time." They smiled at each other bleakly, the wound starting to heal. "But I just don't have the stomach for it." Kate drifted away to a window. "I'm sure you'd do a hell of a job. The points you made, they all sound right. You might win, but—"

"*We* might," Sarah corrected quickly. "We *would*."

"Right—we. But getting into a legal wrangle and seeing it through takes a kind of energy and resolve I don't have."

"Katie, I know how injured you feel. But that's why you must be practical. Who knows when you'll recover? And you've lost your source of security."

"I'm not going to the poorhouse. I'll be teaching again soon."

"I wasn't referring only to money, darling. There's the security of the world making some kind of sense. Of not letting things that are wrong happen without an accounting." Sarah moved beside her daughter. "Losing Jim and the children, seeing you in such pain, it's all unbearable. For me, the only way I can find relief is not to let their deaths mean *nothing*." She paused, her expression darkening. "Yes, I want those responsible to pay. But the most important part is to make them see their fault . . . the needlessness. That could stop a similar tragedy from happening again."

Kate turned back to the window. The rain was over, she noticed. "To be honest," she said finally, "right now it doesn't matter at all to me. But if it's what you believe should be done—okay, I'll go along, sign any papers you need to make your case."

Her mother put an arm around her waist. "It's the right thing, I'm sure. And if any money comes out of it . . . well, if it does nothing for you, there are plenty of good causes." After a moment, she added, "I was glad to hear what you said about teaching, that you'll go back to it."

It struck Kate that she'd never mentioned accepting the position at Ashedeane. Which reminded her the offer had been made the very morning of the accident; she'd never gotten to tell Jim, either. She remembered him, then, standing behind her at the mirror—his voice in her ear, she could hear it now: *there's no one better, Katie. You'll get the job.* Was that her mother's arm around her . . . or his?

"You were right," she murmured, "I did."

"What?" Sarah said.

Kate came back to the present. "Oh, I have some good news. But can I save it for dinner? All that scotch . . . I think I could use a nap."

There was no question Kate should stay overnight and give the rift a chance to be completely smoothed over rather than rush back to where nothing waited. They had dinner out at a modest but reliable Italian place around the corner. Over veal chops and red wine, Kate gratified her mother's hunger for "good news" at a time when there had been so much that was bad.

"Wonderful," Sarah said about Ashedeane. "It's just what you need."

"Something to keep my mind off my problems," Kate observed dryly.

Sarah gave it a more positive spin: "Being engaged in what you love doing."

Kate saw an opening to satisfy her curiosity about Bert. "Speaking of engagements, suppose you tell me more about this man of yours."

"Engagement doesn't enter into it," Sarah replied primly. "But there's no denying Judge Davis and I are . . . involved."

It amused Kate to see her mother blush, but other feelings caused her to frown.

"Do you mind it?" Sarah asked.

"Thinking of you being intimate with someone I've never met?" Kate admitted, "It is a little weird. As if you're . . . someone who brings home strange men."

Sarah smiled off the criticism. "Katie, it's eight years since your father left me. Do you think, in all that time, there hasn't been anyone— that I've been a complete nun?"

Kate knew there were men who'd been attracted to her mother, spent time with her. Without ever letting the notion form fully in her mind, she had assumed the possibilities for a full relationship might be realized. But, as with most children of any age, when thinking of parents there was a mental mechanism that filtered out seeing them too much as sexual beings. What had changed now, Kate realized with an inner shock, was that their roles had been reversed: her mother was enjoying a normal, fulfilled relationship with a man—while celibacy was the condition to which Kate believed she was now ever after consigned. She couldn't imagine desire for a man other than Jim ever awakening in her. She ached for him every night; had dramatized elaborate fantasies of being in bed with him, touching and caressing herself while she pretended he was with her, talking to him all through arousal as if he were there beside her. For the rest of her life it was the most she could ever have, Kate thought. So her strongest underlying feeling as she thought of her mother being with a man was, Kate realized, envy. Pure, poisonous envy.

But she worked hard not to show it. "I guess I felt it was none of my business," she said mildly. "Now can we talk about something else?" She occupied herself with performing surgery on her veal chop.

Sarah gave her a sympathetic look. "In a minute. I think you might feel better about this when you meet Bert. I was going to arrange it weeks ago, but then . . ." She didn't have to say what had happened then. "We could set it up when you come down for Thanksgiving. All right?"

Kate smiled tightly. "If the judge is fucking my mother, I guess I should have a look at him." The poison speaking. And what made Kate feel most ashamed was the way Sarah smiled back so understandingly, accepting this bitterness as if it was going to be a permanent feature of her daughter's personality. It made an apology not only unnecessary but impossible.

"Well, let's see when the time comes," Sarah said. Then, obliging the request to go back to talking about something safe, she said, "So tell me about Nantucket. What did you do up there?"

Ironically, the subject felt almost as precarious as sex. Mention of it brought back at once the mix of hope and disappointment and fury that had surged through her in the encounter with Gabriel Farr. But after being so bitchy, Kate was inclined to make amends to her mother by being honest and forthcoming about the experience. "I went on a sort of ghost hunt," she said.

She told it all, then, step-by-step: the incident with Anne Morrissey that had sparked curiosity about the afterlife; the story she'd heard from Eddie Thorne that had led her to Gabriel. Sarah never interrupted. She propped her elbow on the table and put her chin in her hand, listening with rapt fascination like an avid student.

They were interrupted by a waiter who saw they had stopped eating and came to ask if he could clear their plates. They nodded, and ordered coffee.

Kate resumed at the point where she had found Gabriel at home. She sketched a description of him and the little seaside shack where he lived before recounting the way he'd resisted her plea to assist in her quest, then yielded with seeming reluctance. As she came to telling about his trance, and the visions he claimed to have seen, Kate's account grew more detailed and vivid. Caught up in the story, she barely broke stride as coffee was brought. She imagined herself in the shack again, with all the longing she'd felt to have those spirits hiding in the shadows make themselves known, all the cruel disappointment when Gabriel dispatched her with the revelation that the spirits refused to communicate because they couldn't tell her what she wanted to hear.

"That was the story he gave me, anyway," Kate concluded. "He said the way Jim and the children died, and knowing I was so unhappy, made it hard for them to be at peace. So they couldn't tell me"—Gabriel's very words came back—" 'that it's all fine and they're playing in the fields of the Lord.' "

Kate sipped at her coffee. Mulling in retrospect what had unfolded with Gabriel, she found herself feeling more generous toward him than she had that night.

"So that was the end of the trance," Sarah said, sensing there was more to the story. "What happened then?"

"I got angry," Kate admitted. "I felt cheated."

"Don't you think you were?"

"I sought him out, Mom. He only did what I begged him to do. Afterward, he charged much less than I expected to pay." Kate let out a laugh as she recalled his explanation. "He said it was a much smaller job than getting rid of a ghost."

"Well, you got one very good thing out of it, anyway," Sarah observed. "That's the first time since the accident I've heard you laugh."

"Maybe I got more. I didn't realize it until now, but thinking back, I feel it's possible that . . . somehow . . ." Kate paused, consumed by the feeling. Then, freshly animated, she said: "I was thinking I might try to find a medium while I'm here in the city. New York has everything. There ought to be someone really top-notch."

Sarah didn't like to think of Kate traipsing around the circuit of mediums and psychics and whatever else they called themselves, who were all too ready to provide the solace of a chat with a dead husband and children at a hefty fee. There were all too many hustlers in the city, and they would charge a whole lot more than whatever Kate had paid on Nantucket. Though if it *was* solace for her, then what was the harm? "But you can't just pick anyone out of the Yellow Pages," Sarah said. "If you really want to pursue this, I'll ask around, try to get you a name or two of someone who comes recommended and you can follow up when you're here at Thanksgiving."

Kate agreed, though she told Sarah she would do her own checking as well and might choose to ignore her recommendations.

"I won't mind," Sarah said. "I just want to help any way I can."

But Kate thought she heard more than mere sympathy and concern in her mother's inflection. Wasn't there a trace of pity, too?

15

For a teacher, it didn't get any better than this, Kate mused, as she drove onto the Ashedeane campus. The road passed through vistas of broad lawns and quadrangles of ivy-covered redbrick buildings. At intervals, discreet signs marked turnoffs to the various facilities—THE GYM AND ATHLETIC FIELDS, THE LIBRARY, THE THEATRE—unseen in the inner reaches of the school's vast property. The main drive ended at a parking area in front of the pillared Georgian mansion that had once been the home of the childless banker who bequeathed it, with four hundred acres, to establish the school in 1921. Now, it housed offices of the school's Headmaster and other administrators.

When Headmaster Halaby returned Kate's call, they'd agreed she should come to the school this Tuesday before the Thanksgiving break to settle the details of her schedule, and meet other faculty members at a luncheon. He had suggested Kate might also like to get "the feel of the classroom" by teaching for an hour. "From what I know of your subject range, Katharine," he'd said, "we've got several courses you could easily fit into, giving a lesson in line with what the kids have been studying."

The minute he brought it up, Kate knew the casual suggestion to do an hour in the classroom before she took up her duties was actually on the order of an audition. The school did want to be assured, after all, that in the wake of the accident her emotional state was not so shaky her classroom performance might be affected. It annoyed her—no, in truth it *hurt*, had the aspect of hitting her when she was down—but to argue that it was unnecessary after they had already thoroughly approved her qualifications would only mark her as overly sensitive, even lacking in confidence. And justify their concern.

Kate settled on lecturing in a course entitled "Our English Roots" taught to the fifth form—as eleventh graders were called at Ashedeane—a survey of British history from Roman times to the American Revolution. The class had arrived at discussing the English Civil Wars and the ascendance of Oliver Cromwell, and Kate's lecture would introduce this period. Not an easy task, by any means. The causes of war between the Parliamentarians and the Royalist forces in the mid-1600's, leading to a temporary abolition of England's monarchy, were a complex amalgam of religious, military, and political issues. But Kate had a good grasp of the topic, and felt sure she could make it interesting to a roomful of seventeen-year-olds. The class met at 10:35 this morning. She had agreed to arrive earlier for a short meeting with the Head.

His office was a large, wood-paneled, book-lined room with an ornate desk set in front of French windows looking out on a sweep of lawn, and comfortable seating around a fireplace. Louis Halaby came from behind his desk to greet her. He was short and wiry, with close-cropped, black hair, and lively black eyes, features that bespoke his middle-Eastern heritage. Kate had first met the Head after being short-listed, and they'd gotten along well. She knew him to be fair-minded and liberal, responsible in the twelve years since he'd taken over for making Ashedeane more progressive, as well as swelling the endowment.

A log fire was going, and a tray on a low table by the hearth was set with a silver coffee service and cups. He escorted Kate to a fireside chair, and she accepted his offer of coffee.

"So," he said when they were holding their cups, "how are you holding up?"

"It's been very hard," she replied honestly.

"I can only imagine. I hope you'll forgive me for wanting to know how you're coping—I'm sure it's painful. But I'm afraid, Katharine, it's the elephant in the room, awfully hard to pretend it isn't with us."

She excused him with a smile. "And it's my very own elephant, isn't it? Follows me around on a chain wherever I go."

He smiled back gently. "Frankly, there's been some question among the trustees about whether it might not be too much to ask of you to go back to work so soon. A blow like this, you couldn't be blamed if—"

She couldn't hold it in. "Mr. Halaby, I know—"

"Please . . . Louis."

She set down her coffee cup on a side table. "Louis, yes . . . I know that I'm here today because it seemed a good idea to double-check my classroom performance. I'm not unaware I face special challenges. No doubt some students can see that elephant trailing along with me as much as anyone else. And they will until I can make them forget by doing my job as well as any other teacher. As for whether it's too soon . . ." Kate shook her head, and tried to meet his probing gaze with a confident look. "Without my work to keep me busy, I admit I might be totally lost."

He nodded reassuringly. "Thank you for your understanding, Katharine. I was expecting it to be awkward to explain why I was planning to audit your class, along with Mr. Chambers—the regular teacher. But you've made it easier."

She forced herself to pick up her cup again rather than stare at him. She hadn't anticipated having a jury right in the room, but of course it made perfect sense. How else would they judge her? Hand out performance questionnaires to the students?

The Head stood up. "I have a couple of little chores before your class," he said. "Suppose you head over to Wicker Hall where our history department is located. Al Chambers will meet you there. We'll have a chance after lunch to go deeper into your schedule for next term."

Half an hour later, she was at the front desk of "Wicker 207" as students filled up the desks. The regular teacher, Alfred Chambers, stood by the blackboard, waiting to give Kate a quick introduction. Chambers was firmly in the mold of old-fashioned prep school "masters," a stocky, gray-haired man in baggy tweeds, his rep tie slightly askew. She'd spoken to him on the phone after choosing this course, and he'd done a good job of briefing her so the Cromwell material would dovetail with what the class had already covered. She in turn had made one request of him that she hoped might shrink the elephant a little.

The class filed in. The bell rang. The door was closed. While Kate sat in a chair off to one side, Chambers made his introduction, using her maiden name as she'd requested.

"This morning's class will be conducted by Ms. Katharine Ballard. Ms. Ballard will start teaching at Ashedeane next term, but we thought meeting with a class before then would help her acclimate. Since this class is filled with our friendliest and most brilliant students"—his hyperbole earned a laugh from the class—"and she's familiar with the period you're studying, she's with us today. Ms. Ballard . . . ?"

He moved to a chair in a front corner of the room. The Head still hadn't appeared; Kate expected he'd drop in midway for a sampling. Kate took her place behind the desk, laid out her notes, then looked up to face the array of bright-eyed, intelligent faces. She knew that a generous scholarship program made it possible to diversify the student body economically, and was glad to see a mix of races, as well as evidence of some tolerance for the modern customs of youth—boys with long hair, a couple of girls with eyebrow studs and nose rings.

"Good morning, everybody," Kate said. "Thanks for giving me this time. The period I'll be talking about consists of those decades in seventeenth-century England that are sometimes referred to as the Cromwellian era. You know, I'm sure, the name relates to Oliver Cromwell, the period's most prominent figure, who rose to the position created expressly for him—Lord Protector of England. Some of you may not have read all the text that relates to Cromwell, but I'd be interested to hear what you already know about him." She scanned the class. "Anyone want to tell me . . . ?"

Kate never talked for long without asking a question. She wanted students to be engaged in a dialogue, not just passive listeners.

Hands went up and she collected answers. Cromwell had come to power as a general during the Civil War. He was "very strict." He had ordered the King to be killed. One boy said he was "a kind of fascist."

"So the general impression we have of Cromwell isn't a good one," Kate summed up. "That's the way history usually paints him. But it's always wise to remember there can be differences between history . . . and fact. It might surprise you to know that Cromwell executed the King only very reluctantly—after months of trying to negotiate with him; and that he was much more in favor of religious freedom than the factions responsible for driving out the Puritans who came to our—"

The door opened and a girl slipped into the room. She gave Kate a puzzled glance, then saw her regular teacher, and stole toward the nearest empty seat. She meant to be inconspicuous, but she was slender and fairly tall, and very beautiful. And her long blond hair, Kate noticed, was the same pale, summer-wheat shade as—

Kate fought to hold on to her thought. "Who came to our shores . . ."

It wasn't just the color of the hair that kept her fixated on the girl. It was the modish way she'd gotten herself up—a strip of white silk knotted to one side as a headband, her long blond hair trailing from beneath. Looking at her, the only thing Kate could hold in her mind was the memory of Chloe in the hospital, the hair they hadn't cut on one side trailing from under a white gauze bandage.

"What's your name?" Kate asked, after staring silently at the girl for a few seconds. A teacher's reflex, a hint of discipline for a late-comer. Or was it that fixing the girl's identity would banish this intrusive vision of her daughter?

"Grace Meade. I'm terribly sorry I'm late," she added guiltily.

Mr. Chambers spoke up. "Grace is rehearsing for the Christmas play," he told Kate. "She's permitted some lates."

Kate nodded, and looked away from the girl. It took her a moment to focus again. "I was saying that . . . there are things about that period . . . about Cromwell that we should . . ." For the first time she glanced at her notes. "That tell us he was a better man than history generally gives him credit for. But if the picture we have of him is un-appealing, Cromwell himself is partly responsible. There's some famous evidence he was a man without vanity—who even urged his judges to take the harshest view. Does anyone know what I'm referring to?"

As if to redeem herself, Grace Meade was the first to put up her hand. Kate pointed to her, though she avoided eye contact.

"He said he wanted people to see him 'warts and all,' " the girl answered.

"That's the way we often hear it," Kate said, "but you haven't really got it right." Hearing herself, she paused. It wasn't like her to disparage a student's contribution, personalizing it as a mistake. She could have easily said, *Right, that's probably his most famous saying . . . though there's a little more to it.* Too late now, though. "Let me read to you what Cromwell is supposed to have said." She referred again to her notes. "He was having his portrait done by Peter Lely, a prominent painter of the day, and he told him: 'Mr. Lely, I would desire you use all your skill to paint my picture truly like me, and not flatter me at all; but remark all these roughnesses, pimples, and warts, and everything as you see me; otherwise I will never pay you a farthing

for it.' " Kate looked back to the class. "So, as we paint our own picture of Mr. Cromwell, let's do what he asked, see him as he was. And
remember: because there were warts, doesn't mean there weren't also
good qualities, such as honesty and an absence of vanity."

She moved on smoothly to the next phase of her presentation, lay-
ing out the background of religious rivalries, and regional antago-
nisms that seeded England's Civil Wars. When Halaby entered and
tiptoed to a rear corner, she was doing well. She invited the class into
discussion whenever a point referred back to something previously
covered, like the Puritan oppression, the past kings. From the corner
of her eye, she could see Grace Meade raising her hand along with
others, but Kate didn't call on her, couldn't risk looking at her again
and seeing a vision of Chloe.

"To be a leader in such difficult times required a man to be a war-
rior, too, admired by the soldiers he commanded. Cromwell's rise began with his early military successes. He was able to command
extraordinary loyalty because he regarded his soldiers as comprising a
kind of a religious congregation—a sort of church. Do you understand
what I mean by that?"

No hands showed. Kate felt she'd posed the question without
enough preparation, too eager to impress the Head with the way she
involved the class. But then one hand went up.

Kate had to call on her. "Yes, Grace?" And now she couldn't look
away.

The eyes, too, were the same, the exact same vivid, summer-sky
blue.

"He thought they were moved by God," the girl said. "I mean, by
what He wanted to happen."

—*just what she might have looked like at sixteen or seventeen*—

Her thoughts seemed to be floating away from her, but Kate made a
grab for an idea, clung to her lesson as if to a life raft. "Yes, that's right.
Cromwell was a fatalist, who felt God made His will known by . . . by
the nature of events. . . ."

So was it His will if the nature of events had been to kill Chloe, kill
them all?

Kate stared at the bandage around the beautiful golden hair, and
the blue eyes open now, blinking in bewilderment, scaring her because
she knew Chloe was dead, so the eyes should be closed, had been.
Then the rage began to mushroom up inside of her, rage at the god-

news that Bert would like to join them, Kate was even more certain she couldn't handle the occasion. "I think I'm coming down with a little touch of something," she ad-libbed vaguely; she didn't want her mother knowing she'd suffered a mini-breakdown. "I may just stay in bed."

"Oh, sweetheart, it'll be such a shame if you don't come," Sarah said. "Not just for the holiday; I've also tracked down a couple of those people for you."

"Which people?"

"You know, the kind we talked about. I asked around, got recommendations, even made a couple of appointments for you. You don't have to keep them, if you'd rather not, but since I expected you to be here through the weekend . . ."

The mediums! Occupied with preparing for her day at Ashedeane, Kate had given no thought to pursuing it since. But the mention revived her interest. Reversing herself gracefully, she told Sarah she might be feeling better by tomorrow.

"Do try, dear," Sarah urged. "Let's both try to make the best of things."

As well as it was meant, Sarah's parting wish brought Kate down again. As things were, today the best seemed to be dead herself, unable to feel how miserable she was—and perhaps to be with *them*, wherever they were.

But she had taken an oath to survive. Maybe, in the days ahead, she could at least join them in spirit.

16

"But that's the miracle of this DNA stuff, isn't it?" Judge Bertram Davis said across the restaurant table. "You can analyze the tiniest scintilla of a person's remains and six or seven generations after death, the genetic evidence is still all there, the essence of that individual. Someone speaking from beyond the grave, in effect. And in this case, speaking to rewrite history. It makes the puzzle of Jefferson more confounding than ever, doesn't it?" The judge ate another forkful of his filet of sole.

Catching Kate's eye, Sarah gave a small lift of one eyebrow—soliciting Kate's appreciation of her "boyfriend's" qualities.

Kate sent back a smile of approval. By now, after first meeting over drinks at Sarah's apartment, Kate had formed the opinion that Bert Davis was indeed likable. He was the same age as her mother, tall and erect, with lively blue eyes. His full head of snow-white hair was cut short, not kept long and overly primped as did many older men, vain about retaining full manes in their later years. Bert was also well read, able to bring references and quotations from a range of great works into the conversation. His table talk was stimulating enough to distract Kate from her problems. No doubt, he was tailoring whatever he spoke about to touch on things that would interest her, but she recognized that as part of his gentility. Just as she guessed his choice of dining at a seafood restaurant—even if he insisted the need for fish derived from a heart attack three years earlier—was to keep Kate from facing the painful reminders of Thanksgiving tradition.

At the restaurant, they had gotten into discussing Kate's interest in American history, which led to Bert's remarks on the affirmation—by DNA analysis—of the long-held rumor that Thomas Jefferson had fathered children by one of the slave women he had kept at Monticello.

"It's always been an amazing contradiction," Kate responded now. "At the same time Jefferson is creating the Declaration of Independence, writing into law 'all men are created equal'—he's a slave owner. The question, of course, is whether his relationship with Sally Hemmings was simply an exercise of what was regarded as a right of ownership, or if he was truly in love and treated Sally as his wife."

"What's your opinion?" Bert asked.

"Oh, I vote for love every time," Kate said. A pause fell around the table, weighty with the thought of her own loves lost.

Kate broke the silence herself, veering in a new direction: Bert's earlier use of the phrase "speaking from beyond the grave" had stuck, making her wonder what opinions he might have about the existence of an afterlife. "Speaking of wives," she said to him, "my mother mentioned you'd had a long happy marriage. . . ."

"Yes. Thirty-four wonderful years."

"How did your wife die?"

Sarah shot Kate a look of displeasure. After all the good conversation, this was an unwelcome foray into heavier territory.

But the judge smiled at Sarah to assure her he didn't feel the subject challenged their own relationship. "I lost Judy to breast cancer five years ago," he said.

"After thirty-four years, her death must have been very difficult for you. How did you deal with—"

Sarah broke in. "Kate, today's a holiday. Maybe we shouldn't—"

"It's all right, Sarah." Bert turned to Kate again. "I can understand there's nothing more important on your mind. But I doubt my experience can be helpful to you. Judith and I had a full life. We got to see our three children grow up, marry, become established; we saw a lot of the world together, and shared the joy of seeing our first grandchild born. And Judy died of an illness that gave us time to prepare for the end. It's all very different from what happened to you."

He put his hand across the table, palm up. It felt very natural for Kate to reach out and accept the gesture of this warm, friendly man. "I dealt with my loss simply by going on, and you'll do that, too. All the same, why shouldn't you avail yourself of any form of comfort that presents itself? Whether visiting a shrink, or going on a trek to some maharishi in India, see anyone who offers even the tiniest hope of giving you some peace and acceptance of the way things are—no matter how they say they'll do it. Short of asking you to turn over all your worldly goods, of course." He released her hand, and gave Sarah a contrite glance, which informed Kate that her interest in visiting mediums must have been mentioned to Bert by her mother, probably in hopes of enlisting an ally against the idea rather than a supporter.

Kate went to the crux. "After your wife died, Bert, did you ever think of . . . trying to communicate with her?"

"No, Kate, I never felt any need to do that."

She might have left it there, yet she had developed a respect for Bert's mind. It would make her feel less a fool if he regarded her exploration of the supernatural as not totally baseless. "But do you think these people I'm going to see are charlatans?" she asked. "Or could there be people in this world who are truly able to bridge the gap to an afterlife?"

The judge cast his eyes again at Sarah before bringing his attention back to Kate. "What I think, my dear, is that searching for the truth of that matter is probably much more important than finding it. There was a fine Englishman of letters who expressed it pretty well." The judge got a distant look in his eye as he recited softly: " 'Ah, what a dusty answer gets the soul when hot for certainties in this our life. . . .' "

Kate recognized it right away as a line from the English poet George Meredith. "The same man also said, 'Speech is the small change of silence,' " she remarked lightly. "So perhaps it's time for me to shut up on this subject."

Bert laughed, and Sarah looked relieved.

But behind her casual behavior, Kate was burning with a fever. Never mind what some literary Englishman had recommended a hundred years ago, she was no less "hot for certainties." Or, at least, the certainty that she hadn't said good-bye forever to the people who owned her heart and soul.

It was hardly an exhaustive investigation Sarah had done to come up with the two names. One had been provided by a secretary at Legal Aid, who overheard Sarah telling a paralegal about her daughter's wish to consult someone who could "talk to the dead"; the other had come from asking attorneys she regularly met in the city courtrooms if any knew someone who had ever "successfully" consulted a medium. One of them had provided the name of a woman his wife had consulted once after the death of her sister.

"Not much of a recommendation if she went only once," Kate observed when told this.

"I said the same thing," Sarah countered. "But the wife was completely satisfied. Supposedly, she had some unresolved issues with her late sister, and settled them with that one visit."

From the few particulars Sarah was able to give Kate about the two mediums, it was apparent they represented opposite ends of the spectrum. The first, a man named Matteo Esteban, saw people in his apartment, and charged twenty dollars for a session that lasted—as Sarah was told on the phone by Matteo's assistant—"as long as the spirit is with us." The second, a woman named Jasmine Arthur, had an office off Park Avenue. Sarah had spoken with her personally and she had stated her fee as $400 per hour for an individual session. Group sessions were also available—ten people at a time, each trying to communicate with different loved ones—at $60 per person, but Sarah was sure Kate would want to see the medium alone.

The appointment with Esteban came first, set for nine o'clock Friday night.

His address was a building on West 165th Street, and when Kate saw its ramshackle condition, she wondered if it had been wise to insist on driving up here alone. "That's not a good part of town," Sarah had warned, offering to accompany her, but Kate had been adamant about going by herself. She was motivated less by courage, however, than the same superstitious fear she'd felt with Meg that being accompanied by someone with a negative attitude could affect the outcome.

Sarah had been forewarned the intercom was broken, and Matteo's visitors should proceed through the unlocked entrance, and climb the stairs to an apartment on the fourth floor. Arriving there, Kate saw a small plastic plaque above a button for the buzzer that read: *ABIERTO— SONAR Y ENTRAR.* Her Spanish was rusty, but Kate understood to press the button and let herself in.

She entered a small foyer lit by a dim overhead bulb. A few plain wooden chairs lined the walls, and a coatrack stood in a corner, a blue windbreaker hanging from one of its arms. To one side, the foyer opened to a dark hallway, and opposite Kate were double doors with glass panes blocked by a black satin curtain. From somewhere along the hall came the whistles and bangs of a video game being played. Kate sat down. She had no clue about what should happen next.

After a couple of minutes, a middle-aged Hispanic man emerged through the double doors. With barely a glance at Kate, he grabbed his jacket from the rack and left. Through the open door, Kate glimpsed a room with a figure seated before an altarlike structure where two tall candles burned.

A man's voice, raspy and quavering, called from within. *"Sí? Ninguno?"*

Summoning her, Kate realized. She rose and went slowly through the double doors. She saw him more clearly now, a very old man with a smooth bald head and taut leathery face, who sat hunched in a large, carved wooden chair, a shawl around his shoulders. What had looked like an altar was actually a large-screen television. The rest of the shadowy room was crowded with a sofa and chairs and tables. The two candles atop the TV were all that supplied the atmosphere of a chapel. The old man beckoned her forward, and held out a cigar box in which Kate could see a pile of bills already stacked. She removed her coat, took a twenty-dollar bill from a pocket, and laid it in the box. The old man waved her to a chair facing his and once more addressed her in Spanish.

"I'm sorry," Kate said. "I don't speak your language very well. Can we—?"

Before she could say more, he snatched up a little bell on a side table and shook it vigorously. A door opened at the side of the room and a girl in a plain black dress entered. The old man exchanged a few words with her, then she turned to Kate.

"My grandfather has asked me to translate for you. Will you please sit down?"

She was eighteen or nineteen and very pretty, with long lustrous black hair, dark sparkling eyes and hands that moved gracefully as she gestured to the chair. Her aspect inspired Kate's confidence; surely this girl could be no shill for a con game.

Pulling a chair from a corner, the girl sat beside her grandfather. "You have not been here before, so I will explain. Matteo lives in two worlds. Many years ago, before coming to this country, he was a young tradesman. There was a hurricane, his house was knocked down, and he lay in the ruins for days. When he was found, he was

close to death. So close, it is said he died . . . and then returned. Since
then, he has had the dead always near to him. Yours, that are near to
you, come with you, and he can hear them and speak to them. Whatever you wish to know from them, whatever help they can give you, it
will be made known to you through Matteo." She made a gesture with
her graceful hands, as if sifting water, to indicate she was done.

So. What did she want to know? Kate wondered. Everything. Yet it
was so difficult, getting near any intimate subject in front of these
strangers.

The old man rattled off a few quick phrases to his granddaughter
and the girl translated for Kate. "He sees a man with you. A very nice-
looking man. Perhaps this is the person you wish to contact . . . ?"

It was enough to help Kate past the barrier. "Does this man have
something to say to me?" she asked.

The question was conveyed to the old man and he replied, looking
at Kate. The girl translated his Spanish in bursts. "He is filled with
great love for you. . . . He says he is very sorry for what happened . . .
but you cannot let your own life end. You must know that he can be
happy where he is . . . if you let yourself be happy, too."

True or not, the relief of imagining even for a moment that Jim was
with her was irresistible. "And the children?" Kate said, caught up.
"What about them?"

The girl gazed silently at Kate for a second before turning to her
grandfather and continuing her task. The old man answered slowly in
his raspy voice.

The translation went on. "He sees no children."

"But they're with him!"

"Matteo says they are not here."

Strangely, Kate felt no less alarmed than if she'd lost sight of them
herself, like the times when they were little and she'd taken them to
the beach or to a supermarket and they scampered away. "Why?" she
demanded. "Where are they?" Kate glanced around, looking for the
specter who was supposed to be hearing her question.

The old man spoke, the girl translated: "They are fine and happy,
your man says. But they are with a master now, learning. Children are
pure when they go to this other world, so they have a chance to learn
and to become angels."

Kate managed a faint smile at the image of her children as angels.

And a memory came—the school Christmas pageant Chloe had appeared in when she was four, the wings Kate had made for her to wear out of window screen cut and shaped and painted gold. What an adorable angel she'd been—

Adorable *make-believe* angel. Kate looked down and sat silently. Why go on with this? The old man couldn't guess the specifics of her children, their ages, how many, so he simply said they weren't there. And it was only after she'd revealed she wanted to speak to her husband that he spoke of seeing a man—a "nice-looking" man. What bereaved wife wouldn't accept that description of the man she'd loved?

"You have other questions?" the granddaughter asked.

Kate looked up. "No. Nothing else."

"But your time is not over. The spirit has not left us, or Matteo would say—"

"I'm satisfied," Kate said, rising. Hearing her children were taking lessons to become angels—and what mother wouldn't want to hear *that*?—was such a sweet place to leave it.

She was heading out of the room when the old man spoke again, two or three rapid sentences. Kate looked back.

The granddaughter spoke. "Matteo says your husband encourages you to go over the water. It will be the best thing for you, and it will bring you closer."

And what the hell did that mean? Kate thought. She'd given away that her husband and children were dead. For a woman bereft, travel was a reasonable suggestion—and where could you go that didn't lie "over the water"? Just something extra, she concluded, to help her believe she'd gotten her money's worth.

"*Muchas gracias,*" she said to the old man, and proceeded through the door.

The street was emptier as she walked back to where she'd parked her car, but there were a couple of young men sitting on a stoop near a corner. She thought one whispered some sort of proposition as she passed. She quickened her step, but the sinuous whisper of Spanish words stayed in her mind until she was safely back in her car. Then suddenly, as she put the key into the ignition, she had an insight that made her laugh out loud at her own gullibility.

Matteo Esteban's regular customers—who didn't need translations— might never see the light, but to her the old man had revealed himself as merely a sham. For there was no way he could have truly been receiving and understanding messages from her husband. Dear Jim had always been very good with numbers, but completely hopeless with languages. After three years of high school French, he could barely put together a sentence. And as for Spanish? He'd never learned a word of it, probably didn't even know how to say, *"Olé!"*

17

After hearing about the visit to Esteban, Sarah tried to dissuade Kate from keeping the second appointment: "Surely you have better things to do with that money. Four hundred dollars would cover several visits to a therapist. Or you could treat yourself to a weekend at a spa. Or . . . just buy a piece of art." This last notion because they were meandering past sculpture and paintings as they talked. It was Saturday. They'd gone to Soho for brunch, and were browsing now through the galleries along West Broadway. Kate was due to head uptown soon for her four o'clock appointment with Jasmine Arthur.

"What do they say about trying again if at first you don't succeed?" Kate replied. Whatever had happened with Esteban, she was still affected by Anne Morrissey's story. The image of Chloe's spirit rising kept Kate fixed on a quest to find out where it—*she*—could have gone.

"Katie," Sarah persisted, "you do need to start being a little more careful with money." This morning, when papers pertaining to the lawsuit had been brought out for her signature, Kate had broken down and talked about the fiasco at Ashedeane, then admitted she might not be able to teach again.

Kate brooded on her mother's warning until they had left the gallery. Once on the street, she hailed the first available taxi. "Listen, Mom," she said, as she opened the cab door. "Maybe it is useless to see this Jasmine woman. But if once more gets it out of my system, then it's money well spent. And who knows, maybe something amazing will happen. I just can't let it go without giving it the old college try."

"College is where people know better," Sarah said. But by then the cab had taken Kate away, and she was talking to herself.

Jasmine Arthur's office was on the street level of a town house in the East Sixties; a space, Kate thought, that might as easily be occupied by a Park Avenue doctor. When the woman greeted her at the door, Kate was struck by how much like herself she was. About the same age, build, and coloring—the hair a darker brown, but cut to almost the same length. Gray eyes were the main difference. She was dressed similarly as well, in a two-piece suit, though the one under Kate's trench coat was a medium gray, her blouse pale blue, the other woman's black over white.

"Come in, Mrs. Weyland," the medium said in a low voice with an almost seductive lilt. She pointed to a closet in the entranceway. "You can hang your coat there." As Kate took a hanger, the medium asked, "How did you hear about me?"

"My mother got your name from someone she works with."

"Who would that be?"

"Sorry, I don't know exactly. . . ." Just as well: the medium might be digging for clues that could be used to simulate clairvoyance.

Jasmine Arthur led the way along a corridor, its walls hung on both sides with framed cuttings and reprints from magazines and newspapers; photographs of her with various celebrities, including one being interviewed by Larry King; and dust jackets from two best-selling books she had authored—No End to Love was one title Kate caught as she passed by. The corridor opened to a large room with French doors that looked onto a garden landscaped in the Japanese style, areas of raked white stones around small plantings of shrubs. By the rear wall of the garden, a bronze Buddha faced the house. The room was also under the Japanese influence, a couple of leather chairs, some black lacquered pieces, a bronze floor urn holding a tall arrangement of dry flowers.

"This is very nice," Kate commented.

"It's important for my work environment to have the right spiritual vibration," the medium explained as she crossed the room and seated herself. "Please sit down, Katharine." Kate took a facing chair. "Do you know anything about how I work?"

Kate shook her head. "After seeing all those articles, I'm embarrassed to say I knew nothing at all about you before my mother made the appointment."

"Well, you had no reason to know, did you?" Like her reply to Kate's compliment on the decor, a delivery of plain, good common sense. "I'm a channeler," Jasmine Arthur explained. "This means whatever I can tell you will come from my association with a spirit guide named Leander, a soldier who lived and died in ancient Greece." She gave Kate a sideways look, as if to invite Kate to express any opinion or doubt. When Kate said nothing, Jasmine continued. "Leander first spoke to me when I was in my early teens. At the time I kept it a deep dark secret. Well, a teenager hearing voices, I thought if I breathed a word I'd be sent to a loony bin. But I came to know better, and Leander and I have worked together now for twenty-five years. He is an elder in the place where all souls go, and can guide us to those we desire to be with. So . . . shall we start?"

"What can I expect to see?" Kate asked.

"See? Probably nothing. It's quite rare for spirits to take on bodily form or be audible in human voice. This is why all contact with your loved ones will be effected through Leander—and thus through me. Are you ready now?"

"One more question: how much do you know about why I'm here?"

Jasmine returned a benevolent smile. She seemed to guess that Kate's intent was to ascertain how much of what "Leander" communicated came from convenient foreknowledge. "I did ask your mother when we spoke why you wanted to consult me. She told me about the accident—that you'd lost your husband and children."

All right, that much was blown.

Jasmine read the disappointment in Kate's expression. "But why don't you see what happens here before you judge me?" she said, and reached out to a low table by her chair to pick up a compact tape recorder. "Generally, I tape the session for my client—unless you'd prefer I don't. . . ."

Kate gave a shrug—why not? The medium pressed a button on the recorder, and set it aside again. Abruptly, she sat up straight, hands on her knees like a child scolded for bad posture. Then she closed her eyes. Her features settled into repose.

As the medium continued to sit motionless and unaware, Kate's gaze drifted to the garden overseen by the Buddha—so good for establishing an atmosphere of celestial wisdom. Yet didn't the teachings of Buddha preach a cycle of death and rebirth through successive lives? Not the passage of souls into an eternal afterlife—

"I am before you now, and pleased to assist in your quest."

The voice startled Kate. No longer a husky purr, but deeper, more strident—more like a man's. Turning back to Jasmine Arthur, Kate found her eyes opened wide, looking fixedly into her own. The woman's face looked different, too, somehow. More taut and muscular, more . . . masculine. "Tell me your name, and what I may do for you," the medium said.

Kate was slow to answer, unable to adjust quickly.

"Trust me," the medium said. "I am Leander, a man of honor. Now tell me who you are, and what you wish of me."

Kate found her voice. "My name is Katharine Weyland. I . . . uh . . . I'm here to contact my husband and children."

"They must be called here from where they are. Please give me their names."

"James Weyland—Jim—that's my husband. And Chloe, and Tom . . ."

"We will wait for Jim and Tom and Chloe." The medium shut her eyes, and sat stone still and silent for a minute longer. Kate watched her in suspense. At last Jasmine's eyes opened again, staring fixedly into the middle distance. "They are with us now," she said. "They wish me to tell you first they are in a place of great joy and beauty, and are content—but for one thing: your unhappiness is known to them, and they can never be completely at peace until your sadness lifts. Trust me, there is no reason to be sad. Share their joy. Now, ask what you will of them."

What's the weather like? Are you eating well? Do you remember how you died? A score of questions whizzed through Kate's mind and went unsaid. She still couldn't fix herself into this odd realm, trying to reach her dead family by conversing with an ancient Greek soldier in the body of a glamorous celebrity medium.

"They are here . . . waiting," Jasmine said. "Don't you want to speak to them?"

That notion—that she was in some way rejecting them—propelled her past doubt. "Have you seen Ba?" she burst out, a question formed somehow without thought. The name was what the twins had assigned to Kate's grandfather, who had died at eighty-nine, still lucid, when they were only four.

The medium cocked her head as though listening. "Ba met them when they came. It is the way here. Those who have gone before welcome those who come after."

"How is he, what did he say—?" It was almost as if she was under hypnosis, Kate felt, surprised by the ease with which she fell into the vision.

"Ba has joined us," Jasmine said. "You may speak directly with him." Before Kate could react, the medium gave a throaty laugh. "This man is full of mischief. He is no longer old, he says, and now he can spend much of the time chasing beautiful nymphs. Though not, of course, when Grandma is watching. . . ."

Kate laughed faintly, too. Yes, Ba had been mischievous—that was the sort of teasing he might do. And it struck her suddenly: she'd said nothing about this being her *grandfather*!

She was off and running after that. It felt so good to embrace the myth of the hereafter in the here and now. She stopped testing, measuring words, keeping track, feeling shy. She told Ba how much she still missed him, had read the same book of "Mother Westwind" stories to the twins that he'd read to her. *He'd had a wonderful long life, she should always remember, and now he had a chance to stay with a part of her always by being with the twins. He could even read to them.* She missed him so much, she told Jim, sometimes she thought she'd go crazy. *He knew how hard it was, but she ought to know he really was with her, all the time.* She'd been told the kids were learning to be angels, was that true? *You know I've got a long way to go to be an angel, Mommy—*

That was from Tom, and "Leander" laughed as he passed it along.

Kate laughed, too. And cried. And said whatever came into her head. "Harry's asking if I'd like to come into the business," she said to Jim. "Thinks I'd be good at it. He'd teach me everything I needed to know about insurance. . . ."

We both know that's not your game, honey. Stick to what you do best.

"But teaching may not work out. I'm not sure I can do it anymore."

I'm sorry I never got to take your classes, Mommy.

"Oh, Chloe, honey . . . I'm sorry, too! So . . . very . . ."

Grief overwhelmed her then. Doubled over in her chair, she could only sob out how much she wanted them back. She didn't care how joyful it might be in paradise. She just wanted them back, to hold, feel, watch as they grew, to grow old with . . . !

"They cannot come," Leander said. "But you will always be able to visit them."

Kate lifted her head as the words emerged from the medium. Tears were still streaming down her face and now her nose was running. Stupid, she hadn't thought to cram every pocket full of handkerchiefs! Mindlessly, like a little girl, she brought her arm up and swiped her sleeve across her nose, smearing the cuff with mucus.

The medium let out a husky laugh. "Chloe says, 'You always told me I shouldn't do that, Mommy.'"

"No, baby, it's bad manners, isn't it?" Kate forced out in a whisper.

"The instrument keeps a box of Kleenex over there," the medium said, and pointed to a table by the door to the garden.

It took Kate a second to realize "the instrument" was Jasmine as defined by her "channel," Leander. She went over to the box and plucked out a wad of tissues. Returning to the chair, she sat blotting her eyes.

"They must leave us," the medium said. "Wait—Jim asks something else . . . about something he hopes you'll keep with you. . . ." The medium narrowed her eyes, concentrating. "Something you keep in a pocket or handbag . . . metal . . . with rounded edges. Maybe a watch?"

"Keys . . . ?" Kate murmured. Out of all the things returned from his pockets by the undertaker, she'd picked out his house keys to add to her own key ring, a sentimental symbol of eternal togetherness.

"Yes! The keys. He says keep them with you for luck. And don't be too hasty in deciding what to do with the house."

Kate stared back at Jasmine, confounded.

"They're gone," the medium said. "And now I must leave you, too. Farewell." Her eyelids went down slowly, like shades being pulled over a window. The rigid pose she had maintained throughout her time as Leander's "instrument" softened gradually, over a minute, as if a figure of ice were melting. Then her eyes opened again. Kate was amazed at how different she looked.

Jasmine reached over to the small recorder and removed the tape. She stood and held out the cassette. Kate left her chair to take it. "Was it a good visit?" the medium asked, glancing pointedly at the tissues Kate held with the tape. Her voice was sweeter, higher. "I never know what happens."

"Yes, fine," Kate replied. Her tears had subsided, and she looked for a place to dispose of the Kleenex. She saw a small waste container by the door that led out of the room and moved toward it.

"How did you want to pay?" Jasmine said.

"Oh, of course," Kate felt embarrassed at having to be reminded. "Is a check all right?" She had brought cash, but preferred to keep it if possible.

"I'd rather a credit card. . . ." Any one would do, Jasmine assured her. Visa, MasterCard, Amex—she took them all.

It was dark when Kate got home. Her mother had asked her to stay through Sunday, but Kate longed to be alone now, to savor the feeling of being with *them*. The experience with Jasmine Arthur, the comfort it had brought her, had not worn off. *She ought to know he really was with her all the time,* Jim had said.

Once she was back in the house, the specific advice about it passed along by the medium also came back to her—not to be "too hasty." What else could that be but an admonition from Jim to think twice about selling?

She unpacked, and took a bath. In the warm water, she closed her eyes and fantasized being with Jim, remembering all the way back to their honeymoon. *Damn!* The better the memories were, the harder it was to come back to the reality. After getting out of the tub, she thought of taking a sleeping pill or two—then warned herself if she didn't stop using that crutch, it would become habit. She'd start going to bed earlier and earlier. At times, all she wanted to do was sleep— forever. If they were together in paradise, why not join them? No! She had to shake herself out of that hopelessness. She put on some comfortable clothes, went down to the den, and turned on the TV to divert herself. But it didn't do the job.

Then she remembered the tape provided by Jasmine Arthur. She needed nothing more right now than to relive the sense of closeness to her family the session had given her. Kate got the cassette from her shoulder bag in the entrance hall, and took it back to the den. She put it in the stereo unit, and sat down on the sofa to listen.

Now, removed from the experience, it was easy to judge the medium's performance—and pick out little flaws that revived Kate's doubts. The changes of voice and appearance that came over Jasmine when "Leander" appeared? Nothing that couldn't have been managed by an accomplished actress. As she listened, Kate even mimicked "Leander's" mode of speech by holding her own voice low in her throat, achieving something close to the same effect.

Once reexamined, all the feats of clairvoyance seemed equally unimpressive. Like the thing about "Ba." When she'd first mentioned him, Kate hadn't said he was her grandfather. Yet, how hard was it to guess that her question would be about some beloved elder relative? And it was only after her own reference to him as "he," that Jasmine had identified him, and quoted his reference to "Grandma."

And where "Leander" had reacted to Kate's breaking down by pointing out a box of tissues kept handy by "the instrument," the brand name "Kleenex" had been used. Kate chuckled out loud when she heard that now. Had Greek warriors back in the days of Pericles or Alexander the Great fixed their sword cuts with a "Band-Aid," refreshed themselves after a hard battle with a "Pepsi"?

The thing about a round-edged metal object was only a little harder to figure out. After years of meeting with the bereaved, Jasmine must know there was a high probability they carried some keepsake. Her first guess had been a watch, probably the most common sentimental choice. But a ring would have fit the description, too, or a coin, or a cuff link, or a religious medal. Describing it as having a "round edge" rather than simply being "round," left room for interpretation. In Kate's case, it was keys, and she had identified the item before Jasmine confirmed it. As for the advice about the house, what woman in her position wouldn't give at least some thought to selling the home shared with her family?

Well, for her four hundred bucks, at least she'd gotten a good look at her own gullibility. Kate removed the cassette from the stereo, and dropped it in the wastebasket by Jim's desk.

There are people all over the place who'll tell you they can do it.

The phrase was in her head before she remembered where she'd heard it.

Gabriel!

Gabriel, whom she'd been ready to pay hundreds, and who'd only accepted fifty. *Gettin' rid of a ghost is a whole lot more work. . . .* Gabriel, who didn't just paint pretty pictures and instantly oblige her desperate need to make contact. When she saw him again in her mind, so much of what had seemed negative and even slightly frightening about him when she was in his presence, was stripped away. What stayed with her was a sense that he had truly meant to help her, that in his own way he meant to be sympathetic and compassionate. He was a rough man obviously, yet the hard exterior seemed to be also a protective shell, formed out of the same attitudes that made him a loner— and hinted that perhaps he, too, had been badly hurt by life. Which might be what made him especially sensitive to the deepest hurts of others, and able to provide relief. . . . He had given her none; in fact, had angered her. But when she thought back to their encounter, she felt the root of her anger was that he had denied her what she believed was within his power.

And she could not believe that Anne Morrissey had simply invented that vision of Chloe. . . .

Kate ambled over to the mantel, where a bunch of framed family snapshots were lined up. There was one of all of them crowded together on a single sled one snowy weekend in Vermont, the twins red cheeked in their snowsuits. Another one of the kids in bathing suits and snorkel masks on a Caribbean holiday. Jim with her on his parents' porch in Maine, right after they'd gotten engaged. "Oh, God, I miss you guys," she cried to their pictures, but without bitterness, almost as she might say it over a telephone while traveling somewhere, expecting to see them soon.

She found herself then looking at the old picture of Jim in his whites and team jacket when he'd played second singles for the U. Conn tennis team. Into her head at the same moment came the phrase she'd tossed out earlier to her mother—almost as if the picture were sending a message. "Think I haven't done it yet, mister?" she muttered, bringing her eyes closer to the picture, staring at her husband's young self. "Okay, I will. One more time."

Give it the old college try.

He'd always been smiling broadly in that picture. But damned if the smile didn't look even a little brighter as she stared at it now.

18

No gray apparition this time, the harbor town was an etching cast in yellow gold, transformed by a low winter sun at that moment when it balanced on the ocean's horizon like a juggler's ball on the edge of a blue china plate. When the ferry docked, Kate saw remnant drifts of a recent snow lying everywhere. The day was bitingly cold, but the air was clear, small details so easy to see it was almost as if she was looking through a magnifying lens. The perfect clarity, the beauty of the light, reaffirmed Kate's feeling that this was the place she had to be. She recalled then that the last spirit message given to her by Matteo was to "go over the water." A standard phrase for fortune-tellers, perhaps. Yet finding herself here, Kate had to wonder if it was a decision she'd made, or if there weren't unseen forces moving her, some current of destiny on which she was being carried forward. She had the odd sense that the decision to come was not entirely her own.

Or was that only because her mind had been so battered by events that she couldn't be sure any decision she made was entirely right or rational?

Driving off the ferry, Kate recognized enough of the streetscape to find her way back to the front of the Nantucket Atheneum. She left her station wagon at a meter near the library, then walked the same route she had followed before to bring her to the Captain Markham House.

The man who answered the door had a rangy athletic build, a lean attractive face, and curly black hair beginning to thin. The way he stood and the set of his features suggested he was generally relaxed and contented. Over his tan chinos and maroon pullover, he had on a linen cooking apron, and there were a couple of white smudges on his face. Flour, Kate guessed; she remembered Eddie Thorne saying her husband liked to cook.

"Mr. Thorne?"

"That's me," he answered brightly.

"I'm Katharine Weyland. I was here a few weeks ago. Your wife helped me out with some advice, so I thought—"

"Sorry to cut you short, but I'm busy in the kitchen, and my wife's right here." He urged Kate inside with a quick hand motion, and called up the stairs, "Honeeee! Someone for you." He closed the door, mouthed another apology, and trotted off into the recesses of the house.

Eddie Thorne appeared on the upper landing, wearing a purple-knit sweater-dress over a black leotard, her wild mass of golden hair bunched atop her head with a red alligator clip. A book was in one hand, a finger marking the page. As she came down the stairs, Kate noted the furry slippers on her feet had whimsical bears' heads on the toes. Halfway down, she recognized Kate. "Oh—hi. Still ghost hunting?"

"Sort of. I've just arrived on the island and I know you're closed, but I thought you'd be a good person to recommend a place to stay. I mean, a place with the same kind of feeling as yours."

Eddie stopped on the bottom step. "You want someplace haunted . . . ?"

"No, I didn't mean that. Just charming and quiet." Kate's eyes swept over the period wallpaper and polished wood surfaces. "And homey. I'll probably be staying through Christmas and New Year's."

Eddie's eyebrows went up before she managed to suppress her surprise at this attractive woman isolating herself over the holidays. "Hmm, let me think. . . ." She came down the last step and proceeded through a wide portal into the parlor that served as both office and sitting room. Kate followed her in.

"Just for yourself?" Eddie double-checked as she sat down at an old rolltop desk, laid her book aside, and pulled a notebook from one of its cubbyholes.

Kate nodded.

Eddie flipped through her notes. "Problem is a lot of places close from late autumn to Memorial Day. Others close around now for a few months. Oh, *here,* this is a nice little inn on Cliff Road. . . ." She pinned her finger to something in the notebook and grabbed up a portable phone from the desk. "Karen, wasn't it?" she asked as she waited for the call to go through.

"Kate."

The call was connected. Eddie barely began to explain she had someone seeking a room before she was told the "nice little inn" was closed until April. The next place she tried was already fully booked for the holidays.

After a few more calls to places either closed or fully booked, Eddie said, "It doesn't look good. There aren't a lot of tourists this time of year, but those we have come back again and again because Christmas is such a special time on Nantucket."

"I didn't know," Kate said.

"We have something called 'The Christmas Stroll' when we recreate the old-fashioned celebrations. People dress up like in the old days, and there are shows for children, carolers stopping at each house. . . ."

The talk of a special Christmas made Kate anxious. It was, in fact, the growing flow of holiday greetings in the mail that had confirmed the idea to get away from Fairhaven. Many of the cards were from business connections of Jim's, who clearly hadn't heard he was dead— addressed to him, with penned notes wishing "All the best to the family." As they piled up and she faced the prospect of the Christmas parties, the school pageants with children on the block dressing as angels, the glimpses of decorated trees through windows of other houses, it became unbearable to contemplate remaining at home with nothing but the hollow echo of all that vanished joy. This morning, she'd loaded a suitcase with cold-weather clothes, and driven straight north. She'd call Sarah later to let her know she was away, though Kate wasn't sure she'd reveal where. She didn't want her mother racing up here to be sure she wasn't alone on Christmas. Kate felt a need for solitude, and aside from seeing Gabriel, she had expected the island to be bleak and empty. Perfect for her mood. But now she wondered. Carols in her ears, excited little faces everywhere. That wasn't going to make it any easier. "Maybe coming out here wasn't such a good idea, after all," she said.

Eddie Thorne was studying her. "Do you want me to keep on trying?"

"I . . . I don't know," Kate stammered. "I did want . . . at least once more, to see that man you sent me to . . . but I didn't expect it to be"—a laugh popped out, one of those small bubbles of hysteria— "Christmas. I was trying to get away from all that."

Eddie regarded her for another second, then sprang up from her chair. "Wait here a moment, Kate." She ran from the room before Kate could reply and was back in a minute. "I checked with Danny, and he said it'd be fine for you to stay here."

"Oh, no! I can see you like having this time all to your—"

"Listen, this way you can give it a day or two and see how you feel, or stay longer if you like. And it'll save me the trouble of calling all over the island."

"No. You're terribly kind, but it wouldn't be right."

"Why wouldn't it be, Kate?" Eddie asked quietly. "I don't want to pry, but I get the sense you're going through a difficult time. So if somebody wants to make it a little easier, what's wrong with that? And we wouldn't give you the room free, just the usual holiday rate. I'll also ask you to make your own bed."

"In that case," Kate said after a moment, "okay."

Eddie showed her the room upstairs, the one she'd been decorating on Kate's first visit. It was finished now, the stenciling complete, trim painted ivory, furnished with a maple four-poster, desk, and chair, and a mirrored dressing table. A tapestry rug with a floral pastel pattern, matching bedspread, and curtains completed the scheme. A bathroom was right next door. Kate couldn't imagine anything nicer.

"I left my bag in the car," she said. "I'll go and bring it around."

As Kate was going out, Eddie told her she could use the parking area behind the house and gave her a set of keys, one for her room, and one for the front door in case she came in late at night, or whenever the Thornes weren't around. "Dinner tonight at seven thirty," Eddie added. "In the dining room." She pointed across the hall.

"Oh," Kate protested, "I certainly don't expect you to—"

"Sorry," Eddie said, "it's mandatory. Danny's fiddling with this new recipe—fish and vegetables wrapped up in pastry or something— and he needs an impartial critic. He knows I drool over everything he cooks."

The fish wasn't the half of it. Other concoctions of Danny Thorne's were either made fresh, or pulled from the freezer, to produce a meal that compared favorably with any Kate had eaten at a top restaurant. A colorful corn, red pepper, and beet mousse pâté to start; then the fish *en croute* and, for dessert, poached pears that had been hollowed at the center and filled with a cool lime syrup spiked with peppermint schnapps. A crisp white wine accompanied the meal. What was even more surprising to Kate than the quality of the dinner was to find she actually had an appetite for it. Since the accident, she'd eaten only out of habit, barely even aware of the taste. Tonight, she found the flavors coming through and enjoyed everything.

Perhaps it was the sea air that helped. Or maybe it was being able to forget herself as the Thornes, evidently perceiving Kate didn't want to dwell on herself, carried the conversational ball. They told of meeting for the first time when they shared a chair on a ski lift, teased each other affectionately about their "bad taste" in former lovers, and spoke about the careers they had left behind to come to Nantucket— Eddie as an advertising copywriter, her husband in the executive offices of the corporation that had hired him straight out of Harvard "B-School."

By coffee, Danny was talking about how much he had grown to hate his corporate job, and how pleased they both were with the decision to take up inn-keeping forced upon them by his health problems. "We work like Trojans in the high season," Danny said. "But we love meeting new people, and then there's this wonderful, sleepy time when winter comes. Ed can read all the books she missed while everyone else was lying on the beach, and I can play all day in the kitchen."

"You have a real talent for cooking," Kate said. "I feel sorry for the customers who only get breakfast."

"We're going to change that," Danny said. "The house next door may be coming up for sale. If we can buy it, we'll add rooms and open a restaurant. We needed to start slow, though, to make sure it felt right before jumping in with both feet."

"This should be a nice place to bring up kids, too," Kate said, "when you get around to having them."

That produced the first uncomfortable lull of the evening. A look passed between the Thornes. Then Eddie said, "I can't have my own, unfortunately."

Before Kate could apologize for the gaffe, Eddie went on matter-of-factly. "Goes back to college. One of those infections that went too far and gummed up the works." She looked to Danny, and Kate was touched to see him give his wife a wink and a smile he must have given her hundreds of times before that said beyond any doubt it absolutely didn't matter. Eddie turned back to Kate. "Danny knew when he married me. He still says he doesn't care, but there are so many different possibilities for having kids now, we'll manage it somehow when we're ready. It's hard to cry over that particular spilt milk when life is so good every other way."

Later, lying in bed, Kate kept replaying that part of the evening—a young woman's realistic adjustment to losing the capacity to bear children. It was like looking through a keyhole at a world that lay beyond a door that was closed to her, a world where it was possible to count your blessings and offset them against the hard knocks. Of course, not being able to have children hardly matched having known and loved your kids before losing them. But would she ever be able to open that door, and enter a place where she could count her blessings?

It was one of the questions she hoped to answer by seeing Gabriel again.

She went down for breakfast at nine. In the sunny dining room, a single place was laid, a glass of orange juice, a basket of warm croissants, and a thermos of coffee placed beside it. Through a door to the kitchen, she saw Danny Thorne, in a navy pullover and khakis, at a counter, slicing a banana.

He heard her pull up a chair and came in. "Sleep okay?" he asked.

"Great. Not a sign of the old sea captain."

He smiled. "Disappointed?"

"I might've been if I hadn't slept so well." It was even better than her last full night—and no pill this time. The sea air again, she supposed, and the wine.

"I have a breakfast special this morning. Banana-nut waffles with a pomegranate syrup I'm trying out."

"Oh, no." Kate laughed. "You've got to stop doing this to me."

"I'm cookin' 'em anyway," Danny said.

"Will Eddie have some?"

"She's out. There's a yoga group that meets early three mornings a week."

Kate agreed to "just a taste" of the waffles, and Danny returned to the kitchen. When she finished her juice, Kate brought the empty glass into the kitchen, and rinsed it in the sink. Danny was just ladling his batter into a hinged, cast-iron waffle iron nearly the size of a bicycle wheel, which took its heat from the stove burners.

"That's quite a contraption," Kate said.

"Found it at a yard sale here on the island, must be at least a hundred years old." He heaved the whole iron over to heat the other side and soon produced a gigantic, round, golden-brown waffle. Kate said it was too much for her, and he cut two slices pizza-style, and put them on plates. He warmed his pomegranate syrup in the microwave. Then they went to the dining room table.

The waffle with its ruby-red, sweet-tart fruit syrup was delicious. Kate told Danny how much she liked it, he thanked her for the compliment, and they ate in silence a minute. Kate poured herself a cup of coffee, and drank it black. Strong, Italian style, it was especially good against the sweetness of the waffle.

Danny broke the silence. "Eddie says you came back for another visit to our ghost chaser. So you think he's the genuine article?"

"He solved your problem, didn't he?"

"Seems so, anyway."

Kate caught his uncertain tone. After swallowing a bite of waffle, she said lightly, "You think your ghost might still be hanging around?"

He shrugged. But Kate kept waiting for more of an answer. At last, he said, "I'm not sure there ever *was* a ghost."

"But you saw him."

"Me? No, never. Eddie did."

"And some of your guests," Kate said.

"People see what they want to see sometimes. What goes on inside them, what forms their ideas, their beliefs . . . it can fool them into seeing and hearing things that . . . well, maybe aren't real." He broke off, and took a quick sip of coffee.

"Well, your wife certainly strikes me as having her feet on the ground. And she doesn't seem to have any doubts about what she saw."

"Mmmm," Danny said, as if agreeing.

But it still sounded equivocal to Kate. "You doubt her?" she said, unable to hide an edge of disappointment. They seemed like such a solid trusting couple.

"Of course not," Danny said firmly. But Kate kept looking at him, and then his eyes met hers. "I just wonder if, maybe, this thing about not having kids doesn't have some effect. She puts a brave face on it, but deep down I feel it's got to bother her, and maybe the ghost stuff feeds off that. Long before the night she saw the captain, she was telling me she heard things in the house."

"She mentioned footsteps. . . ."

"Other times, she told me she heard crying coming from upstairs— 'a high-pitched bawling' was the way she described it. Her guess was it might be the captain's wife, or his daughter, grieving for him." From his tone it was clear Danny's interpretation was different.

"You think she might have been hearing the cries of a baby," Kate said. The imagined cries of the child to which his wife could never give birth, induced by her suppressed but overwhelming sadness.

Danny frowned, then stood and swept up the plate Kate hadn't touched for a few minutes. "I can see you've had enough of that. . . ." He headed into the kitchen.

Kate followed him. She could tell he was troubled by his wife's situation, and possibly had opened up to help gain perspective on it. "Have you suggested this to her," Kate asked, "that what she saw comes from her own unresolved feelings?"

"Oh, sure," Danny murmured. He was at the sink, rinsing dishes.

"Well, what does she say?"

He took a moment to reply, as if deciding whether or not to go on confiding in her. "Eddie admits to feeling a sense of loss. She even agrees it could be why she sees and hears things that I don't." He shut off the tap, and turned to Kate. "But she doesn't accept that it's causing her to imagine things. Eddie believes her feeling of loss makes her sensitive to those feelings in others." He gave a wincing smile. "Including others who are dead." He went back to cleaning up.

"That still leaves the guests," Kate said. "How do you explain what they saw?"

"Damned if I know how to explain it. Power of suggestion, maybe, or mob psychology. But there's plenty of ways that make more sense than believing people who died a hundred years ago are still prowling around this house."

"So what do you make of Gabriel? Since he came, nobody's been bothered by any . . . visions."

"Power of suggestion again. He says he's done the job, so people believe it."

"Then you don't think he's the real thing. . . ."

Danny was drying his ancient waffle iron. He kept running the dish towel over the surface as he pondered. "I don't think he's a bad guy," he answered at last. "Somehow he got a reputation for doing this stuff, so whenever he's asked, he does it, that's all. Just the way he does other odd jobs, anything to make a living."

"What else does he do?"

"I see him around town doing carpentry, caulking windows, fixing roofs. And I think he also does metalwork, makes gates, fences, et cetera."

Kate's hope that Gabriel might be sincere was bolstered by hearing he didn't try to reap great profits from it, or rely on it for his living. Still, she wondered: had he done nothing more than perform an exorcism of the psychological demons within Eddie? "So how did he get a reputation for . . . having these special powers?" she asked.

"I don't know. Only part of his story I've ever heard is that he comes from an old Nantucket family. Maybe it goes back to them . . . like some old wives' tale."

For all the doubts Danny Thorne had expressed about Gabriel, Kate was no less eager to see him again and soon after breakfast she set out for Madaket. In just the few weeks since she'd last driven across it, the land had changed dramatically. Gone were the patches of color provided by the last wildflowers and autumn leaves. The fields, blanketed by the recent snow, were white expanses broken only by skeletons of leafless trees and wind-stunted evergreens that looked more black than green against the glare. Under a sky of unbroken gray cloud and glimpses of wind-whipped ocean, it all made for the sort of bleak view that Kate felt matched her inner landscape.

This time she knew the turn to Gabriel's house without searching for it. When she arrived at the rise that overlooked the shack, Kate wasn't surprised to see his truck wasn't parked outside: it was a weekday, and she knew now he did odd jobs. But the place looked so desolate from the outside, Kate wondered, if he could have gone away. Hadn't Eddie mentioned that Gabriel came and went from the island, sometimes staying away for weeks?

Kate left the car, and walked down the knoll. She moved up to one of the front windows for a look inside. Also much the same as on her first visit, neat and spartan. No pot on the stove, dish on a counter, scrap of paper on the table. But then, on the cushion of that same frayed, brocade-covered chair where she'd sat during his trance, she saw a book lying closed. A sign of life, at least. Gripped by a need to know he hadn't gone away, she moved to the front door, and put her hand to the doorknob. She had to see him again. An intuition had taken root that he was the only possible link to those pieces of her heart that had been torn out of her.

The door swung back so easily it was as if an unseen hand were opening it for her. Her heart began to pound as she crossed the threshold. As an invader in the territory of this intense solitary man, she could imagine how he'd react if he found her here. But she went in and pushed the door shut behind her.

She was drawn first to pick up the book on the chair and check its title. It surprised her to discover that it was Fitzgerald's novel *The Last Tycoon*—an oft-read copy from the Atheneum according to a library card inserted in the back inside cover. The incongruity of this reclusive odd-jobs man and part-time medium reading a Jazz Age novel about a Hollywood titan caused her to smile. She was glad, too, to see that the book had been checked out of the library only two days ago. She replaced the book as she'd found it, and scanned the shack again. Was there anything here to assure her Gabriel had the ability to provide what she needed? Her gaze settled at last on the wooden trunk at the foot of the bed, the most likely repository of private things. It was plainly very old, the wood scarred and darkened and worn to a sheen by time. Bentwood braces girdled the ends, and large metal hasps and hinges secured the lid. Kate crossed the room for a closer look. Now she could see the carving in the wooden lid, a design of wheatlike stalks and leaves forming a circle the size of a dinner plate, framing the initials J. F. She knelt in front of the trunk, and hesitated. This would be a terrible violation of privacy, she knew, and she was fighting her conscience. Yet she told herself the punishment she had endured gave her special privileges. Her hands moved to open the front hasps.

Behind her, the door banged open, and Kate leapt to her feet, a jolt of fear and guilt tingling in her nerves as she spun to look toward the door.

The door swung away from an empty frame through which came a gust of cold damp wind. Hadn't closed the door tight enough on the latch, she guessed. The wind had blown it open. But she took it as a sign—perhaps the same unseen hand that had aided her entry was telling her certain boundaries mustn't be crossed.

Kate went to the door. Near the threshold lay a couple of dead leaves that must have been blown in by the wind. She plucked them off the floor, and turned for a last look to be sure there was no other sign of her intrusion. Then she backed out of the shack, pulled the door closed, and tested to make sure the latch had caught.

Climbing back to her car, she still worried that some telltale sign of her trespass might have been left behind. She'd feel less guilty, Kate decided, if she admitted at least that she had come looking for him. In the station wagon, she rummaged in the glove compartment for the means to write a note. The only paper she came across, aside from the registration, was the one with Anne Morrissey's address, and there was a green marker, probably left over from a trip where Chloe took a coloring book. She turned the paper over to the blank side, and wrote with the green marker.

Mr. Farr—I hope you remember me. I was here a few weeks ago, and asked for your help. I've come back to Nantucket to see you because

Because what? How did she explain what had brought her back? It was nothing logical. Just a feeling that there was some comfort to be found here that had eluded her elsewhere. She pressed the marker to the paper again, yet still hesitated. How open should she be with him? After a moment, she continued:

I feel I can trust you, and I still need the kind of help I came seeking before. When I was here, I felt closer to my husband and children than anywhere else, so I'm praying you'll be willing to try once more to help me make a connection. I'm staying at the Markham House B & B on Quince Street. If I do not hear from you in the next

She paused once more to decide just how long she would wait.

two days, then I will leave.

That should give him time enough, if he was willing at all. She signed the note "Katharine Weyland," and carried it back down to the shack. As if it was her first time and she didn't know that it was unlocked, she folded the paper and slipped it through the crack under the door.

19

The few things learned from her snooping heightened Kate's curiosity about Gabriel Farr. His choice of reading, for one. *The Last Tycoon* seemed as far as possible from what she supposed would interest the surly man who lived in that tumbledown shack. And who, she wondered, was "J. F."?

Back in Nantucket Town, she went straight to the Atheneum. The island clearly valued its heritage, so she guessed biographical information relating to its families must be preserved. From the librarian, she learned that a great deal of such material was indeed available, but maintained separately at the Nantucket Historical Association on nearby Broad Street.

Kate found the Association in a two-story brick building, with its own library on the second floor, a large room lined with file cabinets and furnished with several tables for readers. At the moment, the tables were empty. The room's only occupant sat in the corner at a desk covered with papers and office supplies. A heavyset woman with an upsweep of snow-white hair, she produced a welcoming smile as soon as Kate entered, and introduced herself as the collection's "custodian." When Kate said she wished to access the archives "for a research project," the woman was agreeable, as long as Kate paid the access fee of five dollars the Nantucket Historical Association required of nonmembers.

"Now if you'll tell me the nature of your research," the custodian said after Kate handed over a five-dollar bill, "I'll try to steer you to the right files."

"I'm interested in a family named Farr."

"Aha! The Farrs," the woman said heartily. "Got some interesting material on them, all right." She headed immediately for a row of file cabinets.

Kate was soon seated at a table with three manila folders stacked in front of her. The tabs on the edge of each folder indicated that the librarian had gathered an odd assortment of subjects related to the Farrs. The top folder was labeled INDIGO, the middle one, LOST SHIPS, and the third, YONDER POINT. LOST SHIPS struck Kate as the most intriguing, so she started with that. There were approximately fifty separate sheets in the folder, mainly photocopies taken from accounts in old newspapers of whaling ships that had suffered fatal damage in storms, or foundered on reefs. As whaling ships had sailed in the far Pacific at a time when its most distant islands were rarely visited, and populated by natives who weren't all friendly—some even cannibalistic—there were cases in which ships had been boarded and crew members slaughtered. There were instances, too, when a whale, harpooned and frenzied as it tried to escape, had turned on a ship to ram it, caving in the hull. From a college course in American literature, Kate recalled it was such an incident involving a whaling ship named *Essex*, which had provided Herman Melville with the inspiration for *Moby Dick*. She came at last to one story describing a similar fate that had befallen a whaler named *Indigo*. The account of the event was from a front page of the *Nantucket Inquirer* dated "Wednesday, February 10th, 1841":

Reports transmitted via Hong Kong journals inform that the whaling barque INDIGO, after being at sea 28 months, sank off the Marquesas Islands on July 19th when the port aftquarter was stove in by a wounded whale. Three boats were put over and took on survivors including ship's captain Joshua Farr. Due to storms and rough seas, only one boat is known to have reached land, arriving at Nooaheva August 12th. The other boats, including Captain Farr's, have not been seen or heard from and are presumed lost.

Kate closed the folder and sat thinking. The trunk carved with the initials J. F. had the look of being old enough to have been the property

The story continued with an account of the circumstances of the captain's death and the inquest that had declared him legally dead, mentioning that Farr had died leaving no heirs. Without the newspaper stating it explicitly, "the squatter" was plainly being dismissed as an impostor whose claim was fraudulent. However, the fact that Gabriel was occupying the land twenty years later made the final outcome of his claim obvious. Reading through subsequent stories, Kate learned how Gabriel had prevailed in a legal battle that had gone through the courts for nine years. In his version of events, his ancestor Joshua Farr was one of two men among twelve in his lifeboat who had survived storms and starvation to be found adrift by a Portuguese trading ship. Brought to the Portuguese colony of Macao, Captain Farr had then started a journey back to Nantucket. However, weakened by his ordeal at sea, he had gone only as far as Hawaii before his health failed. A young Hawaiian woman had nursed him to full recovery, after which Farr had married her and stayed on. As proof of his tale, Gabriel had produced marriage certificates for his father and grandfather in the name of Farr, and the sea chest the whaling captain had taken with him from his sinking ship. Along with such personal effects of the captain's as an engraved silver compass and a personal Bible, this proof had swayed the court of appeals of the Commonwealth of Massachusetts. The inquest which had nullified Joshua's ownership a century earlier was declared invalid, and Gabriel was awarded the tract deeded to his great-great-grandfather.

"Get the info you wanted?" asked the custodian as Kate returned the files.

"Some," Kate replied. Though not what she wanted most. Gabriel's ability to persuade a court he was entitled to a valuable piece of land didn't strike her as reassuring; it might only be proof that he was an ingenious con man. She started to turn for the door, then paused. "I gather you know about the law case," she said to the custodian. Otherwise, the woman would not have included that file.

"Anyone who's lived out here long as I have probably remembers it. Made a lot of news in its time—fella showin' up from nowhere and tellin' that tale."

"You don't sound convinced it's true."

"Well, he had a lot of stuff that satisfied the judges, but there's ways he could have come by it without it being his. Never mind, though. He's been out there a long time, and never made trouble." She

of Joshua Farr. Yet the nature of such a trunk was to be used
or transport things while its owner was traveling; a ship's captai
certainly have had his trunk aboard when his ship went dc
there must be another J. Farr to whom Gabriel's trunk had bel

She turned to the INDIGO file. It also had photocopies of stor
had appeared in editions of the *Nantucket Inquirer*. Some wer
views done as late as 1842 with survivors of the sunken ship af
had sailed home. These detailed the terrifying experience of h
whale ram the ship until it was mortally damaged, then actuall
lowing some men who jumped into the sea. "That whale was l
man," one crewman was quoted. "He weren't going be killed v
takin' a bunch of us down with 'im." There was also a page of
aries, including one for Captain Joshua Farr. It described its sut
"the son of George and Prudence Farr," and named his moth
three sisters as survivors. None of the sisters' names began wit
A concluding line read, "Captain Farr is mourned as well by
Olivia Stacey, who was to have become his wife on return fro
voyage."

Strange, Kate thought—the only male of the line was not ye
ried, still the Farr name had come down to Gabriel.

The last file, tagged YONDER POINT, was again filled with cor
the local newspaper of record—but the datelines started in the 1
and continued into the early 1980's. The oldest of the articl
scribed the establishment of the "Yonder Point Nature Preserve'
Madaket with a bequest of eighty oceanfront acres by a wealth
zen described as "a longtime summer resident who wished to e
that part of our beautiful wild shoreline is not entirely lost to ran
development."

After zipping through most of the file, Kate began to think t
brarian must have included it by mistake and was about to put it
when she came to a 1983 article headed: SQUATTER CLAIMS PROP
RIGHTS.

The man who was removed forcibly by NPD after camping ill
gally on the Yonder Point Preserve is claiming ownership of
four-acre parcel that includes the land on which he squatted. Th
man identifies himself as Gabriel Farr and claims to be a descen
dant of Joshua Farr, a whaling Captain who held deed to th
land when he died at sea in 1841.

leaned across the desk, lowering her voice, even though there was no one else around. "It's pretty well known, though, that he's an odd duck, claims to talk to the dead. But that's harmless, I suppose."

When Kate returned to the B & B in the late afternoon, a fire was going in the parlor and a lamp was glowing against the gloom of the overcast day, but the house was quiet. She started up to her room, then stopped as she caught sight of the phone on the open rolltop desk. A grandfather clock between the windows said it wasn't quite five thirty. She picked up the phone and dialed her mother's office number.

Sarah answered. "Where have you been?" she asked scoldingly as soon as she heard Kate's voice.

"I needed to get away," Kate answered obliquely.

"Where are you?"

"I'd rather not say, if you don't mind."

"Rather not—if—!" Sarah sputtered. "Kate, I've been worried sick. Why won't you tell me where you are?"

"Because . . . I need my space."

"Your space," Sarah echoed derisively. "That's the kind of thing you used to say when you were sixteen, in full rebellion."

"Yeah? Well, it still means the same thing," Kate said, even taking on the sassy tone of a teenager. "I have to be on my own."

"How long will you be away?"

"I'm not sure. Possibly through New Year's."

"Oh, Katie. I'm sure facing the holidays is dreadful. But won't you let me—"

"Mother, please! I'll come home and be with you if I think I need that. But for God's sake don't sit around and wait for me. Fly out to be with Lisa and her kids if you want a merry Christmas. Live for yourself! That's what I have to do now."

"Well," Sarah said, yielding, "obviously nothing I say can change your mind. But will you at least check in every day or two so I know you're all right? If I go away, I'll have my calls forwarded."

"I'll stay in touch," Kate said, without pinning herself down to any schedule. "Just imagine I'm on vacation somewhere, having a fine time."

"I wish I could, darling." Sensing that the contact was about to be broken, Sarah added quickly, "But Kate, dear, instead of isolating yourself, don't you think it's time you went for some help?"

"That's why I am where I am, Mother," she said. "To get help." Before Sarah could probe any further, Kate promised again that she'd stay in touch, and hung up.

She was starting back up the stairs to her room when the Thornes came in, stomping on a doormat to loosen the snow from their boots. Eddie had an armload of long-stemmed, cut flowers in their florist's wrappings, and Danny was toting a pair of shopping bags stuffed with gift-wrapped boxes. Cheeks rosy from the cold, eyes glistening, the couple had the sparkle of two kids in love for the first time.

"Christmas shopping?" Kate said, grasping at something to be polite before she broke away.

"For my nieces," Danny said, as he and Eddie stowed their coats and gifts in a closet.

The realization struck Kate that she should do something for Lisa's kids, hard as it would be. "Is there a good toy store in town?" she asked.

Eddie mentioned a couple of places that carried toys and craft items for children. Kate thanked her, and mentioned she'd used the phone for a call to New York so they could add the charge to her bill. Then she continued up the stairs.

"Dinner around eight, okay?" Danny said.

Kate stopped. "Thanks, but I'm really not hungry tonight." The Thornes deserved to have the private time they would have if they hadn't kindly given her a place to stay. Looking at them, it was easy to imagine they would prefer to have dinner alone and make love rather than tend to her.

The moment she was alone again, Kate was stricken by a deadening inertia. She had no idea of what to do next. Lie down? Read? Change clothes and go out? It all seemed pointless. The effect, she suspected, of witnessing a couple in a moment that was at both romantic and common—simply coming out of the cold and having each other. She didn't believe she'd ever again have a moment like that in her own life.

Taking a chair by the window, she sat and watched the day fade away. Like shadows stealing in with the dying light, memories began to flow, snagged in the web of her mind for no particular reason. Times from before they'd had the kids. Floating aimlessly in a rowboat when they'd visited friends with a house on a lake. Walking home through a blizzard after a movie. Buying a kite and flying it on a beach. Making love in the attic of his parent's Maine house on a summer afternoon.

Never again. Tired at last from all the hopeless remembering, she dozed off in her chair.

"Kate?" She woke to Eddie calling softly from outside the door.

"Yes . . . ?" she answered drowsily.

"Mr. Farr's here. Can you see him?"

Kate went to open the door of her room. Eddie was in a robe, her hair wrapped in a towel, her face clean and shining as though she'd been in a bath. "What time is it?" Kate asked.

"A little after eight."

"Yes . . . tell him I'll come down. But it'll be a few minutes."

"Take your time. I asked him in, but he said he'd wait outside."

Kate hastily changed from the skirt and blouse she'd been wearing into jeans and a sweater. She went to the bathroom, threw some cold water on her face, and swiped a brush through her hair. She didn't care how she looked: the fact he wouldn't come in made her fear he might drive away if she took too long.

Before leaving the room, she stopped by the window and looked down into the street. His truck was in front of the inn, headlights cutting through a swirling night mist. She noticed a load of stuff in the rear flatbed, much of which seemed to be scrap metal. He was leaning against a fender, wearing a checked wool hunting jacket and a baseball cap, his arms folded as he looked along the part of the street leading toward the harbor. From this angle his face was hidden, but just as she was about to leave the window, he turned around and raised his eyes so they locked squarely on Kate's. It gave her a shock, and she pulled back. Maybe he'd seen her shadow cast from the window, or maybe it was coincidence . . . but it seemed as if he'd known she was watching him. It made her wonder if he could know about her trespass.

She took a few seconds to compose herself, then grabbed her down parka and headed out. Just before leaving the room, she remembered to take the set of keys Eddie had given her.

He walked around the front of his truck to meet her on the sidewalk. "Thank you for coming," she said.

He gave a curt nod, as his hand went to a breast pocket of his jacket and extracted the note she'd left for him. He unfolded it, and read one line aloud: " 'I feel I can trust you.' " He held the note out toward her, as if wanting her to certify her handwriting. "What changed?"

He certainly didn't depend on charm to win people over, Kate mused, though the way he was looking at her made her feel he was truly interested in the answer. A swatch of his dark hair fell across his eyes from under the cap, but his eyes shone through it, bright and watchful.

"I went to a couple of other people like yourself," she replied. "Well, not like you, really, but people who do the same thing, and they—well, I just didn't get the same sense of things that I did with you."

He kept looking at her intensely. "What do you mean—what 'sense of things'?"

"For a start, you're the only one who left me with a feeling that I'm not crazy to be doing this. The things you saw in your trance, spirits hiding because they're not ready . . . I've had the feeling since then that they *are* around me. And like you said, maybe it's as hard for them to cross the bridge between us as it is for me to believe it's there. But I need to be with them again, Mr. Farr, need it so much. They were taken from me so suddenly, that I . . . I'm afraid I'll never find my balance again . . . unless I can know they are with me somehow. So I'm hoping you'll forgive me for the way I acted last time and . . . try again to help us meet in the middle of that bridge."

He gazed back at her stonily. Since Kate had come out to the street, snow had begun to float down lightly, separate flakes so large she could see their miraculous designs on his dark hat for an instant before they melted. He kept staring at her, as she felt the snow settling on her hair, her cheeks. Finally, he looked up and watched the snow falling from the sky for a second. Then, with a shake of his head, he turned away and walked around to the driver's side. Kate's heart stopped. Her appeal hadn't moved him. He was leaving, still angry at her.

But now he looked across the hood of the truck. "Get in," he barked before opening his door and climbing behind the wheel.

They drove several miles along the road toward the end of the island in silence. If she didn't say something, evidently he wouldn't. In the dark cab of the truck, she shifted her eyes furtively to examine him as he concentrated on the road ahead. What had his youth been like?

When had he left Hawaii? How had he discovered he had his supernatural ability? (Or when had he begun pretending?)

Take away his attitude, Kate thought, there was no denying he was an attractive man. In the high cheekbones and almond eyes, Kate saw again the hint of a passage through Polynesia in his family history. She could imagine any number of women must have wanted him in the course of his life. So what had made him a loner? Did he separate himself because he was so truly strange, connected to other worlds?

The snow was coming down more heavily, and he turned on the wipers. Their dull metronomic beat made the silence even more oppressive. At last, Kate took the risk of breaking it. "I came across the story of a whaling captain named Farr at the Historical Association. Was that any relation of yours?"

He glanced over and said nothing before swinging his gaze back to the road.

She dared a bit more. "An amazing story—his boat was attacked by a whale and sunk. A lot like an incident that gave Herman Melville the idea for *Moby Dick*."

He threw her another glance. "You writing a book or something? Folks who go to the Historical Association are usually doing something like that."

Testing her, perhaps—he might have guessed the truth. "To be honest," she said, "I was just being nosy. Mr. Thorne mentioned you were from an old Nantucket family, so I went there and looked up the name."

He made a little sound low in his throat, a grunt of satisfaction at having his suspicions proven. "Joshua Farr was my great-great-grandfather," he said. "Want to know any more than that, Katharine, you'll just have to be a little nosier."

Which made it plain she wasn't going to get more out of him. But he sounded amused as much as annoyed, and she felt oddly pleased he'd called her by name.

When they arrived at his shack, he got out of the truck and headed straight for the door. With the headlights off, she couldn't be sure of her footing, so she waited until he'd gone inside and turned on a lamp casting a path of light through the open door. Stepping out of the truck, Kate was aware of a special tranquillity in the night that surrounded her. Except for the distant whisper of breaking surf, it was so quiet she believed she could almost hear the snowflakes settling on the ground. The snow was steady, but floating down gently, a white curtain dragging across the globe in a way that seemed to slow its turning. Tilting her head back, Kate saw patches of open sky above, making the millions of white flakes appear to be shaken loose from the stars shining far above them. It was a night that made heaven seem as real as the endless vastness of space.

"Gonna stand out there all night?" he called gruffly from the open door of his shack. "I thought you were in such a big hurry to get taken across that bridge."

His voice brought her back down to earth. "I am," she said, turning to the door. "I was just taking the first couple of steps on my own."

20

It wasn't as neat as when she'd last seen it. While she stood near the door, he toured the shack in a sudden flurry of housekeeping, tossing a blanket over rumpled bedclothes, collecting dirty plates from the table. Finally, he dropped the lid of the big wooden trunk which had been standing open. Before it closed, Kate caught a glimpse of a profusion of books and papers inside.

His neatening done, he turned one of the straight-backed chairs from the table to face the chair with the worn upholstery where she'd sat last time. Then he went to the sink and started filling the jug of water. "Take off your coat and sit down," he called back to her.

Kate moved to the chair, but kept her coat on. "It's cold in here," she said tentatively, fearful any deviation from his demands might lose his cooperation.

"Oh," he said, "sorry."

It was the first hint of softness she'd ever heard from him, a true tone of apology.

After setting the water jug on the table, he went to the wood stove, took a couple of split logs from a stack beside it, and shoved them inside. "I don't notice the cold, I'm used to it," he said, peering through the stove door as he waited for the wood to catch. "It should warm up soon, but keep your coat if you want."

She sat in the large chair, and he took the one facing it. "Remember," he said, "I could black out during the trance—"

"Then I wake you up with that water." Kate waved to the jug on the table.

"Right. Ready?"

She nodded.

He closed his eyes and began the series of deep inhales and exhales. It went on for a while, until the rhythm of his loud breathing seemed to cast over Kate a lulling, almost hypnotic spell of its own as she waited for contact from the spirits, *her* spirits.

His breathing ceased abruptly. The only sounds in the room were the faint creak of the shack's timbers leaning into the night wind and the distant whisper of surf breaking on the beach below. Kate held her breath, too. Suddenly his body jolted erect, his neck arched back, and a soft moan emerged from his mouth as his breathing resumed. Then he leaned forward, his head pitched as if to look at her though his eyes were still closed.

"Here now," he said softly. "A man. Husband . . . tells me your husband." Gabriel went quiet then, frozen in position, tilted slightly forward on his chair.

"Yes?" Kate said finally, needing to crack the silence. "What else?"

"Can't . . . so faint . . ."

Silence again. This time Kate said nothing, imagining her words might only interfere with his ability to hear from other worlds. The heat had begun to radiate through the cabin, and she unbuttoned her coat and pushed it off her shoulders.

"Hard for him . . . such pain . . . knowing yours," Gabriel continued in bursts. "Leaving you . . . that way . . . hurt . . . so sorry . . . terrible . . ." His voice seemed to carry all the regret and torment, half crying.

"It wasn't your fault," she burst out, aching to relieve the guilt, though she saw no one but Gabriel. "I know that, Jimmy. I don't blame you."

"Hurts so much . . . makes hard . . . to look at you . . . to get closer . . ." There was another long pause. "So what will you do?"

Not only the change in tack, but a change in Gabriel's voice—suddenly firm, instead of hesitant and breathy—puzzled Kate. "Do about what?" she said.

"About us, Katie. You can't be with me or the children; it's not your time. You have to live. But not half a life." Speaking in a stream now, no more tortured pauses. "Learn to live without us. Not easy, we know that. But you have to do it, have to go on. Don't live just half a life. Live completely. Use the time you're given."

She saw the words coming from Gabriel's mouth, yet she believed—*had to believe*—they were Jim's. Was it even Gabriel's voice she heard, his face she saw? In the shadowy room, his closed eyes were merely pockets of darkness; he didn't even look like the same man who had brought her here. She could only see the face of the man she loved. *Wanted* to see nothing else.

"How, Jimmy?" she shouted back at him. "How do I just go on? For what? So I can hurt like this for another day and another and another?"

"It will get better."

"No!" She hated hearing that! It was like refusing her devotion, denying her heart.

"You'll find things that help, other things to believe in."

"Like what?" she demanded. A worm of suspicion crept back in: couldn't this be coming simply from Gabriel, his bid to keep her as a paying customer? "Is this what I should believe in? Being with you *this* way?"

"No, Katie. Not this."

The suspicion passed. "Then what can help?" she begged. "Faith? Prayer? Tell me. I need something. . . ."

"What about love?"

"What do you mean?" If not religion, love of God, then what?

A short laugh came before the answer. "Have you forgotten what love is?"

Talking about their love—or their *kind* of love? Telling her, maybe, to love someone else now that he was gone? "Jimmy . . . oh, darling, never. I only want you."

"You'll always have me."

"Damn it, no!" she erupted. "Not like *this*. I want you with me, want you so much, it's driving me crazy." She began to cry. "Oh, God," she said in a wracked, whining plea, "I'd give anything if you could hold me right now."

No reply came back. But the silence was an answer in itself, perhaps the gentlest way to tell her that no matter how much she wanted it, how much she would give, it could never be.

In that moment of feeling utterly alone, abandoned even by the voice of the spirit, she was rescued by thoughts of the children. "What about the twins?" she said. "Let me speak to them."

After a moment: "Not . . . here." In a different voice—the medium's, and hesitant again, breathy.

"I want them, too, need them—"

"Not now. Too hard for them . . . see you . . . so hurt."

She was back balancing on the edge of belief. This was simply Gabriel denying her, finishing up, that was all.

"I want to talk to my children," she repeated, almost threateningly.

Gabriel grimaced, his face taut as though he were trying to lift something impossibly heavy. "Not . . . here," he said, slowly, as if struggling for breath. "Can't . . . be."

"But they're with my husband, all killed together. If he can talk, then—!"

"Katie, Katie . . . it's just not right yet. For them or for you." It seemed to be Jim back again, speaking easily, soothing her.

She pulled forward on her chair, hands reaching out. "Why not?" The calls broke from her. "Chloe, baby! Tom! I'm here for you. Come to me! Please!"

There was no response. Gabriel sat frozen in position, tilted slightly forward and to one side on his chair, eyes still shut, face tense with concentration.

At last, she took it as an answer in itself: she would not be given her wish. Was it only to get her back for another session? she wondered bitterly.

Suddenly, Gabriel stood up. Startled by the move, Kate lurched back, nearly tipping her chair. Then she noticed his eyes were still closed. She prepared for him to fall over in the faint he'd warned her about. But, instead, he shuffled forward, sidestepping her chair as if he could see it, and moving to the window behind her. He stood there facing seaward, his back to her. "Look, Katie," he said.

Kate gazed past Gabriel's standing figure to the view through the large window. Outside there was nothing to see but blackness, the ocean invisible under a sky clotted with snow-laden clouds that blocked out the moon and stars.

"Look," he insisted.

Now, studying the set of his head, she saw that he was focusing on a particular point in the seemingly empty black sky. Kate moved next to him and glanced over at him, checking his line of sight.

His eyes were still closed, face tilted upward. "Look," he urged once more.

She tried to follow the same axis of his sightless vision. And now there was something in the sky. A light, no more than a pinpoint, yet clearly visible, tracking slowly across the blackness. An airplane, she realized, flying below the cloud ceiling.

"Remember?" His voice broke into her thoughts. "You thought it would end right there. But it didn't."

Kate stared at him. How could he *know*? Or didn't every couple have a plane scare sometime—if they'd been together long enough? A *trick*. It had to be a trick.

"We had more time than you thought then, didn't we?" he went on. "Not as much as we would have liked. But good times. That's the way it should be. Going on as long as we can. That's what you have to do. Go on. And it will get better, I promise. I promised you then. I promise you now."

She kept staring at him, the passive, unsighted face. *How could he know about the promise?* It must be some sort of trick. All it took, perhaps, was to know the schedule of flights that went along the coast near his little shack. Kate wavered for an instant between grabbing Gabriel and denouncing him, or simply begging him to explain—or just subsiding into acceptance, committing herself to end all doubt.

She looked away from him at last, out the window, her eyes searching across the night sky for the traveling pinpoint of light. But there was only blackness again. No bright star of hope. Had it even been there? Or was it just conjured by the power of suggestion? Like the ghost of a sea captain . . .

She was still searching for the light when he said: "What happened?" Turning to him, she saw his eyes were open. "Tell me! Why am I standing here?"

"You wanted me to see something out there."

He glanced at her. "Not me," he said. "Someone speaking through me." He looked back to the window, the dark empty view. As he looked, Kate became aware that it was snowing again. Or perhaps it had never stopped; she had been so focused on the distant sky she hadn't noticed the swirling flakes just outside the window. "Did you see anything?" he asked.

He asked so innocently. As if he *couldn't* know.

"Yes," she said. "I did."

He looked at her for a moment as though to check her sincerity. Then he left the window, picked up the jug of water from the table, and went to empty it in the sink. Telling her the session was over.

"Don't you want to know what I saw?" she said.

"That's between you and whoever spoke to you."

"My husband," Kate said. "You said it was my husband."

Gabriel gave a little shrug. "So that's who it was. I don't need to know what passed between you."

Abruptly, he strode to the door of the shack and yanked it open wide so snow came blowing into the room. A drift that had piled up by the sill toppled onto the floor. "Bad out there," he said, closing the door, and stepping back toward her. "It'll be hard driving 'til they salt the roads. Shouldn't've brought you out, I guess. But now you're here, it'd be best if you stay the night."

All Meg's dire warnings replayed in Kate's mind. And why wouldn't this man think she'd be easy tinder—after that desperate admission of how starved she was for her husband's touch?

"Now wait a second!" she objected. "I don't care if I have to walk all the way back to town, I have no intention of spending the night here."

"I was just thinking of what's best. I'll drive you back if you want. Just seemed safer to wait 'til morning. I had it in mind to let you have this place all to yourself for the night."

"Where would you sleep?"

"In my truck, bed down out there in my sleeping bag."

She thought it over. Was there a bolt on the door? What would the Thornes think if she didn't return? "No," she decided. "No, I'd rather not."

He shrugged. "Your call."

She went for her coat, felt for the wallet in a pocket as she picked it up. "What do I owe you?" she said.

"Hundred dollars."

Double the last time, she noted to herself. Maybe because it had lasted longer—or because he'd delivered more: she'd "seen something." She took the cash from her wallet and held it out to him.

He was getting into his coat. "Just put it there." He pointed to the table.

Kate laid the money down. Even as a performance, she felt she'd gotten her money's worth. But it didn't seem entirely impossible that she had gotten far, far more. She was suddenly overcome with guilt for her doubts and ingratitude.

"Would you do this for me again?" she asked

"Let's wait and see," he shot back. "You may not want to come."

"I will. I know I will." Remembering that he claimed no knowledge of what had transpired, she added, "The children didn't come this time. I still need to hear from my children."

Without reply, he switched off a lamp and moved toward the door.

She demanded an answer. "I'll come back for the children," she said. "Will you be able to bring the children, if I come back?"

He had opened the door. He stood silhouetted in the open frame, his back to her. "It's not up to me," he said, and continued out.

As she followed him over the threshold, a fresh blast of snow stung her cheeks, forcing her eyes shut. She closed the door and started forward, but the wind was a frigid wall that held her back. Opening her eyes to a squint, she saw the air was almost solid white, half a foot of snow already on the ground. Slogging forward up the incline, she was unable to see more than a foot or two ahead. Kate stopped and called through the wind, "You're right, it isn't smart to drive in this." Ahead of her, he halted, but said nothing. "You really won't mind sleeping in your truck?"

"I'll be fine."

"Then I'll stay."

Stepping back on his territory, she felt distinctly different than she had any of the other times. She was going back because it was the place where she could feel safe and warm on a cold, threatening night.

But she was going back, too, because it was the source of a promise that things would get better.

21

The early morning light woke her with the suddenness of a gunshot, sunbeams glistening off mounds of snow and bouncing through the large window facing the sea so the room around her almost seemed to glow white hot. Kate bolted upright, clutching the sheets to her body, and glanced around, gathering clues to the mystery of finding herself in this strange bed. It came back to her as she saw the chairs facing each other, and the money she'd paid still on the table. Also on the table were a single cup and a pot of tea. Such an odd man, she thought, so gruff and closed off, and yet capable of a considerate touch like making the tea for her just before he'd pulled his sleeping roll from under the bed and carried it out to the truck.

Kate rose and slipped into her clothes. The fire in the wood stove had died during the night and the shack was chilly. At the sink, she discovered there was no hot water. What flowed from the single tap was so cold it stung her cheeks when she splashed it on her face. Glancing around, she could find no clock either, though the angle of the sun told her it wasn't much past sunrise. Maybe Gabriel used only the sun to tell the time. Her survey of the shack's contents left Kate feeling something else was missing, too, something that *belonged*. She couldn't put her finger on it, yet she sensed something had been taken away while she'd slept. That spooked her, the notion Gabriel had come back in while she was sleeping. She checked her belongings, found nothing missing. So what had been taken? Or had he come in only to watch her as she slept?

The thought made Kate anxious to leave. She threw on her coat and went out to wake him and ask to be driven back to town.

The snow had stopped during the night and the air of the new day had a crystalline clarity. Kate paused to take in the scene—sapphire sky over a diamond-bright white world. She recalled awaking to days like this when all had been right with the world—*her* world, anyway—and she could think to herself how good it was to be alive. Here it was, the same world, a glimpse of the same beauty . . . and she could only wish that someday she might have that same glorious feeling again.

She tramped up the incline through deep snow drifts to the knoll where the truck stood. At the center of the truck's load bed, the brass telescope stood on its tripod, aimed at the sky. So *that* was what had induced her notion of a "theft." Evidently, Gabriel, unable to sleep and seeing that the snow had stopped falling, had decided to do some stargazing. Right now she could see him sprawled across the front seat of his truck in his sleeping bag, with just a thatch of his dark hair poking out as his head rested against a half-opened window. He deserved not to be awakened, she decided, and clomped down again through the snow.

In the kitchen area, she found a canister of ground coffee, and made enough for two in the old drip percolator. While it perked, she meandered around the shack, inspecting the few things on the shelves and other surfaces. She was intrigued by noting how old many of the kitchen utensils were made of hammered metal, with long wooden handles. Relics from the captain's trunk, she guessed. Kate noted, too, that the book he'd been reading the other day was nowhere to be found. Returned to the library, perhaps. The thought of Gabriel as a fast reader raised her opinion of him.

Then, lying on a rough-hewn, three-legged stool in a shadowed corner, she spied an amazing object that had previously escaped her notice. It was a piece of ivory, roughly the size and shape of a squash or an eggplant, the top half of its curved surface covered with an elaborately carved scene depicting several boats, each containing several men, surrounding a harpooned whale. Lifting the object—its weight startled her, at least five pounds—Kate carried it to the window. She marveled at the intricacies of the carving visible in the sunlight, the detail etched into what she suspected was a whale tooth. Clearly incised were lines that represented ropes leading from the boats to harpoons

stuck into the whale's hide, with another harpoon about to be launched from the hands of a man standing in the bow of one boat. Most impressive were the expressions on the faces of other men, wide-eyed with terror as the wounded whale surged out of the sea, his maw gaping skyward, and his tail thrashing to one side, cracking another boat in half to send its occupants flying. There was a word that defined such scenes carved into whalebone, Kate recalled, and rummaged for it in her memory. *Scrimshaw,* that was it! This piece of scrimshaw was an astonishing piece of folk art. Did it depict the encounter with the whale that had cost Captain Joshua Farr his ship?

The aroma of coffee beckoned. Kate replaced the object, and poured a cup for herself. As she sat at the table drinking it, her glance landed on the trunk at the foot of the bed. She remembered the books and papers she'd glimpsed within before Gabriel had closed the lid, material that might answer questions about him. The temptation was irresistible—but first she went to look out the door of the shack.

Outside, all was quiet. If he'd been up with the stars, Kate reflected, he was likely to sleep late. She closed the door, hurried to the trunk, and knelt down. Where a padlock might have kept the metal hasp from opening there was none, and she lifted the trunk lid and propped it back against the end of the bed. To the right, the inside of the trunk was stacked with books. On the top layer were volumes on nautical subjects such as navigation, a collection of the poems of William Butler Yeats, and a Bible, all obviously well used. The Bible looked particularly old. It was larger than a modern edition, and had a hand-tooled leather cover, which was worn away at the edges. Like the trunk the leather cover was imprinted with the initials J. F.

Kate pushed the top layer of books aside to peek at the titles on some below—a copy of C. G. Jung's *Psychology of the Unconscious,* and a book titled *Human Immortality,* by William James, the nineteenth-century psychologist and philosopher whose writings were often credited with providing an academic basis for the spiritualistic fervor that had prevailed at the time. Jung, Kate knew, had also espoused notions that reincarnation was a factor in experiences of the human psyche. She guessed that reading these theories arose from Gabriel's desire to understand his own amazing gift.

She moved on to examining the other contents of the trunk. In the far left-hand corner, a jumble of objects lay atop some folded clothes of dark rough fabric—a small silver case like a pocket watch on a

chain, a ring of keys, an iron box of the sort that might be used to keep money or deeds. The nearer corner was occupied by a collection of papers stuffed in helter-skelter, some bundled into packets tied with string, some merely crammed and crumpled into any remaining space. At a glance, she saw envelopes of old mail, and a few stapled packets of pages that looked like they might be legal documents relating to his court case.

Then, amid the clutter, she spotted a newspaper, yellowed with age, folded so that Kate could see only a portion of the front-page headline and part of the photograph below it. The visible portion of the faded news photo showed a man in police uniform, alongside a much younger man. In the dull tones of the newsprint, the face of the young man nevertheless stood out in sharp contrast because of the flashbulbs that must have been centered on him: Gabriel, Kate thought, as he would have looked thirty years ago. Because of the fold, all she could read of the headline was EST IN HULA ML. She reached to pull the paper free for a better look—and froze.

The noise from outside was unmistakably the sound of a truck door slamming.

She barely had time to shove the paper back, close the trunk, scuttle to a chair at the table, and grab the coffee cup before he came through the door. She raised the cup to mask her face, certain guilt must be written all over it.

He didn't even look in her direction. Wearing jeans, but no shirt, boots unlaced, he went straight to the sink and turned on the tap. Bending over, he lolled his head around under the icy running water. After a minute, he straightened and shook his head like a wet dog coming out of the rain. Then he turned, and his eyes found her.

Even with a minute to calm herself, she still felt exposed. "I made coffee for you," she said.

He eyed her a second longer as if trying to remember who she was, then took a mug from the shelf and filled it from the percolator. As he faced the stove, Kate was aware of how strongly muscled his back and shoulders were, thick sinews packed under skin that looked almost as weathered as his face. If he was indeed the boy in the picture, the years since had been very hard ones.

While he was turned away, Kate glanced at the trunk, worried that in shutting it so hastily some telltale scrap of the contents might have been left showing. It was fine—but looking at the trunk brought the fragment of newspaper headline to mind: EST IN HULA ML.

Mindful of the policeman in the news picture, it occurred to her that the whole of that first word could be "ARREST." So . . . for what? The word "HULA" in the headline suggested it had happened in Hawaii, where Gabriel must have been raised. But what word began with "ML"? The only way those letters appeared in sequence was in Roman numerals.

"Sleep all right?"

His voice cut into her thoughts. He was looking at her. "Yes, thanks," she said.

He sipped his coffee, watching her over the rim of his cup. "Dream at all?"

"No. Why do you ask?"

"They come in dreams sometimes. Communicate that way. If you have those dreams and pay attention to them, you don't need me."

Like almost everything he did or said, it made her wonder: did he tell her that only because it made him *seem* more sincere? Or was he sharing professional knowledge, in the way a doctor might advise a patient an ailment could be treated with a simple home remedy instead of an expensive office visit?

"I haven't had any dreams like that," she said. In fact, she'd had few dreams of any kind since the accident—which, now that she thought of it, struck her as unusual. Even if she was on drugs much of the time, the loss was never totally out of her mind. Her subconscious as well ought to be riddled with images of them.

"Maybe you will after this," he said. He finished his coffee, set the cup on a counter, and strode across the floor to the bedside chest of drawers. He took out a folded denim shirt, put it on. "Roads'll be cleared by now," he said, as he tucked the shirt into his jeans. "I'll be outside when you're ready."

"Wait. Gabriel—" He halted on his way to the door and looked back. It took her a moment to realize exactly why she'd stopped him. Fifteen minutes ago she'd been so eager to go, uncomfortable with the prospect of being alone with him, and in the meantime she'd come across evidence that he was guilty of some crime. Yet she was reluctant to let him send her away. Whatever he might be guilty of, she believed he was also a link to the piece of her life that had been torn away. To be away from him, she felt now, was to be cut off from everything, cast back into solitary despair.

But that was too much to explain. "I'd like to finish my coffee," she said.

"I said I'd wait 'til you're ready."

"Nicer to have some company."

"I'm not much for small talk." He turned for the door again.

"Tell me what you saw in the sky," she blurted, anything to keep him. "The telescope—I noticed you took it outside last night. . . ."

He took a step toward her. "Stars, moon, planets. My 'scope's not very powerful, though. I can't see near as much as I'd like. But enough to let me think I'm up there, not bound to the here and now."

"Why should you ever feel bound to that? With your special ability . . ."

He smiled thinly. "You think I use that to take little getaway trips whenever I want?"

"No—I didn't mean anything so trivial. Just—"

He cut her off. "It's not something I ever do for myself, by myself. It's because I'm asked, see? For that reason only: because I'm *asked*." He stressed the word with extraordinary intensity.

"But even when you're asked," she said, "you don't always oblige."

He took the last few steps that brought him to the end of the table. Bracing his arms on the corners, he leaned over, his eyes targeted piercingly on her. "I try to do what's right, Katharine. It's not as if I always *know* what's right, but I do try. With you, though, I've had a hard time figuring it out. Because I see how much you need this . . . I can sure see that. But I sense that there's other things working against it. It seems this may not be the best thing for you—or not the best time, anyway."

"Why not?"

"Well, maybe," he said softly, "because the ones you need to contact aren't ready to be called. Your children, I mean. You don't want to call them if they're not ready. So maybe it's best to leave things as they are." He backed off from the table.

She cried out, " '*If* they're not,' you said; 'maybe,' they don't want it. You don't *know*."

"I'm trying to do what's right," he repeated, his tone harder.

"For *them*—the dead?" She shot up from her chair. "I'm here, alive! Can't you try to do what's right for *me*?"

Now his expression darkened. "For you, too," he said flatly. "You've suffered an awful lot. I don't think you should go lookin' to get your hopes beat down any more." He turned from her. "Whenever you're ready," he repeated as he went out, pulling the door hard behind him.

In a fury of her own, she grabbed up her coat, ready to leave. As she slipped into it, she noticed the trunk again. Stopping in front of it, she considered delving into it once more, then stifled the impulse. How much more did she need to know? He'd been in trouble with the law, and the feats of spiritualism he pretended to perform were the time-worn province of confidence men. She'd never have gone near a man like this if she wasn't so pitifully desperate. She was resolved now to be sensible. His own words echoed in her mind: *I don't think you should go lookin' to get your hopes beat down any more.* Wasn't he practically warning her to stay away from him, confessing that all he could deliver were false hopes?

When she went up to the truck, he was behind the wheel, the motor running. She climbed in, and they rode all the way to Nantucket Town without exchanging a word. The roads had been cleared and salted, but he drove carefully, not too fast.

Only when he stopped in front of the Markham House did she feel something ought to be said. "Thank you, Gabriel. You have helped me."

He kept looking straight out the windshield. "Got your money's worth, then . . ."

She heard the anger in it. Not because she'd blamed him for being merciless, she suspected, but because he knew she remained suspicious of him. "I got more than that," she said.

"Good." He kept staring ahead, waiting until she let herself out.

She watched the truck go up the street, and disappear around a corner. The minute it was gone, she wondered if she'd be able to hold to her resolve. She thought back to last night, seeing the light in the sky, the moments when she'd believed Jim was actually with her. What a precious deception—if that was what it was. She longed to have it with the children, too.

No. That was only hiding from reality, she warned herself sternly as she arrived at the door of the B & B. She reached into her pocket for the keys.

It struck her at that moment—one of those breakthroughs the mind arrives at after working on a subconscious level: the way the newspaper had been folded it wasn't only part of the word that must have been obscured but part of a *letter*. The next word didn't begin with ML . . . but MU.

Now, imprinted on her mind's eye was the full headline that she felt, beyond doubt, must go with the picture of young Gabriel Farr in the custody of a policeman: ARREST IN HULA MURDER.

22

She didn't want to think about Gabriel, the things that had happened with him. As with any addiction, the brand of relief he provided could chip away at her health and self-respect; it was a dangerous habit that had to be broken.

To aid the process, she determined to distract herself like any other Nantucket tourist. The town center had shops selling crafts, antiques, stylish clothes. There were cafes that looked warm and inviting on the winter days. A sizable museum documented the colorful history of the whaling industry. Or there were lovely walks to take. Cobblestone streets still laced the area near the wharves where whaling ships had once sailed in, laden with barrels of whale oil after voyages to the South Seas that could last as long as five years. Along streets in the old section there were lovely houses and gardens, once the property of the shipowners and captains. Beautifully restored, some had been adapted to inns and restaurants; others remained homes, now the property of wealthy retirees and summer residents.

As the Thornes had said, Christmas was a special time on Nantucket. Unlike most popular summer resorts, the island didn't shut down in winter. Summer residents came back with their families to enjoy the holiday, and their houses radiated cheer with wreaths on the door, candles in the windows, lights strung everywhere. All this family joy was exactly what Kate had wanted to escape by leaving Fairhaven, but she reconciled herself to the truth that it couldn't be avoided, unless she went as far across the oceans as Nantucketers had once gone to find whales. And even then her Christmas memories would go with her.

After returning from Madaket, Kate spent the day doing the obligatory Christmas shopping. She bought toys and books for her sister's kids, chose a framed antique engraving of a whaling scene for her sister and brother-in-law, and a "Nantucket Lightship" basket for her mother, an expensive purselike item favored by women of the island a century ago. She had everything gift wrapped, chose special cards, and sat in a cafe through lunch, writing personal messages. Then she went to the post office and sent it all express mail to arrive before Christmas, only a few days off. Each time she drifted into a recollection of her experiences with Gabriel, she shut it down, forcing herself to think of anything but.

Reluctant to impose further on the Thornes, she took an early supper alone at a small restaurant. Innocent as it had been, Kate felt embarrassed to face them after staying overnight with Gabriel Farr. Fortunately, she'd been able to slip in and out of her room during the day without bumping into Eddie or her husband.

But in the evening, after she'd returned to her room and taken a bath, there was a knock on the door. Opening it, she found Eddie outside.

"Hi." Eddie noticed that Kate was in her robe. "Sorry to disturb you, I just wanted to be sure you're okay. We noticed you didn't get back here last night."

"I'm fine, thanks. Mr. Farr thought the roads would be dangerous with all the snow, so he insisted I stay over."

"That's what we figured. Lucky you did. There was an accident out that way last night—a guy skidded off the road and his car flipped over."

"Good Lord!"

"Air bag did its job, thank God. Word around town is the man got away with a slight concussion and a broken arm."

Hearing how dangerous the roads had been calmed Kate's concern about how the Thornes might interpret her night away. "It's kind of you to check on me, Eddie. I was worried you might get the wrong idea about last night . . . think I'd stayed out with that man to . . . well, you know. . . ."

"With Gabriel?" Eddie laughed. "From all the people you meet inn-keeping, you get to be a pretty good judge of character. I don't know much about you, Kate, but I can certainly tell you're nobody's one-night stand."

"Thanks. You and Danny have been so good to me, your opinion matters."

Eddie gave her a gratified smile. "We're going to eat in a while. Just leftovers at the kitchen table, but you're welcome to join us."

"Thanks, but I ate already."

Eddie told Kate if she wanted tea or anything later on to feel free to come down to the kitchen and help herself and they said good night.

Kate got into bed with the one book she'd thrown into her luggage, the latest novel by an Englishwoman whose previous books she'd enjoyed. She'd been reading it at the time of the accident, and hadn't touched it since. Maybe now . . .

But Gabriel was back in her thoughts, along with memories of the visions he'd induced. Kate turned out the bedside lamp, and lay in the dark, thinking. Had she truly been with the spirit of her husband? Could Gabriel really receive messages from the ether that communicated the feelings of her departed children?

Eddie's remark about character judgment triggered reflections about her own abilities in that department. Facing roomfuls of young students had required her to hone perceptions of personality, detect qualities of self that weren't always apparent, even kept deliberately hidden. As she reviewed her assessment of Gabriel, Kate realized it was far from all bad. Yes, he could be gruff, graceless, rude. She could imagine he had a foul temper at times. Yet she felt, too, there was a solidity, an impressive inner strength—something even pure and incorruptible. An impressive appraisal, she thought, considering his phenomenal sideline—not to mention the evidence of a criminal past she'd come across. ARREST IN HULA MURDER. Then again, an arrest was not a conviction.

She found it difficult to believe he could be a murderer . . . though, perhaps, only because she couldn't reconcile a homicidal bent with a man who gazed at stars and read good novels, made her a cup of tea at bedtime, and avowed that he offered the comfort of talking to the dead—never mind if it was real—only because he was asked. By giving him this positive "report card," was she only setting herself up to be victimized again?

Eager to escape from the unanswerable questions into the oblivion of sleep, Kate got up and took a double dose of sleeping pills.

*   *   *

By the time she woke, showered, put on a sweater and jeans, and went down, it was past noon. The house was empty, a note from Eddie taped to the dining room doorframe. "Cleared breakfast, but help yourself to whatever you want." Kate stopped in the kitchen, and poured herself only a small glass of orange juice. Her stomach felt unsettled, probably from the pills.

Outside it was sunny but bracingly cold. Bundled in her parka and a wool scarf, she set off toward the docks, eager to tour the Whaling Museum, one of the island's prime attractions.

The museum occupied a two-story brick building that had once been a prosperous factory making spermaceti candles, a whaling byproduct. Always interested in history, Kate was instantly absorbed in the story, told in pictures and other exhibits, of Nantucket's evolution from a fishing outpost that the early English settlers had peacefully shared with a small tribe of Native Americans to a thriving economic force in the early and mid-1800's. The discovery—derived from the natives who hunted for whales in the nearby waters—that oil obtained by boiling down the creature's fatty tissue could provide a source of light superior to tallow candles had founded an industry in which Nantucket was a central force. This sandy, windblown island, incapable of supporting any agriculture, grew rich by sending forth hundreds of ships to the oceans of the world. The ships roamed farther and longer as demand grew and it was learned that the sperm whales, common in Pacific waters, provided the purest oil, not from their blubber alone, but from the substance called spermaceti contained within a hollow cavity inside their mammoth skulls.

One large room of the museum displayed an authentic whaleboat of the kind that would row off from the larger ship and maneuver close to the beast so the harpooner could hurl his weapon into a vulnerable spot. Also displayed was a replica of a brick "tryworks"—the oven that would be constructed on a whaling ship's deck on each voyage to boil down whale blubber to oil.

Smaller rooms were filled with paintings, letters crewmen had sent home from the other side of the world, and samples of scrimshaw. All attested to the grueling life led by men who sailed away for years at a time. Seeking relief from the boredom of months that might pass while searching for whales had given rise to the art of scrimshaw, incising pictures on such unused bits of a whale as the teeth and bones.

Kate came eventually to a gallery hung with portraits of the most prominent citizens of the island's "golden age," the shipowners and captains. She went quickly past these pictures of stern-faced men in stately poses, until her glance snagged on something in one of the paintings: a silver watch case dangling from a fob draped across a black waistcoat. It reminded her of the one in Gabriel's trunk. She raised her eyes to the face of the man stiffly seated in a broad armchair, gazing forward so that his eyes seemed to be staring straight into Kate's. And even before she had read the placard beside the painting, she knew who he was:

CAPTAIN JOSHUA FARR, MASTER OF THE "INDIGO," 1827–1841

How strange that she'd stopped right here! Glancing around, she saw that many of the paintings depicted their subjects wearing similar watch fobs, common for affluent men of their time. Nor had the one in the trunk borne any special markings. Yet it was Joshua Farr's that had caught her eye. Kate looked again into the face of the man in the portrait. Even after the passage of five generations, the resemblance to Gabriel seemed clear—and those painted eyes staring into hers seemed somehow to convey an assurance that his descendant could be trusted.

"Come with us!" Eddie insisted.

Kate had walked in from the museum to find the Thornes dressed up, preparing gifts to bring to a Christmas party. Danny was just boxing a large cake he'd made; he showed it off, with its decoration of "snow" frosting, and the top half of a candy Santa Claus disappearing down a chocolate-brick chimney into the center of the cake.

"No—really," Kate demurred, "I'll be happier here by myself."

"Oh c'mon, Kate," Danny coaxed, "it's Christmastime. We won't be able to enjoy ourselves as much if we have to think of you cooped up here alone."

She knew he wasn't just saying it: submitting would let them feel they'd fulfilled the spirit of the season. What the hell. She could have an eggnog and leave. If she hid away, she'd just take another pill and retreat into sleep.

"Go and change," Eddie said. "We'll wait."

The streets were filled with happy groups. Twice as they walked, they passed small impromptu bands of carolers standing outside houses where occupants stood at open doors, happily listening. On the way, the Thornes told her about tonight's hosts. A married couple of about their own age, they were summer residents who always returned for Christmas; the wife's father was a technology tycoon.

"Oh, and Anna's brother is very nice," Eddie said pointedly to Kate, "and not attached, as far as I know. You should meet him."

In other words "a catch." Having not yet shared the reason for her lonely trip to the island, Kate realized Eddie must have concluded it was the aftermath of a failed marriage or romance, while her interest in Gabriel was probably to contact a late parent or sibling. This wasn't the time to set the record straight, but Kate gave a thought to saying she really wasn't in a party mood, and turning back. Just then, however, they reached a corner, and Danny said, "Here we are!"

The large house, originally built for the owner of a whaling fleet and now magnificently restored, stood on a plot large enough to be surrounded by gardens. A maid took their coats at the door, and they passed into exquisitely decorated rooms overflowing with guests being served champagne and an endless variety of finger foods by a dozen waiters. Immediately, Kate felt out of place. Celebrations of life were no longer for her. She stared at all the feasting and merriment as if blocked off from it by glass so thick as to be bullet proof. When a tray of champagne came by she ignored it, but Eddie took an extra flute and pressed it into her hand. "C'mon," she urged gently, "give it a try."

Kate knew she meant more than just the champagne.

The Thornes told Kate to stay close so they could introduce her to the hosts, "Anna and Phil," as soon as they were located, and meanwhile they introduced her to people they encountered in the crowd. But it wasn't long before they were absorbed into a conversation with a couple like themselves, and they didn't stop Kate from drifting away on her own. Having made the effort to come, and seeing it wasn't going to work, Kate felt she could disappear now. She headed back to the entrance through a few large rooms. In the last doorway before the entrance hall, a man was standing alone. He was slow to move aside as she approached.

"Excuse me," she said. "I'd like to get my coat."

"You can't be leaving so soon. I just saw you arrive."

She took him in at a glance, a pleasant-looking man with dark curly hair just beginning to thin at the front, a bit heavy set, and slightly taller than herself. "It's too much of a crowd for me," she explained, and tried to edge forward again.

"Me, too." He leaned in to add conspiratorially, "Why don't we run away together?"

The tiredest of party pickup lines. Kate sighed inwardly, and tried to form a put-down with enough force to move him aside. But as she looked back at him, she saw that his dark eyes radiated warmth and intelligence, and he smiled shyly in a way that suggested it was rare for him to make passes—and he knew this one was on the brink of failing. She decided to let him down gently. "I never run off with a man unless we've been properly introduced."

"Does it count if I introduce myself?" He put out his hand. "Paul Levinger." As Kate took it, he gave a small wave at the surroundings. "Anna's my little sister."

So this, she realized, was the "catch." She studied him again. Mid-forties, far from glamorous, but solid looking, a face that was easy to look at. His overall aspect—not too slick, a bit rumpled—and finding him at the fringes of the party hubbub suggested a man who valued contemplation and the life of the mind over seeking the center of the action. An academic, perhaps.

"And *you* are?" he prompted as they shook hands.

"Katharine Weyland."

"Well, I've met your criteria, Katharine. Can we at least run as far as some empty corner where we'd both like it better, and might get to know each other?"

Kate gave a slight regretful laugh. "Oh, Mr. Levinger . . ."

"What?"

"Just . . . the way life works. I was invited along tonight by a friend of your sister's, and she told me I must definitely make an effort to meet you."

"Then what's wrong with the way life works? We did meet—and without any effort."

She didn't have the patience for polite repartee, nor was there any point in encouraging him. "Here's the problem," she said. "I'm sure you're a lovely man, and meeting you at any other time of my life would have been nice. But my husband and my two children were all killed one day not long ago, and I'm not over it. I don't think I will be over it, frankly, for a very long time. So that's what's wrong with the way life works. Now, if you'll excuse me . . ."

She waited for him to move aside, but he didn't and his glance didn't shrink from hers. "I'm so very, very sorry," he said. His sincerity and profound empathy were evident.

Strange. Why did it feel so cruel simply to have told it, report the cruelty of her own fate? "You understand, though," she said. "I'd like to leave now."

He nodded and stepped back from the doorway. But he watched from across the foyer as a maid brought Kate's coat and helped her into it, and when she moved to leave, he came over. "May I offer at least to walk you wherever you're going?"

"That's not necessary," Kate said.

"Not for you, maybe . . ."

She took another moment to decide. "That would be nice."

On the walk back to the Markham House, she answered his sympathetic questions, told him how it had happened. When he said, "It's hard to imagine how you—how anyone—can deal with such a blow," she replied honestly: "I can't imagine it myself. I'm amazed sometimes I haven't died from the sheer misery. But you just . . ." She paused, struck by the words on her lips, the idea they'd been put there by someone else.

"You just what?" he prompted.

"Go on."

"Yes, I know something about that. . . ."

Kate heard the sadness in his voice. "You've lost someone, too?" That would explain why he was alone.

"Yes, though not in the way you mean. My wife left me last year. She'd been having an affair for several years and I never knew until she picked up and went to him." He looked at her to add softly, "I was very much in love with her."

Kate nodded sympathetically. They had arrived in front of the B & B. "This is where I'm staying," she said.

"Are you here through New Year's?"

He was going to ask to see her again, she thought, and as nice as he was, she still didn't see any point to it. "I don't think so. Good night, Mr. Levinger, thanks very much for the escort." She started up the entrance steps.

"Wait a moment—" He extracted a card from his billfold. "Let me give you this, please. If I can help in any way . . . or if you'd just like to talk. . . ."

Kate took the card and thanked him. But she didn't expect to see him again.

On the wide beach, at the water's edge, a little girl was piling sand into a tin pail with a little shovel. Then, far down in the hole, emerging as she took out the sand, there was a little toy car. Suddenly not a toy, but a big car, completely mangled, yet somehow small, too, because her own little hand went at it with the little shovel until she saw the dead children inside. The scariest, most horrible thing she'd ever seen. She wanted to cover it up again, dump in all the sand she'd taken out, but where had the bucket gone? She ran all over the beach, searching for it, not a little girl now, but fully grown. And then a man seized her and the nightmare got worse; he was going to murder her, she knew. But he didn't; he just held her and forced her to face the sea, a blank screen of mist floating above the water. Until far out, through the pale gray air, she could see a small boat, and the twins were in it. She tried to wave to them, but her hands were pinned at her sides. Tried to run into the water, to swim out to them, but the man wouldn't let go of her. She fought to twist out of his grasp, struggling with every bit of her strength until she could feel her heart pounding, her breath giving out, but his hold on her only got tighter.

Kate woke panting as if after a frantic run, her heart beating wildly. The sheets, clammy with her sweat, were twisted tightly around her body. She pulled herself up, unbound herself from the damp linens, and sat in the dark, breathing deeply, waiting for her heart to slow down. She didn't turn on a lamp; the darkness of night was already giving way to the first light of daybreak.

For a while, she sat hugging her knees and she cried. Quietly, the way she had when she was a girl, homesick at sleep-away camp but not wanting the other girls to know. Not wanting, in this case, to lose control because it might wake the Thornes—and because every time she lost control, she was afraid she might never recover it.

As she calmed down, she remembered Gabriel's question. *Dream at all?*

She'd never dreamed about it before; now here it was. The wreck, the horror. And the dead? Was that Jim who'd grabbed her, made her look out into the mist . . . ? *They come in dreams sometimes . . . communicate that way. . . .* So was it because Gabriel had planted the idea,

the power of suggestion? Or did he know—did he *divine*—that the time had come for "communication."

Her tears had subsided. Through the window, beyond the roofs of neighboring houses, she could see the edge of the sky beginning to glow.

If you have those dreams and pay attention to them, you don't need me.

But she did need him. He alone offered a way to know what they were trying to tell her.

23

"They came in a dream," she said, "the children."

He stood in the open doorway, a blanket wrapped around him for warmth, mussed hair over his eyes, too drowsy to look more than slightly peeved about being pulled from bed at sunrise.

"I was afraid if I waited, you'd be gone somewhere," she added apologetically. "And I need . . ." She went dumb, and merely opened her hands in supplication.

"Come in," he grumbled and turned from the door, leaving Kate to close it.

Walking to the chest of drawers, he threw the blanket aside, exposing his full nakedness without any regard for propriety. Caught off guard, Kate didn't take her eyes away as he took fresh briefs and a shirt from the drawers, and started pulling them on. To see a man like this—once so natural with her husband—gave her relief more than any thrill. But she let herself appreciate his body, lean and muscled, surrendered even to a crazed instant of wanting him—not *him*, really, but wanting release from all the longings for her husband that had to go forever unfulfilled. Finally, she looked away. As he moved to a chair by the bed where his shirt and jeans were draped, she could no longer wait to tell him. "They came like you said they might. They were in a boat, far out in a mist. I wanted to go to them, but I couldn't. A man held me back. . . ." She glanced around and saw he was dressed now, and at the sink throwing cold water onto his face. "Doesn't it mean they're ready to be seen?"

He brushed his teeth, pushed his wet hair back with his fingers, then set up his percolator. She waited for him to answer, assure her. He turned to her after lighting the flame under the coffeepot. "Who was the man holding you back?"

"You, maybe. You *have* tried to stop me."

"Suppose it was your husband . . . ?"

She shook her head. If it had been Jim, wouldn't that have been clearer?

Gabriel went on. "Listen: we always want to call back the ones we've lost, and the ones who come are the ones who *want* to come. Remember that. It isn't a good thing to make them come if they don't want it. Do you care about that, Katharine?"

"Of course, I care!" she shot back: they were her *children*! "But, oh, God, Gabriel . . . just once, to be with them again, to know that they . . ." She fell silent, confounded by her own thoughts. What exactly was it she *needed* to know? Simply that their spirits survived? Or to know that they weren't rejecting her. It came to her then that, just as she could not forgive herself for her part in their deaths—however incidental—maybe they could not forgive her, either.

Her silence was broken when the percolator began to rattle. "I'll have my breakfast," he said. "Then I'll try."

He sliced bread from a loaf, and toasted it by holding it on a fork over a stove burner. He put jam on it, and brought it with his coffee to the table. He offered her the same, but Kate declined; she felt the need to be alone with her thoughts, to prepare herself for an encounter—or steel herself for any possible disappointment.

"I'll wait outside, if you don't mind," she said. "Clear my head a little."

She walked away from his shack, not up the knoll, but the opposite way, along the edge of the cliff. Footsteps leading back and forth—Gabriel's surely—marked a path through the snow, and she followed it. The path descended toward the sea, and on the shore below, Kate saw a smaller, even more rudimentary hut than his living place. Moored not far off shore was a small white boat, a sailboat with a single bare mast rising up from a square, enclosed cabin of dark wood. The sea was rough today, and the boat was bucking up and down on high waves, pulling at its mooring. The boat reminded her of the dream, and its battle against the ocean to stay safely moored made her wonder if her own anchors—to reality, to the earthbound solidity she could understand—weren't being strained. . . .

She looked back to where she had left her car, and told herself to go, take the road home. Build on what was absolutely real, tangible, no matter how difficult it would be. Call her mother and plan Christmas together, if she hadn't yet flown west. Kate turned around and ascended until she could see the car on the rise above the shack.

But to reach it, she had to pass his door, and there she turned in.

The chairs were waiting, set opposite each other. He was seated already, facing the large window. The water jug was on the table, placed near at hand. But although it was daylight, the curtains hadn't been drawn. When Kate sat down across from him, the sun beamed over her shoulder and shone into the room, erasing all shadows. Were séances ever held in bright light? she wondered. Would spirits come like this— or did he want a reason for them *not* to come?

"Shouldn't it be darker in here?" she asked.

"It doesn't matter," he replied, looking straight back at her. "Unless you'd prefer . . ."

"No. Not if it doesn't matter."

"Then, if you're ready . . ." His voice was somber, with none of the wry lilt she'd detected at other times.

She nodded.

He closed his eyes and began the deep breathing. With the sun full on his face, the strain was starkly etched into his features as he inhaled and exhaled. Fine creases around his mouth and his eyes, squeezed tightly shut, cut into the skin in a way that made her think of the carved scrimshaw. His respiration became noisier and more labored and he began to rock slightly side to side on his chair.

It went on far longer than the other times. She expected him to break off at any moment, tell her he'd failed, and blame it on the unwilling spirits. But then, along with his exhalations, Kate began hearing faint sounds that might be words, barely articulated. Leaning closer, she thought it was the same word being repeated every few seconds. But she couldn't make out what it was. She leaned closer, trying—

Suddenly, violently, as if he'd been seized from behind, Gabriel snapped backward, his neck arched, and went rigid. His eyes opened wide, staring upward. Even with the preparation of his past trances, Kate was alarmed by the stark, spastic movement. But she relaxed as he spoke, his voice more normal, regulated:

"Katie? Katie, why are you here?"

Jim, it had to be Jim. "To be with you, of course. And the children. I need—"

He cut in. "You should listen."

"Yes. I'm listening. . . ."

"To him. Listen to *him*."

Kate stared at Gabriel, his eyes still rolled upward as he spoke, his body rigid, the hands resting on his knees balled into fists. He looked less like he was in a trance than in the midst of some sort of seizure. "Whom do you mean?" she asked.

"The one who brings me here. Listen to what he tells you: leave things as they are."

"I can't. Not yet. Not until I've . . . been with the children."

"Katharine, you're expecting too much."

The name caught her attention. But Jim had called her that, too, when he was annoyed with her. She had to believe she was speaking with Jim. "Why is it too much? Even without what I'm doing now—I mean, without being 'called'—you've been able to watch. Isn't that right? You're . . . around me."

The answer came softly. "Often."

"There are times, too, I've felt the children could be near."

"Times . . ."

"Then why shouldn't they be with me, like this—as you are?"

There was a long silence. Kate noticed that Gabriel's eyes had closed, though he remained seated stiffly erect, his head back. Was he going to deny her again? Wasn't it *his* denial . . . ?

"Why?" she cried angrily, uncertain of whom she was asking. Only Gabriel, perhaps. "Why won't you let them speak to me?" Her voice broke as she began to weep.

"It's not me that decides. For now, that's just the way it is. But, Katie, that's because it's the right way."

"No. No! It can't be right to leave me like this! It can't. I need them so much. If only once!" The wave of sorrow engulfed her, making it impossible to speak. She fought to regain her composure, possessed by the idea that if she could stop begging, could calmly act as an advocate at her own tribunal, then it would make a difference. "All I ask," she began again more deliberately, "is, just once, to be with them, too. To know they're—" She cut herself off.

"What, Katie? Say it."

Alive was the word she'd swallowed. Stupid. Impossible. She had to accept they were no longer with her. Could never be. Yet wherever they were, if they *existed* anywhere, they were alive. Not *dead*!

But she cheated the answer, asking for no more than what she might be given. "I need to know they don't hurt," she said.

"They hurt only for you, not themselves."

"Then I can tell them I'm all right. Just this, just give me this. It will mean so much. They'll see. I'm begging you. . . ." She stretched out her hands. But who was she pleading with. A scoundrel? A ghost? The timid spirits of her children? It didn't matter. Only that she should be heard, obliged. "Just this, nothing more," she whispered, then weakened again.

Slumped in her chair, she bowed her head and wept.

For how long she wasn't sure, but then she became aware of the movements and sounds coming from Gabriel's chair. Looking up, she was startled to find his eyes wide, blazing, aimed right at her—though it was obvious he wasn't really seeing her, but focused on something beyond. Released from the position of arched rigidity, he was still apparently lost in a trance, gripped by contortions over which he had no control, his features twisted. His arms were raised, but bent at the elbows, the hands curled, almost as though trying to lift a huge weight like a car with someone pinned underneath. His whole body shook with the imagined effort, his boots racketing on the floorboards. Beads of sweat broke out on his forehead.

"What's wrong?" She was terrified. "Gabriel—!"

His mouth opened. Sounds came from his throat, high-pitched, throttled cries. Or were they words? Kate left her chair and crouched in front of him to hear.

The same sounds again, but this time she could make out words: "Try . . . bring . . ."

His face reddened, suffused with blood. The shaking had become more pronounced. "Gabriel—stop!" she screamed.

"Trying . . ."

The water. He'd said to use it if he fainted, but it seemed no less important to jolt him out of this fit. Kate took a step to his side, reached toward the water jug—

"Mama?"

She froze.

"Mommy?"

Their voices! Each different. And *like them exactly*, not calling her the same thing. Chloe had always said "Mama"; Tom, the other. She didn't look at him, couldn't. Better to picture them, to stare at a section of bare wall and remember their faces. "Yes," she murmured softly. "Oh, yes . . . I'm listening. . . ."

Only silence came back.

"Talk to me," she pleaded, "my babies. . . ."

When the silence went on, she turned at last to Gabriel.

She gasped at the sight of him—so pale, the blood all drained from his face, his eyes closed again. He looked dead. She had only a moment to see him this way before he sagged sideways, and fell off the chair, going down hard onto the floor. He tumbled over in his rigid pose so that his head thumped against the floorboards before he came to rest, lying on one side.

Automatically, Kate grabbed up the jug and dumped all the cold water onto his face. He didn't move, didn't flinch, though she could see now the rising and falling of his chest. She thought of shaking him, but he'd always been so specific about the procedure. She ran to the sink and refilled the jug with freezing cold water from the tap. Crouching over him again, she poured half the contents of the jug over his head, careful to keep the water away from his mouth and nose so it didn't interfere with his breathing. His eyelids flickered, and she quickly splashed the rest of the water onto his face.

He groaned, and rolled onto his back. His head lolled over so that the side that had hit the floor was turned toward Kate.

"Oh, God," she said as she saw blood trickling from the wound and running down his cheek; where his face had lain on the floor a small red puddle had collected. She remembered the clean handkerchief in the pocket of her parka, went for that, wet it at the sink, and returned to him. She knelt and, pushing the hair aside, pressed the cloth to the wound. He opened his eyes and stared up at her.

"Don't move," she said. "You cut your head when you fell. Not too badly. The bleeding should stop in a minute." He gazed back without protesting, in a daze. "Do you have bandages anywhere?" she asked.

His gaze moved over her face another few seconds, then he reached up and pulled the hand with the handkerchief away as he sat upright. "It'll be okay."

The feel of his touch lingered on her hand, the rough texture of his fingertips. "You should put something on it." The place she'd swabbed was still bleeding slightly, though it looked less serious than it had at first.

He didn't reply, but stood quickly as if to demonstrate he was fine. Once on his feet, though, he wavered unsteadily, and turned to the table, putting his hands down flat onto the surface to steady himself.

Kate hovered behind him. "At least lie down for a while."

"Don't worry about me. You can go now."

"I can't leave you like this. I feel responsible. I made you do something you didn't want to do, and maybe that's why this happened. . . ."

He made no comment. He looked down at the surface of the table, and lifted his hands from it slowly as if testing his stability. Finally, he walked slowly to the sink, ran the tap, and splashed more water onto his face. Then he leaned in to the mirror above the sink, and parted his hair with his hands to inspect his injury.

Kate's feelings of guilt were starting to be replaced by irritation at being totally ignored. As usual, when he incited her to think the worst of him, she fell back into suspicion. The children's voices? Mere approximations in falsetto. If it sounded like them, that was only because it was what she insisted on hearing. The routine of heavy breathing he went through had lulled her into something like a hypnotic state. Even his fainting could be part of the act—he just hadn't meant to hurt himself.

Angry, she pressed him for an answer. "So how *do* you explain it, Gabriel? Why does it work sometimes and not others? Why can I talk to a man, and not to children? Is the bridge so hard for them to cross— or do you just take a fall when that's easier than playing the whole scene?"

He went stock-still for a second, then leaned back from the mirror, and straightened up. "If that's what you want to believe," he said, his back to her.

"No, damn you!" she roared. "It's not what I *want*! I want to believe you can bring them to me! I want that more than anything else in the world. But you make it so hard." She moved closer to him, and lowered her voice. "You make it seem sometimes—you even tell me— that it's only because you don't want to do this. And I can't understand. If you have this . . . this power, this amazing miraculous way of helping people like me . . . why would you hold it back?"

He turned to face her now and his expression was dark, even

threatening. But she went on, desperate to get at him somehow, get at the truth even if it came in the nastiest form. "Sometimes I think you're *telling* me, in your own twisted way, that I should know better than to be here, to trust you. As if you haven't made up your *own* mind whether to prey on poor sad people like me, or whether you're doing them the biggest damn favor in the world—in *this* world. For God's sake, which is it? Are you trying to hook me in, or chase me away?" He was right in front of her now. She stared boldly back into his eyes. "Just have that much mercy, won't you? Tell me what you're doing? What in heaven's name is real?"

His hands came up to grip her arms, tightly. She thought he might fling her away at any second, but he didn't. He stood there, his eyes blazing into hers. Where his fingers dug into her arms it hurt, but she welcomed the pain as proof she'd cracked through his armor.

Then she saw a change in his eyes, a different light as they shifted slightly from holding her gaze to graze across her features, her hair, her skin, her mouth. He was going to kiss her, she realized, if she didn't fight him off; his need radiated from him as palpably as heat from a flame. She knew what she ought to do. To do anything but obey the rigid protocols of widowhood, honor her husband, was no less a sin than adultery. But she remained motionless in his grip. She wanted him to kiss her. Not for the selfish thrill alone, but for the advantage it might earn for her in mining out the truth.

Then his mouth came down onto hers, and she knew he would go as far as she let him. And rather than make any move to stop him, she urged him on as if possessed by a demon demanding that some perverse hunger be fed. She pressed her lips hard to his, her tongue probing no less deeply. In her core, she felt the desire no longer for the purpose of enchanting him, of gaining the truth. It was simply a headlong plunge into sensation for the sake of forgetting all else, transmuting herself from that mindless organism that was forced to feel nothing but inconsolable grief, to one that felt *something* else, whether it was pleasure, or shame, or both together.

She was clinging even as he suddenly drew away, and straightened his arms, thrusting her back. "No," he muttered, "sorry, that was wrong. I know that was wrong, Katharine. Forgive me. . . ."

Left swaying between opposing desires, she stared at him, confounded. She felt humiliated now, and might have been furious with him if she wasn't so much more furious with herself.

"I did nothing to stop you," she said coldly.

He turned from her, and walked to a corner. "Get out of here. Stay away from me."

"All right. But first tell me: before you fainted, I heard my children—thought I did. Tell me the God's honest truth, Gabriel. Was it just part of an act?"

He didn't answer at once, but she could see him going through an argument with himself—a small shake of the head, a slight heave of his shoulders. "Sure," he replied wearily. "You see right through me." He walked over to his bed and sat down on the edge, hanging his head. "Now would you leave here, please?"

Kate hesitated. The way he'd answered carried no conviction, as though he'd told her only what was necessary to get rid of her; she was no more certain of anything about Gabriel Farr than she had been before.

She might have made a fresh effort to satisfy her craving for the truth, but he had lain back on the bed and put his arms up, crossing them at the wrists so they covered his eyes. Kate thought then that his head might be aching from the fall. Perhaps he was more seriously hurt than either of them realized.

She watched him lying on the bed, his legs bent at the knees, feet on the floor, for a couple of minutes before she finally spoke again:

"I can't go until I know you're all right."

He said nothing. Had he slipped into unconsciousness?

It wasn't certain yet that he wasn't more seriously hurt than either of them knew. Head injuries could be deceiving. But for now, she decided, it was best to let him rest. Carefully, soundlessly, Kate moved the chair nearest the window so it faced the bed. Then she sat down and watched from across the room as he lay across the edge of the bed in a swath of sunlight. And while she kept her vigil, she tried to make some sense of the way she'd behaved.

Perhaps it could be excused as nothing more than a surge of plain animal need in the wake of months of physical deprivation. But, given the quest that had brought them together, wasn't it also possible she wanted this man, this unsuitable roughneck of all people, because he was the best surrogate for a true love lost, the flesh-and-blood conduit for her husband's spirit? So there was the more noble impulse at the heart of her desire, her longing to believe that what she had kissed, held, hungered for, was only the ghost within the shell of a man who meant nothing to her.

But then was it the ghost who had kissed her back? Or the ghost acting through the medium, urging her to know the pleasure of another man?

Or were all these mystical equations nothing more than pitiful excuses for the basic impulses of an animal in heat? Even now, Kate felt the current of desire flowing through her. How easy it was to fantasize walking over to that bed, slipping out of her clothes, climbing naked over the man who lay there, undressing and touching and arousing him. And fitting him into that space within herself that had been so terribly empty . . . that she believed would ever after be so empty. With Gabriel, even if responding to him left her disappointed in herself, perhaps she could find something to mitigate the endless, bottomless sadness that had been her only consuming emotion. Love had nothing at all to do with it. What she needed was simply to be touched by someone, anyone. She needed to be revived into feeling, to know that part of her wasn't forever dead because so much of what defined her had died along with those who had truly possessed her heart.

Kate looked away from him to scan the shadowy corners of the shack. Could *he* be here somewhere? Jim? Could he know what she was thinking? Even these thoughts were an infidelity. As her gaze landed on the farthest, darkest corner, her lips moved in an almost soundless whisper to the possible phantom. "I'm sorry." Not only for what she had done, but what she couldn't promise she mightn't yet do.

Her gaze went back to Gabriel as she kept arguing herself into the right to be there. Should she be consigned forever to self-denial as tradition demanded of widows in more ancient parts of the world, expected to wear black to the end of their days, remaining always at the fringes of joy like crows perched on branches atop the highest trees, forbidden to ever glide down and taste the fruit of the field? Wasn't that the expectation only of less-civilized peoples? Or was it always a fair romantic sacrifice—even if you remained married in spirit, married *to* a spirit—never to break the vows taken at the marriage altar?

"I told you to go."

A long time had passed before he spoke. He was still lying on his back, but the blanket of sun had slid from the bed onto the floor. She guessed now he hadn't been napping at all, simply frozen into inaction like herself.

"You also told me to go *on*," she replied. "Maybe staying's the way to do that."

He sat up and gave her a long look, then sprang to his feet. "I have work to do," he said, and marched to the door without looking at her. "Stay as long as you like." He paused to grab a sheepskin coat hanging on a peg, and went out.

Kate bounded up in time to catch the door before it closed. Following him across the threshold, she watched him head down toward the shore along the path trodden in the snow. He walked quickly, steadily, no sign that he'd been affected by his injury. The cold wet air cut through her clothes, and she retreated inside the shack.

Stay as long as you like. She looked around the room, playing with all the possibilities. There was the trunk, its secrets still to be explored. And the bed. Suppose when he came back, she was lying there, a simple declaration of readiness. The fantasy began to unfold again.

ARREST IN HULA MURDER. Kate glanced at the trunk. To know he was capable of the worst crime might loosen the grip of this attraction she felt—

Yet, did she want to know the worst about him, destroy the belief that he might be the way to make contact, to find peace with the way things were and would always be? She heard the children's voices echoing in her mind . . . recalled the dream it seemed he'd foreseen . . . remembered standing at the window, watching a light move across the night sky.

No. This wasn't the way to "go on." Kate spotted her coat where she'd left it. She snatched it up, and ran from the shack. Crossing over the fresh imprints of his boots leading down to the shore, she went clambering up the slippery hillside to her car, as though being chased by a whirlwind.

24

Returning from Gabriel's to the Captain Markham House, Kate went straight into the parlor to call her mother's office. Making a proper adjustment to her reality, she felt now, required being with family, those who cared most.

"I'm sorry," the secretary told her, "Ms. Ballard is out until after the holidays."

She tried the home number next. The machine answered, Sarah's voice. "Happy Holidays, everyone. I'm away 'til after New Year's, but I'll be picking up messages, or you can reach me directly at . . ." Kate heard the area code and number for her sister's house in Beverly Hills, and lowered the receiver into its cradle. She felt oddly marooned now, wanting to escape from the island, yet with nowhere better to go. Going to Los Angeles wasn't a possibility. Her presence amidst the family would only create a kind of false cheer, everyone else trying too hard to make it easier for her, and she wasn't anywhere near ready to see her sister's children opening presents around the tree, their lives going on in happy normality.

She went up to her room. Hanging from the doorknob was a small straw basket holding a slip of paper—Eddie's charming little touch for delivering a phone message. *Paul L. called. Wants to see you tomorrow nite if you have no other plans. Will call again later.* Nice, thoughtful. But what had transpired with Gabriel had confused Kate enough that she wasn't eager for any more interactions with men.

From somewhere in the recesses of the house, she heard the hum of a vacuum cleaner. Kate tracked the humming noise along the corridor, and arrived at an open door through which she could see Eddie vacuuming a rug in a nicely furnished suite—probably the Thornes' private quarters. Eddie wouldn't hear a knock over the noise of the vacuum, so Kate went in. Seeing her, Eddie switched off the vacuum.

"Sorry to bother you, but I wanted to talk to you about this." Kate held up the note.

"Sure, no bother."

"I don't like to put you in the middle, but when Mr. Levinger calls again, I'd appreciate it, even if I'm here, if you'd handle it."

"You mean say you're out?"

"No need to lie. Just tell him I appreciate his kindness, but I really can't . . ."

"Of course. Whatever you think is best."

Hearing the sympathetic conciliation in Eddie's tone, it dawned on Kate: the elephant was in the room with them. Since she'd mentioned her circumstances last night to Paul Levinger, it must have come up when he called. His sister was a friend of Eddie's, so they would have chatted awhile. Kate felt oddly embarrassed by having all she'd done and said in the past few days reappraised in the context of having her tragedy exposed. "Thank you," she muttered quickly, and started to leave.

"Kate, wait a second. . . ."

Kate turned back. "I suppose you know about my problems, and I'm sure I have your sympathies. You and Danny have been wonderful to me, and that's truly made things easier. It's as much as anyone can do. Thank you." She started out again.

"Kate . . ." Eddie tagged her with a light touch on the shoulder. "Listen, it's not just about going through some polite ritual of sympathy. As little as I know you, to think of what you're going through, all I can say is . . . it hurts deeply. I mean, I hurt for you. And I think . . . maybe, it would help if you could, well . . . just let people . . ." Her stumbling effort finally gave out.

Kate had continued facing away as Eddie spoke. Now she faced her again. "Let them what?" she demanded. *What the hell did she owe anyone?*

"I don't know, Kate . . . let them try to help, let them just be human, say whatever useless, stupid, well-meant things people say when it's the best they can do."

Kate stared back. It was a hell of a slant to put on things—that *she* was being selfish by denying others the chance to unburden themselves of their sympathy. But as she met Eddie's steady gaze, Kate understood and accepted it. To come back from being that mindless, unfeeling organism to which she'd been reduced, to be human herself, there was an obligation to tolerate whatever fumbling efforts others made to give her comfort. She felt ashamed now of the way she'd shut out her mother and a good friend like Meg; had shied away from all who would be moved to commiserate. Of course, they were powerless to change anything—the things she needed changed, anyway—but how mean and small of her to want to punish them for it.

"Thanks, Eddie." Kate gave her a forgiving smile. "Sorry I snapped at you."

Eddie waved off the apology. "I did get a little self-righteous—"

"No. I can do with a lesson in how to be a good widow." Maybe a lesson, too, in not overdoing the self-pity.

Suddenly, Kate was seized with a longing to talk more. Eddie was exactly the sort of new friend from whom she could ask advice without getting answers colored too much by knowing her as she had been. But Eddie had her rooms to clean.

Then, before Kate could retreat, Eddie said, "I was just going to take a break. How about a cup of coffee . . . ?"

"Sounds great," Kate said. Eddie had evidently perceived a thirst for more than coffee.

"So what did you do?" Eddie sat at the large table in the downstairs kitchen, chin propped in her hand. Glued to Kate's account of her visits to Gabriel, she'd kept priming her with questions as avidly as a child listening to a ghost story around a campfire. Kate had already revealed that she'd come back to Nantucket hoping Gabriel Farr could put her in contact with the spirits of her husband and children.

"I did just what he'd told me to do if it happened—dumped the water over his head. Had to refill the pitcher, in fact, and toss more in his face before he woke up."

"Then what?"

"Well, he'd hurt himself a little when he fell, so I took care of that. . . ." Kate paused; the moment had come to reveal the matter she needed most to consult another woman about. "And then he kissed me," she finished in a rush.

"No!" Eddie said, her green eyes widening.

"The thing is," Kate confessed, "I didn't mind. Don't you think that's awful?"

"Not especially."

"He didn't ever try that with you, did he?"

"No. I never got the sense he's some kind of sex maniac, if that's what you're worried about."

"It's not. But you brush it off so easily. This wasn't a small thing for me. I'm a woman in mourning, after all."

Eddie rose and took the pot from the coffeemaker. "Kate, I don't think you have to rake yourself over the coals for letting yourself be kissed. I can see where Gabriel is pretty sexy, after all—the way dangerous men always seem sexy to good girls like you and me. If you gave in to a moment of temptation, that doesn't mean you care any less about . . . what you've lost." She hovered the coffeepot over Kate's cup. "More?"

Kate shook her head. Eddie still hadn't gotten the picture, though perhaps it was her own fault from painting it as more innocent than it was. "Interesting you think of Gabriel as a dangerous man," she observed. "How do you think he's dangerous?" Had any hint of character supported the capacity for homicide?

Eddie sat and poured more coffee for herself. "Not 'dangerous' in the worst sense. I'd never have recommended you go to him if I felt he was a real threat. He's just rough, bottled up . . . and involved with things that are a little unnerving."

"But you do believe his ability is real—that Gabriel is honestly able to communicate with the dead?"

"You know I do. Sounds like you have doubts of your own. . . ."

"Someone in my situation wants so much to be fooled. The things that happened with me—talking to Jim, hearing the children's voices—they could just be tricks."

Eddie looked thoughtfully into her cup for a moment. "I don't think they are, though—any more than I think I'm wrong to believe I saw a ghost right here in this house. Other people may tell me I'm nuts to believe it, but . . ." She looked up at Kate. "It doesn't matter what they think. I know what I know."

Eddie's "they," Kate perceived, was just one person. And since Danny had confided that it was a sensitive issue with his wife, Kate knew she ought to leave it alone. But the need to test belief overruled discretion. "What does Danny think?" she asked.

"He's sure it's nonsense," Eddie said. "According to him, the things I saw were delusions that come out of my unhappiness about not being able to have children."

Kate considered asking Eddie if it didn't occur to her that Danny might be right. But she didn't have to ask. Eddie seemed to know the question had to be answered. After sipping thoughtfully at her coffee, she continued: "I can't blame him for seeing it that way. It's so easy as a rational explanation, isn't it, right out of elementary psych? The crying I've heard is imagined, a sublimation of the cries of my own lost baby. My belief in ghosts comes from guilt, an unwillingness to accept death because of the death I caused." Eddie paused, when she saw the puzzled expression on Kate's face. "Oh, that's right, you got the quick, easy version Danny and I usually give when the matter of being childless comes up. But an infection is only half the truth, Kate. I got pregnant in college. The guy was lovely, but I knew even then I didn't want to spend my life with him. I wasn't ready to handle a child alone. So . . ."

Kate said it for her. "You had an abortion."

Eddie looked down into her cup. "Yeah. And then the infection set in. I regret it now. I wish I hadn't lost the ability to have children. I wonder often about my child, who he or she would have been. It adds up to feeling terribly guilty about what I did." She raised her eyes to meet Kate's. "But it's too easy to say those feelings have screwed me up so much I've lost touch with my own senses. I know the difference between real experience and what's imagined. And I know there were spirits here in this house. I forgive Danny for what he thinks, especially because he's forgiven me so much. But he's wrong, dead wrong, if he thinks I'm fooling myself."

It helped Kate to hear Eddie acknowledge feelings of guilt, yet also deny with such certainty they had skewed her perceptions. Kate had wondered if her own need to forgive herself—and be forgiven by her dead—didn't cause her to deceive herself that they could be summoned to provide that absolution. She saw now that guilt and belief could be separated, needn't be regarded strictly as cause and effect.

Nevertheless, her faith in Gabriel remained shaky. And in the light of Eddie's belief, Kate considered whether to seek her perspective on the alarming discovery she'd made about him. *Suppose I told you that Gabriel might have murdered someone . . . ?*

In the end, she decided it would be unfair to stain his reputation based on the little she knew. "Thanks, Eddie," Kate said. "Listening to you has encouraged me to trust my own intuition." She brought her cup to the sink, and rinsed it.

Eddie followed her. "Will you see Gabriel again?"

For a second she imagined what another session with him might be like—perhaps a breakthrough. "Probably not. I don't think it'd be good for either of us."

As they went upstairs, Eddie said, "You still want me to run interference when Paul Levinger calls? Seems a shame to be on your own tomorrow night."

"I've been on my own a lot. Why should tomorrow night be any harder?"

"It's Christmas Eve, Kate."

"Oh," Kate said quietly, not at all surprised at having forgotten.

And would being alone on Christmas Eve be any worse than at other times?

No. That night of all nights was a time she ought to be alone—available, as in Dickens's *Christmas Carol*, to the ghosts of Christmas past.

25

Soon after talking with Eddie, Kate walked over to the Atheneum; old as the library was, she guessed it must have kept pace with the present. Yes, the librarian told her, there were computers in an upstairs room providing free Internet access.

Kate soon located websites for three newspapers in Hawaii: the *Honolulu Star-Bulletin*, the *Honolulu Advertiser*, and the *Hilo Register*. All had historical information recounting that they had begun publication more than a century ago—in fact, two had been founded to report on whaling activities in the Pacific. But none gave access to archives going back thirty years. Phone numbers appeared, however, and Kate copied them down. Then she returned to the front desk to ask the woman librarian if there was a public phone in the building. "A couple in the basement," she said. "But hurry, we're closing early—in a few minutes. The staff is going caroling."

Knowing her calls would need more than a few minutes, Kate decided to make them from the Markham House, and started out of the library. "You're welcome to join us," the librarian said cheerfully. "Everyone's welcome."

The offer deserved a polite reply, but all Kate could do before rushing out was silently shake her head. It seemed so miserably wrong to be preoccupied with hunting for the truth about a murder at a time that other women could go singing about holy nights, and wrap gifts to perpetuate sweet myths for their children.

During her time in the library, a thick fog had rolled in off the sea.

As she walked through it, Kate felt the damp mist lying cool and wet on her face like old tears. She drifted along uncaring, the fog inside her, too, shrouding her mind. Daylight was beginning to fade, but the streetlights were not yet lit, so people moving along the street around her were no more than vague shapes. A pair of figures came close, a woman with her arm draped protectively over the shoulders of a young girl. The details of their clothes were blurred, but Kate recognized the distinctive outline of bonnets that arced around their faces and cloaks over dresses with long, bell-shaped skirts. The shock froze Kate in her tracks; they were apparitions, she realized, ghosts of an earlier era. The rustle of taffeta faded behind her, and she whirled to see them disappearing into the dense fog. Her yearning to cross over into the world of the dead had misfired somehow, she thought, landing her among the wrong ghosts. Or was her mind crumbling? Afraid and disoriented, she stood motionless, staring into the swirling mist, tempted to chase after the ghosts, but held back by the fear she might be lost forever in the afterworld.

Then, as the shock ebbed, her senses began to gather the realities. A car passed in the street. Electric lights shone in the houses and shops around her. Now it came back to her—the Christmas stroll Eddie had mentioned!—a Nantucket tradition when holiday celebrations were recreated, including people dressed up in period costume! She hovered between feeling relieved and disappointed.

Eddie was at the desk in the parlor when Kate let herself into the B & B. "Oh, Kate! You just missed a phone call from Mr. Levinger."

"I hope you told him—"

"I did. But he asked me to try changing your mind, and said he'd call again."

"I'll be going home tomorrow," Kate said. "That's the best place for me now." The decision was spur of the moment, but it seemed right. Coming away certainly hadn't made things easier. If she needed companionship, Meg would surely take her in. Or maybe she'd get a flight to California, after all: out there, it never *really* was Christmas, no sleigh bells in the snow, the weather too warm for roasting chestnuts on an open fire. Perhaps the emptiness of the holiday would seem less tragic.

"I'm sorry it didn't work out for you here," Eddie said.

"Certainly not your fault. You did everything possible to make me feel welcome." Kate asked then about the ferry schedule, and Eddie gave her a winter timetable from a cubbyhole in the desk.

Eddie apologized that she and Danny had to be out this evening at a small party of close friends, but if Kate got hungry, she could help herself to anything in the kitchen. They'd be up to bid her good-bye in the morning.

Finally, Eddie said, "Wherever you go, Kate, I hope you'll find peace and a way to be happy again. You'll always be in my prayers."

They embraced, then Kate went to her room and began packing. In winter, there were only two ferries daily; she planned to have everything done so she could leave in the morning. As she went through the mechanical routine of folding clothes into her valise, she drifted once more into thoughts of Gabriel. *Could he have the power? Could he be a murderer?* At last, all the inner questioning boiled over. Flinging an armload of clothes onto the bed, she went to her coat and pulled from a pocket the paper on which she'd written the phone numbers for the Hawaiian newspapers.

The Thornes had already left for their party when she went downstairs. It was after seven—but four hours earlier in Hawaii.

"Star-Bulletin," a woman operator answered.

As soon as Kate said she was researching an event that had happened in Honolulu many years ago, she was transferred to an extension that was picked up by another woman, younger sounding and impatient, her words clipped: "Newsroom—Tashiro." It seemed to be the wrong extension—not the archives—but Kate went through an explanation anyway, specifying her interest in a thirty-year-old murder case.

The woman was cooperative. "Give me exact dates. I'll see what we've got."

"I don't have the dates. All I know is it was thirty years ago, more or less, the victim was a hula dancer, and the person arrested for the crime might be named Farr, Gabriel Farr. Is that enough?"

"Could be. How's that last name spelled?"

"F-A-R-R."

The clicks of a keyboard came through the phone as the woman started checking a database. Then Kate heard a man shout from the background: "Sandy, where the hell's that rewrite?"

The woman on the line shouted back, "In a minute!" Then she spoke rapidly to Kate. "Listen, I see something that might tie in, but I don't have time to get details now. Call back in an hour and ask for me, Sandy Tashiro. I'll help you then." She hung up.

After the call, Kate went to the kitchen and filled a pot with water to boil for tea. If nothing else, staying up for an hour to solve the mystery of Gabriel's past gave her an excuse not to seek her usual retreat from sorrow in a sleeping pill. She was just adding hot water to a tea bag when the front door chime sounded.

Paul Levinger was on the doorstep. Beneath his unbuttoned overcoat, he wore a tan cashmere turtleneck and wrinkled slate corduroys; it looked as though he'd dressed quickly.

"Oh, it's you!" Kate blurted out. She was surprised and also a little put off by his persistence, considering he had supposedly been told she preferred not to see him.

He heard it, too. "If it's a bad moment, I'll go. But I bumped into Eddie on the street just now, and she mentioned you'd decided to leave, and I thought if I made a special appeal, you might at least go for a walk with me before you disappear."

Had he truly met Eddie by accident—or had she phoned him, some well-meant meddling to initiate a rescue operation? Kate had no appetite for any kind of company, but decided his good intention deserved better than a door slammed in his face. "I was just making tea for myself. Would you like to come in and have a cup?"

He followed her back to the kitchen. As soon as they were seated with their tea at the kitchen table, she said, "Paul, it's thoughtful of you to invite me out, but I hope you'll understand if I refuse. I'm really not up to being good company for anyone."

His dark eyes settled on her. "Kate, you don't have to be 'up to' anything. The idea is simply for you not to be alone at Christmastime."

"Thanks again, but I'm okay. You don't have to feel sorry for me."

"Well," he sighed regretfully, "all a fella can do is try." He stood, leaving most of his tea in the cup, and picked up his overcoat from a chair. She stood, too, and gave him a smile of appreciation. He turned for the door, then wheeled to face her again. "You're wrong, though," he said. "I've never known anybody who's had to deal with something as rough as you have. So I *do* have to feel sorry, if not for you, at least *with* you." He moved nearer. "Probably no one can understand how badly you hurt, Kate. But that's no excuse to isolate yourself even more. C'mon. It's a nice evening, the fog's blown away. Why not come out for a walk . . . ?"

She hadn't the will to go on resisting. Anyway, there was a bit of time to kill before she made that other phone call, and all she'd do if she remained alone was stare at the walls and think about ghosts.

The night was cold, but not a bitter cold, only the invigorating chill perfect for a winter stroll. Swirling breezes brought flurries of snow down off the rooftops, frosting the old drifts with a fresh clean sparkle. Heading down the sloping hill that led in the direction of the harbor, they walked along Quince Street without speaking. A comfortable silence, though, both of them diverted by the warming sights in the windows of houses flanking the narrow sidewalks—candles and wreaths and trees aglow with lights in rooms with chandeliers and walls painted rose or pale yellow. At one window, Kate saw a little girl with a flop-eared spaniel at her side, wistfully looking out as though on early watch for a reindeer-driven sleigh. It made her smile rather than instilling a pang of loss. Perhaps the difference was in not being alone.

"Thanks, Paul," she said. "It is good to get out."

"There are people caroling around town," he said. "Let's try to find them. . . ."

He seemed to know exactly where to go. They turned a corner, walked a few blocks, and soon emerged onto Main Street, the wide thoroughfare—still paved with cobblestones—lined on both sides with stores and markets and eateries. The sidewalks were crowded with families out to enjoy the festive spirit. Many were participating in the tradition of dressing up in costumes—or even real antique clothes—from Nantucket's whaling heyday. At sidewalk tables, servings of buttered rum and hot grog were being ladled out in plastic cups.

"Like a grog?" Paul asked.

"That'd be lovely."

Sipping the warm spiced wine, they moved on to an intersection where a group was singing "Deck the Halls," a crowd gathered around them. As they stood listening, Kate noticed that one of the singers was the librarian who had invited her along. At almost the same moment, the woman looked up from the songbook she was holding and met Kate's gaze. Her eyes brightened with shared recognition, and her singing became more animated, as if once more urging Kate to join in.

Kate chimed in at the "fa-la-la-las," and kept singing through "Tannenbaum" and *"Adeste Fidelis."* Flashes of Christmases past kept coming, not only with the kids, but before she and Jim had married—the first time she'd celebrated with his folks instead of her own—then the year it got so touchy deciding which in-laws to be with that they'd simply run away to that inn in Vermont. Tears came to her eyes, but still she found herself glad to be harvesting memories, buoyed up by the music. She turned to Paul, singing beside her in a lusty baritone, and gave him a grateful smile. She could foresee the first possibility of a Christmas, someday, without pain.

They ambled away from the carolers eventually, and into the smaller cobbled lanes leading away from the crowded downtown. As a refuge from talking about anything that touched on family, they fell into the topic of their work. Kate spoke of the enthusiasm she'd had for teaching. Paul explained that he had never wanted to join the huge communications conglomerate developed by his father; his own choice had been to pursue the interest in microbiology he'd had since he was given his first microscope as a child. At present, he held a research fellowship at Harvard.

Kate continued to feel glad she'd allowed herself to be persuaded into coming out. The calm, friendly conversation with Paul Levinger was a soothing contrast to all the intense exchanges she'd had with Gabriel, all the doubts and worries and disappointments that being with him had provoked. . . .

Yet, as soon as *he* was back in her thoughts, she could no longer yield herself to this simple, quiet interlude. She remembered the reporter in Hawaii who'd said to phone again, and she was eager to have the answers awaiting her call.

Paul was in the midst of explaining how his research into a certain river parasite in African rivers was a first step in saving the lives of tens of thousands of natives when Kate broke in. "Forgive me, Paul, but I need to get back to the guest house to make a phone call."

"We could find a phone nearby, and afterward have dinner—"

"No. This may keep me busy for a while."

The disappointment was plain on his face, but they headed back toward the Markham House.

Kate's sudden shift of plan had obviously thrown cold water on the conversation. They walked briskly in silence until Kate said, "I'm really sorry to spring this on you. I was enjoying myself so much it almost slipped my mind."

"Then I don't know whether to be glad or sorry."

The perfect gentleman, she thought. Not the least attempt to pry into her business, even if it had forced them to rush off. But she began to feel disappointed he hadn't shown more curiosity. She wanted to share some of the disturbing questions she'd been keeping to herself. Eddie's absolute conviction that Gabriel was genuine had blocked her from sharing the most troubling facts, but Paul was the sort of person who might provide an especially useful perspective—a man of *science*.

As they reached the next corner, Kate stopped and turned to him. "Tell me the truth, Paul: did you show up tonight because you happened to meet Eddie on the street . . . or did she phone and ask you to look in on me?"

"Does that really matter?"

"Yes. I'd like to ask your opinion on something—but I've had my foundations shaken in so many ways. If you're going to be a friend, I need to know you're someone who'll always give me complete honesty right down to the smallest detail."

"Fair enough." He took a breath. "Eddie did call. I fudged it because I thought you'd be annoyed if you knew people were deliberately butting in—conspiring—"

"Damn right!" Kate admitted, then gave him a forgiving smile before walking on. "But I appreciate your honesty. No more manipulations, though, even with the best intentions."

"You have my word," he said sincerely.

"So . . . while you and Eddie were conspiring, did she also tell you why I came to Nantucket?"

"You mean about trying to . . . make contact with the dead?"

Kate nodded. "I'm interested in having your opinion of that."

"My opinion?" he echoed, and walked a few steps in deliberate silence. "I'm a scientist, Kate," he said then. "I put my faith in what can be proved in a laboratory."

"Then you think what I'm doing is silly?"

"No, not at all. I think what you're doing is entirely understandable."

"Not sensible. Just understandable."

"Kate, give me a break—and give *yourself* one. I'm not judging you in any way. Whatever answer you get from this, it's certainly a darn sight better to put your faith in something than to simply surrender to feeling hopeless."

"In your own opinion, though," she insisted, impatient with his polite qualifications, "the idea that anyone—anything—survives beyond the grave is nonsense."

He stopped walking and looked at her carefully. "If you insist on having my scientific view: yes, when we die, that's the end. The people we love may live in our memories, our hearts, and minds. But anything else . . . ?" He simply shook his head.

As if it were settled, they walked on.

"This man I've been going to," Kate said after a moment, "who claims to make contact . . . in your opinion, I guess you'd say he's a fraud."

"I don't know that much about him," Paul said, retreating to his diplomatic stance rather than criticize Kate for being swindled.

"Sounds like you know more than nothing."

"My family has been coming to the island long enough to have heard his name here and there. I can remember when the newspaper wrote about his claim to some very valuable land. Evidently, he proved a connection to one of the old whaling families. It's known he's a pretty odd character—though, I suppose he'd have to be."

"Have you ever heard anyone say he's dangerous?"

"Dangerous?" Paul repeated, giving her a sharp glance. "Why do you ask *that*?"

"Well . . . I've had to spend time alone with him, for these trances. . . ."

"I imagine he's safe enough. I've never heard anything truly bad. Not that Mr. Farr has been exactly popular. Local environmental groups resented his taking that land. But he went through the courts, and won fair and square."

They were back on Quince Street, the entrance to the Markham House visible ahead. As they neared the entrance steps, Paul thanked her for coming out, and told her how much he'd enjoyed being with her. Finally, he said, "I'd like to see you again, Kate. May I call you in the future—after you're home?"

She couldn't see the point to it, really. He was a nice man, yet unexciting. It disappointed her that he couldn't open his mind to consider possibilities beyond what was cut and dried—"proved in a laboratory," as he put it. But she gave a neutral reply rather than be discouraging. "Let's see when the time comes." The future itself, after all, was something she found hard to believe in.

"Until then," he said, and they shook hands on the steps outside.

The house was empty, the Thornes still out with friends. Kate didn't even take the time to remove her coat before hurrying into the parlor to make the call.

26

Though the woman reporter had left to cover a story, she had kept her word to dig out material pertaining to Gabriel Farr. A man who took Kate's call found copies of old news articles on the reporter's desk, and summarized details of the case for her.

It went back to the summer of 1969. An eighteen-year-old hula dancer, named Halea Kameluna, who performed at a Waikiki Beach hotel had failed to show up for work one night, and was reported missing by her mother, with whom she lived. The police learned from other dancers at the hotel that the missing girl had an ex-boyfriend who kept trying to patch up their romance, but the girl had been guarded in discussing her private life and no one could furnish the boyfriend's name. Then police suspicion fell on a former live-in lover of the girl's divorced mother, who had moved out a few weeks before the disappearance. The mother told detectives the man had made unwanted advances to her daughter, and they took him in for questioning.

It was then that Gabriel Farr entered the story. Described in news reports as a part-time fisherman, he had come voluntarily to the Honolulu Police to say they had the wrong man under suspicion, and his conscience would not allow it. He named another fisherman as the guilty party. When police questioned this man, he denied anything more than a passing acquaintance with the girl, and turned the accusation back on his accuser, saying Gabriel had only named him to deflect them from his own guilt.

After exhaustive investigation of both men, the police failed to turn up any evidence against either one. With no body found to prove any crime had actually occurred, the story of the missing hula dancer faded from the news.

Then a fresh development brought it back to the front pages: an anonymous phone call to the mother of the missing girl directed her to search for the body near a beach a few hours' drive from Honolulu. The mother brought the police to the place described, and human remains were found in a shallow grave—identified as those of Halea Kameluna from clothing and physical characteristics. Buried with the body and determined to be the cause of fatal stab wounds was a fisherman's knife, razor-sharp along one edge of the blade, serrated along the other, used for descaling fish. Partial fingerprints on the handle were determined to belong to the man Gabriel Farr had named—who then confessed. But in his confession, he named Gabriel as an accomplice in raping and killing the girl, and helping dispose of her body.

At the 1971 trial, Gabriel's accuser was found guilty of the stabbing. The jury ruled that no evidence had been presented to prove Farr himself guilty of rape, or even that he had been present at the time of the killing. But it was believed he must have helped bury the victim, or how could the crime have been revealed? He was almost certainly the source of the anonymous phone call that had revealed the body's whereabouts.

The man convicted of the murder received a life term in jail; Gabriel, a lesser sentence of fifteen years. After serving twelve years, he was paroled. Nineteen when he was sent to prison, he became a free man at the age of thirty-one.

From her readings of old Nantucket newspapers, Kate recalled that Gabriel had begun to squat on his Madaket land in 1984. Obviously, he had managed to conceal his past when he went to court to claim the land, Kate thought, or it would have surely played a prominent part in the local news.

After finishing on the phone, Kate went to her room and sat by the window, staring out into the darkness, mulling over what she'd learned. The jury that weighed Gabriel's fate had dismissed the worst charges against him. So was he no more than an unfortunate soul who had become embroiled in the deadly passions of an acquaintance when he was too young to know better? Or was he guilty of greater crimes, for which he'd escaped punishment?

Kate dragged herself up at last from her chair and finished her packing. A good thing she was leaving the island, she concluded; she needed to rescue herself from the temptation to give him the benefit of the doubt.

She had started preparing for bed when there were three soft knocks at the door.

Eddie stood outside, holding a slip of paper in one hand. "Sorry to bother you so late," she said, seeing Kate in a nightgown. "Hope you weren't asleep. . . ."

"No, I was packing. I'll be going in the morning, Eddie."

"Why should you be alone for the holiday?" Eddie said with concern. "You sure you don't want to stay just another day or two? Celebrate Christmas with us?"

"I'm sure. Empty as it is, I think home is where I need to be." In fact, she was anxious to get away before having to witness the Thornes exchanging gifts, one more loving ritual that was dead in her own life.

"Well, you know best," Eddie said. "Kate, about the bill . . . I'd be happy if you'd forget it. Let me treat you as a true guest."

"I wouldn't hear of it. You did enough by taking me in." Before there could be any more discussion, Kate hurried to dig her credit card out of her bag. She didn't want gifts given to her out of sympathy. "Take the charge now," she said, handing the card to Eddie. "Make it easier for me to get away tomorrow."

Eddie acceded, and gave Kate a good-bye hug. She turned to the stairs, then stopped. "Oh, I almost forgot the reason I came." She raised the hand holding a slip of paper. "There were a couple of messages for you on the answering machine."

Kate was vaguely aware of the phone downstairs ringing three or four times while she was in her room.

"Both from Gabriel. I wrote down what he called about." Eddie held out the message slip. Kate took it reluctantly. Coming on the heels of her "investigation," she was unsettled by his apparent eagerness to make fresh contact with her. Could he *know* somehow that she'd been poking into his past?

Eddie seemed to notice her concern. "I'll handle it for you, if you want."

Kate fingered the message slip. "Let me look at this, then I'll decide. But thanks for the offer. Oh, and for calling Paul."

"He told you," Eddie said guiltily.

"It's all right. I had a nice walk with him."

Eddie went downstairs and returned in a minute with a charge slip for Kate to sign. While she was gone, Kate had brushed her teeth, taken a sleeping pill, and left the written message from Gabriel on the night table, unread. After saying another good-bye to Eddie, Kate got into bed. She looked at the paper lying on the table beside her, her curiosity balanced by a reluctance to be pulled back into his orbit. She had made the decision to leave; finish it there. But at last she reached for the message. Whatever it said, at least the sleeping pill would save her from churning with thoughts and questions about Gabriel all night.

She held Eddie's writing up before her eyes: *Mr. Farr—something very important to tell you. Asks you to meet him Arno's Restaurant, Main St.—8 A.M.*

Kate laid the paper on the night table, and turned out the light. The pill had begun to dull her consciousness, but a couple of words penetrated the fog. *Very important.* The bedclothes seemed to weigh a ton as she shoved them back, her limbs moving in the dark as if pushing through tar. But she turned on the lamp, and picked up the small travel alarm clock on the night table. Dialing the knob on the back of the clock seemed to take no less strength than turning the wheel of a ship through a gale. But she set the alarm pointer to wake her in time to meet Gabriel at the restaurant, before she fell back into the unworried dark.

Arno's was a large, high-ceiling restaurant on Main Street with a comfortable old-fashioned aspect. Kate rushed in and scanned the people having breakfast. Too late! In her groggy state last night, she'd set the alarm for *eight*, not seven, giving herself no time to wake and dress. Now, after loading her bag into her car and driving over, it was almost half an hour past the time he'd said to be there. He hadn't waited. All for the best, perhaps—

Then her eye was caught by the man at a table not far from the entrance, beckoning— *Gabriel?* Right in front of her and she simply hadn't recognized him at first. His appearance was so altered by his hair being neatly combed rather than wildly tousled, and he was wearing a neat, white, button-down shirt rather than the usual scruffy denims or checked flannels. He wasn't merely attractive in this cleaned-up

mode, she thought, but ruggedly handsome, the hint of something Oriental in his features making him particularly distinctive. He stood as she approached the table, and she noticed his chino pants were freshly pressed. A cup of coffee was at his place.

She sat and apologized for being late. "I thought for a moment you'd left. . . ."

He settled back into his chair. "I would've given it at least another hour."

"You were so sure I'd come?"

"Long as we met where there's other people around."

Was he making reference only to what had happened at his shack? Or could he be aware she'd explored his past? "What do you want to tell me?" she asked.

"Don't you want to order breakfast first?"

He was plainly eager to put this on a casual basis. Kate nodded, and he raised his hand to summon a waitress.

She asked for coffee and toast. He ordered a full breakfast, waffles and bacon, orange juice, more coffee. When the waitress had gone, Kate put him back on track. "Very important, you said."

"In a real hurry to get this over, aren't you?"

"I'm leaving today. There's a ferry to catch."

"Winter schedule, next one's at noon. I won't keep you that long."

Kate sensed a wistful undercurrent in his words. All so different from the way he'd acted before. Maybe he was trying to make up for his past behavior. It broke through her armor. "Gabriel, I haven't been fair with you, maybe. Too demanding, too . . . suspicious. But I'm on pretty shaky ground about everything in my life right now. That's why it seems best—even if nothing you've done is wrong—that I should go." He bent forward as though anxious to reply. "Wait," she said quickly. "There's something else you should know: I've done some more . . . research into your personal history. I know about what happened before you came here."

The way he was looking at her didn't change, she noticed. Not a trace of anger or fear in his eyes. A hint of disappointment, perhaps, but basically a look of acceptance. "You can rely on me not to tell anyone," Kate went on. "I promise you that."

He gazed at her steadily. "Why'd you want me to know you'd been poking into my past? You'd be better off keeping that to yourself, wouldn't you?"

Did that mean he was angry about it, after all? Was he even giving her a subtle warning? It was so difficult to penetrate his shell, Kate lamented to herself, get a reading of his true emotional temperature. "I felt you should be aware of . . . how skeptical I have a right to be before you tell me this new 'important' thing."

"I get it," he said. "If you think I might be guilty of murder, then for sure you can't trust anything I might tell you now. Or anything I've told you before. . . ."

"Oh, Gabriel," she objected. "I do *want* to trust you. I'm being honest with you so you'll know why it's been so hard for me. Even if I hadn't learned about this stuff in your past, it would be hard. Not just because we're dealing with incredible phenomena, either, but because of—the way you behave. Often I get the feeling you *want* me to doubt you. Yes," she said, the notion crystallizing as she explained it, "as much as you act insulted sometimes if I question what you're doing, there are other times it seems pretty obvious you're questioning it yourself."

He looked down at the tabletop and was quiet a moment. "You think I shouldn't?" he said quietly at last, lifting his eyes. "You think I can stop myself from wondering how the hell I—" He cut himself off suddenly, and glanced away to their surroundings, the restaurant full of people, as if urgently needing to fix himself back in the real and mundane. When he turned back to her, he said flatly, "Look, you can trust me or not, that's up to you. I came here to tell you something I thought it was important for you to know. But since you might find anything I say hard to believe because of your research"—he gave the word a bitter twist—"I'll start by telling you something *unimportant*." He leaned across the table and added slowly and solemnly, as if taking an oath, "I never hurt a soul. Never did one bad thing." He leaned back. "And now, since you're in such an all-fired hurry to—"

She broke in. "Gabriel, you're telling me you spent twelve years behind bars for something you didn't do? That's hardly unimportant."

"Isn't it? They said I was guilty and sent me away. Didn't matter a damn to people if I told the whole truth then, and it's sure as hell too late to matter now."

"Try me."

"No. I came for something else. Maybe it'll be harder for you to hear now, but that's your problem; believe whatever you want." More quietly, he said, "They've been around me. I've sensed them . . . close. . . ."

Kate looked carefully into his eyes, searching for the least hint of unsteadiness, any glint of shrewd intent. She saw only the solid light of sincerity. "The children, you mean . . . ?"

"All of them. Together. The man, too—your husband, I guess."

"You 'sensed' them, you said. Didn't *see* them."

"No. It wasn't in a trance. It's just this . . . sense of them being close."

"And why is that very important?"

The way he put it was so vague—a sense, a feeling. She had to quiz him, try to find the flaws in his story as once she might have tried to shake the excuse of some student who came to class without an assignment done.

"It could mean," he said, "they want me to bring them through."

"Why now, and not before?"

"Got no idea. I guess they're just ready. Or they feel *you* are."

"I was ready before."

"Were you, Katharine? Were you truly ready . . . ?"

A fair enough question. In fact, she wasn't certain she was one hundred percent ready now. Yet she understood that probably this contact she was seeking could only be achieved by making a contract to believe; if there was a bridge between worlds, the tangible and the intangible, then the toll to be paid to get across was total and unfailing belief. And she wanted—oh, how desperately she wanted—to commit herself to that so that the souls she loved could speak to her. All this rational examination that she did habitually as a student and teacher of history, events molded by men who lived and died and were replaced by other men, all the scientific empiricism of men like Paul Levinger, had to be ignored, overridden, forgotten, or nothing might happen. She had to go on pure faith alone.

But not just in Gabriel. If the spirits were ready, it was also because they felt *she* was. So faith in *them* was also required. Faith in a universe where life never ended.

The waitress was back with their order. They stayed silent as she laid the plates down. As soon as they were alone again, Kate said, "So . . . now that you've told me, what am I supposed to do?"

He cut into his waffle. "Not supposed to do anything but what you want."

She tried to be just as cool, picked up her toast to butter it. But then

she threw it back on the plate. "You understand why it might be hard for me to go back to your place now for another try . . . ?"

"Oh, yeah, sure. Worried I might chop you up and bury your body in the snow."

"No," she answered sharply, "not that."

He put down his knife and fork, looking into his plate. "If it's about what happened between us, I told you I'm sorry."

"You don't have to be sorry. You just have to realize it mustn't happen again."

His gaze met hers squarely. "It won't."

"And you're not afraid to try another trance for me? You were hurt last time."

"This will be different," he said. " 'Cause they won't be fighting it." When she continued hesitating, he added, "You'll be safe, Katharine. I promise you."

"Tell me again," she said, after a moment. "I need to hear you tell me about it once more."

"I've felt them—"

"Not that. About what happened all those years ago—the truth."

He took a deep breath. It was obviously distasteful to him even to have the subject raised, let alone to have to dispel the cloud of guilt. But he relented. "I had no part in it. I was innocent. Now, will you let me help you? Please."

He'd never said "please" before, either.

27

The room seemed to have been prepared for her, as though he'd been sure she couldn't refuse. It was warm, for one thing, the wood stove evidently stoked up before he'd driven into town. The brocade chair where she had sat during previous trances was already placed with its back to the huge window. The preparations only made Kate feel like a fly snared in a spider's web. The drive from town had been unsettling, too. She'd made another effort to get him to explain his claim of innocence, but he'd grumbled that "talking about it wasn't gonna change a thing," and after that, the ride had been tense and silent.

"Thought you were in a hurry to catch that ferry," he said, when he saw her hanging back by the door.

Kate went forward at last, threw her coat onto one of the spare wooden chairs, and seated herself on the worn brocade. Gabriel grabbed a chair for himself, turned it from the table to face her.

"Close the curtains," she said. They'd been open last time, when things had gone badly.

He went to pull the curtains across the expanse of glass, then lit a few candles before coming back to his chair.

"And the water," she said. "You forgot the water."

He glanced at the bare top of the nearby table, then rose again, and went to the sink. He filled the familiar jug and brought it to the table. "Ready now?"

He sounded annoyed by her insistence on details he'd left unattended. Yet Kate thought of one more. "You didn't tell me how much this is going to cost."

"Don't worry about that."

"I think it should be settled before we start."

"Then suppose we say . . . whatever you think it's worth."

What value could she ever put on it if, indeed, he could truly be the conduit for a visit with her lost family? But certainly it was impossible to decide in advance. "All right," she said. "Let's see how it goes."

Gabriel straightened in his chair, preparing to begin. But then he did something Kate hadn't seen him do before previous trances: he scanned the room slowly, his eyes passing over every corner. It was as though he was looking for some sign the spirits were present before entering his trance. Only after surveying the entire space did he close his eyes, drop his chin to his chest, and begin his deep breathing.

It had taken him awhile to get into it last time, but this time no more than a minute or two passed before sounds began to rise from his throat: little, high-pitched whines reminiscent of the way a dog might cry at a closed door. Kate found it almost painful to listen to.

The words came then, hoarse, breathy: ". . . hey, Katie . . ." He had lifted his head, though his eyes remained shut. "Glad . . . you didn't . . ." He fell into noisy breathing.

"Didn't what?" she asked.

"Give up. . . ."

What Gabriel himself might have said, she thought. As much as she kept trying to relax into belief, she couldn't free herself from what she'd learned about him and the questions it raised. "I don't want to give up," she said. "I wouldn't ever . . . if I could only know—"

He broke in. "It's hard . . . we understand . . . but we want . . . to help . . . you . . . ."

The words came so haltingly this time Kate wasn't sure if and when to speak. She waited until he was silent a long time before responding. Now she forced herself to take the leap into accepting what was being given to her. "Jimmy—you said 'we want to help.' You mean the children, too?"

"Sure."

"Can they talk to me? That would help so much!"

"I need . . . first . . . just us."

Not really an answer to her question, she realized. Looking into

Gabriel's face as the candles sent faint waves of light across its contours, doubt kept flickering in her mind. Yet, even as her trust wavered, the face shaped by the shifting planes of light and shadow
seemed to change before her eyes. It wasn't an exotic stranger looking
back at her through the gloom, but a man she knew better than all
others, the well-remembered face she yearned to see. "Oh, Jimmy,"
she said, sighing. "Talk to me, then."

"Must listen . . . you must . . ."

"Yes . . . I am listening."

"But maybe . . . like some of your students . . . listen, but still don't
learn the lesson."

Kate sat up erect, startled. Had she ever told Gabriel she was a
teacher? No, she was positive: never mentioned. Or could he have
heard it from Eddie?

"What's the lesson you want me to learn?" she asked.

"Things are as they seem."

It struck her now that there were no more hesitations in his speech.
It was flowing easily, conversationally. " 'Things are as they seem,' "
she repeated, in the way she might have made young students do to
imprint a fact. "Is that all?"

"What more do you need?"

"Much more!" she erupted. "Because I can't take the way things
are. It's too hard. I need to believe there's something better. Everything's gone, and the only hope I've got of getting through this is pretending that—"

He interrupted, his tone matching hers. "You call it 'pretending.' Is
that how it really, *really* seems? Is everything really gone? We're with
you, you've got to feel that—we're here."

"Not the way I want!" she cried out. "I need . . ." Her voice broke
to a pleading whisper. "I need to have you with me."

"We're with you, Katie."

"Don't do this!" she blurted suddenly, not knowing exactly whom
the plea was meant for. Herself, to stop letting herself be fooled?
Gabriel, to stop victimizing her? Or was she commanding this spirit to
stop rejecting her devotion, the sacrifice she was trying to make?

Gabriel went on—whatever voice it was kept coming from his lips.
"Believe that, Kate. Believe in life. Believe in ours, so you can go on
with yours."

"Stop!" she bellowed. "Gabriel—" She would have reached out and shaken him, but the anguish and tension sparked an ache that sliced across her middle, made her clutch at her stomach. "Enough . . ." She could barely get out the word as she doubled over and buried her face in her hands, weeping. She was cracking, Kate knew, no longer able to see reality, define it in any way.

"Mommy, don't."

Kate went rigid.

"Mama . . ."

She kept her hands over her face, bent over, unwilling to look. Afraid of the truth. And afraid of the lie.

"We're here."

"Me, too."

The voices were so much *like* theirs. Just to hear them soothed a little of the agony. Though, of course, it must be something he did with the upper register of his voice. Something he wouldn't have dared to do while she was looking at him.

Or was it proof of the madness? She'd gone past the brink.

She jerked upright, throwing her hands aside, and stared at the figure in front of her. "Tell me again!" she demanded, staring at him.

"We're here, Mama. . . ."

She saw his lips move—but the voice was a little girl's. Or *like* one. But no, not *any*— "Chloe," she gasped.

"And me." The voice was different, just a shade.

"My babies," she murmured, her arms opening to the air, the reflex of a time when they could have rushed into an embrace. She squeezed her eyes shut, not wanting to see the emptiness remaining before her— and instantly she had the sensation of a warm pressure against her chest, a fullness that she was holding within her embrace. Or perhaps merely a memory of what it had felt like. But so sweet; she would not open her eyes.

"Is it all right for you?" she asked. "Tell me you're all right."

"It's beautiful, Mama."

Then the boy's voice. "It's fantastic. Fun. It's everything."

Just like Tom—his enthusiasm. "Tell me more," she said, just as she would pry out the details after a first day at school or at camp. "What do you do?"

There was a laugh—a giggle, actually, like a little girl's.

Kate's eyes snapped open. There was Gabriel in front of her, his lips parted, and the sweet high sound was rising from his throat. But that wasn't all; there was such a look of delight on his face. Indeed, it was an expression she wouldn't have thought could ever form on the features of a man with his bitter history.

"We play," the child's voice came from him. "We play all the time."

"Play," she echoed. "So you're . . . you're happy."

"Better than happy."

Tom would have said it just like that—

"Just one cloud, Mama . . ."

"What, baby?" she asked, alarmed.

"They need you to be happy, too."

The return of the man's voice shocked her. Jim? Gabriel? Were the children lost to her again? But she answered automatically: there was only one answer to such a demand, no matter who it came from. "How can I be happy? There isn't any way I can ever—"

"Yes, Katie. You can!"

"How?" The word was a howl.

"Forgive yourself."

She stared at Gabriel. "What?"—she wanted to ask, but her lips moved without being able to expel the word.

Still, he answered. "It wasn't your fault. Don't blame yourself for anything. We're okay. Believe that, and you can be okay, too."

"Jimmy . . ." she whispered. Surely only he could know the burden she'd put upon herself, and only he could lift it.

And with the release of that breath, carrying his name, she let go of the last doubt. After barricading herself for so long against belief, shoring up the supports of her resistance again and again as each new promise of the impossible appeared like piling brick upon brick, it happened: all resistance gave way, the surrender was total, the wall collapsing, washed away as if being swept off by a flood breaching a dam. She had met them on the bridge that spanned the here and hereafter. She was with them, she felt—she *knew*—in their heaven as much as they were in this room.

"You are, aren't you?" she said, her voice lifting, rejoicing. "You're with me!"

What seemed to answer was not one voice, but a chorus, all of them. Had she gone into a trance herself? Entered a dream? Had the pulsing play of light and shadow from the candles put her under a hypnotic spell? No sooner did the questions rise in her mind than they evaporated as the fresh breeze of other wonderings blew in, questions not for herself, but for them.

From that moment, there was no sharp definition to any of it, no dimension. Exactly what she asked or exclaimed, what they answered, how long it went on, she had no idea. What did it look like, what did they play, had they seen Ba? She certainly asked some of that, and they answered, and she felt delight and amusement and fascination with their answers—that much she knew. But beyond knowing, there was the feeling. She was in a profound rapture of the sort that must overtake those who witnessed miracles—statues that cried real tears, madonnas giving benedictions from the clouds. Floating in the shadows around her she could see their faces, loving and happy and radiant. And she felt such absolute gratitude and happiness.

And, finally, at long last, peace.

"Sorry, sweetheart, we have to go now."

The words came from Gabriel's mouth, but it was Jim speaking! "No, no, don't, please," she begged. "Stay with me."

"We're always with you. . . ."

"Just let me say good-bye to the children."

There was a silence. Gabriel's head lolled back.

"Let me say good-bye!" she insisted shrilly.

". . . not . . . here now . . ." The breathy hesitant delivery had returned.

"No! It's too soon!" she shouted, furious again, blaming *him*.

"Katie. Let us go." Firm once more. "This is the way it has to be. Have to leave you now," she heard. "Have . . . to . . ."

Then he slumped forward on the chair, arms dangling down at his sides. But he didn't fall over.

Kate remained seated, waiting for him to open his eyes. The moment he sat up and looked at her, she hit him with the questions: "When did I mention my work to you? Did I ever do that?"

He shook his head.

"What do you think it is—my work?"

"Why—?"

"Just answer me!"

He realized now it was a test, and made a show of it, scanning her carefully, collecting data. "Might involve showing off a little. Like something in TV. Or maybe working for one of those glossy magazines—

yeah, that fits—the kind filled with pictures and articles on what to wear or what kind of fancy furniture to stick in your house, editor or writer for one of them."

No clues, she thought. "Not bad. What did I do before that?"

He frowned thoughtfully, then shot up from his chair. "I don't feel like being put through your third degree. You've got a ferry to catch, right? Just settle up like we agreed, and let's go." He moved to get his coat.

"It's not easy to keep our agreement," she said.

Now he halted, and spun back to her. His expression darkened, and his body grew noticeably more taut. "Why the hell not?"

"You said to pay what I think it's worth. And I don't have that much money."

He studied her, then slowly leaked a smile. It had a conspiratorial tilt to it, she thought, as if he suspected she was flattering him to escape paying altogether. "Well, then," he said, "just make it a hundred."

Kate rose and went toward him. "I've just told you what happened here was incredible, astounding. But you don't even ask what it was. Why not, Gabriel? Is it possible—can it really be you're not at all interested?" She stopped in front of him. "Or do you already know?"

"I knew before I went in, didn't I, said they were ready to come? I'm guessing they did. . . ."

"But where's your curiosity? Why don't you want to know more about it?"

He sidestepped her and moved away. "It doesn't concern me."

She stayed at his shoulder. "Doesn't—? You claim the ability to connect with . . . with some corner of heaven, and it doesn't *concern* you?" Her incredulity was overtaken by outrage. If, by some unfathomable phenomenon, this obscure and uncouth man was endowed with the divine ability to be inhabited by departed spirits, take in their souls so that they might speak and listen through him, to let his body become no less than a portal to eternity, how could he be so arrogant as to declare disinterest? "How do you dare to say that?" she hissed, venting her fury.

He spun to face her. "Well now, Katharine, what do you think would be better? If I boast about it? Write a book and go on one of them TV talk shows to sell it, do little performances with all the hocus-pocus? Or maybe start a whole new religion—get rich making people

line up for a little piece of my time?" He stepped closer, glaring at her.
"I do jobs for people like you—because I can't always refuse. But do
you really think I *like* doing this?"

She thought there was real anguish in his voice. She saw the gift
from another angle then—the burden it put upon him. If it was true he
regarded it not so much as a divine gift but a kind of affliction, that
could explain some of his other reactions she'd found puzzling. The
way he made light of the ability, almost ridiculing himself at times,
could be interpreted as a mechanism to chase people away—relieve
himself of the responsibility—or a symptom of simple embarrassment
at being chosen to bear powers he could never fathom. It might explain, too, the pent-up resentment he carried around, the anger he expressed openly at her repeated doubts—doubts he would always have
to endure, no matter how unfair he knew they were. It all fit with what
could be true: that he felt an obligation to perform this "service" when
asked, even while knowing it opened him always to criticism and
ridicule.

And beyond all this reasoning, she still held in memory—in her
very nerves—the joy she'd felt at the experience he'd given her once
she'd surrendered to belief.

A tide of emotion rose within her, regret for her mistrust, empathy
for his torment, gratitude for the consolation he offered. "I'm sorry,"
she said. "I appreciate everything you've done."

Standing only inches away, she longed to reach out and touch him.
As a gesture of conciliation, as well as for the continuity his touch
could provide to the spirits that spoke through him. Believing now
that they were with her, she knew she shouldn't feel even more isolated
than before. Yet she felt inconsolably alone, needed desperately to be
held, to feel the real-world evidence that she wasn't. She leaned toward
him, the slightest indication of an offering.

He perceived her intention. "No," he said quickly.

"Please." She moved closer.

"I promised you—"

"Hold me, Gabriel."

She could see him trembling, fighting against the urge. Then suddenly he grasped her by the arms. For another moment, he seemed to
hover between pulling her nearer or thrusting her away. Then he gathered her in and kissed her. Not slowly and gently, but with an abrupt

sudden move, his mouth pressed hungrily on hers, as though he had been overwhelmed himself by a force he could not resist. The fierceness of his passion shocked her, yet she yielded to it, surrendering to this carnal element of herself as completely as she had earlier surrendered to the spiritual.

What followed upon the kiss was more primitive and immediate than any sex she'd ever had before. Clothes peeled off hurriedly, left where they fell in layers to provide a cushion between them and the bare floor, a declaration of pure animal hunger. In the way she took him into her, clawed at his back to urge him deeper, was an element far beyond any desire for pleasure; more in fact a desire for death, to have this penetration go so far as to tear into her, split her apart. To be one of those animals, like certain insects or fish whose instinctive mating was their final act, the very thing that took the last of their strength and killed them. In the throes of the act, with no concept of a life beyond, any aftermath or fear of guilt or regret, she was freed to experience pure lust, freed from a need to give or receive tenderly, to be anything but wanton, selfish, shameless, voracious, insatiable. She lost all consciousness of the woman she had been with her husband—a woman who had not only enjoyed sex, but who had made love.

It was over quickly, but the sensations still went on rippling through her in little bursts, a storm in the blood dying away slowly like summer thunder moving off into the distance. Finally, she was aware of him again, lying on his back beside her. She put out her hand, her palm on his hard stomach, then moved it down until she felt what had been inside her. Still shameless, she wanted him again, wanted once more to descend into the cave of sheer mindless pleasure. Her hand moved to hold him.

He placed his hand over hers, imprisoning her fingers so they could not grasp him. But he did not push her away. "I'm not the kind of man who should be with you," he said quietly, almost as if talking to himself.

She pulled free so she could roll sideways to look at him. "You're not like anyone I've ever been with, that's true. Or like any of the men I'd usually meet. But that doesn't mean you're the wrong kind." She paused and almost laughed. "And didn't my husband tell me to accept the love that's around?"

"You don't think that was me just giving you a line?" He was still on his back, eyes aimed at the ceiling.

She stared at his profile. "Not anymore." She raised herself up on one arm, so she could look down at his face. "Though having you say that makes me wonder all over again why you *want* to remind me. Why must you do or say so many things that seem to . . . warn me not to trust you. Yet, when I don't, you're angry. I can't figure that out."

He shifted his eyes so he was looking into hers. But he offered no explanation.

She might have insisted, but before she could, his hand came up behind her, his fingers sank into her hair, and he pulled her down into another kiss. This one, surprisingly, was as slow and soft as the earlier ones had been rough.

When he stood, pulling her up with him, she went with him to the bed eagerly, desire overwhelming any need for justification.

28

With the curtains shutting out the day, time slipped away, forgotten. He left the bed once to put more wood in the stove; another time, he brought two oranges from the icebox, peeled them and gave one to her. They barely spoke. "Ferry's gone," he said once when they were lying quietly, and without a word she let him know it didn't matter.

At last, lying apart from him, spent, Kate let herself wonder where such a frenzied detonation of desire had come from. It wasn't simply physical need, that much she knew. To hold him within her, perhaps, was a way of merging her flesh with the souls that seemed to speak through him.

"Hungry?" he asked finally.

"Yes." She hadn't realized until he mentioned it.

"I'll make something."

It pleased her that he should want to take care of her, even in this small way.

He collected his clothes, went to the small corner bathroom, and emerged dressed, his hair slicked down after a shower. As he crossed to the kitchen area, he opened the curtains across the glass wall. Kate was amazed to see that the day had passed into the deep lavender of winter twilight.

She went to wash, too. The shower consisted of a watering can spout attached to the end of a rubber hose that ran up the wall in a corner of the windowless, wood-sided bathroom. No hot water, she was reminded. Gasping at the touch of the icy downpour, she washed quickly, and dried herself with a frayed, faded beach towel she found folded on a shelf.

Wrapped only in the towel, she went out. He had stoked up the stove and, after the freezing shower, the shack felt deliciously warm. Kate collected her clothes from the floor, and folded them on the end of the bed. She was comfortable in the towel wrap, and hurrying to dress seemed to suggest an element of embarrassment, even regret; whatever had happened, for whatever reason, she felt neither.

"It's ready," he announced, carrying a pan and plates to the table.

He'd made an omelette with peppers, onions, and a canned tomato sauce seasoned with spices. It was very good, Kate thought, just the right kind of simple snack to follow up an afternoon of passion.

They ate for a while in silence. Everything Kate could think of saying seemed fatuous, pointless, bound to irritate him. Could she tell him he was a wonderful lover? Ask him about other women he'd known? More than anything, she wanted him to answer the question he'd evaded this morning: if he was truly innocent of any part in the murder of a young woman, how and why had he been convicted and sent to jail? But he'd already shown an unwillingness to deal with the subject.

"Not your usual Christmas Eve dinner," he said finally.

Again she'd forgotten the holiday until it was mentioned. "Nothing usual about any of this," she said.

"You sorry?"

"No. But I want you to know this is the first time I've ever done this." She caught his little smile. "I mean . . . been unfaithful to my husband."

"That's how you think of this—being unfaithful?"

"In a way. You've made me believe he's not really gone." She pushed some food around on her plate until she realized she wasn't hungry anymore, and put down her fork. "I was wondering if he could even know what we've done. What do you think?"

"I don't know."

"You don't know," she echoed, belief fraying again. "But you feel them when they're around. . . ."

He pushed his plate away and looked at her coolly. "You want answers to everything, don't you? Well, I could make things up, act like I understand the whole thing. That's what the phonies do. But I don't know how the hell any of it works. I don't know why they come to me, not other folks. I can only tell you what I feel, whatever comes through. It isn't all neat and logical, and I'm sorry if that makes it harder for you." He laughed to himself. "Always made it harder for me, too."

"Just tell me what *you* believe, then. Are they here now? Are they always around?"

He was quiet a minute, staring at the floor. At last, he said, "They come when they're called, I think, or when they know they're needed, or when they have a message. And they come sometimes for their own reasons, because there's something they need to know, or that needs to be done so they can be at peace where they are." He raised his eyes to meet hers. "But most of the time, seems to me, they don't want to be here at all. They're in a good place, a better place. So I'd guess there's a million reasons they wouldn't want to look back at this mean, mixed-up world."

It had the ring of truly wanting to share as much as he understood. Which gave her the confidence to push for more: "Tell me why you went to prison." He pressed back in his chair, his eyes narrowing as he looked at her. "You told me you did nothing wrong," she said. "Let me hear your side."

"Is this another test?"

"Oh, Gabriel." She sighed. "Do you think I shouldn't care if you've been treated unfairly? We've just made love."

"So I owe it to you. . . ."

"If you want to put it that way, maybe you do."

He stood and left the table. But he took only a few steps away before turning around. "Told it all before," he said. "Told it, and no one believed me."

"That doesn't mean I won't."

He gave her a cool sideways look, wordlessly remarking on how hard won her belief had been. Then he walked to his glass wall and for a long time he stared out at the sea on which his ancestors had sailed away, and which had brought him back to this island.

"I knew that girl, but not very well," he began quietly. "She was seeing a guy who worked on the fishing boats like I did, an islander named Lekaikai. Him and me hung around together when we weren't working; we'd go out to the beaches together—surf bums, y'know. I knew he had a thing with a girl who danced at one of the hotels, real pretty girl. I'd seen them around together. Then she disappeared. I saw Lekaikai afterwards, and he told me he'd broken up with her, and he figured she took it badly and ran off to the Mainland. But it was in the papers she was missing, and I knew the police were questioning a man who'd lived with the girl's mother."

He stopped. The last of the twilight had faded, and he went on staring into the blackness as if searching for the lights of a missing ship. "She started coming to me then," he resumed. "At first, only when I was sleeping. Didn't take it for anything but a dream. Always the same dream, though. I'd be on a beach, just standing there, and the sand around my feet would begin to move. Then I'd see a hand was coming through, the fingers moving. Then the hand sort of waving—like when the hula girls dance. Suddenly the sand would cave in, and she'd be there, half buried in it, looking up at me, her eyes . . . those eyes . . ."

He trailed off, but it was clear to Kate from his tone that the memory was vivid to him, and the inescapable eyes of the girl had begged his help. He turned away from the window and paced across the room before he continued.

"I'd wake up, and that would be the end of it—just the way a dream ends. Only one night I woke and it didn't stop." He threw a glance back at Kate, and there was a strange glint in his eyes, not exactly fear, but no less in the realm of helplessness. "She was still there, talking to me. She said Lekaikai had killed her, and I had to be the one to tell people." He came back to the table and looked into Kate's face, searching for any hint of rejection. Apparently satisfied, he went on. "First time it happened, I was still lying there in bed—figured it must've been part of the dream. I wasn't really awake yet. So I lay there until it went away and I did nothing about it. But then the police arrested this boyfriend of the mother's, and this . . . ghost, whatever it was, started coming almost every night. I knew it was no ordinary dream by then—hell, I was having a hard time sleeping, scared to close my eyes and scared to keep 'em open—and I thought maybe there's something I can do so it'll end. That's when I went to the police. Stupid—it only ended up with them suspecting me—but I told them I thought the man they'd arrested was innocent and Lekaikai had killed the girl. But there was still no proof of anything, so naturally it looked like I must know more than I was telling."

"How did you explain your accusation?"

"Couldn't tell 'em I was getting it straight from the dead girl, could I? All I said at the time was that I had my suspicions. They asked me why, and I just said I didn't trust Lekaikai." He hung his head for a moment, as if embarrassed by handling it so badly. "Anyway, it died down for a while. The police let the other suspect go, left Lekaikai alone, and stopped pulling me in for questions." He walked the floor a bit more. "But the girl went after me even harder. Not just coming in the dark, or when I was alone. I could be anywhere, and I'd sense something near me, or hear a voice, and I'd turn and she'd be there. Finally, when I was alone, I started talking back to her, saying I couldn't just go out and blame someone for murder with nothing to back it up except I'd been tipped off by a ghost." He let out a short bitter laugh. "That's what really got me in trouble. 'Cause then she told me the details of where she could be found, out by a certain beach, a place not many people went. . . ."

Kate recalled the news stories. "So you made that anonymous call to the police."

He nodded and dropped back onto his chair with the weary resignation of a suspect undergoing interrogation. "After they found the body, they brought in me and Lekaikai, grilled us both. He tried blaming it on me, told them I must've been the one who told where the body was buried. Luckily, once the police took him serious as a suspect, they turned up a couple of people who knew he'd roughed her up, and heard him make threats against her. He couldn't put himself in the clear, and the evidence against me came down to the fact that it had to be me who'd told where the body was buried. I was tried as what they call an 'accessory.' The theory was I must've at least helped get rid of the body."

Kate remembered his saying that he'd declared his innocence, but nobody had believed him. "At the trial, you talked about your visions . . . ?"

"Only way I could defend myself."

And no doubt his testimony had been judged the crazy, last-ditch alibi of a no-good surf bum who'd used too many drugs. "I understand now," Kate said, "why you might not want to advertise your . . . special talent."

"I never asked for it," he said.

"Maybe it started with seeing visions you didn't want, but you've developed it, learned how to summon spirits, communicate through your trances. . . ."

"Seems like what happens is that once they find someone who's open to them, then they use you. If I hadn't known that girl, and she didn't have such a strong desire to get even with who killed her, maybe there never would've been a link to me. Or maybe I was always some kind of freak, but I had to be in a certain situation before I got . . . switched on." He leaned in closer. "Why do you think I'm here? Do you wonder why I got in a boat and sailed all the way from Hawaii to this place?"

"I assume once you were free, you wanted to make a fresh start. And you found out you owned land here. . . ."

"That ain't the half of it."

She sat waiting for the rest.

It would take awhile to tell, he said. Would she like something else to eat or drink while she listened? He admitted to wanting a drink for himself.

Kate said she'd join him in whatever he was having, and he went to a cabinet in the kitchen area and brought back a couple of tumblers and bottle of whiskey. She stopped him from putting more than a splash in her glass, but he nearly filled his own, and took a hefty swallow before he resumed:

Soon after he'd begun his prison sentence, he said, he'd been put into solitary confinement for fighting. While there, other spirits had begun to visit him. A prison was a place that attracted hordes of unsettled souls; there were ghosts of past prisoners, ghosts of men who'd been executed, ghosts of wives and lovers and children of prisoners who'd died without being able to contact the person behind bars. Isolated and surrounded by all these specters, he might have assumed he was going mad—except that he owed his very imprisonment to a ghost. So he had accepted the visions, and spent his time in confinement learning to control their access to his consciousness. He had found eventually that he could shut out the visions from his dreams or his waking moments if they were permitted to come through at other times—through self-induced trance states. Throughout his incarceration, he'd managed to keep these supernatural contacts a secret—often deliberately breaking prison rules so he could spend long periods in solitary confinement. There were too many risks in letting any fellow prisoners think of him as weird or crazy . . . or truly spooky.

When he was finally released from prison, there was a period of parole during which he was required to stay in Hawaii. During that time, he had a visitation from his own ancestor, Joshua Farr. The whaling captain's spirit had begun by appearing in dreams, commanding Gabriel to complete the voyage home to Nantucket, which had been interrupted by the sinking of the *Indigo*. Through repeated trances, Gabriel had learned his ancestor owned the land to which a claim might be laid.

"You're saying you had no idea this property existed," Kate said, "until you were told by a ghost?"

Gabriel pointed across the room. "See that old trunk? That belonged to Joshua Farr."

"And it was passed down to you, along with—"

"No. I got nothing but my name passed down to me. Joshua married an island woman and all their children were mixed breeds. My father was Joshua's great-grandson; he worked on a pineapple plantation and used his spare time to repair boats. Kept me and fed me and a couple of other bastards he had until I was twelve—when he died, but he didn't leave me any fancy heirlooms."

"So how did you get the trunk?"

"I found it on Molokai, one of the smaller islands. It was in the attic of a house missionaries had built two hundred years ago and gone on using ever since. How it got there, why it was never touched, damned if I know. Maybe Joshua sent it there to keep it safe. All I was told was where to find it. When I went, there it was."

"And who told your father?"

"You don't get it, Katharine. It was the captain himself who told me where to find the trunk. But until I did, I hadn't known anything about him, or how we were related. I just had this spirit bothering me, telling me to go and find his 'sea chest,' as he called it. When I did, I found the evidence I needed to come here, and make this land my own." Gabriel swallowed down the last of the liquor in his glass.

Kate sat for a minute, digesting what she'd heard. "That's one hell of a yarn," she remarked at last. Maybe it was Gabriel's seafaring pedigree, but hearing it as he guzzled whiskey conjured images of the sort of wild tales that used to be spun by mariners to pass the time on long voyages—a verbal equivalent of the intricate scrimshaw carved by whaling men. She couldn't help thinking it might all be an embroidery designed to support his claims as a medium.

Yet, rejecting any part of his story no longer meant that he was simply a fraud; it opened the possibility that she had just made love with a murderer.

"What do you want to do now?"

Lost in thought, Kate missed his question. "What . . . ?"

"It's Christmas Eve," he reminded her. "I can take you back to town now."

"You want me to go?"

"No, " he replied, "but I was thinking you'd want to leave."

Kate glanced around the room, wishing she could be told the full dimensions of the unknowable. But the most she could grasp was the impulse of her own mind and heart. She could do nothing but believe him. To do otherwise, was to reject belief in everything that had happened here, reject the forgiveness that had been granted to her, reject the salvation of her future.

With belief, of course, came trust. She felt she would be safe with him. Felt, too, now that she accepted the unfairness of the punishment he'd suffered, a resurgence of the desire to erase his bitterness. "I'd like to stay," she said.

"You sure?" Now he was the one who had trouble believing.

"Yes. Although, right now, I would like you to drive me into town so I can get my car. All my things are in it." She'd feel better with the car close by, able to leave whenever she wished. Then something else occurred to her. "Maybe, too, if you wouldn't mind . . . since it's Christmas . . ." She hesitated.

"What?"

"We could go to church," she said.

"You go if you want. That stuff's not for me."

"You don't *believe*?" she said, incredulous "You're plugged in somehow to eternity, but you cut yourself off from—"

"It isn't that I don't believe," he interrupted quickly, sounding almost offended. "It's just . . . a whole lot simpler for me if I don't let what I do get mixed up with prayers, and vows, and . . . and trying to figure out where a man like myself fits in with some big holy master plan. Any time I've been to church," he concluded quietly, "I just come out confused by what the hell I was put here for."

He'd take her into town, he said, but she could go to church on her own, then drive back in her own car, still parked in front of the restaurant where they'd met this morning.

"That's if you're comin' back," he added. His eyes rested on her, as if waiting for an answer to the unasked question.

She didn't have the answer, though. It was impossible to say what she'd do after she had sat and prayed. Would she want to confess to being wicked? Betraying the vows she had taken as a wife? *'Til death us do part.* Her husband was dead, but not the love. So what would she feel after communing with God about coming back to Gabriel?

She got her coat. "Drive me to church," was all she said.

Yet it did occur to her as they went out into the night that it was the first time since the accident that she really wanted to go—that she was no longer angry with God for what had happened. And in some way, maybe that was because of Gabriel, because of the gift he had been given.

29

When she came back, the shack was dark, with no light to find her way from the car except what came from the moon, its faint bluish glow bouncing off the snow. Kate felt faintly disappointed that a lamp hadn't been left on—a show of faith that she would return. Or maybe what she wanted most was to find him waiting up for her.

Curiously, rather than making her question her own morals, the midnight mass had left her feeling less guilty about her involvement with Gabriel. Joining with hundreds of others to find comfort in the rituals and beliefs that had remained a source of hope for millions after two millenia—and had derived from mysteries and phenomena that could never be explained and had to be taken on faith—gave Kate confidence that her own private search for hope in the mysterious and unknowable was not merely reasonable, but brave.

Inside the shack, it was cold. The stove fire had been allowed to die. By moonlight through the large window, she could discern the humped shape of his body on the bed under the mound of blankets. He had given up, evidently, made up his mind she was gone for good; he'd said he was the wrong kind of man for her, and must assume she felt the same.

Shedding her clothes beside the bed, Kate slipped under the covers. Somehow it felt even more intimate than making love to climb wordlessly into the bed of a man asleep, a presumption she'd never taken except with her husband. She stretched herself out close to him, and felt the warmth of his body along the length of her own. It gave her comfort, relief, but at this moment there was no excitement. Strangely, it was the same blend of sensations she would feel when returning home late after some solo obligation, like a teachers' meeting, to find Jim already asleep.

As she arranged herself to fit more closely against him, he moved. Had he awakened? Kate lay still. She didn't want sex now, wanted only a continuation of this delicious echo of a vanished intimacy. He stirred again, but just slightly, and then she felt his arm curve languidly around her shoulder, bringing her nearer.

There was no word from him, and Kate said nothing. Was he awake or asleep? She didn't want to know. Either way, she felt, she was being welcomed back.

On Christmas morning, she could find no food in the house to make any kind of special dinner. The markets were all closed, so she insisted on treating Gabriel to a restaurant in town. He dressed in the best clothes he owned, an old gray suit jacket with black pants, and they were able to get a table at the Coffin House, where they both ordered a traditional turkey meal.

Their table was in the upstairs restaurant, more formal than the downstairs room Kate had visited with Meg, and crowded with families in a noisy holiday mood. Plainly unaccustomed to dining in such circumstances, Gabriel spent the first few minutes fidgeting in his chair, and switching nervous glances between Kate and the other parties. Before the soup arrived, Kate asked if he'd feel better if they left.

"No. It's a nice place and I want you to have a nice Christmas."

"I want it to be nice for both of us," she said.

"I'll be okay. Not a bad thing for me to be around folks now and then, instead of being such a damn hermit."

Touched as she was by his wanting to please her, Kate was more affected by the hint of discontent and loneliness in the way he referred to his isolation. Until now, she had thought he was satisfied with the life to which he'd consigned himself.

As the meal continued Gabriel appeared no less ill at ease, but Kate did her best to keep a conversation going. She'd only known about the Coffin House, she explained, because she'd been brought here by a friend from her hometown. That led into talking about the life she'd led in Fairhaven, providing enough subject matter to keep the meal from passing in silence.

When they returned to the shack, they exchanged gifts. Neither was prepared, of course; if they were not together, Kate realized, neither would have done anything to observe the holiday. She rummaged in her luggage and pulled out the one thing she had that might appeal to him, the novel she hadn't been able to finish reading. (She managed to catch herself before saying that it was the best thing she could think of for a man who read *The Last Tycoon*.) When it came to reciprocating, he walked over to the whale-tooth scrimshaw and brought it back to Kate.

"You take this," he said, and held it out to her.

"Gabriel, I can't. That's part of your history, an irreplaceable heirloom."

"Yeah, it's special. That's why I want you to have it." He kept it extended to her, cradled in both hands.

Kate kept trying to refuse until it was clear he would be deeply insulted if she didn't accept. Obviously, the gift was meant to make clear that what had happened between them was not a casual thing, even if he might never put that into words.

Kate stayed on. The physical magnetism between her and Gabriel remained overwhelming, but the furious passion of their first coupling became a series of quieter explorations. Each time he was with her, it seemed to Kate he was more tender and patient than the last, his touch more knowing of the needs of her body. She suppressed her widow's guilt. What law of man or nature said she had to be deprived of a man's touch, even if she never stopped loving her dead husband? At moments, even in the midst of intercourse, she found herself contemplating the notion that her husband's spirit could be aware of this involvement—that she had committed herself to a sort of metaphysical ménage à trois, a proposition that was laughable and outlandish and deeply disturbing all at the same time.

In thoughtful moments by herself, she sometimes diagnosed her interest in Gabriel as an obsession, an unhealthy reaction she could never have allowed herself if she was not so bereft and needy. She ought to have the strength to break it off, she would tell herself—just get in her car and go. There was certainly no lack of opportunity. In the days after Christmas, he would leave her alone for hours at a time, driving off to various carpentry jobs, or disappearing to his seaside hut where, he told her, he did his metalwork—told her in a way that made it sound like a sanctuary where he welcomed no visitors. During the times she was alone, Kate sometimes drove her car to town to buy food or a newspaper or to get books from the library: her appetite for reading was coming back. Reassured whenever she made the trip that the option of escape was always available, she would return to the shack. The place that had once struck her as merely cold and uninviting now seemed sensibly uncluttered and tranquil, a place of spiritual retreat with the calming simplicity of a monk's cell. While she waited for Gabriel, she would stoke up the wood stove, and meditatively look at the ocean, or read, able once more to concentrate on a page, a story, the news, events outside of the ones that had reshaped her destiny. Kate no longer felt tempted to pry into his possessions when he wasn't around. If she felt restless in the confinement of his one room, she would go out for a walk. Often she walked for hours, content to be alone on the promontory above the sea, or on the barren moorland— content in the way you could be when you knew there would be someone at the end of the day to be with, to make love with.

In bed, in the silent language of touches, she never felt at a loss for how to communicate with him; no uncomfortable pauses, questions of trust, uncertainty about what came next. None of the things, in fact, that stood between them at every other time. While she had come to accept his innocence of any violent crime, and no longer questioned the authenticity of his spiritualism, she still sensed that there were deeper truths about himself and the reasons for his bitterness than what he had told her. But it would do no good, she felt, to insist on answers. They would be revealed only if he cared enough to tell her.

Just as she tread carefully on his feelings, she had lost the urge to go any other place he didn't want her. She never went down to the hut where he worked. Her reluctance to intrude extended to leaving him to choose when he might aid her in making another contact with her spirits. In fact, she had mixed feelings about what her husband—or her children—might have to say to her if and when they were conjured again.

In the middle of their fourth night together, Kate woke suddenly and found she was alone in the bed. She sat up and turned on the small bedside lamp. For a moment, she was afflicted by the same uneasy feeling she'd had in the middle of the first night she'd stayed over.

Then she noticed that, as before, the telescope had been taken from its place by the window.

She wrapped herself in a blanket, slipped into her shoes, and went outside. The night was clear, the moon bright, and she only had to scan the perimeter briefly before she saw the dark outline of Gabriel not far along the cliff, warmly bundled in a parka. He was bent over the telescope's long tube, aimed toward the speckled night sky. At the sound of her footsteps crunching toward him through the snow, he straightened up.

"What are you looking at?" she said.

"Not at anything. Looking *for* something, more like . . ." He bent over the eyepiece again, forestalling her next question.

Kate moved up beside him. He straightened again. "Want a look?" he said, stepping aside.

She lowered her head to the eyepiece. Even with the optical magnification, within the round field she saw no fine detail, only a sprinkling of myriad stars dusted like powdered sugar across a swatch of blue-black velvet.

He spoke over her shoulder. "That's a little corner of *galaxias kyklos*," She looked up questioningly. "The Milky Way," he explained.

She studied it again. For what was he looking? she wondered, trying to find it for herself rather than ask. The stars were too far away to be seen as anything but twinkling pinpoints of light. His voice came again to her, accompanying the sky's display like a planetarium narration. "Those stars—those gigantic flaming things—are as far away as anywhere from ten to thirty thousand parsecs. At that distance—"

"Parsecs? I don't know that word."

"Astronomical unit of time. One parsec equals three-point-two-six light-years."

So, she calculated as she stared at the white-speckled field, the light emitted by some of these shimmering pinpoints, traveling at a speed of 186,000 miles per second, had taken more than ninety thousand years from the time it flared up into the universe until it was received by her eye. She took it in for another minute while he remained silent. At last, she stood back from the telescope. "You started to say something about the distance. . . ."

"Just that what you saw—what you see right now if you look at the millions of stars filling that little place in the sky"—his eyes shifted upward—"it don't really exist anymore, not like what you see there. A lot of those stars are gone, exploded to pieces. Others are flamed out by now, stone cold, dead." He looked back to her. "But with all the time it took for their light to get here, we see 'em still winkin' at us. You see? It just depends on where you're standin'. From here, they're part of our world. If we were up there, we'd see they were gone. . . . "

She thought she understood now what he was getting at, what he might be searching for by staring far off into the heavens. "You think that's got something to do with how you're able to see the dead? Something explained by . . . the physics of light or . . . time folding back on itself . . . ?"

His shoulders heaved in a big shrug as he kept his eyes trained on the far edges of the universe. Kate waited, hoping for more of an answer.

"Couldn't say how to explain it," he resumed finally. "And that drives me crazy sometimes, crazy with questions I try to answer and can't, no matter how much I read about it, or how often it happens. I'm left crazy with wondering why it's me who can do this thing instead of . . . somebody more . . . more . . ." He fell quiet again for a long moment, as if reluctant to say the word that came. "Worthy. Then the thing that helps me most—gives me a feeling maybe I'm not so strange or crazy—is having *this* experience, right here, one that I know anyone can have, any person on this earth, just by lookin' up there. To see with their own eyes, right in front of 'em, what's been dead and gone for a long time."

He lowered his gaze to stare across the moonlit sea, and shrugged again. "Don't explain nothin', really. Just makes me feel better to know my own thing is only one of a million things there ain't no way to explain. It don't end with those stars up there. Think about how far past those stars you gotta go to get to the end of space . . . except there probably isn't any end." At last he looked at her. "Can you get your mind around that? Or how the whole shootin' match started, where it came from, that maybe there never was a beginning to time?"

Kate might have offered a reply. But she was glad just to listen to him, glad he was opening up to her. She liked, too, the experience of being his student. As simply as he expressed himself, he was grappling with complicated ideas. So she just shook her head, instead of making it a discussion.

And in the silence, he seemed to decide he'd already revealed himself too much. "So that's all there is to it, Katharine," he said. "Same as you, I'm searchin' for answers." As if to clear her vision for that search, he reached out and pushed back a few strands of hair that the night breeze had blown across her eyes. "Now get yourself back to bed. It's too cold for you to be out here in nothin' but those blankets." He turned back to the telescope and slowly, deliberately, bent down to look through the eyepiece.

No sooner did he mention the cold and turn from her, than she began to shiver. She left him staring at the stars, and hurried back inside.

Lying once more in the comfortable warmth of the bed, she thought back over the things he'd said, and she was freshly gratified by the willingness he'd shown to give her glimpses into a depth and thoughtfulness he usually kept camouflaged behind his surliness and all his cocksure pronouncements. Like her, he had said, he was searching for answers.

Rather than lying awake, bedeviled by all the unanswerable mysteries, Kate fell asleep again quickly. Even without him lying beside her, she felt so much less alone.

30

The next morning, Kate went to Nantucket Town to shop. She'd been buying food day to day, never sure she would be staying long enough to plan beyond that. Now she wanted to provision the house. She wanted to get a heavier sweater, too; the temperatures had dipped the past couple of days, and during her winter walks by the ocean, the chill air cut through to the bone.

As she drove away from Madaket, she was aware of a different attitude than on the other days. No longer the faint relief of making an escape, the flow of mental reassurances that she didn't have to go back; she was reconciled to returning even before she left. The insight she'd gotten into him last night, the first glimmers of seeing deeper into the man had formed a bond that went beyond the physical.

Kate was on Main Street, walking toward a clothing shop where she'd seen sweaters for sale when she heard her name called out. Glancing around, she spotted Eddie just leaving her car at a parking space.

Eddie crossed the sidewalk. "Well, hello!" Her enthusiastic greeting also carried a lilt of surprise.

"Hi," Kate said, her own hello restrained by embarrassment.

"I thought you'd gone home. Or are you back again . . . ?"

Kate hesitated. Reluctant as she was to state the facts, she decided Eddie deserved to be treated as a friend. "I never left," she said. "I've been with Gabriel."

"Oh." Unable to hide her shock, Eddie's green eyes widened.

In the silence that followed, Kate was sure Eddie was filling in the blanks; she knew about the kiss, the rest wouldn't be hard to guess. "I know," Kate said, and smiled sheepishly, "it doesn't make any sense."

"Don't be so hard on yourself," Eddie said. "I told you I can understand being attracted."

"For the thrill," Kate reminded her. "Because he's 'dangerous.' "

"Girl talk, Kate, don't hold it against me. If it's good for you, fine. I'm not making any judgments."

Once again Kate felt chagrin in the face of Eddie's plain decency. "Sorry. Running into you, having to explain . . . I thought I was feeling okay about it, but . . ." Kate turned away a second, shaking her head. "Truth is, I'm not sure why it's happened. He's not someone I would have ever imagined I . . ." She broke off again.

Eddie grasped her arm lightly. "You want to talk some more? We could grab a coffee somewhere."

Kate considered it. If she sat down with Eddie and started pouring out her troubled feelings, she'd surely bring Gabriel's past into it, exposing what she'd learned about him, asking for an opinion about his guilt or innocence. And right now it seemed to Kate the revelations would be a betrayal, a breach of trust that would trouble her no less than the uncertainties she was living with now.

She smiled gratefully, but shook her head. "Thanks, but this is something I've really got to figure out on my own."

Eddie gave an understanding nod. "You've got a rain check, if ever you need it."

They fell naturally into a brief hug and parted. But Kate had taken only a few steps before Eddie called out to her again. "Hey—what are you doing New Year's Eve?"

Another forgotten day of celebration. Before Kate could say anything, Eddie went on: "Danny's cooking up a feast and we're having some people over. Please come. With Gabriel, of course. Anytime after nine." She waved, and walked away.

The shack was empty when Kate returned, but Gabriel's truck was on the knoll. She supposed he must be working in the smaller hut at the base of the cliff. She'd never before thought of disturbing him there, never gone farther along the path down to the shore than the point where she could see the small wooden building. But today she headed straight down along the track marked by his passage through the snow. Past a turn where the path dropped more sharply downhill, she saw the hut below on a base of piled rocks at the inner edge of the beach, a plume of dark smoke rising from one end of the pitched roof. She marched ahead, unconcerned now if she would be violating some unstated rule not to go where she hadn't been asked. So much the better if he was annoyed, even furious at the violation.

Until the encounter with Eddie, Kate's constant reviews of her relationship with Gabriel had dealt only with trying to define it for herself: to determine if it was good or bad for her, if it derived from nothing more than a selfish sexual need, or whether there was an empathetic desire to join him in his isolation, two wounded souls punished unfairly. Or was she clinging to him because of his rare ability and the promise it offered of some form of occasional reunion with the beloved family that had been torn from her? Just this morning—because of their conversation under the stars—she had allowed herself to feel for the first time that even if any or all of those things were true, there was also one more basic element: she was indeed attracted, not only physically, but by qualities that he kept hidden behind a facade of surliness and discontent.

Yet she had been thrown back now into doubting that it made any sense to be with him. Having revealed the affair to Eddie, seeing the effect it had on her, and knowing the news would be carried back to Danny and discussed, Kate had awakened to the light in which other people would regard this liaison with Gabriel. The invitation to appear with him at a New Year's party gave rise to visions of the way they would be seen when they went out in public, how they would be gossiped about—the sex-starved widow from the suburbs who'd thrown herself into the arms of an eccentric island recluse. All the while Kate had made her rounds in town, and during the drive back to Madaket, she'd run through that scenario again and again, walking into Eddie's party, facing the judgments of others. Her imaginings went beyond New Year's to future times, when she might be seen with him away from the confines of this island. What would it be like to explain the involvement to Sarah, to introduce Gabriel to her, or Meg—?

It seemed to Kate finally that being out in the world with Gabriel, being anywhere but safely in the cocoon of his room at land's end, was inconceivable. While ashamed of whatever strain of conformity or snobbishness within herself made her regard the idea as absurd, she still couldn't picture herself including Gabriel in the situations which had been a part of her usual life. So there was nothing to do but break it off. Better sooner than later. If she hadn't the sense or the strength to leave on her own, then perhaps she could force him to cast her out—offend him, pick a fight, whatever it took.

As she approached the hut, she could see it was constructed of wood on only three sides. The smoke rising above the roof came not from a stovepipe, but a brick chimney that was a continuation of a curiously uneven brick wall at one side of the structure, the bricks laid so that there was a greater thickness at the base, and a bulge in the wall at its center. Kate noticed then there were also a couple of small iron hatches in the wall a few feet above the ground. She realized now that the brickwork must enclose a furnace, the hatches giving access for cleaning.

There was a single window on each side of the hut, and a door at the end opposite the furnace. Kate approached a window to observe what he was doing.

He was facing away from her, fortunately. It must be hot inside the hut, for his shirt was off, and she could see the sweat glistening on his back as he hammered a long piece of iron stretched across an anvil. To one side, she could see a white-hot fire glowing through an opening in the hive-shaped furnace that extended from the brick wall. A mound of coal was heaped in a corner. Everywhere else around Gabriel, leaning against the walls, piled along the floor, were pieces of metal and samples of unfinished ironwork: grates, fences, gates. Scattered among these were a number of unidentifiable objects for which Kate could discern no purpose, assemblies of metal, large and small, some shiny, others rusted. Also, leaning end-on in a corner by the door, were a number of long rods with barbed ends, made of silvery and golden metals polished to a gleaming finish. As she looked at them, Kate recognized the shape from samples she had seen at the whaling museum—harpoons.

Gabriel moved suddenly, lifting the metal which he'd been hammering on the anvil to bring it to the open furnace. He pushed a third of its length into the white-hot fire, and turned to perform some other task.

Afraid to be caught spying, Kate dodged away from the window, then stood for a moment, wondering whether to leave without confronting him. Her decision made, she went to the door and threw it open without pausing to knock.

He was at the furnace again, in the act of removing the long piece of metal he'd been heating. At the sound of the door banging open, he spun around so the rod in his hands, its almost molten tip glowing, pointed toward Kate. Feeling the intense heat that radiated from it, she was suddenly aware that if angered irrationally by her trespass, he could easily skewer her on that piece of white-hot metal.

"What—?" he exclaimed, assuming it must be some trouble, some emergency, that had caused her to make this explosive entrance.

We've been invited to a party, she nearly said—the instigation, after all, for coming here, her rash plan to cause a rupture. But all that came out was, "It's crazy . . . the whole thing's crazy."

He eyed her for another moment, thrust the metal back into the furnace, and faced her again. "Mind closing that door," he said mildly. "Wind's blowing in."

Not the reaction she wanted or expected. Off balance, she teetered momentarily between retreating, or slamming the door and accusing him of taking advantage of her, attacking him in any way that produced an irreparable breach. But as he stepped toward her, she read his expression as one of genuine concern. She was affected, too, by the way he'd reacted to her intrusion—no anger, not even annoyance. Only concern. And curiosity.

"You don't mind?" she said "My coming down here . . . ?"

"Should I?"

"I got the impression you wouldn't like it."

"Why?"

"You never invited me, for one thing. And the way you live . . . you make it pretty clear you don't want to let people into your life."

He regarded her thoughtfully, then moved closer. "So is that why you came charging in here? To see just how much I wouldn't like it?"

No need to confess, he had her pegged. As he moved closer, sweat shining on his bare chest, Kate's thoughts were blocked by a surge of desire, the memories in her senses of how well he touched her. She pulled back and looked away, trying to focus again on her purpose. The jumble of metalwork filled her vision now. She waved her hand around. "What is all this stuff?" She spoke merely to keep talking, keep herself from clutching at him, surrendering pathetically to her desire.

"Things that I've made."

"Those, too?" She gestured to the harpoons in a corner. "What do you make those for?" He didn't reply, and she glanced over at him. "Somebody still looking to catch Moby Dick with a golden harpoon?"

He answered at last. "I don't make it all to use. Some things I make . . . just 'cause I like the way they look. Other things . . ." He shrugged. "Don't even know why I make some of the things I do. Maybe it's what they want me to make. Maybe they got a use for those. . . ." He nodded at the harpoons.

They, she imagined, would be his whaling ancestors.

Was he teasing her again? Either way, Kate thought, there was a mystical element to the crafting of something that had no purpose other than to release the urge to produce it. Looking again at the odd metal creations buried within the piles of grating and other useful metal-work, Kate realized they were, in fact, what would be called—among those who would define as "art" the making of things without any practical use—sculptures. Regarding them as such made her wish she could see them without all the clutter piled over and around them. She wondered if the art Gabriel made was good art, if he had a true talent.

"Why . . . ?"

His voice pulled her out of the thought.

"Why'd you come?" he said when she looked back to him.

"You were right," she said evenly. "To make you mad. To make something ugly happen between us. Because I don't know what I'm doing here with you, Gabriel, I honestly don't. But I haven't been able to pick up and leave."

"So you were hoping I'd help it along." He came closer. His gray-blue eyes seemed darker, the sea under a gathering storm. "Well, what would it take? Should I throw you over my shoulder, carry you up to the road and just dump you there? How ugly do you want it to be, Katharine? You need me to take a hand to you?" He half lifted one hand as if he might swipe it across her face, and she shied away. "Or would it be enough if I just told you that you'll never be safe with me, 'cause I've already killed one woman and you just never know when I might take it into my head to do it again. Would that do it for you? Would it?" His hands shot out and gripped her arms tightly as he re-peated the question in a seething hiss, and his stormy eyes bored in on her. "Would it?"

Yet what she perceived behind that piercing gaze was still not anger. Only pain. Even before he released his grip and thrust her back, she knew she had nothing to fear.

"Well, damned if I will!" he roared, and strode off to the other end of the hut. "Go if you want. Go to hell and gone! But it won't never be 'cause I told you to." Facing into a corner, he bowed his head, and muttered softly, "I want you here."

She went toward him. When she was very near, she stopped. Her fingertips hovered over his back, the muscled surface gilded with perspiration, as fearful of making the final contact as she might be of lighting the fuse on a bomb.

But he felt her there and spun around. "What do you think this is for me? Just a little piece of Christmas candy, a nice little treat I helped myself to, good as long as it lasts, never mind there'll be another one along any day?" His voice broke to a whisper. "Lord, what *did* you think?"

She was stunned by the force of his emotions. "I don't know what to think. You've told me so little."

"Have I really?" he said bitterly. He lifted his hand again, and she nearly flinched, but it reached out slowly, sliding through her hair to hold the back of her neck, and then gently pull her mouth to his. She didn't resist.

His kiss was tender, then ravenous, then soft, then furious and demanding, then restrained, even shy. She did nothing but submit, eager to know about what change would come next.

He finished it quietly and eased her away. "What did that tell you?" he said. "What do you think I've been telling you all along?"

"Oh, Gabriel . . . no . . ." She didn't want to hear the word "love." Though maybe he knew that; maybe it was why he wouldn't put it into words.

But he knew she understood. "You can't believe it's good, I know. You think I'm not someone you could be with for anything more than . . ." He shrugged, left the rest of that charge unsaid. "But I can't help what I feel, Katharine. Truth is, I felt it the first moment I saw you. I knew right then it was wrong, too—did as much as I could to keep you away. Except you wouldn't let me." He hesitated for a moment. "And neither would they. Had to do what they wanted, too."

They. The souls that spoke to him, he meant—and these in particular, she knew, were her very own.

It no longer surprised her to hear him blaming his actions on commands from the beyond. But for him to claim nothing less than loving her as the dictate of the ones she mourned was so audacious she was left staring at him, speechless.

He filled the silence. "They told you, too, didn't they? *He* did. Remember? You mentioned it to me. Said something about love being near you . . . taking it. . . ."

She glared at him. Shouting the reply inside her head: *You said it. Those words came from your mouth. That's how you seduced me!* But she held it in. She hadn't been seduced; she'd wanted him. Nor did she harbor any longer the same suspicions of his supernatural ability. Not all trace of skepticism had vanished; it still crossed her mind that there could be explanations for the phenomena that occurred during his trances that were less fantastic than believing in contact with the dead. It might derive from some extraordinary sensitivity to the thoughts of the people for whom he did his "readings," extrasensory perception. Or perhaps, even unwittingly, the mood he established put his "clients" into a sort of hypnotic state in which they told themselves the lies they wanted to hear. Whatever the mechanism, Kate could no longer ascribe the words and visions of the man who was her lover to deliberate deception and sheer trickery.

"And now that I've taken the love," she said, "do you think they're glad? Do you think they'd tell me that there's more to this than . . . grief therapy? Would they say this is where I belong?" As she posed the questions, Kate knew it was the only thing that could keep her here: if he could convince her it was what "they" wanted. She realized, too, it was why she had avoided asking him to do the next trance. Enjoying the interlude, craving his touch, glad for a change from plain sorrow, she feared the spirits he called forth might condemn her. Even if they encouraged her, would that be better? Would it only leave her in a limbo of doubt?

Now, though, she had issued the challenge.

"Are you ready to ask?" he said. As if, perhaps, he had already guessed the answer.

She nodded.

He turned away and grasped the end of the long metal bar he had left in the furnace. "There's work to finish here," he said. "Get out. We'll do it later." He sounded now the way he had the first time he had ever spoken to her, gruff, unfriendly.

A stranger.

As she went to the door, he kept his back to her, rolling the metal rod in his hands, heating it evenly. She said no more before walking out into the cold. The only words that could make a difference now would have to come from another world.

31

She had everything ready by the time he came. Pitcher of water on the table, chairs positioned, candles lit. She'd closed the curtains, then opened them again as darkness fell. It was almost ten o'clock now. Perhaps he'd delayed coming, also reluctant to learn what the spirits would tell her.

Waiting, Kate had done nothing but ponder what she wanted for herself. Over these past few days she had found not only physical satisfaction, but a rare measure of peace and an appreciation of solitude, of a simple existence. What awaited her if she left, returned to Fairhaven? The fresh collision with memories of a shattered life, another failure at work, a return to solitary grieving, loneliness?

Yet to remain with this man, to accept the love now virtually declared, and with it the obvious bargain of returning it—trying, at least, to return it—seemed no less daunting. As she imagined sharing her days with Gabriel, Kate reminded herself of how complicated he was, and speculated on what facets of his character might yet be revealed. Not only the bad. Just today she'd discovered he might be—in the most genuine and unself-conscious way—an artist. What might emerge from him if he was finally, completely, trusted, nurtured, encouraged . . . loved?

When he came through the door, he went straight to the sink and stayed there a long time, washing his hands and face. The noise of the water splashing into the iron sink seemed meant to keep her silent, too. At last, he shut off the tap, dried himself, and turned to her. "You're sure you want this?" he asked.

"I'm not sure of anything. But if it wasn't done, I'd keep wondering what would've happened." Her gaze roamed the shadows around her. "They may want me to . . . know something. And," she added, "I still miss them."

He looked at her coolly another second or two, then walked briskly across the room. "All right," he said, "let's go." His familiar prosaic invitation to bond with the incredible.

Kate took her chair, and he sat across from her. His reluctance had been evident, and she wondered if it could interfere with the outcome.

He closed his eyes and went into his routine of deep breathing.

It went on and on, far longer than the last time, but she remained patient, watching and listening for the first sign he was into the trance. Eventually, his breathing became more labored, the inhalations and exhalations deeper, louder. Even with his eyes closed, his features were not in repose, but appeared strained, lines etched around his mouth and across his brow, teeth gritted.

Perhaps fifteen or twenty minutes had passed, far longer than ever before, when he spoke. "They won't come. I can't do it . . . can't get through. . . ." He went on breathing deeply, though, for another few minutes.

Kate said nothing, afraid she would only disrupt the flow at the moment he might suddenly succeed. But then he slumped back, and opened his eyes to regard her bleakly. "I can't," he said once more, his voice a dry rasp, his throat raw from all the air he'd forced through it.

"You don't want to," Kate said. "You're fighting it. That's the reason, isn't it?"

"Maybe," he muttered. "I guess that could explain it." He rose and grabbed up the pitcher on the table, and spilled some water from it directly into his mouth.

"Once more," she said. "Just this once. I'll never ask again." She felt certain there was some final revelation that would come out of it.

Without reply, he went back to the sink, emptied the pitcher, and put it on the shelf.

She followed him. "You didn't really try, did you? Something would have happened if you tried. Did you try, Gabriel? Or are you afraid to let them come?"

"I tried," he said quietly, and walked away from her.

"I don't believe it. You can do this whenever you want. You've always gotten something, never a complete blank." He kept moving away from her, but she dogged his steps. "Afraid of what they'll tell me, isn't that why? Afraid they don't want me here. Answer me, damn it! You won't keep me with you by avoiding this! I needed to hear from them. If there's any chance I'll stay, it can only be if you—"

"I can't!" he exploded, whirling around and seizing her by the arms. His eyes blazed into hers as his mouth opened as if to shout at her again. But the fire in his gaze suddenly cooled, and the words emerged in the quiet tone of an apology. "Don't you get it? I can't do it anymore." His voice sank. "I just can't do this to you."

She stared back into his eyes. *To* her, he'd said. Not *for* her.

She understood instantly the huge meaning of that small difference, but still she tried to block it from ramming fully through the barrier guarding that sanctum of her mind where her most treasured beliefs were kept. She had been so careful in guarding the gates to that sacred place, keeping out what was false, demanding proof. History was her standard, after all, the record of events—of what, in fact, had been *known* to happen. And she had come to believe in Gabriel, even in what all science and logic contradicted, because of what had undeniably happened with him, between them. All that she had seen, and heard. And felt.

She needed to hear it again. For the historical record. "Do what to me?" she said quietly.

He let go of her and turned away, avoiding her again.

"Answer me!" she demanded.

He moved farther away, alienating her as much by his silence as he had with his words.

Then in the silence, hearing in her memory so many other things he'd told her, events so thoroughly explained with so much conviction about how his ability had been revealed to him, she supplied an answer for herself.

"You're letting me go—that's why you're doing this, isn't it? Because I've told you once too often I shouldn't be here. That's the *real* truth. You're doing this to make the break. Right, Gabriel? Tell me I'm right." She could hear her own voice, its tone of pleading growing more pronounced. But after all she'd come through to believe in him, having those beliefs dashed would be unbearable. Like enduring another death. "You're lying about this for my sake. Being noble because you care. Everything you've said and done is true, except—"

He faced her and shouted back, "I care, right! Cared from the beginning, like I said. So I wanted to help, kept giving you what you wanted so you'd feel better. But now it's more than just caring, more than I can say. Hell, no—I will say it, even if I know you won't like hearing it. I love you, Katharine!" This, too, emerged in a shout that sounded oddly both exultant and tortured. Then he said it again. Quietly. "I love you. Never in my life loved anyone but you. . . ." He gazed at her a long moment, as if giving her a chance to reciprocate.

But she couldn't speak. Beyond the declaration, she needed to hear him recant the confession that he was simply a fraud.

He lowered his eyes and bowed his head. "So that's why I won't go on with this. I want you to have something better than that."

He'd made it even clearer, and still she wouldn't accept it. "I heard them," she said. "The children. Both of them. Different voices. That couldn't have been—"

"Heard what you wanted to hear," he said gruffly, lifting his eyes. "That's always what makes it work."

"There were things you couldn't have known . . . private things. . . ."

"I take guesses. Sometimes they're right. The person hearing them wants them to be right, even if they're not. You made them right." He looked at her as if challenging her to prove she hadn't.

"There has to be more to it," she insisted.

He moved away and stood at the window looking out at the sea. "Oh, sure, much more. It takes . . . a certain talent, I guess." His tone had lightened, and taken on a bragging edge. "I suppose there's some real intuition that comes into play. I don't even know how I do it sometimes. All I know is I make it happen, all of it." He glanced back at her. "Make it up, that is. . . ."

She was reexamining every moment now, remembering how many things she'd questioned, even at the time, how carefully she'd held herself back from belief. The airplane . . . the promise? Didn't she guess that the odds favored every couple having some sort of overwrought fear of dying on a flight?

As for the rest . . . ? Good acting, voice control, and, of course, setting her up so goddamn perfectly with all that playing hard to get, all his fine denunciations of the fakers.

"You sonofabitch," she said, her eyes pooling with tears. "You complete—" Words failed then and she rushed at him, her fists raised. It was the first time she'd ever felt the desire to thrash a man.

He caught her by the wrists. "Listen, I never dreamed it would get to this point. A woman like you—with me. I've been mixed up about what to do and say since you walked in. Couldn't you tell? I wanted you right then, the minute I saw you. Wanted to chase you away, and keep you close, all at the same time. Wanted so bad to help you stop hurting, but . . ." He shrugged.

"But what?" she cried harshly. She knew he'd only stopped himself from reiterating the same hateful confession, but still she needed to hear it said. Needed to hear it as many times as it would take for her to be sure she could never be hurt like this again.

"But I could only help you," he said slowly and deliberately, "by going through my act."

She stared into his face. She thought she could read remorse there, a wish for forgiveness, even the longing to be loved. But none of it could win her back. "You miserable, low-down bastard," she muttered, tears flowing, and her throat becoming so tight she could do no more than whisper while her entire body quaked with rage and grief together. "You pathetic shit."

He stared back, offering no defense.

She fought down one more urge to strike him, then whirled away and started gathering up her clothes from around the shack. She couldn't stop crying, and heedlessly used whatever garments were in her hand to keep blotting her cheeks.

For a while, he stood where he was and watched her. "You begged me," he said at last. "Don't forget that."

She had just lifted her suitcase onto the bed to cram her pile of clothes into it. She turned to him. "I won't forget either that you came after me! Even when I was ready to give it up, you didn't let me. You came after me, told me you felt they were near. . . ."

"Yeah, I did," he replied. "After I'd kissed you."

"Damn you," she said after a moment, and kept whispering it over, "damn you, damn you," while she hurriedly finished packing and collecting whatever belonged to her, impatient to get away as quickly as possible.

He remained rooted to one spot, silent once more, until she had carried her packed suitcase to the door, and was about to take her parka from the peg where it was hanging. Then he said, "I had to do this, didn't I? I couldn't love you and not tell you the truth."

That made the rage boil up. She looked back to him. "Couldn't you, Gabriel?" she roared. "So what the hell am I left with now? What's the great prize I get from this beautiful love you've given me? Nothing! I'm left with nothing at all to believe in. And no one. You've made me hate you—and made the people I truly love die all over again!" Her coat was on now, and she went to pick up her suitcase. He took a couple of steps toward her, as though he meant to help, but the glare she turned on him was enough to keep him at bay.

She paused before she went through the open door, and looked back. "Damn you forever," she said once more, quietly. "Why couldn't you just go on lying to me?"

In Nantucket Town, the sidewalks were rolled up, most houses already dark. The Christmas celebrations past, New Year's yet to come, people were turning in early. Kate drove slowly up Quince Street. Passing the Markham House, she could see a yellow glow behind one second-floor window. Eddie would take her in, Kate knew. But as she thought of having to account for her late night, the unavoidable confession she'd have to give for the pitiful way she'd been gulled into a humiliating affair, Kate couldn't face it. Nor could she bring herself to go around knocking on other doors. All the hotel rooms must be booked for the holidays.

She spent the night in her station wagon, parked in the lot where cars lined up for the ferry. Cold as it was, she didn't turn on the heater. Tonight, it suited her to be without any comfort at all. Numb and hopeless, Kate stared at the ocean through the windshield for hours, running through all that had happened with Gabriel in an endless, repetitive loop.

Her fury ebbed, so that each time the loop returned to his plea for mercy—*I couldn't love you and not tell you the truth*—she got caught up in imagining a different reaction she might have had, a better ending to the scene. Couldn't she have forgiven him? Wasn't there some nobility in making his confession, some courage, to be recognized and rewarded? It could be true that he'd pretended only to please her, to soothe her—

Except it was a pretense he'd begun long before he met her. A way of making a little extra money. Harmless enough, he could tell himself, since he didn't go overboard trying to build it into a full-time business, and the act he performed was simply one that people yearned to see. Or was that where the self-delusion ended?

When she thought back to the way it had begun for him—as he'd explained it, anyway—it wasn't just the launch of a mere con game. It was nothing less than his alibi, the "evidence" he'd offered that he was innocent of any part in a murder. So admitting his contacts with spirits were mere fakery left him with no alibi.

Did he truly think she'd be more ready to love him once she believed he was guilty of murder? It was a question she would have put to him—if it had occurred to her before she walked out. Now that it cropped up, it kept nagging at her. His urgency to "come clean" with her didn't seem consistent with the fact that by doing so, he was acknowledging some responsibility for a crime far more heinous than a spiritual sham.

When she recalled, furthermore, the way he'd talked about his visions of the murdered girl, Kate couldn't write them off as just one more well-rehearsed part of his act. The trances, voices speaking through him, yes, all that was easy to discount. But those descriptions of his dreams, of hands coming up through the sand, of being haunted by the murdered girl even in his waking hours, of being visited in prison by the shades of all the miserable souls who'd died there, could he have made up all these details of the torments he'd endured?

Hearing it again in memory, Kate still believed it.

So perhaps that much was true, and had been the inspiration for his fraud.

She was still wide awake, turning the same questions over and over in her mind when, not long before dawn, a pair of headlights appeared in her rearview mirror approaching slowly from the rear. He could have easily guessed she'd be here—especially if he'd checked first at the Thornes'. If he'd come to make a final appeal, she wasn't sorry; there were questions she was eager to ask. She wanted at least to know that the man who'd made love to her for a few days over Christmas couldn't have killed anyone. The headlights pulled up right behind her, then the shadow of the driver loomed up through the seaside mist. He knocked at her car window, and she turned to him—

A stranger stood outside, his face framed in the fur collar of his jacket, a police cap on his head. Kate rolled the window down and frosty, ocean-scented air spilled into the car.

"You all right, ma'am?"

"Yes, thanks. I'm waiting for the ferry,"

The cop cracked a smile. "A bit early to get on line. There's only one midday this time of year, and always plenty of space, not like high season."

"I know, Officer."

"Listen, there'll be some warm places opening up soon. You can get breakfast while you wait."

"I'm okay right here," she said.

He lingered. "You sure . . . ?"

She nodded again. "Just playing it safe. I don't want to take the smallest chance of not getting off the island."

He shrugged and backed away. "I'll leave you to it, then. 'Night, ma'am."

Kate was already rolling up the window when she heard him call out, "Happy New Year."

32

Returning to the empty house was every bit as hard as Kate expected. The answering machine was full of messages from friends, acquaintances, and neighbors wondering where she was, invitations to come and share Christmas dinner and, latterly, to spend New Year's Eve with them, but the only calls she was tempted to answer were Meg's. Though even that she decided to postpone. She didn't want to answer questions about where she'd gone and what she'd done and whom she'd met.

New Year's Eve she stayed home by herself. Her only planned ritual was to pull out all the family photo albums and look through them, spending the last moments of this year in which her life had been destroyed in an orgy of nostalgia. She sat on the floor of the den before a log fire and turned the pages, sometimes talking to the images as they passed in front of her. "Wow, kid, weren't you something!" she said to Chloe as she posed at the ice rink in her first skating outfit, blue with white fur trim. To Tom at Little League, coming across home plate, all smiles after an easy pop-up to the pitcher somehow turned into a bases-loaded home run, she whispered, "Way to go, Slugger,"—an echo of that same cheer she could remember shouting from the stands.

And Jim came in for the whole gamut of ridicule and admiration as he went past in his wedding tuxedo, bathing suits, Halloween costumes, candids from vacations and birthdays and backyard barbecues. It was hard at times, but Kate stayed with the pictures, being with her family in the only way possible as a new year approached.

Filling her mind with the past was also a way of keeping Gabriel out of her thoughts.

When the clock on the mantel struck eleven, she considered whether to stop now and take a couple of pills, or if she could endure being awake at midnight—the first time in sixteen years without a kiss from her husband. At last, she went down to the basement to fetch a split of champagne from the basement stock. The bottle was cool, and she opened it, poured two glasses, and went back to looking at the albums. If she could get through tonight without a pill, she thought, it might set an example for the year ahead. She drank a toast to that— her first resolution; no matter how tough it was going to be, she had to stop retreating into unconsciousness.

At a minute or two before midnight the phone rang. Meg or her mother, no doubt, calling to offer a personal New Year's wish. Kate let the phone ring twice while she took a sip of champagne, and then made another resolution: stop punishing the people who cared most. She went to the phone.

But when she answered, no voice came back. She could tell the line was open, though, someone at the other end. A faint background whooshing noise was audible; a passing car, maybe, or a gust of wind rustling a tree. The call was certainly coming from an outdoor phone.

"Gabriel? Is that you? Gabriel, if that's you, I'd like to—"

The line disconnected.

Afterward, she couldn't settle again. Maybe he'd wanted to speak to her and had lost his nerve—but there was another possibility: he was angry, couldn't let go, wanted to harass her. How well did she know him, after all? Stalking might well be the reaction of a violent man. Could she be sure that phone call came from far away?

Yet the unfinished wish she'd wanted to express to him had been a positive one, absent the ill feelings that had boiled over when she left him. Because her words had been cut off this time, remaining unsaid, she couldn't be sure exactly what they would have been, how much she would have dared to admit. At the least, she would have told him she'd like to say she was sorry things had ended so badly and apologize for insulting him. Maybe, too, she would have agreed that the ultimate concern for her expressed by his confession deserved to be appreciated.

Or were there even deeper feelings that might have poured out? He had been good to her in many ways, she reflected. He had—she did not doubt it—loved her.

She kept expecting the phone to ring again, and vacillated between hoping for it, and fearing it. But midnight passed, and the next half hour. Kate finished her own champagne, and the glass she'd poured for her lost partner. She put away the albums, and went up to bed.

For a long time she lay awake thinking about the call. Could it have been anyone but Gabriel? She recalled that a year or so back—when her only reason to be interested was common curiosity—she'd read a magazine excerpt from a bestseller authored by a psychic, one of the many recently popular accounts of after-death experiences and contacts with the dead; it had recounted more than one story of someone in mourning answering a telephone and hearing (always distant, and through a staticlike sound) the voice of a lost loved one.

But Kate couldn't soothe herself anymore with the fantasy of a call from the beyond. Gabriel had taken that from her. The darkness around her was empty. You couldn't tap into AT&T from the hereafter.

She made one more resolution for the New Year—maybe the hardest one to keep. To survive. Simply that.

Then she broke her first, and got up to take a couple of pills.

Her mother returned from California, and Kate went down to the city to have a restaurant dinner, along with Bert, then stay over so the two of them could, as Sarah put it, "catch up."

Over dinner, the conversation remained neutral: the menu, politics, the rampant overcommercialization of the holidays, the way the whole world had changed in the past year. Kate was glad to see Bert again. One positive result of her time with Gabriel, at least, was that she was able to enjoy knowing about her mother's romance with the judge rather than resenting it because of her own deprivations.

As soon as she and Sarah were back at the apartment alone, Kate was subjected to an extensive account of the lavishness of Christmas and New Year's at her sister's in Beverly Hills, featuring a full report on how spoiled Lisa's children were—"Davey got a little electric car to drive around their patio? Can you imagine? Four years old and he's got his own miniature Mercedes! And Lindsay got stud earrings, *diamonds* no less—for a child of six!"

Of course, what Sarah expected in exchange for dishing Lisa and her family was to discuss where Kate had gone over the holidays.

"Will you tell me now what all the mystery was about?" she asked as they sat in her kitchen, sipping pre-bedtime cups of herb tea.

Not *all* the mystery, Kate decided. "I told you: I just needed to get away."

"But why Nantucket?"

Kate was startled by the revelation her mother already knew where she'd gone. Had Sarah hired someone? "How did you know where I was?" she asked suspiciously.

"Darling, you sent Christmas gifts. I simply looked at the postmark."

Kate nodded, placated.

"Did you go to stay with Meg?" Sarah prodded. "I thought you said you wanted to be alone."

"I was. Meg's house is closed up."

"Then tell me: why there? It's a summer resort."

Kate remembered recounting her first trip to the island to her mother, including a mention of discovering Gabriel. Even if she'd ended that report by ridiculing the experience, it might not be much of a leap for Sarah to guess the trip back involved another visit to the medium. But Kate was desperate not to get into discussing the humiliating result of her return. She tried to answer in a way that signaled Sarah to keep any guesses to herself. "It happens to be very nice at Christmas. They have a tradition of doing things the old-fashioned way—hot grog, caroling in the streets. The kind of old-fashioned holiday spirit you can't find anymore in too many places."

"And you didn't mind being alone in the middle of all that?"

The vision of being grilled on the witness stand came over Kate again, her mother breaking down her testimony to get at the truth. "I was only alone when I wanted to be. I stayed at a guest house owned by a young couple who were very friendly." To throw Sarah further off the scent, she added, "They brought me along to a fabulous Christmas party where I met a very nice man."

"Indeed?" Sarah plainly wanted more.

"A biologist at Harvard. Smart, and quite rich as it happens. . . ." Sarah kept looking at her expectantly. "Well, what else do you want to know, Mother? When our next date is? If we've already slept together?"

"Good Lord, Kate, I wouldn't have—"

"Can we just drop this? Mom, I know you don't want me to be

alone. But there isn't any choice for me right now." Kate left the kitchen table to dump the rest of her tea in the sink and rinse out her cup.

"I'm sorry, Katie. It's hard for me, too. I just want to help, and I don't how."

"You can't. So it would be better if you just stop trying so hard."

"Well, what about one of those support groups?" Sarah persisted. "You know, there are meetings of people who've suffered the same kind of terrible loss—"

"The same kind," Kate echoed ironically. "Let me tell you something, Mom. There's none the same, not one. Everybody's tragedy is their very own, every heart breaks in a different way. If I sat down with ten other women and heard each one say they lost everyone they loved in a fire or a skyscraper collapse or even—like mine—in a car crash, I can't imagine it would make me feel one tiny bit better."

"Except you'd know you weren't—"

"Alone?" Kate put in quickly. "No. It might work that way for some people. But not for me. Okay? So just let me work it out my own way." She hurried to offer a quick embrace before heading for bed.

Sarah kept holding her. "There's one more thing we should talk about while you're here," she said. Her eyes went to the empty chair at the table, inviting Kate to sit again, but Kate hung back.

"At least one of my efforts to help isn't turning out so badly." Sarah explained. "I've had a call from the Fairhaven town counsel. . . ."

About the law suit, Kate understood. She thought of telling her mother to keep it for tomorrow—*any* other time—but she'd already been truculent enough for one night. "Go on," she said tiredly, though she remained standing.

"It's unusual at such an early stage, but they're talking of a settlement in the case. They must realize if this ever comes before a jury, chances are you'll win big, and until then, it'll go on being a blot on the town. Getting it out of the way now, they can settle for a relatively insignificant part of what we're claiming. So they've offered a hundred thousand. Coming this early, it's certain I could easily get it up higher. Would you like me to start negotiating?"

Kate had little feeling in the matter. She'd never wanted a lawsuit in the first place. But, since she hadn't read through any of the legal papers, merely signed her name when they were put in front of her, a detail mentioned by her mother piqued her curiosity. "You said what they've offered is relatively insignificant. Exactly how much are we suing them for, Mother?"

"Combined punitive and compensatory damages? Forty-five million dollars."

Forty-five million, Kate mused. How strange it was to hear such a particular and absolute value affixed to her suffering, a price put on the lost lives of her nearest and dearest. And how utterly meaningless. Every ounce of gold on the earth, every denomination of wealth in the world, didn't add up to what she would have paid to ransom them out of oblivion. In fact, it seemed to her now that taking any money at all carried a risk of diminishing the value of their lives rather than emphasizing it.

"What do you want me to do?" Sarah prodded. "I could close it out fairly quickly if that's what you want."

Kate might have just said to drop it, profiting out of her pain was abhorrent, but she was aware that her mother had worked hard and skillfully and with a genuine wish to ease the burdens. Whatever her own feelings, it was past time to let her feel appreciated. "You're my lawyer. What do you recommend?"

Sarah checked her daughter with a glance, as though she hadn't expected to be given a vote. "I'd say think it over. It won't hurt to keep them dangling for a few weeks, and you want to be sure that however it comes out, you'll be satisfied."

"Good advice," Kate said. "Sensible as ever." She leaned down and gave her mother the delayed good night kiss and another hug. "Thanks, Mom. Congratulations on a job well done."

Back again in Fairhaven, Kate kept herself in motion. She followed through with putting the house on the market, giving an exclusive to a broker who was the mother of a girl in Chloe's class at elementary school. She went to supper at Meg and Harry Parker's a few times, sat through half the movies at the multiplex, and boxed up the unneeded clothes and old toys and other stuff all over the house, calling a couple of charities to take it away. She called in people that the realtor had recommended to do a little sprucing up on the house before buyers started walking through.

And she went to the insurance agency to clear out Jim's office, and sit in the conference room with Harry, while he summarized the commission payments due to her on Jim's open policies, and outlined his plans for finding a new partner. A portly, avuncular man, he did his best to discuss the necessary matters in the most considerate way. Kate had to laugh, though, when he repeated the idea that, as long as she was "on sabbatical" from teaching, she might take a crack herself at coming into the agency to fill the gap left by Jim's death.

"Me—sell policies? Harry, if a man was standing on the deck of a burning boat in the middle of a typhoon, I don't think I could get him to buy Fire, Flood, or Life. I've seen a great salesman in action, and I know I don't have what it takes."

"Sure you do. You must know how to talk to people, Katie. You stand up in front of them and teach, for chrissakes."

"Used to," Kate said. "Anyway, my subject was history. You don't have to sell anyone on history, Harry; there's no way to say 'no' to it."

They concluded with practical details. Harry agreed to arrange for the boxes of Jim's records and personal things to be delivered to the house; she told him he could keep any of the personal furniture, or sell it and send her a check. As Kate was leaving, he said, "What *are* you going to do next? Meg and I are both concerned."

"I haven't figured it out yet. When the house sells, I may move down to the city where my mother lives . . . or possibly travel for a while."

"A time like this, sweetie," he said, "you shouldn't be roaming the world on your own. You should stay where your roots are."

She replied with a nod and a smile. Perfectly fine advice—if your roots hadn't been torn out along with your heart.

Wounded as she still felt, Kate finally began going to church again. She was ready to make peace with God, to accept that she had not been singled out for punishment. She was ready, too, to mingle with her neighbors, let herself be seen and accept their condolences, and not hide from the well-intentioned concern of those who wanted to ask, "How are you doing?" She was able to answer honestly. "It's hard, but I'm managing." In fact, when she took stock of the change between the way she felt now, and the way she had felt before the holidays, she realized she had indeed made progress. She also believed it was more than just the passage of time that had made the difference. It was the trip to Nantucket, the people she had met, the things that had happened there. Like the insight Eddie had given her into the selfishness of refusing the sympathy of others.

And, yes, what Gabriel had given her. As betrayed as she had felt by the revelation of his pretense, as time dissipated her anger she could assess more easily what had without doubt been genuine—his feeling for her. In the vacuum of not being loved that was left after the loss of her family, his love, even if she could not return it, had put some warmth into the place in her that was cold and dead, lighting a candle to chase the darkness. She was grateful to have had it; grateful for it still.

She'd been home nearly a month when the package arrived in her morning mail, an eight-inch cube, neatly wrapped in brown paper, addressed with a black marker. No return address, but Kate noticed it was postmarked "Nantucket," and her name had been written K. Wayland. That ruled out the Thornes as senders, she thought, since the register at the B & B had the correct spelling of her last name. Which left Gabriel, whose spelling might be more casual.

She left it unopened on a kitchen counter, tossing worried glances at it, while she had her juice and toast and coffee. Trying to think the best of him in retrospect was a whole different kettle of fish from letting him back into her life in any way. That voiceless phone call—the possibility it had flowed from resentment—opened Kate to the idea that he might have sent something dangerous or, in any case, emotionally hurtful. The best thing, probably, would be to simply mark it "return to sender" and bring it back to the post office. Without a return address, though, her only choice for its disposal if she left it unopened was to dump it in the trash.

By the time she'd finished breakfast, she'd come around to feeling less wary. Any fear he might be capable of stalking her, or worse, was based on knowing he'd been charged and punished for a violent crime. But it was a crime for which he had always denied guilt. No matter what other lies he might have told, Kate could not bring herself to reverse her belief in his claim of innocence. Despite his denials of performing any supernatural feats, the explanation he'd supplied for knowing the whereabouts of the murdered girl's body had been imparted to Kate with such detail, and in a voice that had the ring of truth. To reject this was to accept that he'd been involved in a killing, and no matter what else he'd done, Kate felt certain the man with whom she had made love could have taken no part in a murder.

Her perception was colored, too, by her memory of that night under the stars. Conceivably, before he had made the decision to confess his pretense, all that he'd said about questing to understand his psychic gift was meant only to further convince her. Yet—at least as she remembered it now—it rang truer than mere performance. If he were only pretending to commune with spirits, why also concoct the lie that he was puzzled and troubled by such a talent? If it was all a falsehood, wouldn't it be easier and wiser to pretend confidence and certainty?

At last, she took a paring knife from a kitchen drawer, and carefully cut through the sealing tape to peel away the wrapping paper, baring a cardboard carton. Separating the interleaved flaps of the carton, she looked in on a tightly packed wad of crumpled newspapers. She pulled away the paper, and found at last the object it had been used to protect, the whale tooth with its remarkable scrimshaw carving.

She had deliberately left without taking it—and since then hadn't given it a thought. No way she could banish him from her life, yet keep such a gift. But once again, he wasn't allowing her to refuse.

When she lifted it from the box, Kate was freshly amazed by the intricacy of the etched scene of a whale hunt. Then she noticed the plain envelope lying at the bottom of the carton. Kate grabbed it up and tore it open, impatient to see what he'd written. Forgiveness no longer seemed completely out of the question.

But the envelope contained no letter. Only seven fifty-dollar bills. A full refund.

She went through the rest of that day, and all of the next, thinking about him in every idle moment. A few times she stopped by the whale tooth, still on the kitchen table, and picked it up, letting its amazingly vivid cartoon of a battle with a harpooned whale pull her away into daydreams of everything and anything to do with him, and her time on Nantucket: the story of Joshua Farr, the harpoons Gabriel made in his shop, the strength in the hands he used to work the metal—

Hands that had touched her so tenderly. More than that: lovingly.

In the evening, when the phone rang well past the time she usually got calls, she answered to hear a man say, "Kate—?" and her pulse began to race even before he concluded the greeting with, "it's Paul Levinger."

She tried not to sound disappointed as they talked in the most general way about what they'd each done in the month since New Year's. Then he explained the reason for his call. The week after next, he had to be in New York for a conference of biochemists at Columbia. He was thinking he might drive down on the Sunday instead of flying, particularly if he could stop along the way and visit her.

"It's nice to hear from you, Paul. But I really don't think you should be making any plans around me."

"They're not big plans, Kate. We could simply go for another walk, if that's all you're in the mood for. . . ."

"Paul, that's awfully nice, but . . . it's still too soon for me to . . . well, to encourage any man to—" She was going to say "pursue me," and realized how conceited it would sound. The only other words that came were old-fashioned, yet they struck her as exactly right. "To come courting," she finished.

"Kate, I haven't forgotten about your twenty-year embargo on anything serious. But the last time we were together, you asked my opinion about something, and since then I've learned things I wanted to tell you—as a friend."

Of course, put that way, it felt too churlish to go on making excuses. "Well," Kate said, "I can always use a friend. But you've got me curious now—"

"Good. It's a bit complicated, though, so can it wait 'til Sunday?" He went on to say he'd be leaving Cambridge mid-morning, which would put him in Fairhaven around noon, and they could have brunch together if that suited her. In the end, Kate told him she'd just as soon have brunch at her house as go out.

After the call ended, she thought back to their last conversation on Nantucket. The main thing she could remember talking about was Gabriel. Paul's characterization of the "complicated" things he'd learned as being things to pass on "as a friend" suggested it would be advice of some sort, perhaps including a warning. Yet, even without hearing it, Kate was ready to reject it. As she went upstairs for the night, she was still wishing the voice on the other end of the line had been Gabriel's, and there would have been a chance to clear the air with him. To thank him for his gift. To let him know she believed his fakery could have been motivated by wanting to ease her torment. To probe further into his claim of innocence, and the circumstances on which it was based. The last thing she wanted to hear was anything that put her back into doubting him, feeling betrayed.

She was undressing, standing before an open drawer at her dresser, when she heard the voice inside her head, the fragment of a sentence sounding out of memory—

I'm a lucky man.

The voice was so clear it was almost as if it had not risen from recall, but had been murmured into her ear. It took her only a second to link the words to their moment of origin, and she lifted her eyes to look into the mirror. The memory came back with such clarity, the whole picture. She could visualize him against the shadowy background of the darkened bedroom, standing behind her as he had that last morning, her eyes meeting his in the mirror—

She spun around, strangely expectant that she would see him, be able to relive the kiss, too, to collapse into him for comfort. But there was nothing to be seen or heard or felt. There was only the empty room, a lamp on beside the double bed that waited for her to climb into it alone.

What had triggered the illusion—that memory of a voice so vivid it reactivated some auditory nerve, making it seem absolutely present? Could it be the jealousy of a spirit, anxious to chase those thoughts of Gabriel out of her mind? God, the words were still there inside her head, the last things Jim had said that morning in the last moments they were alone . . . and, oh, the *very* last before they'd gone downstairs: *I'll find the earring later, I promise.* Yes, that did it, made her wish only for him.

"But you broke your promise, you bastard," she whispered to the empty room. "Left me to do it myself . . . everything, all by myself. . . ."

In the next instant, by reflex, she was down on her hands and knees, once again searching the floor, around furniture, in the crevices of the box spring, pulling up the carpet at the baseboard. Though she did it calmly this time, slowly and methodically—and without really hoping to find the earring. She'd come to accept that, whether or not it made any sense, certain things, even something as solid and precious as a jewel, could disappear forever into thin air.

33

Potential buyers had begun coming to view the house. It was wrenching to see the critical eyes they turned on everything, to realize the choices she'd made, that the home her family had loved would be dismantled and changed to suit others. So Kate tried to stay away when prospective buyers were being walked through.

It was to avoid a broker bringing a client that she made two appointments on Thursday that would keep her out of the house until past one o'clock. The first was to have her hair cut and set—a rite of personal maintenance she'd ignored since a hairdresser had come to the house right before the funeral. Next, she had agreed to meet Dave Kronin during his lunch hour at a coffee shop near the high school; the high school principal had been trying for weeks to get Kate to sit down with him and hear another pitch for coming back to teach. Kate didn't feel it was possible to simply pick up where she'd left off, but Dave deserved a personal explanation. His interest and encouragement had remained steadfast while she hadn't heard a word from anyone at Ashedeane since her classroom debacle.

Through most of lunch, Dave's talk consisted of general school news, griping about budget cuts, harmless gossip about other teachers, and crowing about the number of early admissions the senior class had already chalked up at Ivy League colleges.

"Sounds like it's all business as usual without me," Kate said when she sensed he was about to make his pitch. "I'm flattered you still want me, David, but you can take it as final that I won't be returning to Fairhaven High."

"Then you've settled things with Ashedeane? I wouldn't have kept hounding you, but I'd heard from a friend over there that your position was still up in the air."

"Your friend was misinformed. Nothing's up in the air. Dead in the water is more like it."

"But then . . . why wouldn't you come back to us?"

How did she explain it? She did so love teaching. "Dave, my life's a vacuum; whatever goes into that vacuum is going to expand to fill every bit of the available space. I'm afraid that going back to this work because it's all I've got, all I can care about will . . . let it take me over completely." He started to speak, but she hurried ahead. "I know, I know—'keep busy, do this to take your mind off things.' That's the usual pep talk; take satisfaction in giving to the community. It's not bad advice. But if I go back to teaching now, I feel I'll never get things in balance. I'll accept being a teacher as my whole identity because . . . it's easy for me. But before, I was so much more." *Woman, wife, mother*—the list went through her head, though she didn't spell it out for him. "I need to be sure I can be at least some of the other things again, before I settle for just being a teacher. Am I making any sense at all?"

"Honestly?" he came back. "Only some. A woman like you, Kate . . . I can't imagine you'd ever settle into just being the old maid schoolteacher."

She shrugged. "Maybe it's an irrational fear. Except, teaching comes closer than any other profession to parenting. It would be awfully easy to sink into it as a complete substitute for . . . everything I no longer have."

"Is that so bad? If it helps to ease your loss, fills the vacuum, and does some good for kids at the same time?"

"Other people's kids," she said, unable to hide the edge of bitterness. "I shouldn't admit it, but that's the thing I'm most afraid of—that I'll resent them much more than I value them. Deprive them of my best."

"I don't think you could."

"Thanks for the vote of confidence. But you have no idea how hard it is some days not to resent every last child I set eyes on."

That stark admission reduced the principal to silent acceptance.

Honest as it was, the feeling shamed Kate, and she didn't want to leave it as her last word. "I'd feel differently, maybe, if I knew these were students to whom I was vitally important; that I was giving them something no one else could, or would, and it was absolutely crucial for me to be on the job."

Kronin brightened. "But that's what I've tried to tell you, Kate. You *are* that good."

"It's not a matter of how *good* I am! The kind of importance I mean, Dave, is what used to exist when, say, some frontier community would send to the East for a 'schoolmarm' to go to their godforsaken town on the prairies because that was the only hope their children had to grow up with some idea of law and culture and decency. Kids around here don't need anyone that much."

"Kate, that was over a hundred years ago. In this country, anyway."

"I know. But that's what it would take to get me back. To mean that much to ... someone." She laughed to herself. "Dear God, if only the King of Siam was still advertising for someone to teach his children."

Kronin signaled his surrender by calling for the check. "There are still places in the world where you could be that useful," he observed, as the waitress toted up the bill. "Maybe you should look into the Peace Corps, or working for some missionary outfit."

Kate didn't reply, but she drifted away on the notion for a second. Maybe it was the only way to live now without constant grieving, to dedicate herself completely to others and accept the impossibility of ever finding happiness for herself. She imagined herself carrying enlightenment into some dark distant corner of the globe—a Peruvian jungle, a muddy Afghan village—a version of retiring gracefully from the world by entering a convent. There, she might have the love and admiration of desperately poor and ignorant children she couldn't possibly compare to her own, or resent for the wonderful lives they would grow to fulfill. Far away, cut off from the familiar, wouldn't it be easier to forget?

"Ready to go?"

Or would she only be more lonely and miserable?

"Kate—"

She looked across the table blankly, until she realized David had finished paying the check. Ready?

To end the lunch, anyway; not to become a nun or a missionary.

*   *   *

Returning from town, Kate recognized the massive SUV pulled up in the drive as the real estate broker's, evidently involved in a longer tour than usual. She almost drove on around the block, but today she rebelled against the obligation to stay out of the way. Life had already relegated her to a limbo of keeping busy just for the sake of avoiding discomfort. She parked her car at the front curb, and steeled herself to go in, even though the broker had practically said in so many words that Kate's presence could be a negative factor, since it brought unpleasant associations with the house into buyers' minds. The exchange had occurred after there had been two offers from among the first few people the realtor had shown through. In both cases, the amounts had been too far below the asking price for Kate to consider them at all, even as a basis for negotiation.

"I can't believe I'm asking too much," Kate had said. Using a couple of other recent sales in the development as benchmarks, she felt $345,000 was already set on the low side to invite a quick sale.

"It's a wonderful property," the broker explained, "but the history of a house can affect its marketability."

"This house is too new to have any history," Kate scoffed, her idea of the word formed by her occupation. The Windridge development was only four years old.

"I meant," the broker said, "the associations people make with it. . . ."

Kate got it then: there could be superstitious antipathy to living where a previous family had evaporated in catastrophe. "I've loved living in this house," she said in defiance. "My family loved it. So tell anyone who's interested it's worth what I'm asking, and I won't take a penny less." She thought a second and changed her mind. "No—it's worth *more* than I've been asking. Put the price up another thirty thousand."

The realtor had tried to talk her out of it—the brochures had already been printed, the higher price would slow the sale down, the economy was soft so she might even be pricing herself out of the market.

But Kate stuck to her guns. "Let's see what happens. I don't mind dealing with anyone who wants to be fair, but not people who'd take advantage of my situation. What happened to me had nothing to do with this house." She'd paused to look around at the walls. "I was very happy here."

As she entered now through the front door, the broker and her client were just descending the stairs to the entrance hall, having finished a tour of the second-floor rooms. June Ehrlich, the broker, was a petite, carefully coiffed blond woman who always wore tailored suits and spoke in a voice that was surprisingly deep and robust for her size. She was escorting a tall, thin woman with shaggy brown hair and an open friendly expression, whose clothes made no effort to impress—jeans, running shoes, and a faded black jogging pullover with the hood pushed back.

"Oh, Kate," the broker said. "I was hoping to be out of your way before you—"

"It's fine, June. I'll stay out of your way. Look around all you want."

"This is Patty Mosconi," June said. "Her family's about to multiply, and she's been looking for something with more bedrooms for the new children. . . ."

Patty put out her hand. Kate could tell at once from the way the other woman looked at her that she knew the whole story. Whether or not June thought knowing the "history" might hurt, Kate guessed it must provide a topic of discussion that was hard to avoid once buyers asked—as they did inevitably—the reasons for the sale. Shaking hands with the client, Kate gave a quick glance to her figure and saw no sign of the pregnancy, surprising since it sounded like a multiple birth was expected. *Would she want to bring new twins into this house?* "Looks like you've still got a good while before you'll need the nursery," Kate observed.

A look of bafflement flickered across Patty's face, then she laughed. "Oh, the new ones aren't coming *that* way," she said. "I'm divorced with two of my own, and getting remarried in April to a widower with three."

"Congratulations."

"I'll accept congratulations if I can get through my first year as a stepmother without a breakdown, and Stan and I can have an occasional night out on our own without worrying the kids will kill each other."

Kate smiled, and started to move off. She'd already marked the client down as an unlikely buyer, since there were only three bedrooms upstairs, and it sounded like she'd need four or five.

June stopped her. "If you have a minute, Kate, Patty has a couple of questions. You could answer them better than I. . . ."

"Sure."

"We went up into the attic," Patty said. "It's a very nice space. I was wondering if there's any reason you left it unfinished."

"We just didn't need more rooms," Kate said. "The developer offered a good saving if we took it this way."

"But it could be converted if we wanted?" Patty asked. "There's no zoning rule against it, or anything?"

"None. Matter of fact, it's built for easy expansion. The plumbing stacks go right up under the attic floor, and the roof is already framed to prepare for dormers. It'd be easy to put in two more baths, cut out windows, and make three more rooms. My husband and I planned to do it if . . . if we'd . . . ever . . ." She trailed off.

There was a heavy silence. The broker prodded her client. "You wanted to ask about the den."

"Right. I see the upholstery in there matches those floor-length curtains. It's a very nice fabric. I was wondering if you'd have any interest in selling those curtains and the furniture?"

Kate stared back without replying. The woman's inquiries indicated she was a serious buyer, a realization which sent Kate off into a sudden confrontation with the idea of being homeless, still not knowing where to go.

"I'm hopeless at decorating," the woman continued, "and I'll have my hands full getting the kids settled, so the less I have to do in that department, the better. Whatever you don't want to take with you, frankly, I'd like to talk about buying."

The more a sale seemed likely, the more anxious Kate became. Like a bubble forming in her mind, threatening to burst out in an hysterical announcement, she felt a mushrooming urge to tell the broker and her client it was all a mistake: she didn't want to sell her home, didn't want to part with anything in her life, wanted it all to stay exactly as it was . . . exactly as it had been *before*—

But she held it in, and managed to react agreeably until the broker— perhaps sensing that Kate might at any second say something to knock things off the rails—got her client out the door, leaving with a promise she'd be "in touch soon."

Barely five minutes later, while Kate was upstairs changing into jeans from the blouse and skirt she'd worn to the beauty parlor, the doorbell rang.

June Ehrlich was at the door. Her SUV was still in the drive, and Kate could see the client sitting in the front seat. "She wouldn't let me leave without making an offer," the broker said.

The fright hadn't waned, yet Kate had adjusted to accepting the move as inevitable. "Don't bother saying a thing, though," she warned, "if it's another of those insulting—"

"No, I'd already told her the *new* asking price. She'll pay it— subject to confirming it with her . . . what should I call him? Fiancé? But she told me he wants her to make these decisions, and she'll make the offer official with a binder by tomorrow morning. Oh, furniture and fittings aren't included, but subject to good faith negotiations. Is all that okay with you?"

Kate nodded dumbly, paralyzed by an odd mix of relief and regret.

"Keep your fingers crossed," the broker said. "Talk to you in the morning." She started away from the door.

"The history," Kate called after her, emerging from her daze. "The history didn't bother her . . . ?"

"Quite the contrary," the broker answered exuberantly. "Actually thinks it's a plus—you know, that lightning couldn't strike twice. . . ." She waved, dashed to her car, and drove off.

For a long time afterward, Kate ambled through the rooms, making a haphazard inventory of things she could happily dispose of, and those she could never bear to part with. At last, she went and sat in the large rear yard to contemplate her home seen whole, from the outside. In a corner, farthest from the house, a big tree had been felled by the developer not long before she and Jim had first been shown the still uncompleted house. The stump was still there, and the agent had assured her it was due to be pulled, but Kate had asked for it to be left. The irregular shape of the five-foot diameter, and the bumpy gnarled roots pleased her, and she thought the core could be chiseled out to make an interesting garden seat. She'd never gotten around to doing it. Still, it made a nice stool of sorts, and she sat there, looking at the house and thinking of all that had been, and might have been, and never would be.

Yes, time to let it go.

Finally, she went back into the kitchen. Slightly chilled from sitting in the yard, she made herself a pot of tea. While it brewed, her glance fell on the whale tooth perched on the kitchen windowsill. Which category did that belong in: something to keep or something to sell? It didn't really feel like a possession, something she owned. She hadn't actually accepted it from Gabriel; had never sent back any acknowledgment that it had been received and appreciated.

But her failure to do so struck her now as selfish and unkind. If she was going to keep it, she owed him a note of thanks. And looking at it, she decided it was definitely in the category of things she would always want to keep. Aside from being a remarkable piece of folk art, it was a gift made out of his decent impulse to right the wrong he'd done to her.

But how to thank him? She had no address to write to. Nor did he have a phone where he lived or worked.

Kate went to get the receipt Eddie had written for her after her recent stay, and called the number for the Captain Markham House. The phone rang five or six times, and Kate was about to give up, when Eddie answered, plainly having picked up on the run. "Hi," she panted. "I'm here."

"Eddie, it's Kate Weyland. . . ."

"Kate! Let me catch my breath. I was in the basement doing laundry—"

"Sure. I'll do the talking for a minute." But when it came to asking what she wanted, Kate felt a twinge of chagrin. "The reason I'm calling . . . well, I was thinking I might . . . that I'd like to write to Gabriel, but I don't have an address. Would you be able to give me one, at least a box number or something?"

"Gee," Eddie took in another couple of deep breaths. "I'm afraid not. But there's a little post office down at Madaket. If you just send it there, it would probably find its way to him."

"I was wishing I had something more specific," Kate said. Thinking back, she realized she'd never seen recent mail lying around his shack. Even if it went to a post office, Gabriel was the sort of man who could ignore his mail for weeks at a time, might never even stop at the post office. "Maybe I shouldn't worry," she went on, "but the way we left things, he might never write back to me. In which case, I'd never know if he got my letter or not. And . . . I would like to be sure."

"Tell you what," Eddie said. "Send it here. I'll drive it out to his place, and put it through the door."

"Seems you're always delivering messages for me," Kate said gratefully.

"Happy to oblige." She paused momentarily. "As long as it's what you want. Tell me if it's none of my business . . . but I got the impression it didn't work out with Gabriel, and maybe it's best to leave things as they are."

Kate knew the advice was well meant, and tried to sound appreciative. "Maybe. I'll think about it." But then she added quickly, "Eddie, whatever you think of Gabriel, and my relationship with him, you do promise to—"

"Kate, the only reason I put my two cents in is because I care about you. But I'd never interfere with doing what you want. You can trust me."

"I do, Eddie, sorry if it sounded otherwise. But to be honest, where Gabriel's concerned, there are times I don't quite trust myself."

They stayed on the phone awhile, chatting as friends. Eddie talked about the myriad culinary experiments that amused Danny on the long winter afternoons, and her own projects for improving the guest rooms. Kate mentioned the likely sale of her house, and admitted to her uncertainty about where she would go next.

"Well, anytime you just need a place to get away, you're more than welcome here," Eddie said. "Clean your own room, you'll always get a special rate." She concluded with a pledge to give Kate a call after the letter had been received and delivered to Gabriel's place.

As soon as she was off the phone, Kate started for the den, intent on sitting at the desk at once to set down her thoughts for Gabriel. But she was halfway there when she turned and went back to the kitchen to get the whale tooth and bring it with her. If she was to write, she needed to have it right there in front of her, the reminder of all the history that had created him—all the way back to the sinking of Captain Joshua Farr's whaling ship.

34

Dear Gabriel,

I hope you'll forgive me for taking so long to write. I should have written to thank you the day I received your gift, for which I am deeply grateful. It's here in front of me at this moment; I look at it often, and each time I realize it is the most amazing thing I will ever own. The scene carved so beautifully into the tooth of a whale helps me to understand what brave and unusual men they were who once went to sea from Nantucket. You can be proud to be the descendant of such a man.

I want to thank you, too, for returning the money.

But the thing I want most to say with this letter is that I'm no longer sorry or angry about anything that happened between us. I feel very differently about the things you finally told me than I did when I left. I understand that you wanted to help me, and you only did what I asked you to do. I believe, too, that it was truly because you cared for me that you may have deceived me, and for the same reason that you finally told me you had done so.

Yet I wonder at times, Gabriel, if you told me the whole truth? Or do you even know it yourself? Just as I know you did not mean to hurt me, I believe you have never harmed anyone else.

I wish when I'd had the chance I had spent more time listening and trying to understand these mysteries along with you.

Someday, maybe, there will be another chance to find out,
perhaps even with you, what is in the stars.

Your friend,
Katharine Weyland

By the time she finished the handwritten letter, it was evening, and the floor around the desk in the den was littered with crumpled pieces of the engraved personal stationery she'd used—not to put on airs for Gabriel, but to treat him as no less important than any other friend. Each time she'd started the letter, she imagined it would be only a few lines, and not so hard to write. Then she'd decide at the midpoint that, in one way or another, the tone was wrong and she would have to start over. She'd debated longest over whether to make any mention of being "deceived" by him, but decided it was sufficiently softened by adding the words "may have"—which accurately conveyed her suspicion that, in fact, it could have been his final confession that was the deception. And, at the end, she wondered if it was unfairly provocative to speak of being with him again at any time, for any reason. Yet she had been willingly intimate with him, and now she wanted him to know she retained kindly feelings: why wouldn't she leave the door open to seeing him again someday?

So that was how she left the letter finally, still not quite satisfied, but resigned to the probability she could never find exactly the right tone to take with Gabriel. How should she talk to him, this stranger— who had been her lover? She sealed the letter in an envelope, wrote "Mr. G. Farr" on the outside, and folded the smaller envelope inside a larger one, along with a piece of notepaper on which she jotted "Dear Eddie, Thanks again, Kate." Then she addressed the second envelope to Eddie at the Captain Markham House.

As she returned from a walk to the corner mailbox, the phone was ringing. She answered in the kitchen. It was Sarah.

In all their conversations since the possibility of a settlement had been mentioned, her mother always came around to asking if Kate had any further feelings about the lawsuit. No doubt it would be raised before this call was over, and even the prospect of having to talk about it made Kate anxious. The idea of fixing a monetary value to her loss and suffering remained abhorrent.

To head off the topic, as soon as the preliminary chat petered out, Kate said, "I've sold the house."

Sarah approved immediately. A quick sale was lucky, the terms sounded excellent, and it was the right thing to do.

Still, Kate fretted. "I just hope it wasn't a mistake," she said.

"You have doubts?"

"I still haven't decided where I'll go. . . ."

"You can set the closing to give yourself time to think about it," Sarah said. It didn't have to be said that her own preference would be for her daughter to move to the city. "I hope you realize, Kate, that even if you get the full asking price, you'll need more to live on if you move here. There's still your mortgage to pay off, and rents in the city are fairly high, and as for buying—"

"I know, Mother. New York isn't the right place for me."

"I wasn't saying that, darling. I just wanted to urge you to—"

"Keep pressing the lawsuit," Kate jumped in, "until I get a few million."

There was a brief silence before Sarah said, "Katie, I don't want us to argue about that anymore. I've been thinking you could look at the whole issue more clearly if you had another lawyer."

"Oh, Mom, don't get all huffy. You've done a great job. If I'm having trouble with this, it's not because of any problem between you and me."

"I know, Katie. But I've realized I'm too emotionally involved with this case to handle it effectively. I've consulted an attorney Bert recommended, a man named James Benedict. He's a specialist in civil negligence actions, and he's won some huge judgments for his clients. He's reviewed our papers, and he's willing to handle your case on contingency." Sarah paused for Kate's reaction. When the pause went unfilled, she added, "There are just a few more papers you'd have to sign."

Kate mulled it for a second. "Mom, why are you picking this moment to resign? What's been happening in your negotiations with the town?"

"We're stuck at two hundred and ten thousand. It's ridiculously far from a fair settlement—certainly far from enough to make any difference for you."

"Maybe." Kate said. "But could we hold off on this other lawyer for a few more days?"

"That's what I've been doing for weeks—holding off."

"You said it wouldn't hurt."

"It could hurt if we lose a chance to have Benedict on our side. He's a top—"

Kate cut her off. "That's enough now," she said firmly. "Let me sleep on it."

There was another silence. Kate guessed her mother was considering whether or not to make one last appeal to being practical. Before she could, Kate said a quick, " 'Night, Mom, talk to you tomorrow," and hung up.

But she was practical enough on her own to round up every scrap of financial data she had around the house that evening and go through it, keeping track this time with pencil and paper and adding in the expected proceeds from the house sale. After deducting the mortgage, and other outstanding debts—there were still funeral expenses to be settled, and the hospital was dunning her for a gigantic bill relating to Chloe's emergency operation—the amount she had left was a bit over two hundred thousand. Double that if she figured in a settlement at the current level. A fair-size nest egg—if you also had a salary coming in. But how far would it stretch if she couldn't pull herself together to work?

She went to bed worrying. Maybe she was wrong to sell the house. Staying close to the memories, learning to live with them, might be more therapeutic than moving away. And where should she go? Was there any place, any situation, in which she could hope to be happy again?

The worries went around and around in her brain until she worried herself down into a strange sleep, a sense of spinning that continued as she dozed off. Then she was standing on a platform that turned and turned, scenes and faces from her recent life going by quickly. Then, abruptly, the faces of the twins were right in front of her, not passing by, but going up and down in a regular cycle, until she saw they were on a carousel, riding the horses up and down, both of them laughing, as she stood in front of them. After the misery of losing them—and the awareness of that misery which prevailed somehow in the dream—the joy of being on this carousel, seeing the children so happy, so seemingly real and alive, produced a feeling of calm and relief nearly miraculous in the way it suffused every part of her being. She knew in some corner of her mind it was a dream, too good to last, yet Kate felt that some of this calm and relief would survive beyond the dream's end. As she smiled back at the children to convey this feeling, the carousel horses suddenly revealed wings and, bearing the children on their backs, flew up and away into a golden light.

You're not wrong.

It wasn't a voice she heard this time, no words audible to the ear, but something said directly to her senses, perceived in that lower stratum of the mind where the dream transpired. It was Jim communicating to her, though, that much she knew. But the oddest thing of all was that she wasn't left wondering what he meant. It didn't seem to matter. Whatever she thought or believed, he was telling her, she could trust it. She came awake gliding on that smooth wave of calm assurance.

They come in dreams sometimes.

She could still see the faces of the children, joyous, riding the carousel. She still had that voiceless message relaxing her like a soothing melody. But awake, she had one brief moment of wondering what it meant, exactly. What wasn't she wrong about?

Then, just as quickly, she had the answer. Lying in the darkness, she smiled.

Let me sleep on it. What else was she trying to decide? Kate raised herself on her elbow and glanced at the numbers on the digital clock. Only a few minutes past midnight. She considered calling Sarah right now to tell her, then realized it wasn't wise. Probably she shouldn't tell her either that she'd been given the answer in a dream; just let her think the decision was the result of careful consideration. Of sleeping on it.

Kate lay back and almost instantly dozed off. No dreams this time, a perfect rest.

"Are you perfectly sure?"

Her mother must have asked the same question five times by now, with only small revisions. Are you completely certain? Absolutely . . . ? Of course, first there had been all the questioning about how and why Kate had made her decision. Kate had called early, catching Sarah before she had left for the office.

"Well, if that's what you want, darling. It's certainly a . . . a charming idea. But at least wait until after you've talked to Mr. Benedict. I'll make an appointment with him this morning. You'll certainly do well enough if you continue the suit that you could make this a part of the terms."

"Forget that, Mother. This is all I need to feel satisfied. Nothing else, not a thing." She almost added that she felt it was all Jim and the children would want, but she was afraid it might be a tip-off to the part of her decision that wasn't rational.

At long last, Sarah agreed she would take up Kate's wishes herself with the Fairhaven town counsel and picked up a pencil to write down the terms specifically. The money the town had offered could be allotted in entirety to the building of a playground on any of the town's public land, the facility to be finished within the next year. A plaque should commemorate the playground as a memorial to the twins, and mention the date of their death. If possible within the budget—or with the addition of money up to a total of $250,000—a carousel was to be included with the playground facilities, children under seven to ride free. On those terms, Kate would be willing to settle immediately, with nothing for herself, and all the funds to be used for the benefit of this improvement to the town.

"Now," Sarah said, when she had finished jotting the terms on paper, and read them back once for Kate's approval, "you're a hundred percent—"

"Mom, don't ask me again. This works for me." But then came an afterthought. "Just one more thing, though. The place should be called 'Tom and Chloe's Park.' "

She thought the children would like that, too—that it would even encourage their spirits to come and ride the carousel when other children were dreaming.

35

By the weekend, she had already begun the first phases of packing, putting favorite books in cartons, taking pictures off the walls to wrap in cardboard and newspaper. She was in the middle of this when the doorbell rang shortly before noon on Sunday. At the sound, she remembered Paul was expected for brunch. He'd called two days ago to get directions to her house, and she'd shopped yesterday for bagels and smoked salmon. But this morning it was forgotten.

Kate rose from the floor of the den, and brushed book dust from her jeans and T-shirt. On the way across the entrance hall, she caught herself in a mirror and saw her hair was too hopelessly flyaway to even bother attempting a quick repair. Well, she mused as she proceeded to the front door, wasn't it Freud who'd theorized there were no accidents? This must be one more subconscious effort to persuade this man he was wasting his time. Or perhaps she'd shut him out of her thoughts because she didn't really want to hear what he had to tell her about Gabriel.

He stood on her doorstep, dressed quite conspicuously for a date. Heather tweed sport jacket over a black cashmere turtleneck, and gray flannels barely creased from a couple of hours behind the wheel of the silver Mercedes coupe she could see parked in front of the house.

Observing her dishabille, he said, "Oh—am I too early?"

"Not at all," she confessed as she ushered him inside. "Truth is, it completely slipped my mind."

"Well, you did warn me I shouldn't expect to be in your thoughts very much."

"Please, Paul, don't take it personally. My mind's pretty slippery territory in general these days." She guided him from the entrance hall into the kitchen. "Let me get coffee started and lay the table. Then I'll duck away for a minute and try to make myself look less like a stevedore."

He surveyed his surroundings and what he could see through the doorways as she crisscrossed the kitchen. "Your home is lovely," he said.

"Not for much longer," she remarked. "My home—that is. I've sold it."

"Where will you be going?"

"Believe it or not, I haven't the faintest idea."

He looked at her with concern. "But you have . . . possibilities . . . ?"

"Nothing but."

"Well, I suppose you have time to decide," he said.

Kate realized he was measuring the dimensions of her problem to determine if her apathy—along with today's forgetfulness—might be symptomatic. "Don't worry, Paul, I won't wind up on the street."

"But don't you think you should have a plan?"

She paused as she finished measuring out the coffee. "I should, I suppose. But since September, plans are something it's hard for me to believe in." She glanced at him and smiled. "Or maybe I'm just waiting for a sign."

He eyed her curiously and was plainly on the verge of another question, but she quickly switched on the coffeemaker, told him to make himself at home, and excused herself to change.

Upstairs, as she did some quick work on her hair and face and put on a peach silk blouse over charcoal slacks, she reflected privately on the remark she'd fled from explaining to him. Only after it was said did Kate realize its truth: she was waiting as if for guidance from the spirits. Though why not? Hadn't a dream told her what to do in the very practical matter of the lawsuit? Why shouldn't she expect a sign to steer her along other paths?

She went downstairs, and laid out the food and place settings in the breakfast nook while they exchanged inconsequential chat on what had kept them busy since they'd seen each other on Nantucket. He declined scrambled eggs, so they were soon seated.

As Kate passed the food and poured coffee for him, he said, as if casually, "Too bad you had to miss the Thornes' party. It was a lovely way to bring in the new year. Eddie said she'd invited you. . . ."

Since Eddie had also invited Gabriel, Kate guessed mentioning the party was Paul's polite way of indicating he'd learned that she had actually spent a few days living with him. "I left the day before," she said. "I should have let Eddie know, I suppose. But it was . . . a spur-of-the-moment decision."

Paul poured cream in his coffee. "This man you asked me about, he didn't hurt you, did he? I mean, I hope that's not why you ran off so—"

"I didn't have to run, Paul."

"Forgive me for bringing it up, but I was concerned. I couldn't forget that you'd asked if I'd heard anything about this man being 'dangerous.' "

Was this all a prelude to confirming that Gabriel was indeed to be feared? Kate wondered. She didn't want to be the first to cast suspicions, however. "There was no trouble, Paul. I was never in any danger."

"Good."

To Kate's relief, that seemed to conclude his "investigation." Paul occupied himself for a minute putting cream cheese and salmon on half a bagel, remarking after a bite how good it was. "If you don't mind my asking," he said then, "was he able to help you at all with . . . the thing you went to see him about?"

Kate smiled faintly. In his reluctance to define it clearly, she heard an echo of her own difficulty in speaking plainly of something so strange and unreal. "No," she said. "No communications with the dead were arranged."

"But you gave him money—"

"No," she interrupted, "Mr. Farr took nothing from me."

Paul examined her curiously. "I thought you mentioned paying him."

Kate was growing irritated with this probing, but she tried to answer reasonably. "At my request, he did attempt to make contact with my husband and my children, but he couldn't, so he didn't feel it was fair to keep the money. It's over and done, Paul. So can we talk about something else now?"

He put the bagel on his plate. "I'm sorry if this subject is distressing to you, Kate." He wiped his hands with a napkin, pushed his plate away, and fixed her with an earnest gaze. "But ever since you asked me about it, I've been more aware of all this stuff about an afterlife, contacts from the beyond. I know I wasn't very sympathetic when we talked about it before. I wanted to see you today to tell you about something I've learned since."

Kate's attention sharpened. She perceived that this was truly something he'd been anxious to get off his chest.

"I've always dismissed all this psychic stuff as malarkey," he continued. "I'm a scientist—and there's simply no way to fit a belief in life after death into a scientific understanding of the way the world works. But sometimes you come across things that can't be so easily . . ." He was absent a second, using another sip from his coffee to ponder the collision between science and faith. "A good friend of mine recently came back after a trip to Vietnam. He's a research biologist, somewhat older than I am, but we've worked together for many years. As close as we are, there was an important part of his life I never knew about until I asked the reason for his trip. He told me he had a younger brother who'd been drafted into the army thirty years ago to fight in Vietnam. A few months into his tour of duty, the brother was declared missing in action and he's remained one of the thousand-odd Americans listed as MIAs from that war." Paul looked down and his expression grew even more somber. "On the Vietnamese side, the numbers are much worse. Some three hundred thousand soldiers who fought against us are still missing—and not long ago my friend learned that one method relatives of those missing soldiers have used to locate them is to consult psychics." He turned to Kate again. "The method has reportedly been so successful, the Vietnamese government actually sponsors a program in which psychics visit relatives of the missing in their homes so they can speak to their dead in hopes of learning where to find their remains."

Kate had set her own cup aside and was concentrating on Paul, fascinated. "You mean the dead reveal where they can be found?"

Paul nodded. "According to my friend, the government claims seventy percent of those who use these services to find their dead have been satisfied. There's no way to certify the claim, but my friend was intrigued enough to try the same method for locating his brother's remains."

"What happened?" Kate asked impatiently.

"He went to Hanoi and met with one of the government psychics, a woman whose regular job is working as a hotel accountant. She told him—well, his brother told him, speaking through her—that he was buried in a cemetery outside a certain village in the hills along what was once the border between North and South Vietnam. My friend was directed to go to a particular unmarked grave located among all the others. When he returned here two weeks ago, he brought with him the bones he found there. He's convinced they're his brother's and he's reburied them here. He says it has brought him some long-awaited peace."

"You said the grave was unmarked," Kate said. "How can he be sure they're not just anybody's bones?"

"He's satisfied, that's all I know. And remember, he's a scientist like myself."

"So he did DNA tests. . . ."

"No, he didn't feel the need for that."

"Did he find dogtags? Identifying marks? A fracture line on a bone where the brother broke his arm falling off a swing when he was a kid?"

"I asked the same things. He didn't look for that kind of proof."

Kate gave a baffled shake of her head. "Paul, I don't see what would change your scientific viewpoint. It sounds quite possible the psychic simply sent your friend to a cemetery where there were a load of unmarked graves and picked one at random."

"Except for the test that was done at the grave."

"Test . . . ?"

"A Vietnamese thing. They believe that if you're standing over the grave of a true ancestor or blood relative, then you should be able to put a chopstick upright in the earth, and balance a fresh egg on the tip."

Kate regarded him with disbelief.

"And my friend was able to do it," Paul said.

For another very long moment Kate gazed back at him, this logical man of science, then a smile crept over her face. And when he met her smile with a puzzled smile of his own, she couldn't help breaking into laughter.

He went on staring back at her, happily confounded. "But that *is* what he told me. I'm not putting you on, Kate. It was all he needed— he *swore* the egg balanced on the end of a chopstick. Now, you try to do that—"

"I don't have to," she said, her laughter only beginning to subside. "I'm sure I couldn't do it in a million years."

"Then . . . what's so funny?"

"Gosh, I don't know exactly. People. Life. Death. Everything. Most of all. I guess, it's just such a great big load off my mind to know everyone else, no matter where they are in the world, is as mixed up about this as I am. They believe what they want to believe, and avoid the things that prove otherwise. From today, I think, from this minute, I expect I'm going to start feeling a whole lot less confused. And I have you to thank!" She threw her hands across the table and grasped his. "You and your friend and your scientific minds!"

At last, he laughed, too.

For the rest of their time together, they talked easily about books they'd enjoyed, travels they'd taken, other favorite pastimes. But there was no more talk about Gabriel or life after death.

At last, Paul said he needed to be in New York this evening for a preliminary gathering of conference attendees, and she saw him to the door.

"I'd like to see you again soon," he said, before going out.

"I can't promise anything, Paul. I don't even know where I'll be."

He smiled ruefully, acknowledging her polite disinterest. "Well," he said, "I hope you get that sign you're waiting for. When you do, maybe you'll let me know where I can find you."

As she watched him go down the path to his car, Kate asked herself if she was making a mistake not to give such a good man much more encouragement. If she ever hoped to re-create a new version of the existence that was lying in ruins, there might be no one better than Paul Levinger with whom to build it.

But for the first time, too, she realized that what she wanted was not simply to fashion a mere reproduction of what had once existed and had vanished. If she couldn't have the original, she knew now, she would never settle for a copy.

36

For several days, she felt a level of well-being that hadn't been present since that moment at the high school when, even before knowing exactly what it was, she realized something catastrophic had happened. With few doubts or second-guessing, she was able to deal with important matters that needed to be settled. The details pertaining to the sale of the house were negotiated and the documents prepared. Obeying Kate's firm instructions, her mother obtained an agreement from the town to build the playground and dedicate it to the twins. (The carousel wasn't promised—the expense of that alone might be more than the agreed settlement—but the town agreed to sponsor a fundraising drive to raise the extra money required.) Kate knew it wasn't truly a practical solution, but she was more than satisfied. To have waged a lawsuit for the next few years, whatever money might come out of it, would have only sustained her grief and anger. This brought closure.

You're not wrong.

It was as if it applied to everything. Not wrong, even, to go on with her life—or believe that there was some ineffable guidance available to help her: a dream, a whisper, a glimpse of the beyond, that could shine a bit of light into a dark corner when she needed it. Her confidence extended even to believing that, when necessary, she would decide the right destination to head for after leaving the house. Or at least she would know the absence of a destination was a freedom she needed to experience.

Then on Thursday morning, there was a phone call from Eddie. "Your letter came yesterday," she told Kate. "I drove out to leave it at Gabriel's place a little while ago. I thought you'd want to know right away, Kate: he's gone."

"Gone?"

"The door is padlocked, and there are plywood panels across those big windows on the ocean side. And you know that sailboat he keeps moored below his place? The mooring's empty."

Empty. The word resonated within, describing what she felt. "When did he go?"

"I have no idea."

"Does anyone know where he went? Did you check the post office to see if—"

"Yes, I found out he does have a P.O. box, and I left your letter there. But he hasn't been in for a week or two. There's a bunch of other mail waiting for him."

"He left no forwarding address . . . ?" Kate asked, though she could guess even before Eddie answered.

"Nothing."

The regret that knifed through her for not writing sooner seemed on the edge of becoming an actual stabbing pain through her middle. If he'd only heard from her, he might have stayed. As long as she could count on finding him there, Kate realized now, one idea for the future would have been to return—if for no more than a visit.

"But he's done this before," Eddie was saying. "I mentioned that, didn't I? He comes and goes. He'll be back eventually."

Eventually. Or maybe this time, Kate thought, he'd feel differently about coming back. Maybe he'd stay away on this voyage for years, as his ancestors had. Maybe he had gone off to hunt a whale with one of those golden harpoons he made for no reason he understood.

"Sorry," Eddie said, after Kate had remained silent. "But he's bound to come back. Such a beautiful spot he's got out there. Do you think he'd just abandon it?"

The question hung in the air without an answer. It wasn't just the place he might want to leave behind, Kate reflected, but his shame, his failure, his rejection, the whole history. It was in that place that he had loved her. Told her he'd never felt that way about anyone else; there was no other person he'd ever cared enough about to take the risk he had with her—the risk of telling the truth. The perils of sailing away alone on an ocean could seem small by comparison.

"I should have told him sooner," she lamented. Though, as she heard her own words, Kate wasn't sure exactly what she meant. Told him what? That she was grateful, that she wasn't angry? Would that have been enough?

Or could she have told him what she knew he hungered to hear? She had thought at the time it wasn't true . . . but she was less sure now, confused by the emptiness she felt inside.

"He's not gone forever," Eddie repeated once more. "He's a Nantucket man, the sailing's in his blood. But this is his home."

Kate gazed around her at the walls of a house she was preparing to abandon herself. No, she thought, home was something more than a place you inhabited. Home was the place where your heart lived.

"It just knocked the stuffing out of me," Kate said, shaking her head as she gazed off at nothing.

Meg Parker looked across the glass-topped table in the tree-filled solarium at the back of her house and nodded sympathetically, encouraging Kate to go on pouring out her feelings.

"I can't make sense of it, " Kate said. "I never realized it was so damn important to me."

"It?" Meg questioned gently.

Kate gave her a wan smile. "Him, maybe. Crazy, isn't it?"

"Unlikely, unexpected, unusual," Meg allowed. "But not so crazy."

By now Meg knew everything. Once Kate had decided she needed to seek the perspective of her best friend, she had held nothing back. In the two hours they'd been together, Kate had recounted what she knew of Gabriel's past, described his quirks, what it was like to spend time with him, confessed to the humiliation she felt when he'd admitted his deception. She had even revealed—with more candor than ever in the past when they talked about sex with their husbands—how passionate and satisfying the physical relationship with Gabriel had been.

"But I always knew it had no future," Kate said. "Right from the start, there was never any doubt about that. So why do I feel I've lost so much?"

"What made you so sure there was no future?"

"Meg, have you been listening? Me . . . with a man like that?"

"From everything you've told me, hon', I'd have to agree he's not the sort of man your mother ever wanted you to bring home. Nor one you'd have picked for yourself, going strictly by the book. Jim was the guy who filled the bill perfectly on those counts. But, Katie . . . somebody threw the book away when it comes to figuring out what's best for you now. The future you thought you could count on disappeared overnight, so maybe the future that's going to take its place won't have a thing in common with the one you lost."

Meg paused, searching for any hint her candor was unwelcome. When it met with no resistance, she went on. "I read a piece in the *New York Times* a year or two ago by a fairly successful writer, a woman about your age. I forget her name, but the article told how, after doing well in her career, she'd gone through a couple of bad marriages and moved to somewhere quiet like Montana or Wyoming. Out there, she'd met a cowboy and fallen in love with him. A real cowboy, I'm talking about, a guy who just rides around on a horse taking care of cattle. They were living together, and she admitted they didn't have a whole lot in common. They didn't always have a lot to talk about, and that most of her friends couldn't figure it out. Yet she said it worked because of what was good. No doubt, that included the sex. That wasn't everything, though. She seemed to like having someone who was plain and strong and reliable and accepted himself—liked it as much, anyway, as she'd once liked being around clever people who could trade repartee and talk national politics at dinner parties. She'd come to respect his life as being as worthwhile as hers. Their differences didn't keep her from doing what she liked: reading, writing, going off now and then to see the dinner-party crowd. Your situation with this Gabriel guy sounds comparable."

"Not exactly. This writer-woman fell in love with her cowboy. I haven't said anything about being in love."

"No," Meg acknowledged, "you haven't." But she gave it a wry twist that intimated the omission was all the more reason to suspect the opposite.

Kate reared back wide-eyed. "C'mon!" she protested. "I should know how I feel!"

"Unless you're afraid to feel it."

"Afraid? Why should I—"

"Because it's too soon. Because you think it's . . . disloyal—that caring for another man means you didn't love Jim enough."

Kate dropped her gaze. Her shame wasn't just in the truth of those feelings, but in remembering that her "disloyalty" had gone so far as to give her body to another man.

"Katie," Meg said quietly. "What do you think Jim would tell you if he could? Lock up your heart? Keep saving yourself for what you can no longer have? Or to take whatever joy and adventure and relief from loneliness you can find. . . ."

"I don't know what he'd say, damn it!" Kate burst out. "God, how I wish I did! That's why I wanted so much to believe I could hear it straight from him!"

"I know, hon. But, if you didn't, it's okay now to decide for yourself. Even the marriage vows tell you that. Remember? Where it says ' 'til death us do part.' "

Kate looked away silently. Whatever the vows said, she didn't feel parted from Jim. She still felt he could speak to her . . . had been. Even without Gabriel. Or was that only a form of denial?

Yet the messages she'd been getting did hint at the kind of permission Meg was advising her to accept. And if these messages were only imagined? Then even so, in some way she was trying to give permission to herself.

Gabriel . . . yes, she did long to see him again. Thinking back now to those few days she'd spent with him, it was clear they marked the beginning of her ascent out of the depths of despair. In retrospect, she recognized that the solidity of his presence, the comfort of his desire for her, had meant as much as any belief in him as a conduit to her dead. She still appreciated those things—in spite of his confession to her. In fact, having her perspective altered to see him as more fallible and human and less phenomenal could have made him more accessible to her emotions.

"Too bad he went away," she said at last. "If he'd stayed around, I might have been able to figure out what I feel."

"And if he comes back . . . ?" Meg prodded.

"He won't. I'm pretty sure."

"As sure as believing you had no future?"

Kate replied with a skeptical glance and stirred in her chair, preparing to go. She wanted to be alone now to think things through, not badgered with all this optimism, however well meant.

"I've got an idea," Meg said quickly. "Harry and I don't open the summer place 'til Memorial Day. It's winterized, though; there are electric heaters if the nights get chilly. So maybe you'd like to go up there and spend a few weeks."

Kate looked at her askance. "You're suggesting I should go and wait for him to come back like one of those Nantucket whaling wives from olden days—stand on the widow's walk and keep looking out to sea?"

"I just thought it would give you more of a chance to see what it's like in the quiet season, get to know it better. So then if—" Meg had been rolling along, but broke off suddenly and simply shrugged.

Kate got it: if Gabriel came back, she would already know it was a place she could make a life.

And if he never came . . . ?

An island might still be a good place for her. She imagined herself enjoying the solitude and quiet—living, indeed, as Gabriel had, alone, simply. Certainly, she wanted a change from Fairhaven, a reprieve from being pigeonholed by those around her as a tragic figure. She had toyed at times with the idea of trying to write history, a biography of one of the historical figures that intrigued her. This could be a chance to get started. The Atheneum would be a good resource, a nice place to do research. Come to think of it, Nantucket—so much less appealing and less inhabited in winter, the school months—came closest to being the sort of place where she felt her teaching skills might be especially valued.

And if Gabriel *did* return . . . ?

Meg was looking at her with bright expectancy, pleased with the opportunity she was providing. But the uncertainties and fears Kate felt about any further involvement with Gabriel still outweighed all her visions of a tranquil, productive existence. An island was not the place you wanted to be isolated with any situation—or any person— with whom you weren't completely comfortable.

"It's a very generous offer, Meg. I appreciate it. But . . . I don't think so. . . ."

"At least think about it, sweetie, don't rule it out. You did say the island appealed to you, and you don't seem to have any better idea of where to go next."

Kate yielded a nod and, to escape her friend's persistence, said that she'd already left her packing for too long and headed for the door.

*   *   *

But the news of Gabriel's disappearance continued to affect her. She made no change in her closing date and went on preparing to move, yet the comfortable level of confidence that existed before had suddenly fled. Now again she questioned every decision, uncertain of whether she knew—or ever would know again—her own mind. She felt an even more urgent need for a sign, an omen, to tell her what was right, and often found herself in the middle of some task subsiding into a moment of stillness, listening—for what she wasn't sure. That soundless voice in her mind? Or merely the memory of some particular reassuring words that had once been said within these walls. Each night, she went to bed, hoping a fresh dream might point the way. One evening, she stood in front of the mirror on her dresser for nearly an hour, consciously trying without success to recreate that moment when she'd had the fleeting sense that Jim was there with her, resurrected and reassuring.

The absence of any affirmation for the course she was taking became so troubling that several times she went to the phone, on the brink of telephoning the real estate agent or her lawyer to request a postponement of the move, or even a cancellation of the sale. She was only deterred each time by knowing it would be a step backward, and if she took it, she might continue along that trajectory to total defeat.

A temptation began to grow in her to revisit a medium, to ask the questions for which she was awaiting answers. It was strange, but in the wake of the initial cynicism resulting from Gabriel's deception, Kate found herself still receptive to the idea that contact with her spirits was possible. After all, it was in a dream that they had told her how to resolve the lawsuit. Why shouldn't she rely on those who loved her most to point her toward other sources of peace?

But what stayed with her, too, were all the warnings Gabriel had spouted against the charlatans. She realized his "advice" might have arisen from guilt at his own pretense, a roundabout way of confessing. But she was still nagged by an intuition that there could be more to his involvement with spiritualism than he had admitted, more even than he understood himself. A conviction grew within her that the confession he had made of deceiving her had been deliberately intended to send her away, nobly contrived only after she had revealed her belief that she didn't belong with him—and her own lack of willpower.

Though, even in that her confidence failed. She might once again be letting the yearnings of her heart overrule the simple truth. And what exactly were those yearnings? Did giving Gabriel the benefit of the doubt spring from the desire to be with *him*—or to be with the ones who might come through him?

Mired in all this uncertainty, yet still pushing herself to fulfill whatever fragments of constructive planning existed, Kate was on a trip to the hardware store one afternoon to buy twine and other packing materials when she noticed she wasn't far from the hospital. The large modern building could be seen beyond the low-rise shops that lined the downtown streets, and the sight of it suddenly brought all the awful memories swimming vividly into her mind. Hearing the news from that doctor. Chloe's lifeless body stretched out on the bed. The nurse accosting her in the hallway—

I saw her rise.

What had happened to that nurse? Kate wondered. Had the hospital reinstated her, or had she been punished for the professional sin of offering her own brand of analgesic? Or had she seen another vision, and found it impossible to maintain silence?

Five minutes later, Kate was at the nursing station on the floor of operating rooms, making the inquiry.

"Yes, Nurse Morrissey is on duty today," said the floor supervisor, a large woman with a cold officious manner, whom Kate couldn't recall seeing before. "She's currently assisting in a procedure, though. You wouldn't be able to talk to her."

"I don't mind waiting 'til she's done."

Glad as Kate was to learn that Anne Morrissey hadn't been deprived of her job, once the question was answered, she realized she'd come because there was something much more important she needed to hear from her.

The supervisor was running her gaze over a chart in front of her. "Nurse Morrissey is assisting Dr. Shaheen. He's in the OR doing an emergency appendectomy, I think. That might keep her another hour. . . ."

"I'll wait. But would you catch the nurse when she's done and tell her I'm in the cafeteria?"

It pleased Kate that the supervisor asked her name to include in the message; nice not to be a celebrity anymore, famous simply for a tragedy.

*   *   *

In the cafeteria, Kate bought a small salad and took a table within view of the entrance. Anne Morrissey had been the instigator of her quest, provided the first vivid glimpse into the possibility of life enduring into eternity. Kate hoped that talking to the nurse would bring things full circle, allowing her to feel the effort to make contact could be ended without any lingering guilt that she was abandoning her spirits.

The nurse arrived in less than an hour, still in her OR greens, minus the sterile skullcap and shoe coverings. Her aspect today struck Kate as entirely different than when she'd last seen Anne Morrissey in her home. There, ministering to her bedridden mother, she'd seemed marked by the forlorn pathos of the aging spinster. Here in her professional milieu she looked more vigorous, even younger.

The very way she greeted Kate, waving to her cheerfully as soon as she entered the cafeteria, clasping her hand affectionately when she arrived at the table, was imbued with energy. "Katharine! How nice to see you!"

"I'm very glad to see you, too, Anne. Especially to find you're still on the job."

Anne laughed. "Don't worry, I'll be here 'til I drop. Do you mind if I get a cup of tea before I sit? I've done two ops back to back. I could use a little pick-me-up."

"Let me get it for you," Kate said. But the nurse waved off the offer and darted away.

"Ah, that's what I needed," Anne said, after she was seated and had taken the first swig of tea she'd sweetened with four spoons of sugar. "Now, tell me: is something wrong? The message they gave me upstairs said you needed to see me, and you'd wait as long as it took."

"Nothing's wrong. I was passing the hospital, and I thought of you . . . and I was anxious to know that you hadn't been let go because of what you did for me."

"Well, as you see, I'm fine." The nurse smiled at Kate, then went on gazing at her expectantly, as though aware there must be more.

After a moment, Kate yielded. "I'm not sure if you want to talk more about it, especially here"—Kate glanced around at tables where other doctors and nurses were sitting—"but there are things about what you told me, the visions, I've wanted to ask . . ."

"I don't mind answering your questions," the nurse said. But she indicated it was for Kate's ears only by moving closer to the table and lowering her voice.

Kate wasn't sure where to start. "Since we've talked," she said at last, "I've been trying to make a connection to ... my family. You made me believe my daughter—all of them—really could be existing somewhere."

"And so they are," the nurse put in, quiet but firm.

"My own experiences haven't made me nearly as confident as you seem to be. I've never had the kind of experience you have, never seen anything for myself. I'm left ... balancing on the edge, not knowing whether to keep trying or give up."

"So what were you hoping, Katharine, that I could make up your mind for you? I don't know anything more than I've already told you."

"You haven't had any further experiences like the ones you told me?"

Anne shook her head. "Even those were very rare. Remember? Only a few over many years."

"You'd tell me if you'd seen anything more, wouldn't you?" Kate persisted. "You're not holding back because you're no longer allowed ... ?"

"No," the nurse said, and smiled softly.

"But that's something I wonder about: if every person has a soul, a part of them that goes on, why wouldn't you have those experiences more often, even all the time? Why would you see my daughter's spirit leave her body, but no one else's?"

"I did see others. I told you—"

"But not since," Kate said, more forcefully. "Haven't other people died in this hospital? Have the visions stopped simply because you can't afford to have them anymore?" She looked searchingly now at Anne Morrissey. She was aware her probing might be regarded by the nurse as an affront, a fresh accusation of insincerity, even instability.

Anne Morrissey gazed back steadily. "Katharine, I wish I had answers for you. But there are no rules about this. If you look into the experiences of people who've actually had their own loved ones appear before them, you find that it may happen an hour after death, or months later, or even after they've been gone twenty years. Why isn't it the same for everyone? I can't explain that, any more than why I saw what I did when I did. It could be my eyes were more ready to see at those times. It could be there was some quality in those souls that made them more visible—a purity in them that shines. Wouldn't that be true of your daughter?"

Kate resisted the tempting picture. "I need more," she said urgently. "Anne, I'm making decisions now, contemplating steps in my life I might not take if I thought there weren't unseen forces pushing me in certain directions. . . ."

Anne nodded sympathetically. "My dear, I sincerely wish I could tell you something to make it easier for you. But the very nature of faith is that we're asked to believe these things without ever being given any reason or proof. There's no accounting for miracles."

Kate stared at her bleakly, unable to summon any further plea for help. The silence was broken by the beeping of Anne's pager. The nurse extracted it from her pocket and glanced at it. "I'm terribly sorry," she said. "They need me upstairs."

Kate quickly apologized if anything she'd said had seemed harsh and distrustful, and thanked Anne Morrissey for her kindness.

The nurse said she'd be glad to talk again any time Kate thought it would help, and started away. But she stopped and turned back to offer one more attempt at comfort. "You did say you feel forces pushing you, Katharine. Maybe you shouldn't be asking for any more proof than that?"

Kate watched her hurry off—a capable woman, doing her job, working to save lives, even if she truly believed there was a better world waiting for everyone.

37

O n her last Saturday in the house, her mother arrived before lunch-
time. They'd picked this time for Sarah to bring the settlement
papers she'd prepared for Kate's signature. Then Sarah would stay for
the night. This would be a last chance to spend some quiet time together in the home that was disappearing. Next week would be hectic,
with the closing scheduled for Tuesday and Kate needing time to prepare for the movers who would come Wednesday to take things for
storage.

They ate tuna sandwiches in the kitchen, then Kate took her
mother on a walk through the rooms, pointing out things she'd decided to part with or put away, inviting Sarah to take any of it she
might want for herself.

"Thanks, dear," Sarah said, "but at this point I need less, not more."
Though, when they passed by the French doors facing the backyard,
she paused to look out. "That patio furniture is nice. Could I buy that
from you?"

"Mom, whatever you want is yours. Just take it."

"But that's almost brand new. . . ."

Kate stared at the table and four chairs neatly placed on the stone
patio, a set she and Jim had picked out together only last July. With no
happy backyard barbecues on the horizon, it had been left sitting outside through months of rain and snow. "It's a little beat up now, and
I've no use for it," she said. "But where could *you* put it?"

"Bert has a penthouse with a big terrace that faces south. He's neglected it for years—his wife was the gardener—but I've been waiting my chance to do more with it." The remark hinted at some advance in her mother's relationship with the judge, Kate thought, but before she could even ask, Sarah turned to her and added brightly, "He's asked me to marry him."

Much as Kate approved of her mother's companion, there was a sting in being given this news at the very moment when the last solid symbols of her own dead marriage were being sold and scattered. For a moment, she was robbed of words.

"Well," Sarah prompted, "what do you think?"

"You're not asking my permission, are you?" Kate said with a touch of vinegar.

"I'm asking," Sarah said stiffly, "what you think, that's all. I haven't given my decision yet, and your opinion matters to me."

"Well, he's a fine man, and you two get along fine, and you're already sleeping together a lot of the time, and I suppose that's fine. So why even hesitate?"

"For one thing, I've become accustomed to my independence. Being able to get away and be alone whenever I want is something I think I'd miss." She went back to gazing at the yard.

"Bert's no clinging vine," Kate observed. "He's not the sort of man who'd deprive you of your independence."

"Not on purpose. But we're at a time of life when committing to someone can also involve taking care of them sooner or later. He's had heart problems. I could end up being his nurse."

"Is that a good way to plan your life, Mom—ruling out a chance at happiness on a worst-case scenario?"

No sooner was it said, then the fact Kate was actually living out a worst-case scenario lodged in both their thoughts, freezing them again into silence. It ended with Sarah walking away from the window, saying, "We don't want to forget to sign those papers. . . ."

Kate trailed her into the kitchen. "So which way are you leaning on Bert's proposal?" she asked. "Yes or no?"

Sarah busied herself extracting a manila envelope from her briefcase, pulling out the legal documents, and arraying them on a cleared spot in the dining nook.

"Mom, you brought this up," Kate persisted. "Why are you suddenly avoiding the subject?"

Sarah hesitated. "It's not just about me, Kate. You're a factor in my plans, too. But anytime I bring up your life, your needs, you're so quick to reject whatever I say. Even mentioning Bert's proposal obviously touched a nerve—it just seems better not to get into it." She sat down, and picked up a copy of the settlement agreement. "Now, look this over and—"

Kate interrupted. "What are you saying? How do I matter in what you decide?" Sarah looked down at the table surface, avoiding a reply. Kate slid into the nook across from her. "I want you to do what's best for you. What did you think—that I need you so much you should turn down Bert's proposal for *my* sake?"

Sarah kept her eyes down as she replied. "Actually, my thoughts ran the other way. I was thinking if we married, I could live with him at his place—it's much nicer than mine." Now she looked up at Kate. "Then I could give you my co-op, free and clear. Living in the city would be so good for you—the stimulation, the opportunities, a much better place to meet . . . new people. And that would make it easier economically, right?"

Rebelling against the way her mother had started mapping out her future, Kate felt she had to raise the barricade here and now. "Your offer's very generous, Mom. But don't marry anybody on my account. I've already made arrangements to live somewhere else."

"Oh? I thought your plans were still up in the air."

The words kept coming now automatically. "Meg's offered me her house in Nantucket. Not permanently, but if it works out, I'll stay there and find something of my own."

Sarah gave a slight nod, but her mouth was arched down in a frown. Kate couldn't make out if her mother was merely disapproving or possibly even feeling rejected and hurt, but she had no apology to give. She hadn't spoken only to stake out her independence, Kate realized. It was the decision she'd been too afraid to make, the course that didn't seem sensible until she was backed into it, and the only place she really wanted to go.

After Kate remained silent, Sarah asked quietly, "What's there for you, Katie? Tell me: why do you keep getting drawn back to that island?"

"Because it *is* an island, maybe. Because being there lets me feel more separated from the things that hurt. I know, too, my life there won't be anything at all like the one I've had here. If it were at all the same, I'd always be comparing, always too aware of what I've lost. I need to re-make myself into someone who has a very different existence."

Sarah regarded her shrewdly. "Is that all there is to it? To re-create yourself?"

On the witness stand again. Kate wondered if her mother had surmised it had something to do with a man. Though, after all, Gabriel wasn't there anymore. "Seems reason enough to me," she said crisply.

Sarah studied her for another second, then picked up one of the documents. "All right, let's get this done," she said.

They went quietly through the formality of reading the agreements and signing in triplicate, but all the while they attended to the task, the silence was filled with explosive vapors. After Sarah gathered up the signed copies and squared them against the table, she suddenly tossed them down and let loose:

"Just what in heaven's name is going on with you, Kate? Don't I deserve an explanation? I've been making an effort not to interfere too much. I understand the pressures on you, how hard it is to think constructively. Why do you think I held my tongue about this playground thing? Not that it isn't a lovely idea—but doing it at the expense of your own security! Mr. Benedict was certain your case merited an award of two or three million dollars if you went to trial. You could have had that money, donated your playground, and never had to worry. But you barely gave it a thought! Senseless!"

The indictment froze Kate and kept her speechless while her mother's tirade gathered momentum. "Now you want to go off half-cocked and isolate yourself in a place where you hardly know a soul! And give up your teaching, of all things, something you have such a gift for! Does it strike you at all that none of it's rational, that what you're really doing is simply running away, running from reality? Moving so rashly because you're afraid to stop and think. Ready to turn yourself into a different person, you say! Darling, you need *help*! You are who you are, and nothing can change that. God knows it's no picnic to be that person right now, but you can't—"

All at once Kate clapped her hands over her ears, and erupted in a long piercing wail, followed by a plea. "No! No more! Please! Stop!"

Instantly silenced, Sarah sat staring across the nook, her eyes wide with shock until Kate sprang up and ran from the kitchen.

Sarah shouted after her. "Darling, I'm sorry. But what I'm saying is for your own good. . . ."

Kate was aware of Sarah continuing to call out appeasements, but she kept running straight up the stairs and into her bedroom, slamming the door behind her with the fervent wish it would bring down the whole house in a pile of splinters.

Fuming and crying hot tears as she paced aimlessly around her room, she felt cast back to those times as a child when the only way she could deal with disagreements with her mother was to run and hide. Reechoing endlessly in her ears was Sarah's accusation—as Kate viewed it—that she was guilty of "running away from reality." Lord Almighty! Given the reality she had to face, why the hell shouldn't she try to escape from it? And why not to a place where she'd been given the only medicine for her pain that had brought any relief whatsoever? What was wrong with that? *What—?*

Having walked off some of her fury, she stopped at the center of the room to look up and silently repeat the questions: *Why not? Why shouldn't I? Is it so wrong . . . ?* Tell me, she appealed to the heaven above, to *them*, what else should I do now?

One more appeal that went unanswered.

Finally, her fury abated, Kate realized that behaving as she had with her mother would only provide her with more ammunition to assume her diagnosis was correct. What she must do instead was demonstrate maturity, show that she was in control of her life—at the very least, *act* as if she was. After sitting tautly on the edge of her bed for another twenty minutes, Kate went to wash her face, then returned downstairs.

The smell of brewed coffee guided her back to the kitchen. Sarah had made a pot and was sitting in the nook with a cup, turning pages of the *New York Times* she had brought to read on the train. Kate sat down again. They gave each other pained smiles of regret. Sarah started to put it into words, but Kate stopped her.

"I know you're sorry, Mom," she said evenly. "So am I. Now I need you to do me a favor."

Sarah nodded willingly.

"Go home," Kate explained. "Now."

"Oh, honey—"

"Please. I'm not going to stay mad, I promise. But the last thing I need right now is having to justify the choices I'm making."

"All right. I'll keep my opinions to myself."

Kate gave her a weary smile. "I won't have any trouble reading your mind."

"Katie, I shouldn't have spouted off like that. I'm terribly sorry. But it just worries me so to see you—"

Go off half-cocked. Kate cut her off. "Let's not start again." She reached across the table and laid a gentle hand over her mother's. "You have to understand something, Mom—something very important that I've only begun to understand myself. I'm not the same person I was a few months ago. I can't ever be that person again. I wish to God I could be, but I can't. The things that have happened have changed me so much. How could they not? If I look for different things now, a whole different life, it may not be one that ever makes any sense to you. To be honest, I can't be sure it'll make sense to me, not until I try it. All I know is I *do* have to try."

Kate's calm assertiveness had the desired effect. Sarah made no further objection. She agreed to go home, telephoned for a taxi, and immediately started collecting her things.

At the door, with the cab waiting outside, and good-byes and promises for a next meeting already said, Sarah stopped for one more question: "What made you decide on the playground, Katie? You never said . . ."

That was all her mother needed to hear, Kate thought, that she was taking her cue from her dreams. She shrugged ambiguously. "I don't know. Doing something for other children just seemed a great way to honor my own."

Over the next couple of days, while she moved through the world engaged in the task of dismantling one life to prepare for another, she would think again and again of Sarah's charge that she was running away from reality—an echo that replayed in her mind with all the righteous force of a prosecuting attorney accusing an embezzler of absconding with the life savings of a starving widow.

Yet balanced against that memory, and supplying just enough fuel to keep her moving ahead was the remembered advice from another conversation. *You did say you feel forces pushing you, Katharine. Maybe you shouldn't be asking for any more proof than that?* Those last words of Anne Morrissey's made the difference, encouraging Kate to proceed along the path she was following. It might be because the major decisions had already been made, a plan already formed that she had only to obey. But as she prepared her boxes and made her labels and picked up keys to the Nantucket house from Meg, there was a sense of moving effortlessly, as if she was being easily borne forward to her destiny, much as a sailor might head to harbor before a gentle breeze. Kate could even believe it was such mysterious forces that had put the words on her tongue, were even speaking through her, when she had announced so impulsively to her mother that her mind was made up, she was going away to live on an island, ready to "re-create" herself.

Would it matter if Gabriel never returned there?

As the day approached that she would finally cut the last ties of all that had anchored her to an old life and depart for the new, the realization became more and more inescapable that he was indeed a part of what she hoped to find. To accompany the solitary work of preparing for the movers, Kate often had music playing on the radio, and more than once when some romantic old favorite came on, she found herself thinking of him, remembering his heartfelt declarations . . . and wondering if it was fair to him, or herself, or her memories to think that the emotions stirring within her now could be called love. Was she afraid, as Meg had suggested, that to love again would be a treason of the heart?

Or did she reject the idea only because it was too soon? Each time that question formed in her mind, she was also reminded of another thing Anne Morrissey had said:

There are no rules about this. If you look into the experiences of people who've actually had their own loved ones appear before them, you find that it may happen an hour after death, or months later, or even after they've been gone twenty years. . . .

The words had referred to the materialization of spirits. But they could apply as well, Kate thought, to encountering love. It might happen at any time. There were no rules.

38

It was almost with surprise that she found herself on Wednesday evening closing the door on the movers and turning to face the empty echoing spaces, stripped of every belonging that had made her feel this was where she belonged. It was done, a part of life declared over.

She went to the kitchen, made herself a last supper of the food she'd kept aside—a canned vegetable soup, the ends of a loaf of bread, tea—then washed and boxed up the last of the crockery and glassware and utensils, and cleaned the refrigerator. She put out the garbage, and fiddled the remaining boxes into the already overloaded station wagon. Next, she went through all the rooms, opening windows to air them, and gathering up stray bits of packing material. The realtor had arranged for a cleaning service to come in and do a thorough job after she left, but even now she had that funny house-proud need to clean *before* the maid came.

Finally she wrote a note to the new owners, not just to wish them well, but giving the phone number on Nantucket in case they wanted to contact her. She also detailed all those odd quirks about the house that you could only know from living in a place—like the way the builder had put the separate fuse box for the boiler inside the broom closet. On the way up to bed, she left the note in the stairway niche propped up against a vase of yellow tulips she'd bought just for the purpose.

Just as she came to the landing, she was stricken for the first time in days with a fresh failure of nerve. It was as if she had ascended not a mere flight of stairs, but to some airless summit, where she found herself not only out of ground, but too weak to descend. How could she leave this place? If there *were* ghosts, wasn't this where they would go on living, the house they would always haunt? Here, she would have always been accessible. She felt a burst of panic that selling had been an awful mistake—that it was even more wrong to be heading back to Nantucket. It was expecting too much of herself, of fate, to provide a happy future—even a satisfactory one—in an isolated place where she hardly knew anyone.

The house was sold, that couldn't be undone. But fortunately, nothing else was irrevocable. Most of her possessions were in storage. The station wagon packed with the clothes and books and kitchen supplies chosen for her island life could as easily be driven in another direction. Or all of it could be sent along to storage and she could take off on a journey to the other side of the world.

Running away from reality? If so, why not go all the way—to the ends of the earth, to the most fantastical places? The pyramids, the Taj Mahal, the Himalayas. When, if not now . . . ?

She moved along the hallway, suddenly feeling—in her own house, yet no longer her own—lost. An image came to mind of Captain Joshua Farr adrift in a boat after his ship had sunk, his goods had been lost, his crew had died. This was what that must have felt like, to have lost everything and to be at the mercy of fate and nature to bring you to a landfall. Practically dizzy with that feeling of rootlessness, Kate put out her hand to feel the wall as she made her way toward Tom's room, where she had decided to spend her last night in the house. Her own king-size bed had gone to storage, but the children's beds were in the assortment of furniture she'd offered along with the house, and both had been gratefully purchased, since there were so many children moving in. (She might have chosen Chloe's room, but an odd notion that it would represent some vestigial evidence of favoritism—Chloe had been so much more in her mind because of that scene at the hospital—made her choose Tom's instead.)

She headed straight to the bed, peeled off her clothes, and sank into it. Most of the sheets that fit the single beds were the colorful prints inspired by some toy or movie that the kids had clamored for, so she found herself lying down between a set printed with planets and stars and spaceships, licensed tie-ins dating from a few years when the last *Star Wars* film had come out on video. She remembered how the films had captured then four-year-old Tom's imagination, how he'd spoken of wanting to be an astronaut. Thankfully, when she turned out the light, her first thought was not that her child's ambition was a dream never to be fulfilled, but the consoling notion that in some sense he had become a traveler in the stars.

Rolling her head toward the window, Kate gazed out at the night sky and the memory came of standing with Gabriel under the stars, his remark about things we could still see twinkling in the sky that had been "stone-cold dead" for millions of years. Perhaps it was not so strange that she should have been attracted to him; that it was out of more than sheer desperation and neediness that she had given herself to him. Behind the rough stolid facade he showed to the world—to all but her—there was a sensitive, thinking man.

Still, to let him possess her heart still seemed too big a step to take. And was there any other reason to go north tomorrow, except to wait and hope she might see him again?

Tell me what to do, give me a sign, she pleaded soundlessly to those riders in the stars.

Then the mingled weaving of wish and apology burst out of her into the night: "I love you, always will . . . but I'm so alone. . . . Tell me it's all right. . . ."

Outside the window a wind stirred the trees. The stars—bigger than worlds, seen as no more than pinpoints—went on twinkling, the dead and gone indistinguishable from those still flaming somewhere near infinity.

At last, Kate drifted down into sleep, gratefully sinking away from all the menacing uncertainties of her future like a small fish darting down into the deep to escape a school of predators.

She came back to full wakefulness abruptly. Sitting upright in bed, she stared into the darkness, listening hard. Cognizant that some small thing could have shattered her frail sleep, a movement in the house, even a faint intrusion of wind, Kate waited for her senses to detect it again. Then, as she gazed around her, she noticed the bright moon shining through the window onto the floor of the room—though there had been only stars out there when she closed her eyes a moment ago. Now she glanced at the small alarm clock she'd left beside the bed: the hands showed it was past four in the morning—she'd actually been asleep several hours. Which only made the danger seem greater. If it wasn't a moment's light doze that had been interrupted, then this sharp consciousness came from no small stimulus, but something larger and more immediate.

Someone was in the house with her! She was sure of it. Perhaps more than one person. It struck her suddenly that when the movers had gone out for a lunch break, they'd taken away the doorstop and left the door closed. But they must have thrown the latch, because they'd come back and resumed work without having to ring. And she couldn't remember whether or not she'd reset the self-locking mechanism when they left. Anyone could have walked right in. Maybe they were emboldened by seeing the moving trucks, knowing she was alone. . . .

Should she call out to scare them off?

Wiser not to give herself away. She couldn't stay where she was, though; she ought to hide—or try to get out of the house. Slowly, stealthily, Kate turned back the covers and began to ease herself out of bed. Then she froze. Without a doubt another noise had come from along the hallway, a whisper, rustling, something like feet scuttling across the floor.

Frightened as she was, she forced herself to resume moving. Though she couldn't believe they wouldn't also have heard her by now. Her own heart sounded like a drumbeat in her ears, her breathing seemed as loud as a howling wind.

At the door of the room she stopped, then tilted her head out slowly until she could peer along the corridor to the head of the stairs and beyond that to the open door to the master suite. Since its windows faced in the same direction as Tom's room, a swath of moonlight traveled through the door and striped the bare floor of the hallway. A shadow or two danced languidly across the pale light, and Kate realized then that her own shadow was being projected similarly onto the floor in front of her. She ducked back, pressing herself behind the door.

Standing there, barely breathing as she fought to keep still, quiet her heart, her eye caught a patch of darkness flitting across the floor right in front of her. She started—then realized it was only the moonshadowed branch of a tree outside the window shifting in a breeze. As the seconds passed into a minute, and she kept straining fruitlessly to detect another noise, Kate began to suspect that it was only the play of a bough across a moonbeam that had thrown the shadows she had seen along the hall. The sounds that had frightened her could have been the scrape of branches against a sill, the rustle of leaves—sounds transmuted in unfamiliar ways by a house empty for the first time. Kate took a deep breath and ventured out from behind the door, then out of the room far enough to flip a switch that turned on a light in the hallway.

All quiet.

To reassure herself, though, she scuttled down the stairs to check the front door. Locked.

Her "night prowlers" were nothing but the jitters of a lonely woman in an empty house.

Climbing the stairs again, still alert after her foolish panic, Kate doubted she would be able to get back to sleep. The best thing now might be to dress and start driving. The image of speeding along empty roads, cocooned in a car with some late-night DJ playing requests on the radio, gave her a nostalgic lift; she hadn't driven alone at dawn since college days.

But at the thought of going anywhere, the same doubts rose up that had plagued her before sleep. *Go where? Why?*

She switched off the light in the hallway, and took a step back toward Tom's room. Then she stopped and looked back at the stripe of moonlight falling through the door of the master bedroom. Perhaps the same impulse to certify that all was secure that had sent her to check downstairs made her walk to the other end of the darkened hall until she stepped into the center of the pale silver rectangle. She stopped there, for some reason still wary, and looked cautiously through the doorway. . . .

Her eyes went straight to it. On the bare floor, squarely in the middle of the path of moonlight that extended away from her to near the window, lay a small object that caught the muted beams and turned them into a bright spot of glowing lavender ringed with dull gold.

Kate stared at it for at least a minute—it could have been two or three times that long—before she padded forward and knelt down in front of it. She started to reach out, then hesitated, fearful her attempt to grasp it would reveal it to be nothing more than an illusion. But at last her hand continued forward . . . slowly, *extra* slowly, all the more because she remembered that it was only reaching out too quickly that morning, too carelessly, that had made everything else vanish, brought her at last to her knees in this empty room.

She touched it now, solid and real, and picked it up as gingerly as if she were plucking a flower. Holding it between two fingers, she held the earring higher until her eye could see moon through the amethyst, and then she considered the miracle.

Of course, it could have dropped out of some cranny in a piece of furniture as it was carried away. That was the way Meg or her mother or any realistic, practical person would explain it. But Kate knew better. She'd gone through the rooms after the movers left—she wouldn't have missed it then, lying square in the middle of an empty floor.

The mirrored dresser was gone to storage. But as if it was still in its place against the wall, Kate rose and walked over to stand before it. And, as if she could see in that ghost mirror the beloved man just behind her, looking over her shoulder, she clipped the earring to her right ear, the one it had been meant for at that moment, that morning. She smiled at the memory, at him.

"Kept your promise, after all," she said, looking into those remembered eyes. It was, she knew, the sign she had asked for.

Then she turned around and spoke to them all for a while, to thank them, and share memories of the place she was leaving, and explain where she was going and why.

Nothing but moonbeams filled the room, but she never doubted they heard every word.

39

It couldn't have been a better day for a drive and a ferry crossing. The skies were clear, the sea unusually calm for March. Kate coasted all the way on the exhilaration she had felt since finding the earring.

The small accident as she drove off the ferry hardly put a dent in her mood. Coming down the off-ramp, she hit the brakes too hard when her wheels bounced over the metal hitches anchoring the ramp to the pier, and because the boxes and mounds of clothes filling the car blocked her rear view, she couldn't see in the mirror how closely the next car was following. When she stopped short, the station wagon was bumped from behind. A minor bump, yet Kate felt it was prudent to pull over as soon as she was off the boat and inspect for damage.

The other driver also stopped, and hurried over from his car. A middle-aged man in a dark overcoat and fedora, he had a mild, pleasant face behind metal-rimmed spectacles, and was instantly solicitous. "My fault completely, I'm terribly sorry. Are you okay?"

Kate was anxious to reassure him. "I'm fine, don't worry." After they inspected the rear of the station wagon, she said, "Not a scratch."

He pulled out a wallet and started rummaging in it. "Take my card, anyway, in case anything turns up later."

"That's really not—"

But by then he was holding out the card. Kate took it automatically and thanked him. He apologized again, she repeated that she felt fine, and they parted.

The card was still in her hand when she got back in her car, and she glanced at it idly as she was about to toss it in the glove compartment. At once, she let out a laugh, not so much at the name printed at the center, of all coincidences—ALLEN BUMPERS—but the words just beneath it: PRINCIPAL, NANTUCKET CENTRAL HIGH SCHOOL.

She tossed her gaze skyward. "You really do have plans for me, don't you?" she cried out playfully. The card went into her purse. Perhaps she'd call in a day or two, just to let the principal know she might be available if and when a substitute teacher was needed.

Kate drove off the pier, thinking her first stop would be to buy groceries before going to Meg's house. But as she recognized the streets around the docks, she decided before leaving this part of the island to say hello to the Thornes, if they were home.

Mounting the few steps to the door of the B & B, Kate was reminded of what Meg had told her about the local stairways that flanked either side of a street door—"welcome stairs," they were called, designed to signify that visitors were always welcome, whether arriving from land or sea. The small detail reinforced Kate's belief she was starting over in the right place.

It was Eddie who answered the doorbell. "Kate!" she exclaimed. "I'm so glad to see you. Come in, come in . . ." She pulled Kate inside. "This explains why you didn't answer the phone," she said then. "I must've called your house half a dozen times since yesterday afternoon—"

"The phones were all packed up," Kate explained. "The house is sold. I walked out this morning."

"To come here?" Eddie said. "You don't do things by halves, do you?"

"I'm going to try it out for a while."

"Did you want to stay with us? We'd be happy to—"

"No need, thanks. I just came by to let you know I'm here and give you my phone number. I wanted to thank you, too, for handling that letter to Gabriel."

"Nothing to it," Eddie said. "Have you seen him yet?"

"Seen—? But you told me he went away."

"I thought that's why you were here—that you already knew."

"Knew what?" Kate said, the idea dawning, but still needing to hear it.

"He's back."

Kate looked at her without speaking. The news was a lot to process.

"You didn't know . . . ?"

Kate shook her head.

"That's what I was calling to tell you. I don't know when he got back, but he came here yesterday asking for you. He'd gotten your letter, but because I delivered it by hand to the Madaket post office—no stamp on the envelope—he assumed you were already on the island."

Kate kept thinking to herself.

"I told you he wouldn't stay away," Eddie added. "Too bad I didn't know you were coming or I could have told him."

"No problem," Kate said. "Now I can tell him myself."

Eddie invited her to stay and have tea—Danny would be back soon from an errand and glad to see her, too—but Kate was eager to move into her own place, and they agreed to get together in the next day or two. Before leaving, she asked Eddie for paper and pen to jot down the phone number at Meg's. "This is my friend's house," she explained. "I'll be staying in 'Sconset 'til Memorial Day."

"In 'Sconset," Eddie echoed. "So you're not . . ." She let the question hang as she took the paper.

"Moving in with him?" Kate gave a good-natured laugh. "Eddie, I hardly know the man."

She did her grocery shopping, went to Siaconset, unloaded the car, and began settling in. A local caretaker who worked for Meg had already come in to open the pipes and turn on the heat.

She took a hot bath to refresh herself from the trip, then dressed in some casual clothes, opened one of the boxes and put out the books she'd brought along and placed her family photographs in several rooms. Gabriel's remarkable scrimshaw she set on a bedside table in the room where she would sleep, its carved drama a more than adequate substitute for television.

It was dusk by the time she made herself face the question of whether to go to Madaket now or wait until tomorrow. She was impatient to see him, but arriving by night might spur him to assumptions she didn't want him to make. In the daytime, though, he could be away doing some job.

She opened some boxes of kitchen things and spent an hour storing them away. Still restless and uncertain of what to do, she went out to her car to fetch more boxes. But she was arrested at once by the perfection of the night. Mingling in the invigorating air of early spring were the scent of beach grasses and the first growth of wildflowers, and the sky—oh, the sky! Where she'd lived before it was usually bleached out at night by the lights of clustered houses, streetlamps, even the glow rising from shopping malls miles away. In the blue-black canopy arching above her now from one side of the ocean's wide horizon to the other, the speckling of stars was so brilliant, so tremendous, she believed she could almost see the universe expanding as she stood there.

It came back to her then, what it had felt like to stand with Gabriel beneath the stars. And she remembered the last thing she'd written to him. . . .

She ran back inside and changed quickly into other clothes, not too special, but not so casual either, taking some care to look the way she wanted him to see her. She was about to leave the house when one last thought occurred. She put on the earrings this time without even standing in front of a mirror. She didn't need to see how they looked. They were only for luck.

A skein of smoke was curling up from the stovepipe, yellow light glowing softly behind the windows, the same as that first night she'd come here. He'd probably finished supper, perhaps he was reading now—she wondered what books could have followed *The Last Tycoon*.

The ground was still a bit slippery where the last snows had recently melted, so she went gingerly down the slope of the knoll to his shack. At the door she paused, and looked around, then up to the sky. Delaying a bit . . . but no longer asking. Finally, she knocked.

It seemed to take forever before she even heard his footsteps crossing the boards, that sturdy stride that made the whole place shake a little. Then the door opened. He opened his mouth, but there were no words, only the catch of his breath.

If she didn't say something quickly, Kate thought, she was in danger of throwing herself at him. "Can I come in?"

He nodded and stepped back quickly.

As she started to remove her coat, she said, "Only for a while, though . . ."

"I know. I mean, I understand."

He moved behind her to take the coat and she could feel him leaning in, his warm breath on her neck, as her arms slipped free of the sleeves. A longing rose in her, but she took a few quick steps away before turning back to him. He put her coat on a peg by the door and faced her again. So much to say, too much, she didn't know where to start.

"I was told you sailed away. . . ."

"A short trip."

"Where did you go?"

"Nowhere. Out in the ocean. It helps sometimes, just being away from everything."

She gave out the first truth from her heart. "I was afraid you weren't coming back."

"I always do."

She tried again to frame the more important words, but while she worked at it, he filled the silence: "I got your letter." She gave him a knowing nod and he went on. "The things you said there—about if I'd told you the truth, or knew it myself—that part meant the most to me. It told me you understood. You did, didn't you, Katharine? I said what I did to make you go, that's all. I thought . . . it was what we needed, both of us."

"I know."

"For me . . . my need . . . it was 'cause I couldn't give you what you wanted from me—couldn't promise, anyway, 'cause it's not something I've ever really been sure—"

"It's all right," she broke in. As he stumbled through his effort to explain, she could hear the anguish in his voice, see it in his eyes, and she wanted only to reassure him. "I really do understand, Gabriel."

"But listen—please. I need to get it clear now, for me as much as for you. About this thing I do, it never mattered so much before whether I understood how it happened. I mean, there weren't all so many people who came to me for help . . . and I knew it made them feel better. So I just went on with it. . . ." He looked away from her, and began ambling around the floor as he talked. "But I was always mixed up about it, too. Why should I be someone . . . chosen? I wondered so often if it was even real. Seemed just as possible I was a little crazy, imagining things. But I read a lot of books, too"—he waved toward his trunk, the repository of those explorations—"stuff by good people, smart people, religious people. And they believed. So when anybody showed up and wanted me to try, I couldn't say no. Understand? I didn't feel I had any more right to turn 'em away than I did to think of myself as special. It was just something I could do, and people wanted me to do it, so I did it. And then you came. . . ."

His meandering had taken him to the window. He paused now and looked out into the night, but Kate could tell the darkness was simply a screen for his memories of their time together. "With you, right away I didn't want to do anything that wasn't true. And if I couldn't be sure what the hell the truth was . . ." He shrugged heavily.

"You did help me, though," she said. "Remember, there was a bridge I wanted to cross, and I made a start with you, Gabriel—I took the first real steps. It's because of you, really because of you and no one else that I . . ."

He turned to look at her questioningly.

And she told him. "I was able to get the rest of the way across that bridge."

He peered at her intently. "You've seen them?"

"No—not the way you mean. But I know they're with me."

"You know . . . ?"

"Beyond a doubt."

"How?" He took an eager step toward her.

"You have to ask?" she answered quietly, smiling. "I learned how from you, what you told me. Don't expect proof, don't demand it. Just believe. The rest will follow." She moved closer to him. "That's what you have to do, Gabriel. Trust yourself, trust the very same things you told me to trust. Don't ask how, or why. Believe in what you do—just the way you do it. Be here for whoever comes and asks. Go on as before, and know that you *do* help."

Slowly, he closed the remaining gap between them, as if afraid she might back away with each new step he took. But she didn't move.

"So that's why you came," he said, right in front of her now. "To ask me again—"

She laid her fingers lightly over his lips. "No. Oh, no, I won't need that anymore."

"Then why . . . ?"

She thought for a few seconds about how to say it. "Because someone gave me the idea that this is the place where I belong."

After a moment, he smiled at her for the first time. She lifted her face slightly, and his arms went around her and he gave her the long and gentle kiss she had been missing.

"But you're not going to stay," he said when he released her, not with disappointment, simply acceptance.

"Tonight, no. I'll be on the island, though. And after we've spent some time together . . ."

"Sure," he said. "Sounds like the right way to go about it." He glanced around the room. "Give me a chance to get this fixed up a little nicer." His eyes came back to her. "Though maybe it could never be nice enough."

"It's much too soon to be worrying about that, Gabriel. But, for the record, you live in the most beautiful and peaceful spot I know." He smiled again, proudly but in a modest way. "Hot water would be an improvement, though," she added.

He gave a little laugh. "Hot water, right. Should've had it long ago."

For a few moments they gazed at each other, sharing an easy silence as they contemplated the mysteries that had brought them together.

"Before I go," she said at last, "there is one more thing I'd like very much to do with you. I mentioned it in the letter. . . ."

His brow furrowed as he went back in his mind over what she had written to him. Then he realized what she meant, and his eyes brightened. "Well, sure," he said quietly. "There couldn't be a more perfect night for it."

Quickly, he fetched her coat and held it for her while she slipped it on. Then he put on his own, and shouldered the telescope on its tripod. "No telling what we'll see on a night this clear," he added as he opened the door.

And together they went out to look at the heavens, a universe of brilliant blazing suns, still visible in the night sky though not a few had ceased to burn millions of years before the earth was born.